RENAISSANCE MANN

A NOVEL

BY

GARY K. WALLACE

First Edition originally published by Page Publishing, 2024

Second edition, Ingram Spark, Publishing Pros, 2025

ISBN 979-8-89157-345-1 (pbk)
ISBN 979-8-89157-362-8 (digital)

Printed in the United States of America

DEDICATION

FOR SANDY,

WHOSE SUGGESTIONS STARTED THIS 40-YEAR JOURNEY

AND TO MY DAUGHTERS FOR THEIR LOVE, SUPPORT, AND ENCOURAGEMENT

ACKNOWLEDGEMENTS

Special thanks to my beta readers, Jaime Signorino, Orest Zalopino, and Deborah Haas, for their invaluable critiques. Many thanks to my writers' groups, whose feedback guided and encouraged me to become a better writer. I couldn't have finished this book without them. I also appreciate Danny Sheiman, whose editing insights smoothed the dialogue and made this book much more readable. Lastly, I thank my wonderful daughters, Amy and Lisa, for their encouragement.

TABLE OF CONTENTS

PART I

NICK

CHAPTER 1

(Earth, Summer 1984)

An odd smell stirred me to consciousness. Not a hospital smell. More like freshly cut summer grass mixed with the earthy scent of sunflowers. I heard a low-pitched hum in rhythm with a whining mechanical sound. At least I can hear, I thought.

"Phil," a muffled voice called. "Try to open your eyes."

I couldn't open them or talk because my eyes and mouth were like the rest of my body: numb and unresponsive. A wave of panic washed over me. *I'm paralyzed. For God's sake, someone, please help me!*

"Phil, if you can hear me, nod." He sounded clearer.

I knew that voice. Nick? What in the hell was my barber doing here... in my hospital room? Concentrating on moving my head did no good. Hopelessness overtook me as I lay engulfed in blackness. Death seemed better. At least it would put an end to the terror.

Nick said, "It's okay, Phil." his voice was a welcome relief. "I know you can hear me. Relax. Stay calm. I need to make a few more adjustments. Don't worry. Everything will be fine."

A few adjustments? What was he talking about? Where was I, and what was he doing to me?

Nick's chattering, although annoying, kept my drowning mind afloat. An ear-shattering, high-pitched squeal followed a sharp glare of light.

The lights softened. My eyes focused on a bright ceiling. As if someone had thrown a switch, my senses snapped back on. Being able to feel again delighted and disoriented me. Nothing made sense, but it didn't matter. As I pondered my situation, a bizarre sensation rushed through my body. A euphoria welled up in me, followed by a sudden surge of energy that merged into a pleasure-pain tingling. The tingling grew in intensity to a point of discomfort, then stopped.

"Very good," Nick said.

My left leg jerked up and down, followed by my right leg, then both arms. All at once, my arms and legs were jerking up and down uncontrollably. I felt like a stringed puppet being jerked around by an intoxicated puppeteer.

"Stop it. Stop it," I shouted at the ceiling, realizing with conflicted joy that my voice was back. "Nick, what are you doing here? And what in the hell's going on?"

His face appeared over me. "Excellent, everything seems to work correctly." He had that same expression after all my haircuts. I wanted to punch him right in his smiling puss.

Lying angry and confused, I realized how different I felt. Keeping my voice low and calm, I asked, "Nick, what happened?"

"It's a little complicated, and I'm not sure you're ready for the full explanation."

"What?" I tried to lift my head again. It still felt as heavy as lead. After several attempts, I gave up. "The accident," I screamed as the image of the falling SUV flashed through my mind. "Elaine... what happened to Elaine?" My body trembled as I recalled the surreal sensations of the impact, the flying glass, and the pain, all replaying in vivid detail. It broke me out in a cold sweat. I lay exhausted for a few minutes, trying to make sense of what Nick said. But the accident and Elaine hovered in my mind. My head throbbed with questions.

Nick came to my side and placed his hand on mine. "Phil, you've come through a most traumatic experience, but you're all right now." Squeezing my hand harder, he asked, "Can you feel that?"

"Are you my doctor now?" I snapped, pulling my hand away.

Nick looked me square in the eyes and said, "Oh, I'm much more than that."

His dark eyes stared with a severe intensity that told me to back off. So, I changed the subject. "Where am I? Is this a hospital?"

"No questions... please." His stern gaze softened, and his eyes turned to a gentle shade of brown. I tried to sit up. Nick held me down. "You need to rest. There will be plenty of time for explanations." He pulled out a small cube-shaped device and placed it on my forehead.

"Sleep."

CHAPTER 2

During that induced sleep, I had a wonderful dream. I stood by the open French doors, taking in a deep breath of crisp, fresh air. When I walked out onto the spacious terrace, three moons greeted me. They looked close enough to touch. One had a coppery color; its crescent glowed on the horizon, looking like a leviathan arching its back. The other two were more distant. The largest one was the most striking. It appeared large enough to be a planet, glowing like a radiant pearl with a thin gold ring about its equator.

I turned at a soft touch on my shoulder. A beautiful woman smiled at me. She wore a sheer lavender gown that clung to her angular body. Her large, hazel eyes held me under their seductive glow. Her eyes grew darker, and her mouth with full, round lips shrank. Tiny ridges formed, replacing her thin eyebrows, and her small ears disappeared. Her alien features didn't shock me. They seemed natural and only enhanced her beauty.

She took my hand before I could utter a word. We lifted off the terrace, then soared into the starry sky. We flew high into the air, far above puffy white clouds that appeared to fade as we climbed. There were no sounds or any sensations other than the warmth of her hand in mine.

Hundreds of oval-shaped buildings spread as far as I could see. The sprawling metropolis glowed in a spectrum of colored lights. Tiny, lighted objects darted in and around the towering structures.

I turned and looked at my mysterious companion. Her hazel eyes turned dark gray and glowed with a fiery passion. I pulled her to my side, and she rolled under me. We floated in the silence with our bodies entwined.

The dream shifted. I was back on the terrace, standing under a bright midday sun with my arms spread wide. Thousands of people crowded far below in the city streets, chanting. At first, it was unclear what they were chanting. I listened closer. Thousands of voices all intoning a single word: *Uzil*. It sounded like a stunning chorus that struck an odd chord.

The masses of faceless people continued to sing that single word as if I were a conquering hero being praised for vanquishing a dreaded enemy.

I turned from the cheering crowds. My mysterious lady was lying on an enormous bed. She gazed at me with sensuous lips parted. Her gown was replaced by a scanty, silk nightie that showed enough for my body to pulse. With her head tilted, and one brow ridge arched provocatively, I felt myself floating to her....

A gentle kiss on my cheek. It disturbed me at first, being awakened at that moment until my eyes focused, then fixed on her.

"Elaine? You're alive?" She stood by the side of the bed, beaming. Seeing her there looking happy made me wonder if she was part of the dream.

She looked angelic, dressed in all white, a lacy cotton blouse over tights. I blinked a few times to be reassured it was her. Elaine going out without any makeup was odd. The way she looked, shining blue eyes and long blonde hair spilling over her shoulders, took my skepticism down a notch. Seeing her intrinsic beauty reminded me of how lovely she always looked in the mornings.

Without waiting for me to speak, she leaned in and gave me a long, hard kiss. I put my arms around her neck and pulled her in for another lingering kiss. Another thought occurred. How is she alive?

"Oh, Phil, you look incredible," she said in a breathy voice. "Have you seen yourself?"

"Yeah. I'm taller, have bigger muscles, and my hair is darker and wavier."

"That's true. But your eyes are still green, your hair dark brown, with a body like an Adonis. Not that you weren't all that bad looking before the accident." She giggled, then covered her face, blushing like a schoolgirl.

I squinted my eyes. "Is it really you?" I sat up to take a closer look. "Elaine?"

"Yes?"

She looked like Elaine. The kiss was good but different. Something was off. Under Elaine's bright smile, she seemed uncomfortable with my heavy stare—another troubling thing. Elaine never giggled or blushed in my company.

"How did you know I was here?" The sudden question appeared to take her by surprise.

Her smile weakened. "Nick located me and told me what happened to you. He hoped you'd be more at ease if I tried to explain things." She sighed. "What he described shocked me."

"He told you about the accident and all? Why? You were there."

"No, Phil. Remember? You were on your way home," she blurted, sounding almost defensive.

I shook my head. "No. No, we were west of the Intracoastal Waterway." But searching within my fragmented memory, the clarity of the events of that evening had diminished. "I'm unsure of everything now." I lowered my head and sighed.

"It's understandable." She gave my shoulder a reassuring squeeze. "From what Nick told me, your confusion about the details is logical. Look what you've been through?"

After she said, "Nick," my mind stirred. The mere mention of his name created suspicion. Narrowing my eyes, I said, "So, Nick told you everything."

"Yes." She hesitated with lines forming on her forehead. "What's wrong?" She took my hand. "I promise, your confusion will fade, and things will become clear again."

"You think I'm confused?" I laughed. "I'm way beyond that." My voice rose. "Insane would be closer to what I'm feeling. "Elaine, forgive me. My nerves are shot, I'm bewildered... and taking all my frustrations out on you. Please, tell me what he told you."

"Sure, I understand. No need to apologize." She stared down; a finger pressed to her lips. "Let me see." She absently wrapped a strand of hair around her finger. "To begin with, you're at his place. He brought you here after the accident."

"He told you how he found me?"

"Yes. But you knew that.

I nodded.

"Nick believed the only way he could save you was through cybernetic, biomechanical-engineering… whatever that means. He claims to have rebuilt you." She reached inside her blouse and pulled out a familiar-looking cube, and held it up. "He said all the technical stuff is on this. Nick hoped that I could convince you to use it."

She handed it to me. I gave it a curious glance, then returned my attention to Elaine. "Did you buy all that crap?"

"Not at first, but after a while, he convinced me. The truth is incontrovertible. You're here."

It would be hard to disagree with what she'd said. I can't explain how I knew the woman sitting next to me wasn't Elaine. Over the eighteen months before the accident, Elaine and I had built a close friendship that evolved into love. The woman talking looked and sounded like Elaine, but it wasn't her. So, who the hell was she?

"You haven't told me much, Elaine. Nick showed me my new, wonderful body but didn't tell me how he did it. What I want to know is how and why." I heard my voice getting sharper while glaring at the impostor.

"What Nick did was miraculous. He's a remarkable man. When he found you in the morgue, he salvaged usable organs, tissue, and even blood. He said the car that landed on you had damaged you beyond repair. So, he combined your organic material with cybernetic implants and rebuilt you." She frowned. "By your expression, I can see you find this too fantastic."

"You're not Elaine, are you?"

She stood and took a few steps back with her mouth open in surprise, then sighed. "No. I'm not Elaine."

For a split second, Elaine's image grew bright. The brightness clouded into a blur of light, then poof, goodbye love goddess, hello little weirdo. A complete metamorphosis right before my eyes.

It didn't surprise me that Nick was behind the Elaine façade. But seeing him transform stunned me. It was the ultimate proof of my insanity. I curled into a fetal position on the bed and cried, "I'm nuts... I've lost my mind."

Nick sat next to me. He placed something on the right side of my head. It clicked. A few seconds later, a gentle vibration started, followed by a burst of high-pitched sound. A sudden euphoria had me feeling so good that nothing could bother me.

"Feeling better?" Nick said.

I nodded, grinning like a happy idiot.

Nick laid his arm across my broad shoulders and said, "Would all of this be more convincing if I told you you've been abducted by aliens who want your body for their research?"

I looked at Nick, still grinning and not giving a shit. Right in the middle of a nervous breakdown, I was having the best high of my life. A tingling sensation coursed through me. The tingling changed into a powerful surge of vitality. I didn't know if I wanted to run, jump, or eat. The only thing that mattered was not being crazy.

"You're not insane," Nick said as though he read my thoughts. "Nor are you hallucinating. You're experiencing major changes in both your physiology and mental makeup." Nick pulled the cube from the side of my head. The surge and euphoria dissipated, leaving me relaxed.

"What was that?" I asked.

"You were running at such a high emotional rate, you overloaded your processor. Humans, you're so emotional and complex. You make me wonder why I even started this project."

"I'm a project?" I glared. "Wait, a second... What do you mean by a processor?"

He shook his head. "No, no. That's not what I meant."

"About the processor or me being a project?"

"You're not a project...." He scratched his thin mustache. "Well, at least not in the terms you're implying. And yes. You have several processors networked throughout your brain. But it's too complicated to get into now." He lowered his head, a hand pressed to his right temple for a second, and added, "Due to circumstances beyond both of our control, you have become a key player in a vital plan. It's a desperate one that I'll explain to you. But Phil, I need to beg for your trust or at least time to put everything together in terms you can understand."

"So, Nick, if I'm not out of my mind, then what's wrong with me?"

"Questions, questions. I'm not sure I have all the answers…" He took a deep breath and exhaled. "Okay, here's what you want to hear." His face became passive, and he spoke in a low voice. "As to where you are. You're at my place, enjoying the comforts of my guest quarters."

"Very nice," I replied. "Okay, when can I go home?"

"You won't be leaving…." Nick walked to the curved wall.

"What do you mean I won't be leaving?"

"Because you're traveling with me at a high velocity and are approximately 6.2 trillion miles from Earth." He spoke into a small panel, and a section of the wall slid back.

"Oh my God," I gasped, transfixed by the sight of blue streaking lines and shimmering stars in the blackness of space. Nick took a few steps back as I turned, narrowing my eyes, feeling like a trapped animal. I wanted to pounce on Nick and tear him apart.

"How could you do this?" I yelled, rolling my hands into tight fists.

"How could I?" Nick snapped. "You don't get it. Let me explain it to you once more. You were dead." He stabbed a finger at me for emphasis. "I brought you back to life. I gave you a new and wonderful body; I enhanced your mind. You're ten times stronger. And with a little programming and training, you'll be many times smarter than the average human. You'll never get sick, and you'll live for hundreds, if not thousands, of years. So, that's what I did to you, Philip Mann."

"I awaken from a terrifying accident only to discover that I died and have been reborn as a cyborg. How'd you expect me to feel?"

"You're not a cyborg!" he shouted.

I gazed through the transparent wall, thinking my former life and who I was were as distant as the Earth.

"You're not a cyborg," he repeated. "You're technically an enhanced-humanoid."

"And that's supposed to make everything better?"

He shrugged. "You humans are so damn emotional. In time, you'll come to appreciate me. You can't imagine the wondrous things ahead of you. Come, Phil, I want to show you your temporary home."

I didn't want to follow him. My mind was preoccupied with being an *enhanced humanoid*. I looked at Nick and thought, I'm alive because of what he did. And for that alone, he deserved my gratitude. Nick stood by the door with a long face. I felt a little ashamed of my overreaction. How was I ever going to adjust to being Nick's creation as we travel on his ship, taking me to live on his alien world? The gravity of that thought frightened the crap out of me.

"Are we displaying human petulance?" he said.

"No. Human fear of the unknown."

"That's absurd," Nick laughed. "The unknown has been the inspiration for humanity's greatest discoveries."

"Yes," I agreed, then whispered, "Also, our greatest follies."

"All discoveries have their risks," Nick said.

"Damn, you've got good hearing."

"Yours is even better."

"Really?" That surprised me. "What other enhancements did you give me?"

"Oh, more than you can imagine. And think of all the fun we'll have in discovering them." Nick winked at me.

CHAPTER 3

Nick took me on a tour of his enormous ship. There were no visible electronic or mechanical devices like Star Trek, full of panels with blinking colored lights and instruments. There were lots of different bays, though. I took a peek inside one of the medical labs. It was one of the smaller bays and had couches of varying sizes spread throughout the room.

"Why are all these bays so barren of equipment?" I asked Nick.

"The ship creates whatever instrumentation is required."

"How?"

Nick stopped walking. "Phillip, once your processors are updated and synchronized, all your questions will be answered."

After touring three decks, I needed a break. Nick took me to a food station. He pointed to a round table with four high-back chairs inside a curved alcove.

"You look hungry," Nick said. "What do you want to eat?"

"I can have anything?"

He nodded.

"Okay. How about a hamburger and fries with a Cherry Coke?"

Nick spoke into a small silver plate on a flat wall next to the synthesizer. Its blue crystal blinked as he spoke. The ship's automated voice said something I didn't understand.

The curved wall behind me slid back, and the mesmerizing inky blackness of space came into view, with a large yellow-white star shining in the distance. A minute later, a slot opened beneath the synthesizer. A tray filled with steaming food appeared. Nick took the tray and handed it to me. A second tray slid out. He took it and sat.

"What are you waiting for? Eat," he said, pointing his fork at me. His lunch consisted of a small salad with a glass of water.

I inhaled the mouth-watering aroma of the burger with a pile of golden-brown, natural-cut fries. I grabbed the tall, frosty glass and took a sip. The sweet taste was like real cherries. The burger was cooked to perfection, and the fries were crisp. Even the ketchup had a rich tomato flavor.

"This is amazing. It's like you read my mind... or the computer did."

Nick cocked his thick, black eyebrow with a faint smile.

"So, it was the computer."

He shrugged, looking like there were more things than I suspected.

"That's part of all that programming you keep referring to?"

"Yes," he said, stuffing a forkful of salad in his mouth. He leaned back in the chair and eyed me for a second as if considering his answer. "The computer is learning your habits and dietary preferences and all your mental and metabolic functions—"

I opened my mouth to ask a question. Nick held a finger up as if to say hold that thought, and continued. "The ship is also updating data into your processors necessary for your survival while in deep space."

"Wow. So, I'm not that different from the ship's computer. I'm just another machine it's communicating with."

"Aww, Phil, we're all machines. We're self-aware biological units, taking in and using energy as we go along our journey through life. Once we get all that stuff in your head organized, you'll see how much better you'll feel about your new body."

"How in the world did you create this?" I said, one side of my mouth full of the burger, the other stuffed with fries. I didn't want to think about programming and processors. I only wanted to enjoy my burger. "Oh, man... what an amazing meal." I wiped my mouth with a napkin made of a strange material. I noticed the food stains from my mouth fade before my eyes, and it was clean again. "What is this napkin made of?"

Nick smiled. "It's a self-cleaning synthetic composite. One of a multitude of new materials you'll discover as we journey to your new home."

I stared at it for a second in awe of the technology that created it. Then another thought occurred. "Why does the dispenser in the guest quarters only offer bland-tasting crap when I could've been dining in style?"

"That was deliberate. Your digestive tract needs time to build up sufficient bacteria for proper digestion. All that bland crap was a combination of pro and prebiotics, proteins, and complex carbohydrates you needed to metabolize solid food. So, how do you feel after eating your first meal?"

"Full," I said, patting my belly with both hands. "Now, tell me what I really ate?"

Nick smiled again, as if each new question delighted him. "You enjoyed it?"

I nodded, then squinted my eyes at him. "Come on, tell me. What did I eat?"

"The ship's library has Earth's entire dietary and culinary databases. The synthesizer goes out to the database, and then an algorithm combines plant protein infused with synthetic fish oils, antioxidants, and a lot of seasonings. The synthesizer replicates the mixture into a palatable taste and texture. How does that sound?"

"Incredible. The one in my quarters can do the same, right?" I asked, popping the last crispy fry into my mouth.

"Of course. Can't have you running all hours of the night in search of a dispenser. You'll not only have an updated one in your quarters, but another has also been installed between our quarters in the corridor. Then in a timid voice, "Just in case you would like to dine with me from time to time... or alone if you prefer. Think of it as dining out."

Nick gave me an odd look. His thick eyebrows arched up high, his mouth closed in a tight line. His look distracted me for a second with an uneasy thought. Was Nick coming on to me? I dismissed it and, in a perky voice, said, "You bet we'll dine. I hate eating alone."

Nick's eyes glowed, looking relieved and excited about us dining together. After reflecting for a second, it occurred to me. Nick has been alone on this enormous ship for decades... maybe longer. He must be desperate for companionship.

The simple agreement to eat together seemed to make all the difference in his attitude. He had been acting stuffy, formal, and guarded. Even when telling me about Venubia, he seemed detached, robot-like, stuffing my head with databanks full of their history, science, art, and culture. But when we're just talking about ourselves, he's relaxed, congenial, engaging, and so full of knowledge.

Nick seemed as though he wanted to tell me something. Each time I tried to discover what it was, he deflected to another subject. I decided to wait until he was ready.

CHAPTER 4

When we entered the main Control Center off the Command Bridge, there were no visible controls. The large bay, like my quarters, had hundreds of small square panels covering all the walls.

"This is the main controller," Nick said, pointing to an array of hundreds of colored crystals. They varied in size and were embedded in a waist-high platform that stretched along an entire wall. "All primary functions are voice-actuated and interactive through these crystals. They will store and learn your voice and habits. Once you're acclimated to the ship, you'll have complete access to everything."

As we walked and talked, a feeling about Nick grew in me. I discovered I liked him. The strange circumstances that brought him into my life created an undeniable bond between us.

We continued to walk for some time before he told me the truth about his mission. His mouth tightened for a beat, then he sighed. "My planet's male population had become sterile. We're dwindling at an alarming rate."

That worried me. "What happened?" I said.

"A virulent virus broke out. It only affected our males." His voice and face were full of tension. "I can't go into all the details about the cause of the virus. It happened a long time ago. There's a Venubian proverb that states: The follies of the fathers become the children's burden."

"Yes, we have a similar saying. It seems to be a truism of any developing civilization."

Nick nodded. "There's another way of looking at this, though. Great advances are often born out of a great crisis."

"True." I narrowed my eyes at him. "So, what really happened?"

His brow lined, and his expression grew heavy with thought. "We allowed our technology to outstrip our ability to control it. Without going into all the complexities of how it happened, suffice it to say that our arrogance almost destroyed our world. The virus that doomed our males was only a side effect of something we refer to as a Technological Singularity."

"Sounds complex," I said. "What does it mean?"

"It describes a point where a civilization's technology advances to a state of self-awareness and takes control over its creators."

"Are you saying your machines became alive and took over?

"In simple terms, that's precisely what happened. We created a race of androids that grew so intelligent they became self-aware and found their creators too flawed to govern themselves.

"In trying to deal with what we'd conceived, we had to endure through a most horrific period of death and destruction." Nick's eyes grew wide, and his lower lip trembled as though he were reliving the horror he was describing. "Ironically, the virus saved us from total annihilation. For reasons that have remained unclear, our nightmare turned into salvation in that those same androids saw the harm they'd caused and gave us back our planet. They created a Utopian world for us. But the virus is still a threat to my species' survival."

"In all this time, you still haven't found a cure?" I said, almost afraid of his answer.

"The androids worked with our scientific community to find a cure. By the time they isolated the virus's origins, over eighty-seven percent of the male population was infected. It took another twenty planetary cycles, that's equivalent to thirty-two Earth years, before an effective vaccine was developed. Although a cure was found, the damage was irreparable." Nick wrung his hands as he spoke in a solemn voice. "All the data pointed to one unimpeachable conclusion. Our species will die off in less than three generations. At the time, our scientific community went into a panic. Cloning was the most viable and immediate option, but it only provided a short-term solution. Also, for many reasons, most of my people disapproved of it."

"Why such reluctance toward cloning?" I said. "If it could buy you time, why wouldn't they want to use it?"

He dismissed my question with a wave of his hand and said, "It's too complicated, and I don't want to talk about it now."

"Are you saying I won't understand, or are you afraid to tell me?"

He shook his head. "Too painful to talk about. Also, cloning has fundamental dangers and limitations. It doesn't provide enough genetic diversity. And gene manipulation has inherent traps. I, along with many of my colleagues, believe there are more natural solutions to pursue."

Nick was holding something back. I could see it in his eyes, but I dropped the subject.

"I have a plan I want to discuss with you," he said.

"Okay. What do you have in mind?"

"First, we need fresh genetic material. Think of it as seeds for a new population. My original plan was to find worlds with compatible genetic materials. Primarily to recruit male subjects for the reseeding process."

"I gather that the plan hasn't gone as expected."

He shrugged. "I came to Earth and set up the barbershop to screen human male subjects."

"I'm curious. How do you screen subjects with a haircut?"

"Simple," his eyes crinkled with a smile. "When I combed out their hair, I'd analyze their hair follicles for live cells for whatever criteria I needed. If the unsuspecting subject met the criteria, they would have been invited to Venubia to help provide genetic material to repopulate the planet."

"What would you do if the individual declined the offer?"

He scratched his mustache in thought, then blurted, "I would've abducted them." Seeing my shocked expression, he let out a hearty laugh. "Don't look so surprised. I only wanted to see your reaction. Humans are obsessed with alien abductions. The truth of the matter is, I was planning to take some recent cadavers, but after further analysis on human genetics, I decided against it."

"What were you going to do with the cadavers?"

"Harvest stem cells and basic genetic materials for development. However, the trip so far has been a complete failure." His eyes dimmed.

"So, what went wrong?"

"While human DNA could meet our basic requirements, humans do not. You present us with too many variables in your genetic behavioral makeup."

"Is this your way of telling me we're too unpredictable as a species?"

He nodded.

"Would you care to elaborate?"

He shook his head.

"What aren't you telling me, Nick?"

"You're too violent and haven't developed enough emotional stability to ensure a suitable interspecies joining."

"Are you saying we scared the crap out of you?"

"My people are still paying for the errors made in those earlier experiments. I don't wish to repeat them."

"Okay. I get that. But it begs the question of why you chose me. After all, I'm a perfect example of human unpredictability. You said it yourself—I'm too emotional." I noticed Nick's complexion flushed. "Did you realize you just blushed?"

Nick lowered his eyes and, in a timid voice, said, "I became too attached to you."

"What was that?"

"I admit it. I became close to you. Can't explain it. It's something like a human finding that adorable mutt and taking it home. I have feelings for you."

"Using your analogy, I'm your mutt?"

"Well—more like my favorite enhanced-humanoid," he winked. "Come, I want to show you something you'll find most interesting."

CHAPTER 5

We stopped at a large double door. "This's where we'll spend most of the trip," Nick said. He whispered something at the doors. They opened with a quiet hiss.

The bay looked like a massive storage area. Hundreds of long metallic cylinders with clear domes were lying flat on the floor. Nick walked to the closest row and said, "Units thirteen and fourteen, open."

Two of the unit's domes in front rose. I looked inside one of them. The interior was padded. There was a small pillow at one end and lots of stuff connected to its base. More mechanisms were connected to this unit than anything else I'd seen.

"Do you know what this is?" Nick asked.

"Some sort of sleeping device," I said, feeling uneasy. His eyes fixed on me, as if he were deciding. "Nick," I said to break his stare.

"Uh, yes." He cleared his throat, blinking his eyes. "To be more precise, it's a hibernation chamber. It will be a long journey, and it will go much quicker and safer in there." He grinned. "I will be right beside you." He pointed to the chamber to the right.

"By the look of things, I guess you were expecting a bigger crowd."

"Yes. You could say that." He tilted his head and gazed at me with that same funny expression he had during lunch. "But I didn't completely fail. At least I have you."

"Thanks, Nick," I said, sensing he was struggling with something.

"I need to fit you into a special suit that will protect and maintain all your bodily functions while you're in hibernation."

He gestured for me to follow him. He led me to a low platform in front of the first row of chambers. The platform was oblong and had a gold disk on top.

"Step up onto the platform, placing your feet squarely on the disk," he said.

As soon as my feet were in position, another disk came out of the ceiling, then stopped centimeters from my head. I heard a hissing sound from above.

"Take off your pajamas," Nick said.

"How? I nearly peed in them trying to get them down in the bathroom."

Nick chuckled. "I guess in all the confusion, I forgot to instruct you on voice-actuated clothing. Say, '*pajamas off.*'"

I reflected on the bathroom incident and how I got them to open when I said the word *open*. I straightened my body and said, "Pajama's off." They fell to my feet, then dissolved. "Wow, disposable clothes. Is everything on the ship like that?"

"More or less. To be more precise, the pajamas weren't disposed of but recycled. The ship will absorb the material's atomic pattern, then store it until needed again. Everything on the ship is similarly recycled, including biological waste. Urine is reprocessed into water, and feces are broken down into fertilizer, probiotics, and energy. Nothing is wasted. You'll learn all about these things soon."

He told me to close my eyes. The hissing sound grew louder. A spray of warm, moist air covered my body. When I opened my eyes, I found myself covered from head to toe in a gray, skintight coating. The only things exposed were my mouth, nose, ears, and eyes. It felt weird, as though I'd grown a layer of gray skin.

Nick came up and gave me a close inspection. "Very good," he said. He whispered something at a panel on the wall. "Now, please close your eyes."

When I opened them, I found myself naked again on the platform. "Done?" I asked.

"Yes. You can come down now."

As I stepped off the platform, I couldn't help noticing my genitals. I mused to myself, seeing them exposed for the first time since my, let's say, alterations. Nick had also enhanced me there. I was almost giddy with being so well endowed.

"Nick, why did you make me so... um... well-hung?"

"Well-hung?"

"You know," I said, looking down while pointing at myself.

"Oh, you mean you don't know?" He looked surprised. "After all I've told you?"

"Well... no," I said, scratching my head, feeling I had missed something important. "Nick, I'm lost."

"It's because you'll still be seeding the next few generations of my people."

"Oh?"

"Yes. And I'll be your first trial participant." His body glows brightly for a second before a sustained flash of glaring light blinds me. While obscured by the intense whiteness, Nick said, in a high, melodic voice, "My name isn't Nick, it's Nickada. But my close friends call me Nicki."

"Nicki...?

Nick had transformed into the mysterious woman in my dream. Now she was staring at me. Nicki had long, silky black hair that flowed about her shoulders. An oval face accentuated by large, gray-tinted blue eyes and a small nose, almost like a button over her full, round lips. Her skin was the color of milk with a blush of pink. It's practically impossible to describe her in human terms. Although anatomically she was feminine-looking, she also had striking alien qualities. Her forehead, for instance, was quite large. She had no eyebrows or lashes, and except for the hair on her head (which she later explained she grew just for me), she was hairless. I didn't understand why, but like in the dream, I found her alien features to be beautiful and seductive.

"Nicki?" I repeated, wondering if this was another illusion or Nick's true form.

"No, Phil, this is my natural morphology," she said.

"How'd you do that?"

"Hearing your thoughts?"

"No. How'd you transform the way you.... Wait a second. You can read my thoughts, too?"

"Oh, that's easy. In time, you'll be able to do that also."

"Morph? Like you just did?"

"No, silly," she laughed. "Read thoughts."

"I will?"

"Yes, with a little training, it will become almost natural."

"How about morphing? Can all Venubians do that?"

"No. My ability to manipulate my morphology is scarce and beyond your capabilities. I'm able to change my form, but not body mass, and I can only hold the conversion for a few hours at a time. That's why I have been making excuses to leave you from time to time. It requires a great deal of mental and physical energy to maintain the new shape."

Before I could ask another question, Nicki approached me. She placed her arms around my neck, pressing her firm breasts against my bare chest; it aroused me. She smiled and said, "It looks like the equipment is working."

I nodded and ran my hands down her back and felt her firm buttocks. I didn't know where to begin or how to act.

Nicki gave me a gentle kiss on the lips. "Relax," she whispered in my ear, sensing my nervousness. "Before we test our joining, there's something I need to tell you."

Oh no, here comes the bad news.

"Bad news?"

"Ah... Yeah, it's an expression that refers to something that will be unpleasant to hear."

She narrowed her eyes. "Is telling the truth considered bad news?"

"Sometimes, especially when it deals with something unpleasant or sad. Sometimes the truth can upset whoever is on the receiving end."

Nicki became silent and looked at me with those large eyes that turned dark gray, then to dark blue, and back to gray again. The smooth fluctuations of her eye colors had an almost hypnotic effect.

"There's a truth I must tell you." Her voice brought me back from drifting within her mesmerizing gaze. "Humans can often hide their thoughts behind their emotions, but we cannot. You must always be honest, Phil—in heart and mind."

"But you haven't been honest with me. You've deceived me with the Elaine imposter. Took me without my knowledge—"

"Yes. That's true. I'm sorry. All of that was against my nature. The truth be told. You didn't meet the minimum requirements for what we're seeking. I've broken many rules in rebuilding and bringing you with me. In time, I hope you'll understand and appreciate my motives. I also hope you'll come to appreciate me. We have a long journey ahead of us, and we'll spend a lot of time together. I don't want you to resent me for taking you from your home. Believe me, I had no other choice but to leave you dead."

"Do I have a choice now?" I said.

"I'm truly sorry, Phil. The only other option is dismantlement."

"Yeah, I see your point." It was at that moment that I realized I was no longer Phillip Mann from Earth. Now, I was Phillip the Earthling. For some reason, that thought didn't disturb me as much as being dismantled. "Well, now what do we do?"

"For starters, let's check out your hibernation pod and get to know each other a little better."

CHAPTER 6

We were traveling at unimaginable speeds to Nicki's homeworld, Venubia. Sometimes I wonder if I wouldn't have been better off dead, rather than being this alien's experiment she's taking home to mama. Then I looked into Nicki's enchanting multi-colored eyes and said, "What the hell, I'm having an adventure of a lifetime." Then I remember why Nicki came to Earth and the reason she's taking me home, and I get scared all over again.

After my first few weeks aboard this incredible ship, I got a sense that something was always watching over me, like an invisible angel looking out for my welfare.

One morning, I woke up early. Nicki was already at work. I showered and dressed, then grabbed coffee and a bagel from the small galley. I walked into her lab, sat down, and watched her for a while. She talked to all the instruments and systems as if they were crew members. The nav computer was telling her about all the adjustments it was making. Its gruff voice sounded like an engineer complaining to its captain. After a few minutes of listening to that complex discussion, something to do with the ship's energy signature, I asked, "I'm curious. You said Venubia is next door. So, how far is your homeworld from Earth?"

Nicki arched a brow ridge, looking a little surprised. "It's only ten thousand light-years."

My mouth opened with the magnitude of that distance. "How in the hell are we going to travel ten thousand light-years in less than ten thousand years?"

"Not to worry. The journey will only take a little over twenty-two Earth months."

"Only twenty-two months?" I repeated while trying to get my head around what she said. "Nicki, I don't understand. How are we supposed to travel such a vast distance so fast? Recalling my high school science, Einstein insisted that nothing can travel faster than light."

"And he was right. However, our scientific community discovered a means of traversing great expanses of space almost instantaneously. We call them *Swashvee.* or *Corridors*."

"Wow, that's amazing. Corridors? Are they the same as wormholes?"

"No. Wormholes are too small and unstable. Think of them as gravity corridors."

"How do you find them? I mean, is there a sign that says, Gravity corridor straight ahead?"

Nicki smiled. "In a way... We can only detect their energy signature. Their interaction with the surrounding negative energy creates antineutrinos. It has a distinct signature or a signpost."

She said all of that as if I understood her. I guess she noticed how lost I looked. Nicki requested a holographic display that appeared right before me. It looked like a virtual space chart of our part of the Milky Way. There were many blinking colored dots scattered throughout two of the outer arms.

"These highlighted areas are the gravity corridors," she said, pointing at a blue dot. "This one is Corridor-44. It's the closest to your star system. The way it works is the ship has the coordinates of the corridor's approximate location—"

"Wait a sec. Approximate location?

"The strong gravitational forces surrounding the corridor cause space-time to shift a little. The ship needs to find the identifying signature, then we slip through before the surrounding gravitational forces stretch us out like strands of one-atom-thick spaghetti."

"That doesn't sound like a nice way to die."

"Nicki frowned. "The corridors present many dangers. They have side effects that can be harmful to humanoids. So, when we're close to the gravity wells, we must hibernate for protection."

"Can't the ship's hull protect us?"

"Not against everything," Nicki said, chewing on her lower lip.

"Okay. I know that look. What are you not telling me?"

"There are many side effects that only hibernation can protect us from. Besides, as you already know, there's not much to do on an automated ship. Some hibernation periods will last as long as four or five Earth months.”

“I don’t know, we’ve found some interesting ways to spend our time.”

Nicki’s pale complexion turned a rosy color, and her large, greenish-gray eyes turned bright blue. Over the past few weeks, I’ve learned some of Nicki’s moods through her eye colors. Whenever they get wide with a single bright color, it usually elicits a strong emotional response. Blue was both excitement and joy, amber anger or fear, and a pale gray or hazel meant she was calm. I haven’t figured out all the other various multicolored responses yet. When I asked how she controlled them, she said it was an involuntary response similar to blushing in humans, or the dilation of the pupils under stressful situations.

***

The ship has a magnificent arboretum filled with exotic alien plants and trees. I’d often go there to think. One time, while gazing through the leaves of a sprawling oak tree, my eyes caught a flash of bright light. Staring out of the giant, clear dome in the direction of the flash, a bright ring of bluish-yellow light surrounded a tiny white speck. It was a mesmerizing sight as the ring expanded, forming into a new nebula. While watching, I realized that the speck was the large star I first saw while on Nick’s tour of the ship.

The sound of the automatic doors opening told me Nicki had entered. She always goes to her favorite section with all the pungent smells and sweet aromas from her Venubian garden. Nicki selected the vegetation, flowering plants, and bushes from her homeworld. “This little section of the arboretum is my little piece of Venubia,” she told me while staring at a turquoise zeferia bush. Throughout her journey, she has plucked sample plants, bushes, and a few large trees, almost like souvenirs from her travels.

She told me that the oak tree she planted was for me. She said it was a seedling and, using what she termed super nanites, got it to maturity in two weeks. That alone is amazing. Its arching branches have already stretched throughout Earth’s section of the enormous domed structure.

Nicki further explained that she had the arboretum built into the ship's belly to give the ship a more feminine profile. After reviewing the ship from all the available camera angles, I can confirm that it resembles a well-endowed mermaid. The hull seems to go on for kilometers. Nicki summed the ship's dimensions by saying, "Think of her as a small city traveling through space." In the five weeks I've been aboard, I've only visited a tenth of the upper decks and none of the lower ones. The lower bays are where all the juicy stuff is, like engineering and life support. Nicki hasn't given me a reason why those areas have been off-limits. Like many of the things I ask, she either changes the subject or deflects. Something's up, though. I'm just waiting for it to happen.

Usually, Nicki would meditate for hours under her favorite Yeiikshii (pronounced *Yeeshee*) tree before coming to me. But today she came over and sat next to me on the wooden swing I had replicated, along with a picnic table and a putting green.

"You've been wanting to ask me something all morning. Sorry, I had to handle a problem. So, now you have my undivided attention." She smiled brightly.

I squinted my eyes in surprise. "This is most unexpected. Since when have you been worrying about my questions?"

"When haven't I answered any question?"

"Okay. Why are the lower decks off-limits to me? And why haven't you shown me engineering?"

"I haven't?" She shrugged, her eyes turning dark gray.

"See." I pointed an accusing finger. "See... right there. You're deflecting."

Nicki's lower lip curled while staring pensively. "Is this what's really troubling you?"

"You're hopeless."

"Why am I hopeless?"

"Let's drop the lower decks for now. Here's something you can tell me. In all our conversations and some of the more heated ones—"

"Yes. You must learn how to restrain your temper."

"I'm working on it. What made you think of a barbershop? Of all things, you morphed into an Italian barber named Nick."

"I was going more for effect. Besides, aren't Italians known for their hairstyling skills?"

"Now you're stereotyping. That's beneath you."

Nicki's eyes turned to a dark blue and in a timid voice said, "Sorry."

Stop stalling. Tell me why you used a barbershop?"

"Please, forgive me..." She tapped her lips with the tip of her index finger, her face tightened for a beat before she continued, "I did do some unauthorized testing on humans."

"What kind of testing?"

"When I first came to Earth, I searched for a noninvasive way of analyzing a small segment of the male population. While walking in downtown Miami, I came across a barbershop. Fascinating, I thought, seeing men sitting in chairs, engaged in energetic conversations, and looking relaxed. It seemed a most workable solution. After a five-mile search of the vicinity, I discovered an empty store on Lincoln Road in Miami Beach."

"So, that's how you settled in my neck of the woods."

"What do you mean?"

"Never mind. Continue."

"It was a small storefront with a quaint wooden and glass door. It all appeared perfect for my needs. Then I took one of the telemetric couches from the ship."

"Oh, how I loved that couch."

"I know. You spend far too many hours in it watching that brutal game."

"Basketball is not brutal... well, maybe a little."

"May I continue?" Nicki said.

I nodded.

"I modified it into a barber's chair with lots of built-in analytics. I further modified the couch to resemble an old-fashioned barber's chair with a leather seat, metal footrest, all trimmed in a wood-like material mounted on a bone-white porcelain pedestal. I tested it out the next day on a few men."

"Clever girl. How long were you in business before I came in?"

"About two weeks."

"You told me you screened males by analyzing their hair."

"As I described, hair follicles contain live cells. Mostly, I needed to study male DNA. The easiest way to collect follicles is with a good combing."

"Ah, I remember those comb-outs. They were great."

"Best to relax your subject first. My comb had built-in analytics that performed a DNA screening on each male. I could extrapolate their entire physiological, genetic, and mental state from a few follicles. That middle-aged man would have been my last customer of the day. I didn't like him. Bad genes." She smiled at me. "Then you came in, carrying all your woes and troubles about you. You fascinated me."

"Really?"

"Yes. You were so different from all the males I had screened. They all seemed preoccupied with themselves, but you…" Her eyes glowed as she looked at me. "Because I was unfamiliar with human males, I wanted to experience one up close. That's when I implanted a neurogenic transmitter into the base of your skull. Remember that sharp prick in the neck?"

"So, it wasn't an ingrown hair? You lied."

"All for a good cause." She gently patted my face.

"Interesting. How does it work?"

"It's like a transmitter that links us telepathically. Once the connection is established, I can experience everything you do." She gave me a sheepish look.

"Okay. You're holding something back. Out with it."

"I enjoyed helping you and watching your confidence grow with your successes. The more I helped, the better you became as a person. All those burdens you were carrying dissipated."

"You helped me? How?"

Her gaze turned downward. "It's not important to know how. What's important is how well you handled it all. It brought you closer. I wanted to be with you."

"That's what's still troubling. You morphed into Elaine. Imitated all her moves, her voice, even down to the way she ate. Was I ever with her?"

"Yes. I only took her form when I felt your pain. She was a shallow opportunist who was only interested in your sudden rise within the organization. Elaine wanted to mold you into someone incompatible with your nature. When she couldn't affect the changes in your personality, she started losing interest in you. Elaine wasn't a good person and would have hurt you."

Anger rose in me, recalling Elaine's beauty and sexuality. "You sound like my late mother," I barked. "I would have liked to have found that out on my own," I shouted in her face, turning my back to her. After a bit of reflection, it irked me, thinking she was right. Elaine was shallow. But I still resented Nicki's deception by pretending to be her.

"You're still angry with me. I'm sorry. I only wanted to get closer to you. That's why I morphed into Elaine."

I narrowed my eyes, wondering how long she had been in my life before the accident.

Nicki's face flushed as if she had read my thoughts. "I must be truthful," she said in a small voice. "It was me you had dinner with at that wonderful restaurant the night of the accident. You didn't imagine it. I was in the car, not Elaine. When the accident became imminent, the ship's auto alert transported me out. It broke my heart seeing your shock when I vanished. There was no way to get you out. The device was programmed for me." Her eyes welled. "There was no time," she cried.

I didn't console her. I was too preoccupied with the revelations she had laid on me. One thing became clear, though. The accident was the catalyst that drew us closer. Through that device, she experienced my terror and pain. She said she had never had a nightmare. Since the accident, she has had them regularly. That sudden and devastating crash had profoundly changed both of our lives.

"I'm responsible for all that has happened to you," Nicki said, with watery dark blue-gray eyes. "I want to remove those horrifying memories from both of us."

"No, you're not. They are a part of our history now. In each tragedy, valuable lessons are learned."

She sniffed back her tears. "I don't understand. Why would you want to hold on to such terrible memories?"

"I don't know how to explain it. But... I... I feel like all my memories will be lost. Nicki, you're lucky. You can pick any memory you want in virtual, detailed reality."

"But over time, you'll have the same ability."

I nodded, then looked out at the great expanse of stars, wondering what I would become in my new body and life. "Because of you, I'm alive. For that, I'm eternally grateful. But because of you, I'm neither all human nor machine but something in between. Maybe someday I'll come to terms with what I am... but it'll take a while."

Nicki nodded with a solemn frown. She stood and squeezed my shoulder. "Someday, I hope you'll forgive me, Phil." She left to attend to the ship. I pondered everything that had happened as I walked back to my quarters. By the time I reached my workstation, I had decided to record all my recollections and reflections of this incredible journey. I'll title it: *The Journal of Phillip Mann from Earth*.

CHAPTER 7

Later that day, Nicki came into my quarters. "Having regrets?" she asked.

I was sitting at my workstation, staring at the large viewscreen with the nebula's bright colors glowing in the distance. "No. Just reflecting on things while enjoying this magnificent view."

I turned and watched her make herself comfortable on the bed.

"After our talk, I realized how difficult this is for you," she said. "I can't imagine all the mental adjustments you're making. You know you won't be doing it alone. I'll always be here for you."

I smiled, then looked back at the viewscreen and sighed. "Fate is so strange. It moves us forward in constant linear motion through time, opening and closing doors. It gives us opportunities to seize for better or worse—"

"That's something new."

"What is?"

"You sounding... philosophical."

"Yeah. I get that way sometimes."

"You have many regrets, but never express them to me. Why?"

Nicki was right. Despite her being the only one in my universe, I didn't feel comfortable discussing my inner feelings with her. From the hazel-gray mix in her eyes, I knew she sensed it.

"My only regret is you didn't give me a chance to choose to be with you."

"That's true. But it's not fate that moves us. It's the universe...." Nicki stared at me and sighed. "Sorry, seems an inadequate word for what I feel about all that has happened... because of me.... Please, Phil. Believe me. I had no other choice." She got off the bed, came up behind me, and leaned her head on my shoulder. "I'm glad I saved and then abducted you. There was no way I would leave you in the morgue. You still had some electrical activity in your brain stem. So, I snuck you out. Got you on my ship, where I put you back together."

"You did more than *put me back together*. You made me into a goddamn cyborg."

"How many times do I have to tell you? You are not a cyborg. You are an enhanced humanoid..." Then she added, "with cybernetic implants."

"Stop. I don't want to talk about myself. Besides, there's nothing I can change." I gave her a side-eyed glance. "Can I?"

She leaned over my shoulder and looked me in the eyes. "You have changed me as much as I have changed you."

"Oh? In what way?"

"I had no idea that love could feel this way. Venubian marriages were mostly matches made to improve and or perpetuate bloodlines. Rarely were they done out of romantic fulfillment or mutual love. Now, our few survivors marry solely to procreate. Before the war, we were learning how to love nature as much as ourselves. We also were a thriving, almost utopian civilization." She let out a low moan, then moved around and sat on my lap. "The virus changed all of that. In just a few planetary cycles, we went from the brink of greatness to abject despair. We were trying so hard to save our species, we forgot how to live and love. You redefined how precious life is—how important it is to have someone to love and share life with. Now, you can teach an entire planet how to love and live again."

"You had to say that. Like, there wasn't enough pressure on me already." I felt my face burn with my anger rising.

"Why are you so red?" Nicki asked.

"Because I'm trying not to lose my temper. As you've so often pointed out." I clenched my jaw.

"Breathe, Phil. Breathe with long, deep breaths."

After a few deep inhalations, I got outward control of my rising emotions, but my inner self was still churning with anger.

"See. You aren't red anymore. Remember, when you feel angry or out of sorts, breathe. It works every time."

I nodded, still inhaling deeply, pushing each breath out with a nervous spasm.

"Breathe slower and not so hard. Concentrate on each breath and nothing else. Nice, steady inhalations...." She moved her hand in a slow, rhythmic wave, speaking like a hypnotherapist, keeping her voice in a low, melodic tone, "...filling your lungs and then releasing each breath with the same continuous stream. In... out.... slower... good. Now you've got it." She patted my cheek and started to stand, but I held her down.

"Not ready to let you go yet." I pulled her back onto my lap but continued to stare out into the awesomeness of space, thinking about how tenuous and precious life is. And yet we often take it for granted. We live from day to day, making choices and living with their consequences.

"What are you thinking?" Nicki asked with concern.

"Reading my thoughts?"

She arched a brow ridge. "You know I can't read your thoughts without your permission."

"Yeah. Well, it doesn't seem that way at times. But that's not what I was thinking about. Fate has brought us together.

"No such thing as fate."

"Stop interrupting. I need to get this out. You're bringing me to a strange world where I'll only have you to guide me. After studying about Venubia, I can't help wondering what my life will be like."

Nicki caressed my cheek, then got off my lap. She sat on the edge of the bed and gave me a wide-eyed stare. "You'll live like a royal stud in an almost Utopian world and want for nothing."

"That all sounds wonderful," I said with a groan. "But I can't help thinking about all the things I'd miss."

"Oh? Like what?"

"Some of my most cherished things. Like baseball and hot dogs on muggy August nights, and even more regrettable, denied the rights of being a weekend couch potato during football season, eating junk food, and taking long walks on the beach at sunset. I'll also miss my weekend pickup basketball games with my few friends. Not to mention the challenge of finding a date for Saturday—"

"Oh?" She curled her lower lip.

"Well, on second thought, that's one thing I won't miss. Now that I have you."

She smirked. "I never tire of that, though." She pointed at the blossoming nebula in the distance. "That is why I'm out here. It's a constant reminder of the universe's awesome power and beauty. It inspires me and gives meaning to everything."

I nodded in agreement.

"It's around dinner time. Are you hungry?" Nicki asked.

"Always. I'll meet you in the small galley. Just want to finish up my log entry."

After Nicki left, I thought about what she had said earlier. She wasn't the only one struggling to understand what I was feeling. Everything still seemed surreal. I'm not sure I'll ever make sense of my new life. Maybe after a hundred years, I may even learn to enjoy myself in my new world.

Odd, though, the only thing I really wanted was a good haircut.

35

PART II

BIOMEI

CHAPTER 8

Ship's Date 1553.30 Present Day

It's the state basketball championship game. The crowd's chanting my name as I take the ball up the court. I pass it off to the center with five seconds left on the clock, then I cut hard to the basket. The center makes a no-look toss back to me as I get into the low post. There are only three-tenths of a second left in the game. With the ball in hand, my body is lifting in slow motion up and over the rim. The crowd roars as my body twists to do a reverse dunk—

"Phil... Phil, wake up." Nicki's voice breaks through, disrupting my glorious dream.

"You couldn't wait one damn second? —I was about to do a reverse dunk in slow mo—" Nicki's dark green eyes (a new shade) gaze at me with a serious scowl.

"We have a problem," she said, staring past me.

"What kind of problem?"

"It's the ship. She's... how can I put it? She's sick." Nicki rubs her brow ridge.

"How could the ship be sick? You mean, broken. Don't you?"

"No, sick."

"Ships don't get sick. People and animals do."

"Well, this one can. All living things can get sick, and this ship is unwell."

"Take it easy." I pull her onto the bed and give her a reassuring hug. Her body felt tense as she looked at me with her mouth in a tight line. My heart's beating a little faster, realizing if she's this worried, then we must be in a lot of shit.

"Explain what you mean by sick." I'm trying to stay cool.

Nicki's eyes widened. She sat up on the bed and gave me a pensive look as though gathering her thoughts. "The ship's a biomechanical organism. Like any other organic being, she takes in basic elements such as hydrogen and helium and converts them into energy. She's also intelligent, responsive, and self-aware."

"Wait, a minute. You keep referring to the ship as *she*. Are you telling me the ship's a female and alive?"

"Exactly."

My head throbs with this new reality. "I was just getting used to being not human. Now, you're telling me our ship is alive and unwell." I narrow my aching eyes at her. "The ship is sick, as in having an illness?"

Nicki nods slowly, staring outward.

"Do you know what's wrong with eh... her?" Before she can answer, I say, "How does a ship get sick?" I jump off the bed and pace around the room. "How in the hell does a ship get sick? This is friggin unbelievable. Only I could get stuck on a ship that's sick."

"That's it!" Nicki says. "I'd never considered the variable that human microbes would have had on her biosphere. You were supposed to be decontaminated and then placed in hibernation."

Her jaw tightens, and her eyes narrow. "Oh, this's much worse than I had realized." She glances at me and sighs. "You both may be in trouble."

"Both? What'd you mean by both?"

"Although, if that's the problem, we may have a way around it.... Maybe." She hops off the bed, grabs a jumpsuit from my closet, and tosses it to me. "Get dressed and meet me in the central core, Engineering, Level-3."

She stops at the door and looks back as if she's about to tell me something, then turns and rushes out.

"Wait. Where's the central core?" I call to her back.

"Ask the ship. She'll direct you," she answers without turning.

I look down the empty, dull corridor, thinking I spend half the time trying to keep up with her and the other half trying to figure out what in the hell she's talking about.

Dressed in a panic, I rush into the corridor. Checking up and down the long, dark passageway, not knowing what to do, I shout, "Where's the damn central core?"

"Follow the lighted areas on the floor," a soft, feminine voice says.

I look around to see where the voice came from. A narrow line of yellow lights on the floor blinks on. The lights on my right side flash on and off. As I move toward them, they stop flashing. Nice, I think, and run through a maze of intersecting corridors, following the well-indicated path.

Running at a rapid pace for at least two hundred meters, I come to a set of bow-shaped doors. An amber light is flashing over them.

"Okay, now what?"

The doors open.

"Please, step in, Mr. Mann," the disembodied voice said.

The small interior, like everything else on the ship, had no visible buttons or an intercom.

"Destination?" The voice asked.

"Central core, Engineering Level-3."

There was no sensation of movement. A few seconds pass, and the lift opens. A set of tall, translucent doors is in front of me.

"Now what do I do?"

"You are in the decontamination area. Step forward onto the activation pad."

An oval disc rises a few centimeters from my feet. I take a careful step forward. The lift closes, and all at once, I'm in motion. Moving through the first set of doors, my clothes disappear under a bright white light. My skin is glowing, and the whiteness is clinging to me like a fine coating of baby powder. Entering the next section, a high-pitched sound is making my ears ring. The piercing sound stops, and all the white has turned to a scorching red color, but it doesn't burn. I'm moving into a third area. It looks like an ordinary white tile shower. A blizzard of fine spray is covering my body with a thin glaze of green, slimy stuff.

"This shit smells like raw fish."

"Please, remain still and silent during the decontamination process," the automated voice gently scolds.

Another ear-piercing noise, and I'm clean. "What was that?"

"A sonic rinse."

The pad is moving me through columns of warm air. *Rinsed by sound and dried by air. Neat.*

"You are entering the final stage," the voice stated. "At the tone, close your eyes and stand straight."

I hear the tone and close my eyes. A low-humming sound, along with something warm and soothing, passes over me.

"Decontamination is complete. Please, step forward and wait for further instructions."

Despite it being a bizarre experience, I must admit that my skin and hair have never felt this soft and clean. "Jeez, I look like a freshly bathed baby with clear, rosy skin," I quipped, smiling at my reflection while passing through the last set of doors.

I'm looking into an enormous room filled with empty workstations. Clear-pane monitors glowed suspended in midair. It's the most equipment I've seen so far.

"Please step onto the disc in front of you," the disembodied voice instructed. As soon as I center my feet, another disk comes down from above. A second later, I'm dressed in a snappy bright blue jumpsuit with silver piping on the cuffs and down the sides of the legs.

Nicki, still dressed in that same drab green jumpsuit she's been wearing for the past two weeks, is busy working at a large console. She's waving her hands over the three-wide screens filled with unfamiliar symbols and writing. The symbols flow off the screens, creating an exploded view of some complicated device. Hundreds of numbered parts populate the interior of the device. "What took you so long?" Nicki asks, not looking up.

"Didn't you have to go through decontamination?"

"Oh. The ship must have anticipated the problem. Lie down over there," she points at a long couch reminiscent of Nick's barber chair, only larger and with a lot more equipment attached.

"So, this is what engineering looks like."

"Technically, this isn't engineering. It's a workshop. Now, lie down."

"Are you going to tell me what's happening or just keep ordering me around?" She didn't answer or look up. "Nicki, I don't enjoy being treated like a dumb subject. You at least owe me an explanation."

"You are anything but dumb. I hear you."

"I didn't mean that dumb. I... meant ignorant. And you knew that. Dammit, Nicki, stop ignoring me and explain what in the hell's going on."

She sighs heavily. "There's not a lot of time for explanations. Please, lie down on the analyzer."

I look around and shrug.

"It's the couch in front of you," she says, noticing my confusion. "You'll find a telepathic interomitter in the right-side compartment. Please attach it to your left temple."

The couch, like the barber chair, automatically adjusts to my comfort. I peer into the compartment and spot a familiar cube. "So, that's what this is," I murmured while attaching the small object to the side of my head.

"Phil, can you hear me?" Nicki's voice is clearly in my mind. It sounds different. Along with her voice is an added element. Her mood. Also, her use of language subtly changed. She sounds stiff and controlled.

"Oh my, had no idea this is how telepathy worked. You get the emotions along with the words. It's fascinating and weird at the same time. Nicki, why do you sound different?"

"Up to this point, I was talking in American English. In telepathic communications, you're hearing translated Venubian. It's a more formal language."

"Not sure if I like this."

"You can't say I didn't warn you about being open and truthful. Can't hide your feelings behind your words anymore."

"See what you mean. It'll take a little getting used to. So, I'm asking for forgiveness now for all the transgressions to come."

"I will always forgive you."

Nicki's emotional state came right through. We rarely talked about our feelings. Now I see why. There's no need. They're all there, flowing through me like waves of sensory perception. Remarkably, all her thoughts are fixed on my well-being. The ship is weighing on her more, though.

"Hello, Mr. Mann," the pleasant voice of the ship greets me.

"Hello. Are you part of the automation system?"

"No. I'm the ship. Can't you feel me?"

Still dazed by Nicki's link, I only sensed her. I concentrate for a second, wait, I'm picking up another presence. It's separate from Nicki's but unmistakably alive. *"Yes, I can,"* I transmit with a sense of accomplishment. *"Please, call me Phil."*

"I'm so sorry for the inconvenience, Phil." The ship's apology sounded sincere with a real sense of concern for my well-being. *"I was certain that my bio-filters would have been sufficient in cleaning out all harmful, humanoid microbes. It appears I've underestimated their resilience and adaptability. It's strange, though. They don't act like normal microbes. They must have mutated and are causing problems with my biochemical processes. It's most puzzling. I'm confident we'll find a solution in time, though."*

My heart skips a beat. *"In time? What will happen if we don't find a solution quickly?"*

"Our systems will become irrevocably infected and will malfunction."

"And then what?"

"Then we will be in real trouble," Nicki interjects. *"Need to do a few tests, Phil. Please, try not to move. A scanning device will float out of the ceiling and move close to your head. Do not be alarmed. It is a heavy neutrino field imaging spectrometer. Something like an fMRI, but much faster and more comprehensive.*

"What are you looking for?"

"Polarity and sub-atomic lattices," Nicki answered.

"Polarity? You mean like negative and positive?"

"Yes, but also the spin of the elemental particles," the ship adds. *"All matter generates magnetic fields created by the quantum elements that make it up."*

"Okay? So, what does that have to do with me?"

"Your microbes are not harmful in themselves," Nicki interjects. *"We can protect against infection. It is the destabilization of the ship's*

symmetry that would compromise most of her systems. It would be equivalent to a human becoming infected with a radical carcinogen that instead of causing cells to replicate uncontrollably would instead make them fly apart."

Nicki tried to mask her concern with scientific objectivity, but the interomitter permitted me to read right through her. It's evident that time was a critical factor, and we gathered that we didn't have much of it.

I call out, "Are you finished with your examination?"

"Almost," Nicki says.

"Are you finished tinkering with me?" I jump off the table with a blossoming idea.

"I'm not finished."

"What if we neutralize my magnetic field? Wouldn't that stabilize me?" I say, ignoring Nicki's irritated scowl.

"Nicki, Phil may have a practical hypothesis," the ship says. "We've been avoiding this possibility, but it may be the best alternative. Phil must go through the transformation process."

"No. It presents too many problems," Nicki snaps. "We'd always be compensating for your magnetic field. No, it's too risky."

Clutching Nicki's arm, pulling her close, I say, "Okay. What's bothering you?"

"It is too risky."

"I don't understand. Didn't you change my magnetic field before I came aboard?"

"Yes. But a complete biological and physiological alteration is a different thing. And despite what you think, you're still a biologically based organism."

"So, why can't you do it?" I probe into Nicki's thoughts. It surprises me how easily I get inside her head. My sudden intrusion annoys her. *"You're holding something back."*

"Yes."

"Why?"

She didn't have to answer. Within her thoughts, I see a glob of goo that resembles a humanoid body. I gasp, then swallow at the graphic vision. There's no doubt what that glob of goo is.

"Now you see?" she says. "Do you understand?"

"Oh, yeah," I say with the vision still fixed in my head. Then I sense Nicki's emotional state. "You won't let that happen."

She tries to smile through a long, solemn face. "You realize you must go into stasis while we prepare you for the biogenetic procedure? I wanted to put this off until after we go through Corridor-44."

"Yes," I say, naïve about the risk.

"I should explain—"

"It's unnecessary. Sometimes it's better not to know everything and go on faith."

"Faith?" She wrinkles her brow. "Faith," she repeats, looking at me in surprise. "You are willing to risk your existence on belief?"

"Yes. I trust you. You'll let nothing happen."

"What if something goes wrong?"

"You and the ship will fix it."

"How can you be so certain?"

"Because of the trust I have in you. Also, it's not my time to die. I can't believe that after surviving a resurrection, I'll die of runaway microbes. That makes little sense. So, in my ignorance, I have to trust you. That's what faith is, instinctively knowing when something's right."

Nicki's eyes welled up, and a thin stream of tears ran down her cheeks. She holds my face between her long, graceful hands and gazes at me with deep, watery blue eyes. "That was beautiful, Phil. Not sure of the veracity of your argument," she smiles, "but I like it, anyway." She kisses me as if I'd never been kissed before. Her emotions run through me like a rushing tide. I'm wondering if this is what love feels like.

How could I be in love with an alien? Somehow, I keep Nicki out of my thoughts while my intellect and emotions collide over my feelings for her. It's obvious how Nicki feels about me. But am I only reflecting her affections, or is it because she's the only girl in my present universe?

"Why have you closed your thoughts?" she asks.

"Sorry, I needed a moment to myself."

"You're having second thoughts?"

"No, only mental preparation."

"I'm sorry to interrupt," the ship says. "We're at a critical juncture, and we must make a decision...."

The ship becomes quiet. The lights dim, flicker on brightly, then dim almost to darkness.

Nicki and I look at each other in alarm.

"Biomei?" she calls.

"Biomei?" I repeat.

"That's the ship's name. It's an acronym. I just realized that is the first time I called her by name."

"An acronym?"

"Yes. Biomechanical-enhanced-integrated-intelligence," Nicki rattles off. "It is not exact, but it has a nice ring to it. It sounds better in Venubian."

"Interesting, but what happened?" I say, looking around the dim room.

"She's offline." Nicki's complexion reddens. "Quick, get into stasis chamber-4. She points to a single row of open chambers in the back of the deep bay.

I run to them and count from left to right. "This one?"

She nods. A cold chill seizes me with the enormity of our situation. A moment of truth confronts me. I'm not sure if I'm ready to face stasis. Not wanting to appear like a coward, I turn to Nicki and give her a confident smile. She glances my way and nods. My eyes fix on her, trying to gather all of Nicki in a mental snapshot. While gazing at her, a thought comes to mind. Will this be the last conscious act of my existence?

"I love you, Phil." Her words wash over me as I get into the chamber.

The interior adjusts to a perfect comfort level as the translucent dome lowers, sealing me in. I feel a slight prick on the back of my neck. Warm fluid is coursing through my body. She looks at me as the stasis chemicals take their effect.

I feel uneasy with these fluids running throughout my body. A rush of euphoria has me on cloud-9.... My eyes are getting heavy....

CHAPTER 9

I wake with my arms and legs strapped to a gurney in a dim and barren room. I'm shivering with a burning chill. Straining my neck, I get a glimpse at tiny, colorful stones covering my chest. Something is attached to the side of my head. Now the burning is getting more intense, the trembling more violent. Each breath is an effort as if I were breathing underwater. *I... I'm.... No. Something's wrong. Where am I? What has happened?*

"Phil, you are in stasis-shock," Nicki says.

The lighting in the room brightens a little. "It will pass." She runs a scanner over me, then checks the display. When she looks up, our eyes meet. The trembling is subsiding. I reach out my hand and run it down the side of her face. *You're real. Not a dream.*

Nicki takes my hand and holds it to her breast. The warmth of her touch has a soothing effect. I feel safe, not so anxious.

I open my mouth to speak, but only make a grunting noise. Nicki kisses my hand; her face radiates with a beaming smile. "Well, your body made it through stasis," she said, sounding happy and relieved. Her smile weakens into a sorrowful frown while stroking my head. "I missed you," she whispers.

I wanted to tell her not to worry, but I fell asleep before I could say it.

***

I'm in my quarters. Nicki is sitting on the edge of the bed. She's trying to hide her feelings behind a big smile, but her dark gray eyes are telling me things weren't better. Overall, I felt well-rested. Using my elbows, I push myself up higher on the pillows and narrow my eyes at her. "Things are still screwed up, aren't they?"

Nicki arches a brow ridge.

"That's good, huh. How long was I in stasis? It feels like I was in longer than expected."

She doesn't answer.

"So, how long?" I nudge. "I've never seen her in this type of mood. Her silence was making me uneasy.

"Forty-four cycles," she blurted in a timid voice.

"It was only supposed to be two weeks," I say, puffing out a long breath, jumping out of bed. While pacing back and forth, I shot her an angry glance. "You had me in stasis for forty-four days. So, what the fuck happened?"

"Stop cursing. It doesn't suit you."

"You're deflecting."

Nicki stared at the floor.

"Tell me what happened?" I repeat in a stronger voice. Seeing Nicki's dour expression, I got back in bed, flopped on the pillows, rubbing my left temple.

"Do you have a headache?"

"Yeah. It just started. It's like a sharp, stabbing pain behind my left eye."

"It's nothing to be concerned about," she said, pulling out the familiar cube from her jumpsuit. She places it on the left side of my forehead. "Better?"

"Yeah, that little cube is amazing. Okay, my headache is almost gone. Start explaining."

"Where do I begin?" she sighs, rubbing the back of her neck. Her mouth pursed into a line.

Looking into her weary eyes, I realize she must have gone through a lot of crap herself. I softened my tone. "Turn. I'll rub your shoulders while you tell me what I missed. We still must be in trouble because I can't feel Biomei. For that matter, I can't feel anything. Nicki, come on. Tell me."

"Ah, that feels good," she purred as my thumbs pressed into her neck. "You're right. Biomei is still offline. But we have temporary power to most of her auxiliary systems. All the primary engineering systems are at sixty percent. Both muon and plasma drives are down, so we're operating with conventional turbine-produced electricity. Navigation is fully functional, as are life support and communications."

"Sounds like you've been busy. Wait, a second.... You said turbines power us?"

"Yes."

"Where in the hell did you get turbines?"

"I programmed them into a 3-D imager, and the ship stores provided the materials. I had the synthesizer replicate the required machinery on Engineering Level-4, where the turbines are now functioning."

"I get it. Whatever is needed, the ship can replicate."

"Pretty much. However, we still don't know what's inhibiting Biomei's biogenic functions. It's most perplexing. One positive, though..." She closed her eyes and bowed her head. "Rub a little harder with your thumbs pressing into the base of my neck."

"You were going to tell me a positive— Wait, what did you mean by we?"

"What?"

"You said we were clueless. Who else is here?"

"Oh, I must have forgotten. I activated a few droids to assist me."

"We have droids?"

"Yes... Ahh, right there... oh, that is good."

"So, what were you going to tell me?"

"Huh?"

"Nicki, you're drifting on me again. Please focus."

"Sorry, but something occurred to me." I stopped rubbing her neck. Her expression turned pensive.

"Nicki, you're doing it again."

"What's that?"

"You're starting one thought, stopping, and then beginning another. It's confusing as all hell and annoying. Please, give me the short version of what's going on in that sexy brain of yours." Her face went blank, looking lost in thought. "Nicki, talk, damn it!"

"It just occurred to me that you were never the problem."

"What!" I jump off the bed, knocking Nicki to the floor. "You're telling me being placed into an induced coma was unnecessary? Oh shit, Nicki. What other surprises do you have for me?"

"Stop cursing," she says as I help her up. "It is unbecoming of someone of your stature to use such unsavory language."

"I have stature. Since when?"

Nicki held her palm up for me to stop talking. Then she bows her head and mumbles something in Venubian. She looks up with wide, intense dark brown eyes. "If what I am thinking is true, then we are in real danger."

"Real danger? Are you kidding me? Like we haven't been in danger this whole friggin time!"

She calls out, "VSD05 and '07, meet me in Engineering Level-2." She points at me. "Get dressed and meet me there. You must use the service corridors and passageway tubes. All the lifts are offline to conserve energy. Here's a data interomitter," she handed me the familiar small cube. "It will update you on what has transpired, along with my log entries." She kisses me on the cheek, then frowns.

"Why the long face?"

"I was not prepared for all of this," she whispers.

"All of what?"

"I have to go. The droids are waiting for their instructions. On second thought, meet me in Cargo Bay-5. I need to activate a few more. We can talk there."

"What about the droids in engineering?"

"I transmitted for them to stand by."

"So, the droids are also telepathic?

"Yes. But limited to only receiving and acknowledging command instructions. Full telepathy is beyond their capabilities."

"We have droids. That's so cool. Can't wait to meet them. So, how do I get there? You said all the turbo lifts are down."

"It's all in my logs," she calls back, then dashes out of my quarters.

"I hope the damn droids are more helpful than you," I yell at her.

CHAPTER 10

Nicki's logs explained that Cargo Bay-5 is one of six central equipment bays. An odd smell greeted me as I walked into the enormous area. It smells like ozone with a metallic texture that sticks to the roof of your mouth. I inhale, realizing this is the first noticeable odor outside of food. All the areas of the ship I have been in were sterile and odorless.

A slight vibration through my deck boots reminded me I was close to the central core. Nicki described the core as being Biomei's heart.

One-half of the expansive bay had rows of different-sized heavy equipment and many interesting vehicles. As I walk around, taking in all the drilling and hauling equipment, I find most of it looks familiar. Next to the big equipment are racks of neat-looking power tools. A few appear like conventional drills and hand tools. As I progress toward the droids, I see a wide range of unfamiliar instruments and devices stored in cubby holes built into a wall.

Nicki was busy working on a droid in a rear corner of the bay. Racks of magnetically locked droids ran across and up the wall behind her. They're arranged with the largest ones close to the deck, with smaller frames ascending almost to the ceiling.

"Believe me, when I tell you these little zwouns can be aggravating," Nicki greets me, not looking up from the droid.

"Zwouns? That doesn't sound very nice," I say, studying the droid over Nicki's shoulder. "What does it mean?"

"It is like... critter in English. A little pain-in-the-ass, as you would put it." She threw me a glancing smile and then dove back to work.

"Why don't you like them? They're so cool looking."

"Because they've been programmed by mindless idiots to emulate humanoid characteristics."

"Why's that a bad thing?"

"The problem lies in their personality subroutines." Nicki's head pops up, then her arm rises, shaking a tool at me. "They installed social adaptability subroutines to make them more pliable. Droids can't handle all the contradictions that arise in social interactions."

"I still don't see the problem. You said that they're smart. Why can't they learn from their experiences?"

"There lies the problem, my dear. The droids store all the contradictions until someone erases them from their memory. The tech-idiots never considered how all that extra storage would affect processing ability in a standard VSD.

"What's a VSD?"

"Venubian Service Droid. They thought they were doing me a favor by loading the new series on Biomei to experiment and report on their adaptability. Know what I found?"

I shrug.

"Most social behavior appears aberrant to an outside observer. The techs overlooked the need for giving the droids a context in which to guide them through the mental quagmire of interacting in various social gatherings. Having no higher-order logic functions to help them negotiate through the complex social medium, they store everything into their virtual memory."

"So, what happens? Do they start malfunctioning?"

"Malfunction is an understatement. When they run out of operating memory, they erase low-priority files, but not the virtual ones. Within a few weeks, all that is left are random memories of aberrant social behavior."

"That doesn't sound good."

"No, it's not. The little zwouns went wild after the first month. They randomly started breaking anything they could get their hands on. I caught one in the plasma reactor core trying to alter its flow."

"Wow. I see the problem. You have to fix them before you can put them into service."

"Yes. This is the last one for now."

"They're still cool looking."

Nicki let out a heavy sigh. "I'm sorry for venting my frustrations. It feels like I'm always having to improvise on the run. I spoke to deaf ears when I begged the techs to give me unprogrammed droids."

"Your frustration is understandable. No one could've predicted we'd be dealing with such a crisis. Sometimes I think the universe wants to test our resolve."

She pulls a small towel out of the rear pocket of her baggy coveralls and wipes the sweat from her face. "That was the most beautiful nonsense I have ever heard. You almost sounded profound."

"You know, despite your distaste for the little zwouns, I see how they can be handy. Almost invaluable in times like these."

"I agree. That is why I will probably reprogram four more into service.

"Now we'll have little zwouns running all over the place. Does Biomei feel the same about them?"

Nicki arches a brow ridge. "Don't start with the Biomei thing again."

"Well, in the scheme of things, won't she be like their mother or aunt?"

"Do you have to anthropomorphize everything?"

"Just trying to loosen things up a bit. We have been dealing with a lot of stress. And you haven't been the nicest person to be around. You could show me a little love."

"You're not helping." Nicki walks to a central console next to the rear bay doors. The droids she wants are magnetically docked along a separate section of the rear wall.

"VSD11, '12, and '17..." She pulls out her scanner and then glances at it. "There you are," she mumbles. "And 81; enable, release, and come forward." The sounds of magnetic locks clicking open resonated through the cavernous room. The droids glide down to the floor, then walk upright in a single column to Nicki, stopping two meters in front of her. They align themselves into a single row facing Nicki. The droids stand perfectly still, appearing to be waiting for their instructions.

"Impressive," I say. "Especially their hands. They appear almost human right down to their pinkies and thumbs."

"The humanoid hand is most efficient for doing almost any task," Nicki says, coming to my side. "Have to give them credit, the engineers got things mostly right."

"It appears you appreciate them after all."

"They have their uses and will be invaluable in helping us with Biomei's illness."

Nicki walks to the engineering command console and speaks Venubian into the audible input module. Four clear, octagonal-shaped crystals materialize on top of the console. She reaches into a pocket that opens in her overalls and pulls out an interomitter. Nicki places it on the side of her head. She picks up the first small crystal, gives it a quick inspection before telepathically transferring her instructions into it. The clear quartz turns a pale blue. She repeated the instruction process for each of the three remaining ones. With crystals in hand, she walks behind the droids and inserts one into a receptacle in the upper section of each droid's torso.

As I watch the process, I'm wondering if humanity could ever reach this level of advancement without destroying itself. The droids have impressive designs. Most have squat torsos with long, segmented legs and arms. The majority were short, little over a meter and a half tall. The topmost row is filled with wide-bodied automatons. They look like heavy-lifters with big, round heads and oversized three-fingered hands.

Nicki studies the droids while pulling on her earlobe.

I ask, "What are you waiting for?"

"For the crystals to initialize, bring the droids online." Their oval heads with transparent rectangular displays all lit up at once. A small white ball begins bouncing back and forth within the displays. It reminds me of that early computer game: Pong.

Nicki takes a deep breath and exhales slowly. "Here we go."

I look on with growing interest.

"VSD01 and '02 execute your instructions." The two droids power up with a low whine and walk out of the bay. "VSD05, enable and begin diagnostics in lower sections of engineering." The droid, like the others, lights up and walks out of the bay. Nicki watches as they go out. She squeezes my hand. We look at each other with hopeful excitement, then back at the droids.

Placing my arm around her slender hips, I pull her closer. The droids move out at a synchronized, rapid pace.

They almost appear animated," I say, as the last droid exits the bay.

Nicki nods and says, "07, you're with me."

CHAPTER 11

Nicki has moved in with me and enlarged my quarters. She added another workstation, a small dining area, and a nice study with grav chairs. It feels like you're floating on a cloud while sitting in them. She also hung a little artwork from Earth and Venubia. Seeing Venubian art for the first time is most puzzling. I didn't know what to make of all the constantly changing colors moving through 3D squares and circles, along with other complex geometric shapes. The best description I can come up with is to imagine if Dali, Picasso, and Pollack collaborated on the pieces.

We both awoke from a restless sleep. The ship is still in night mode. Nicki and I go to the food synthesizer in a small galley across from our quarters. She orders a Venubian herbal tea and dry-tasting protein crackers while I try to drink myself to sleep on Venubian synthetic brandy. Great taste, no kick. Neither of us can get back to sleep. So, we sit in the study, staring at each other through bloodshot eyes.

"Let me see if I understand this," I say, trying to get my head around the problem. "The infection leaves no discernible markers. Nor can it be traced back to a common source. And it doesn't interact with any other biochemical agents within Biomei's systems?"

Nicki nods.

"That's crazy. We've been at this for weeks. Why can't we inject her with a unique isotropic tracker and follow what happens?"

In a weary voice, she says, "We did all that, several times, using different isotopes and contrast mediums."

"Jesus, this is unbelievable. All those different isotopes didn't tell you anything?"

"The only clear aspect of the infection is its effect on Biomei's biochemical makeup. At first glance, we believed it should've been a simple problem to identify. Isolate the mysterious mechanism blocking her biochemical processes and use an appropriate counteragent to absorb it."

"And you came up empty?"

She frowns with a heavy sigh. "You have to understand. Biomei is like all living organisms. The infection is blocking her ability to synthesize essential elements. Whatever it is, it must work on a quantum level."

"If you know that, why can't you detect it? You must have the technology for such analysis."

"We have. But all our efforts to uncover its subatomic signature have led to one dead end after another. Based on what little data we have gathered, it is neither viral nor bacterial, which... infers... an inorganic organism..." Nicki stares outward while winding a long strand of hair around a finger. "Biomei's complex mechanisms can evolve inorganic organisms like computer viruses—" Her lips close into a tight line, looking full of thoughts, "...Or even a nanovirus that could have evolved from a breakdown in any of her physiological systems..." Her eyes get wide.

"You have an idea," I say with sudden excitement.

"This is only hypothetical, but we may be dealing with a novel virus. I'm worried that it might have evolved within Biomei's systems," her voice raised as she speaks. "Like an autoimmune infection that has a subtle migration path." Her voice fills with enthusiasm while speaking faster. "Phil, we must hurry. There is not much time before..." Her expression turns pensive again, then she starts for the door.

"Wait. What is it?"

She glances at me, then takes off without an explanation.

"Where're you going?"

"I know you're starving," she calls back. "Get something to eat, then meet me at the main engineering level 2."

"The central core?"

"Yes. Hurry."

I grabbed a sandwich and coffee and ate it on the run— what Nicki described before she ran off to engineering worried and confused me. If the infection originated within Biomei's biogenic system, why couldn't it be traced or identified? If it's a virus, how could it be so obscure?

After going through a short decontamination procedure and having to put on a sterile gown, I enter the central core. It's the cleanest room I have ever seen. It looks more like a surgical unit than an engineering level. The circular room has alabaster walls and shiny deck plating all the way around. Everything appears as if we are the first to ever enter this pristine area.

I peer through a transparent dodecahedron structure. The core is a large iron ball spinning in a pool of liquid triterium. Nicki explains that it's a rare liquid metal. She said it replicates Venubia's central core, producing a powerful magnetic field. Nicki tells me the energy it produces could power several Biomeis.

"Biomei has two propulsion engines." Nicki points to a system of colored pipes flowing around and through the core structure. "These pipes transport high-pressure gases that are converted into plasma as they pass through the strong magnetic bottles, which condense the plasma into a powerful stream. The pipes continue through the outer bulkhead, into the engine thrusters, and then out the tailpipe. The plasma drive is for standard spacetime travel. The fusion drive is for reaching the corridors. The distances between them are quite far in certain regions." Her face tightens when she glances at the unmoving iron ball. "The fusion drive went offline when Biomei went down. If we can restore the plasma drive, it will get us home. But it will take a little longer."

"How long will it take us?"

"That's the problem with plasma drives: velocity builds over time. The fusion engines can attain .78 lightspeed in a matter of seconds. That is why it's our main propulsion. Without the boost from the fusion drive, it will take a hundred and fourteen years to reach home."

"A hundred and fourteen…? That's a long time."

"You'll be in hibernation during most of it."

"And you'll be?"

"Working on the plasma engines."

"Not on Biomei's biogenic systems?" I say, still grappling with being in a near-death state for over a hundred years. I checked my universal translator to make sure I heard it right.

"The droids are working on that. I suspect the real problem is with the plasma matrix. It is the most obvious place to start."

"I'm not leaving you while Biomei is down." I hold my hand up to stop any objections. "Don't even start with me about hibernation. I'd rather you explain the problem, and let's see what we can come up with. Biomei is our first and only concern now."

Her brow ridges rise, looking surprised. "What has gotten into you? You even sound sincere. Do you really care that much about Biomei, or is it something else?"

She had me there. I just blabbed the first thing that came to mind, and now I have to prove it. "Of course, I care. She's our lifeboat, and without her, we'll perish."

"Is that all?"

"I care because you care. Besides, I hardly know her."

"You may not be aware of her, but she is influencing you. Biomei told me she saw greatness in you. She sensed it when I brought you aboard. I'm still wondering what she saw."

"Thanks a lot." Her snide remark had me thinking about Biomei. Was she alive? That's what hangs me up the most, regarding the ship's status as a living entity. Nicki believes it, so why didn't I?

I watch in fascination as Nicki plugs different instruments into couplings along the base of the clear domed structure. She looks up at me and smiles, her face wet with sweat, looking exhausted.

"Let me work with the droids," I suggest.

She narrows her eyes.

"Where can I help?"

"Give VSD05 a hand with opening those distribution nodes over there." She points at a set of double doors that lead into the adjacent bay.

"Sure, there's nothing I can help you with here?"

"I'm almost through. I'll join you in a few minutes."

I walk up to a droid working on one of the nodes.

"Good day, sir," the droid cheerfully acknowledges me. "It is a pleasure to finally meet you," it added with a flash of colors across its optical sensor.

It appears more alive than mechanical and different from what I'd imagined in the cargo bay. "Good day, VSD05. It's a pleasure to meet you as well. Where do you want me to begin?"

"You will need this." It hands me a device that resembles a long screwdriver with a tiny opening at its head end.

I'm considering the device, trying to understand its workings. Then I notice the droid's right hand was configured like the tool I'm holding.

"If I may illustrate for you, sir," the droid says as though it understands my uncertainty. It turns to the node next to it and holds the device up to a corner of the front panel. It presses the screwdriver against it. A second later, the front of the panel dissolves right before my eyes.

"Wow. That was cool. What happened?"

"This is a quantum destabilizer," it explains. "It disrupts the molecular bonds of the panel and absorbs the atomic pattern into its memory for later reassembly."

"Remarkable." I walk to the next node in line and say, "May I?"

"Of course, sir."

Grinning like a kid, I go to work with my new toy. "How many of these panels have to come off?" I call Nicki as she enters the bay.

"All of them," she answers.

"All of them?" I mumble, surveying the room. There are nodes everywhere. The nodes are double-stacked, one-meter cubes with a small status display on one side. "There must be hundreds of them."

"1024 on this level, sir," the droid says.

"This level?"

"There are five additional levels above this one."

I look up and see a narrow ladder going up five levels. The nodes in the first few rows of each level are all I can see. "How many in total?"

"6234," the droid answers.

"Sorry, I asked. Guess we got our work cut out for us," I say to the droid with its optical sensor blinking at me. "Okay, guess I'll start here, and you go up to the next level.

"Belay that '05," Nicki says. "I need you here to run a full diagnostic for comparative analysis." She shrugs. "Sorry, but you will have to work on your own for the time being. As soon as the other droids finish with their analysis, I'll send them to assist you."

"Other droids? How many are there now?"

"I have thirteen others working on critical systems. They should be finished in a few hours. Work quickly. We don't have a lot of time."

"What are we looking for again?"

"Anything out of the ordinary." She comes to me and squats in front of the open panel.

I look over her shoulder into the node's interior. "Holy shh—"

Nicki's brow ridge rises, giving me the evil eye. She hates my cursing.

"That looks more like a living organism than an inorganic device. What are all those bags and tubing for? There's nothing electronic in this thing."

"I keep telling you, Biomei is a living organism. The nodes take in raw elements like hydrogen, helium, and oxygen from space, then convert them into usable biochemical elements, distributing them throughout the ship for processing. Just like within any organism. Each section of nodes has a specific function—everything from power to food, waste distribution, and recycling."

Nicki has been trying to explain Biomei's uniqueness to me from the start. It was too fantastic to accept until seeing it up close. "Okay. I admit it. It took me a while, but I see it now. Biomei is alive."

"She will not be for long if we do not figure this out."

Nicki's body stiffens, and her eyes darken to deep gray. In hopes of quelling her sudden anxiousness, I wrap my arms around her small waist and pull her closer. She lifts her face, and in that full-spectrum lighting, I see Nicki's weakened condition. While holding her in a tight hug, I caress the side of her pale cheek. It feels damp and cold. "You're exhausted." I kiss her. She locks her arms around my neck, standing tippy-toed, and she kisses me back.

"We'll have time to catch up later. I promise." As I turn, she touches my shoulder. We gaze into each other's eyes. She pulls me in for another long, passionate kiss. "I promise," she repeats as though she's reassuring both of us.

We both looked in surprise when a strong tremor ran under our feet. Heavy metallic shields and doors slam into place, sealing us in the central core. Then the explosion. The ship shudders violently. Thankfully, the room's blast shields contain most of the shockwave. Biomei rocks to port, throwing us off our feet. A second, more intense eruption rips through the room. Sending equipment flying in all directions. Something sharp pierces my back. My body goes numb, and my head hits the deck hard.

"Nicki," I call with my heart running like a rabbit. "Nicki," I shout. A sudden lightheadedness has me thinking my injuries must be worse than I realize.

The bay becomes dark and silent, giving it an eerie, ghostly feel. "Nicki? Nicki, where are you?" A wave of panic runs through me. *Oh, Nicki, please don't be dead.* I try not to cry, but the tears come anyway.

I swallow my fears down and concentrate on trying to move. My legs are dead. I roll onto my belly to get a better view of the bay. The lightheadedness intensifies. The room blurs with my eyes growing heavy. A part of me wants to sleep, and the other is fighting to stay awake.

All of a sudden, my vision gets sharper. It's as if I had built-in night vision. While searching the room with my newly discovered enhanced optics, I realize my headache is also gone. "One of these days, you'll have to tell me about all the damn enhancements," I shout, hoping Nicki responds.

Everything is illuminated in a light gray background. Under normal circumstances, my paralysis would have been alarming. Somehow, in the back of my mind, I know Nicki could fix me. She wasn't dead. I could still feel her.

It seems like hours that I've been fighting my heavy eyelids to stay open. At about the time I lost all hope, a light shines in my face; it's one of the droids. He easily moves large pieces of twisted metal panels off me, then squats down and asks, "Do you need assistance, sir?"

"What the fuck happened? How's Nicki?"

"Which inquiry shall I answer first?"

"Where's Nicki?"

"If you are referring to Nickada, she has been taken to the medical bay." He runs a medical scanner over my body. "You have a four-by-two-centimeter shard of altirium embedded between your eighth and ninth cortical segments. You have also lost much blood and fluids. You require immediate medical attention."

"Forget about me. How's Nicki?"

"She is in surgery."

"Surgery? Who's doing it?"

"The automated surgical attendant."

"Wonderful. Help me up."

"Sorry, Mr. Mann, I cannot comply with that request."

"I must see, Nicki."

"And you will after her surgery. Oh, look, sir. Your grav-gurney is here."

CHAPTER 12

I woke in a panic and screamed, "Nicki!"

A droid with a frosted oblong head and a metal-frame body stands over me. It's looking at me with its optical sensor, bouncing back and forth, holding a scanner. It seems like parts of it are missing. It has two arms with standard hands, but also has two additional arms lower down its erector set-like body. "Mr. Mann, I am your medical assistant," it says, sounding like a Harvard Medical School professor. He runs the scanner over my body.

"Where's Nicki?"

She is currently working in Bioengineering.

"She's okay?" I push out a long breath. "She's all right?"

"She was most fortunate. The explosion threw her across the bay. She only suffered a mild concussion and lacerations on her face and extremities. No major organs were damaged. However, your recovery will take a little longer."

"Oh? Why?"

"We have to replace a section of your cortical interface. That is why you have no control over your lower body."

"What's a cortical interface?"

"It emulates a humanoid disk in the spinal column and communicates directly with your primary processor. Nickada requested that I also add a new interface that will increase the electrical response within your neural network."

"I don't know what any of that means. Just do it."

"First, I must perform a diagnostic on your network. Once I have finished, you will be cleared for surgery."

"How long will the surgery take?"

"Three minutes."

"Are you kidding me?"

"No. I'm most sincere."

"Do whatever you have to do and get me the fuck out of here."

"I was about to, sir."

"So, do it already," I shouted.

Another droid came around me. I must have been on a mag-gurney. It's this cool thing that's suspended in a magnetic field. It looks like an ordinary gurney without wheels. Nicki told me Biomei can control a magnetic field in such a way that any object can float on it.

My recovery time was surprisingly long for such a short procedure. But I'm whole again.

***

Two droids met me when I rushed into bioengineering. One was '07. He gives me his usual cheerful greeting and tells me Nicki is at the central console working with '04. It points to a dome-shaped instrument suspended above a long table in the center of the bay.

I run up to Nicki. She glances at me and says, "Need two more minutes and then we can catch up."

Her cool attitude surprises me. *I wonder what I did this time to piss her off.* "'07 gave me a better greeting."

"I modified his personality routine."

"That's not what I meant. Please, look at me."

"Give me one minute."

Her mood felt sharp and distant, so I started to leave, feeling dejected and confused.

"Phil," Nicki calls. "Where are you going?"

"You're obviously busy, and I seem to be in the way. When you have time, we'll talk. Finish what you're doing, then come to our quarters."

Nicki runs up from behind, wraps her arms around my waist, and stops me. I turn. She gets on her tippy-toes, then plants a big, juicy kiss. My heart skips a beat, looking into her big eyes.

"Oh man, I needed that. Can I have another?" I say, pulling her back. We embrace and kiss, holding each other in a tight hug. We both sigh as if feeling the same thing; all the tension is melting away.

Nicki smiles brightly. "You look good," she says.

"You still look tired," I say, holding her face between my hands.

Nicki moans. "It will make things much easier once your internal processors are all enabled. I promise, as soon as Biomei is back to full operation, you're going through the transformation process. We cannot continue with all these handicaps."

She didn't mean to hurt me, but her words were piercing. When she mentioned *handicap*, I had no idea what a drag I had been on her. Yet, she never complains. Even when things were at their worst, she stayed positive and on course while towing me along.

"I'm sorry I was a little disagreeable before," she says. "You caught me at a critical juncture. I had to finish."

"I only wanted to see you. Now that I know you're all right, I'm okay. So, what's going on?"

"We have a hull breach. A team of droids is placing a temporary patch over it. The patch will need to be replaced soon, something we will talk about. The explosion... There is no clear reason for it."

"Could the virus have caused it?"

"Unlikely. But it still presents a threat to Biomei."

"If the explosion is separate from the virus. Then what's the virus all about?"

"If '05 is successful, we may get our first look at it."

"You found it?

"We'll know shortly."

"Nicki, something's been bothering me. It's been nagging at me for a while."

"What is it?"

"Have you considered... sabotage?"

Nicki's face turns dark as if I hit a nerve. "Why sabotage?"

"Maybe I have a devious mind, but it's the only thing that fits. We have been running in circles, trying to come up with logical answers to a series of events that, on the surface, seem unrelated. Sabotage is the best answer. Think about it. Biomei's biogenetic systems are failing due to an unknown cause, and then we have a major blowout in the central core... Please, tell me I'm making sense?"

"As scary as it sounds, you are making a lot of sense. Just a minute. '05 is transmitting its findings from the few functioning biogenetic nodes on level one." She listens, and then her face flushes. "Bring them to Biolab-2 at once."

"You're a nice rosy color, what's up?"

"Sabotage. You may be on to something."

Biolab-2 sat at the end of a long corridor about one hundred and fifty meters from Bioengineering. Biomei felt as empty and dim as her long, winding corridors. Not feeling the light vibrations of her powerful engines made me pause, musing on Biomei's absence. Her presence is always around me like a constant hug of reassurance. Without her, everything feels ominous and vacant.

Two droids acknowledged us as we walked into the small lab.

"We are on batteries in here," Nicki says.

"What are those droids doing?" I ask.

"They are extracting auxiliary power packs from droids not in service. The powerpacks will provide enough energy to do the diagnostics on the samples that '05 is bringing us.

VSD05 walks in and stops in front of one of the droids. A slot opens in the lower right side of its torso. A tiny rack of six small vials, containing yellow liquids, slid out. '05 hands the vial samples to another droid and tells it to prepare a series of spectroscopic slides. A slot opens, and the droid places the rack inside.

'05 goes to the second droid, and another slot opens in '05's torso. It hands the other droid a round, coiled object.

"What is that about?" I ask, Nicki.

"The coiled device the droid is installing is a power cell. We hope it will be compatible with the medical scanner."

Within minutes, the automaton had the scanner powered up. The droid that was given the vials produces a series of clear, paper-thin discs and hands them to Nicki.

She places the slides along the top of a glass table. The dome hovering over it lowers a few centimeters, positioning itself over the slides.

"What's that?" I asked.

"It is a tunneling neutrino spectrometer with a built-in imaging scanner," Nicki says.

"Neutrinos?" I repeat. "I thought neutrinos don't interact with matter. That they pass right through everything."

She nodded. "We have developed a process of fattening them up, so they interact with the photon detectors. Our detectors are sensitive to the energy signature of the discharge. Within a few minutes, it can build up a picture from the aggregate of the electron vectors bouncing off the neutrinos."

She made some final adjustments, and a holographic image appeared above the tabletop. One slide is full of crystalline-shaped objects that have fine hairs jutting out one end and a single, thicker hair coming out of the other. They circled other, more petite balls covered in pimples with fine hairs. A larger, crystalline-shaped object engulfed the little balls, absorbing them. The next series of slides was clear.

"Clever," Nicki says, as she stares at the image.

"What are they?"

"A nanovirus," she says. "You know. You were on to this from the beginning. Some of your processors appear to be working."

"Thanks. It seems your suspicions were correct."

"Not entirely. These are not from Biomei."

"Oh? So, how did they get into her system?"

"Somebody put them there."

"Then, it is sabotage."

"Exactly." Nicki squints her eyes at the image. "03, give me a grid over this one." She highlights one of the crystalline nanites with a wave of her hand. The image had a grid map superimposed over it. "Enhance sectors A23 through F30." A group of squares brightens, then enlarges. "I guess this artist didn't want to sign his work. '03, do you recognize this construct?"

"There is no record of this architecture."

"Interesting," '07 interjects as he enters the lab, holding a larger collection vial in one hand. "That nanite architecture is much like Klaxon Zhetanons used in their industrial anthropoids. Their molecular composition is composed of biodegradable materials. They are simple in design and would never have been detected if the designer didn't overlook Biomei's inherent autoimmune system."

"Remarkable," Nicki replies, almost sounding impressed, but her eyes are full of distress. "What are you suggesting, '07?"

"Biomei's biogenic systems are designed with specific subatomic symmetry. Although she was not consciously aware of the virus, she must have sensed subtle fluctuations in her magnetic field caused by the nanites' activation. When activated, there is a brief and tiny discharge in Biomei's bladders. That small discharge momentarily creates a slight imbalance in her biochemical construct. The cumulative effect of the discharges caused a gradual buildup in salinity in her waste." The droid holds up the vial and adds, "I have verified my hypothesis by performing a quick chemical analysis of Biomei's waste collection and discovered a .0152 increase in salinity. I also collected additional recycled materials for further analysis."

"Fascinating." Nicki takes the vial from '07 and hands it to '03. "Good work, '07." The droid's optical sensor flashes in acknowledgment. '03, do a spectral analysis and a biochemical functionality diagnostic. I want to know everything we can gather about these nanites. They are one of the most advanced I have ever encountered."

"As you wish, Nickada." The droid makes a respectful bow and goes to a small table in the rear corner of the lab. An array of instruments appears on and above the table's top.

"You seem to admire those little bastards," I say, mystified about her attitude toward them.

"I admire the technology, not its application," she explains. "Make a full log of this, '07, and upload it as soon as the central core is back online."

"Okay, we've identified it, now what?" I ask.

"First, we need to rid ourselves of the virus, but we cannot accomplish that until we understand its complete design and origin. We need to tag a few and let them run through their cycle. Once we see their mode of operation, then we can trace their activity back to its source. If successful, we will be able to cut them off from their primary power and kill them."

"What the hell are they?"

"Robots about the size of a proton, and they're killing Biomei."

"Why can't we kill the little bastards and be done with them?"

"Because whoever designed this virus knew exactly how to attack Biomei without leaving a trace. It is a sophisticated design. You know I considered Biomei's illness to have been caused by a nanovirus but dismissed it as too far-fetched."

"Why?"

"Because it could only be initiated into Biomei's system by someone familiar with her biogenetic design. There are only a few who possess that knowledge, and they are all trusted friends and allies. I cannot believe any of them is capable of such treachery. Whoever sabotaged Biomei did not know everything about her..."

"What's wrong?"

"Whoever did this must have wanted us to find it. Under normal circumstances, this virus would have remained undetectable if not for that one simple flaw. Biomei's salinity is a natural byproduct of her metabolism. The virus must have been building up since I left Venubia."

"I don't understand. Why would someone design an almost perfect virus with a detectable flaw?"

"Someone working under extreme duress and for some reason wanted us to find it."

"Wow. Any idea who that could be?"

"A few possible suspects come to mind, but none of them have the technological skills... However, the Klaxons have the technological capability for such a virus. And it did possess Klaxon design elements. But as far as I know, the Klaxon scientific community does not have the facility to design such a subtle and lethal virus. Besides, the Klaxons have as much at stake as we do. Also, they are sworn pacifists." Nicki bows her head and sighs. "Damn, this is frustrating."

"Let's get rid of the nanites and worry about the possible vandal later."

"Biomei's biogenic functions are dangerously low, and if we do not get her an infusion of fresh nutrients and clean energy—" Nicki closes her eyes and shudders. "If we lose her, we will be stranded out here for a long, long time."

My heart ached as I pulled her close and held her to my chest. "I don't like the sound of that at all. Let's make sure that doesn't happen."

She looked up at me and half smiled. We hug, then Nicki rests her head against my chest. In a small and wispy voice, she says, "I'm glad you're here."

CHAPTER 13

"I'm having the droids apply positron tags to the vial samples, then inject them back into Biomei. This will enable us to follow the virus's pathway back through her biochemical synthesizer," Nicki tells me as I enter Main Engineering.

"Sounds like a good plan."

"We need to flush out all Biomei's systems and then sterilize them before we can reboot her."

"After you clean her out, will we be able to continue to Venubia?"

"Sorry. It's not that simple."

"What else needs to be done before we can power her up and go?"

"Once she is clear of all harmful pathogens, we'll need to replenish her systems with a fresh molecular medium. We also need to replace her H3 supply to ensure against any other possible contamination from virtual free radicals."

"Please, Nicki. Take a break. Let the droids do the cleanup and get some damn rest."

She nodded and gave me a weary smile. "As soon as everything is in progress, I'll rest. But we are at a critical juncture, and I must ensure we do not overlook anything."

"Where are the droids?"

"I have a team manufacturing the flush. I am using two of the service droid's power-packs to run the berteon generator to sterilize Biomei's systems. Another team has completed a particle collector, which will be converted into a temporary fusion battery. It should produce enough power to maintain Biomei's memory core, protecting all of her data banks."

"That's good news."

"I have more good news. In a few hours, we'll have sufficient power to run all the auxiliary systems at full capacity. So, you can take a hot shower and listen to your weird music."

"Jazz isn't weird."

Nicki arched her brow ridge and smirked.

"How can I help?"

"Work with '03 and '05 to launch the particle sail they have constructed."

"A sail? How'll that work?"

"All we need is two hundred kilometers of nanocarbon fiber and a large particle generator. It's old technology, but it will get us moving until we can get Biomei back. It will be slow going for a while until we gain some decent velocity. Once the hull breach has a permanent patch, we'll place the fusion engines back online and try to make up some lost time.

"The droids assured me we will reach the Delius System within thirty ship cycles. Based on our most recent telemetry, there are several habitable planets in that system."

"Maybe we'll find some edible food sources," I say, thinking it would be nice to eat something real for a change.

"I hope so." She frowns. "I know this has not been easy on you." She comes closer, looking closely at me. "You have not complained about any of this."

"It's been much harder on you. So far, I feel like extra baggage. I want to carry my weight."

"You have helped me in immeasurable ways, my love." She kissed my cheek.

"Thanks, Nicki. In my heart, I know everything is going to be fine. The universe is just testing our worthiness to be out here."

"You always know the right thing to say. So far, you're my best experiment."

"So, that's what I've been reduced to?"

She narrowed her eyes. "On second thought, I think you're still a work in progress."

After a brief discussion with '07, she comes back to me. She says, "'07 stated that we need to conserve as much energy as possible until they have completed the installation of the particle collector and recharged the auxiliary power nodes." Her expression becomes solemn. "I have decided to place us into intermediate hibernation until we reach the

Delius System. The droids will remain active during this period to prepare Biomei's systems for clean-up."

"That's it? That's all you're going to say?"

"I don't understand. What more can I say?"

"How about let's get a bite to eat and make love before being placed into Never-Never Land?"

"Is that all you think about? Food and sex?"

"Is there anything else on an automated ship?"

Nicki's weary eyes brightened with a corner of her mouth turned up.

CHAPTER 14

I'm standing while gazing at a magnificent alien sky full of brilliant reds, greens, and blues. Moons of varying sizes loom above, curving away from the horizon like a Duchamp painting. The landscape is full of vibrant flowers and foliage glistening under a bright sun.

Nicki's presence is close. After a short search, I find her sitting on a patch of bright blue-green grass. She smiles and gestures with a wave of her hand to join her. The landscape turns into a beautiful park. It feels like an early summer's day. The air is dry under a steady, warm breeze.

A nearby lake with shimmering, emerald green water has Swan-like birds congregating at one end. A large white one comes down and lands, barely disturbing the water's surface. It flaps its long wings a few times, then folds them against its body and glides over to the other birds.

Nicki has created an Earth-style picnic complete with a wicker basket and a red and white checkered tablecloth she's spreading onto the plush grass. She pats the ground for me to sit. Nicki reaches inside the basket, pulls out a sandwich, and hands it to me. I study its contents. There's a mysterious white substance between two thick slices of dark bread.

I pulled the upper slice back and gave the white stuff a sniff. It had no odor. "What is this?"

"Whatever you'd like it to be."

"Really?"

"Yes. What would you like more than anything at this moment?"

"Anything?" I ask.

"Go on, close your eyes and think about what you would like to eat."

I close my eyes. A sly smile grows while holding a vision of Nicki's naked body wrapped in my arms.

"No, Phil," she laughs, covering her mouth. "I meant in the way of food," her face brightens. She whispers, "I am still waiting on your food choice."

I concentrate for a second before the memory comes to mind. I take a small bite of the sandwich. "Oh wow, that's incredible. It tastes just like

I remember." I take a larger bite and relish each mouthful of the remarkable sandwich.

"What's corned beef?" she asked, studying me as I devoured the sandwich.

"Corned beef," I repeat, chewing down the last mouthful while savoring its taste and smell. "It's one of the best-tasting meats of all human experience, except maybe for a kosher hot dog at a baseball game in late August."

"It seems I still have a lot to learn about human tastes."

"You'll never be able to appreciate these things until you experience them firsthand and not vicariously through me."

"Firsthand?" She wrinkles her button nose. "I don't understand."

"It means for real. The experience of eating a hot dog at a baseball game."

"Oh, I understand. We must arrange that when we get to Venubia."

"Venubia. Every time you say it, I wonder how I'll fit in."

Nicki casts her eyes downward and frowns. "I've been so busy with all the problems with Biomei, I've never stopped to consider all the adjustments you'll have to make. It will be a real culture shock for you. We must finish your transformation procedure."

"I've been viewing some holographic material in the ship's library. From what I've learned, your people aren't going to like me at all. They'll see me as a barbaric, primitive from a backward, little world."

"You underestimate my people's objectivity. And once they get to know you, they'll appreciate your primitive beauty as I do."

"Was that a joke? Are we trying to be humorous?" I grab her arm and wrestle her onto the thick grass, caressing her neck. A cool breeze washes over us, and the sky darkens. "What's going on?" I say, looking up at the ominous sky.

Nicki says, "We must wake up."

"What's wrong?"

"It's Biomei. She's trying to contact us."

"How? We're dreaming, aren't we?" I stop to think for a second. I could sense what Nicki was feeling. "You're right. Biomei is trying to contact us."

Nicki ran to a console as we entered engineering.

"I check the ship's chronometer. We were in hibernation for fifteen ship cycles," Nicki says. "Biomei induced the dream to bring us back to consciousness."

"How, she's offline?"

"Biomei and I are telepathically linked. Even in an unconscious state, we remain inseparable."

"What's wrong?"

"Biomei's sending me data on her condition. She's programmed to alert me to any change."

"Well, is it a change for the better or the worse?"

"Being in a powered-down mode, she has to relay the information in quanta-code. We must download the data streams before I can interpret them. It will take a little time. Why don't you get something to eat? You must be starving."

"I was enjoying our picnic. Sorry, we didn't have time to finish."

She looks up and squeezes my hand.

"Never a dull moment around here." I frown and sigh. "I'll get something to eat and you some nutrients."

"Thanks, dear."

"Be right back."

On the way to the food synthesizer, my head buzzes like an electrical circuit, and then a notion begins to stir. At first, I dismiss it as nonsense. But the damn feeling is floating around me like dust bunnies from my unconscious. It's as if little nondescript hints at a solution were popping into my head. But I can't seem to get it into focus.

"Glad you're back," Nicki says. "The data—"

"I know what's happening."

"You do? How?"

"On the way to the food synthesizer, Biomei has linked into my internal processor. By the time my order slides out, a sudden odd sensation grabs hold of me. I try to dismiss it, but then my senses heighten. When I fetched our food, my mind was full of new knowledge. Biomei has linked into my processors and is downloading a lot of information."

Nicki's brow furrows.

"I can tell from your expression you're not buying my explanation. But it's accurate. Biomei is talking through me. Our entire situation is clear."

"Biomei must have linked with you while in hibernation. That's how we shared the dream. She synchronized our minds so she could bring us out together."

"She just told me she had less than a minute to get it to me before being corrupted in her low-powered condition."

Nicki stares while chewing on her lower lip. "We need to get that data out of your processor right now." She grabs my arm and pulls me to a bioscanner bed. "Lie down. I need to pick your brain."

"Was that supposed to entice me?"

"I don't want to seduce you. Only retrieve the data."

"Too bad. I was hoping you'd do both."

I lie under the gray glow of the bioscanner's sensors. The machine works fast, literally plucking petabytes upon petabytes of Biomei's data from my neuroprocessors. Suddenly, I feel like I'm in tunnel vision with everything narrowing into a vanishing point. A sound like a phonograph record being scratched and then....

I'm sitting upright on the scanner bed, wondering what in the hell just happened.

"Now that wasn't too bad, was it?" Nicki says with a pleased expression.

"Bad? That term is not analogous to the procedure. It was merely necessary." I'm talking through my teeth like a Princeton English professor. "Now, my dear, if you are quite through tinkering with my mental apparatus. I wish to return to my quarters."

Nicki is staring at me with dark brown eyes, her mouth slightly agape. "Yes. That would be most prudent," she says, her brow creasing into lines.

Nicki looks as shocked as I. My mind seems to have split into two distinct personalities: the enhanced humanoid on the right and Phillip the Earthling on the left.

CHAPTER 15

We worked nonstop for two cycles deciphering the compressed data from my head and loading it back into Biomei's core memory. Best of all, my personality was whole again. What a relief.

"So?" I ask as Nicki studies the holographic image of my brain.

"It appears the transfer didn't corrupt any of your memory streams. How do you feel?"

"Whole again."

She smiles, looking relieved.

"That was a tedious process for you. You must be tired. Get some rest, and I'll join you when I'm finished here."

"You're the one who needs rest. You're pale as a ghost and exhausted."

"I need to conduct a full diagnostic on Biomei's primary and secondary systems."

"Damn it. Let the droids do it."

"I wish I could, but I'm looking for specific..." She closes her eyes and sighs. "It's too complicated to go into. I promise. It won't take long."

"You always say that. You know where to find me. In bed, dreaming of you."

She raises a brow ridge, then goes back to work.

My body feels heavy with fatigue, and my stomach's growling. On the way to our quarters, I grab a sandwich and a protein shake from the food synthesizer. When I enter the bedroom, I don't even bother to take off my jumpsuit and dive into bed, falling right to sleep.

***

I wake, hearing Nicki come into our quarters. She lies down next to me, gazing at me with dulled eyes, grimacing.

"Why the long face?"

"This whole ordeal..." She sighs."

"Come. Lie down next to me." She moves up close, lying her head on my chest, then mumbles something in Venubian.

"What was that?"

Nicki doesn't answer.

I lean closer to her and hear heavy breathing. She was sound asleep. "Finally," I whisper. While lying on my back, reflecting on all the stress and turmoil we had endured. "I hope the rest of this voyage is a little less stressful. I'm ready for a long period of dull tranquility mixed with fun. You remember fun. It's the opposite of mayhem," I say to Nicki's closed eyes.

"No," Nicki shouts, flailing her arms outward, almost hitting me in the face.

"Nicki." I catch her arms, holding them against my chest, "You're okay. It's only a bad dream."

"They're close. We must warn everybody," she cries, her body trembling.

I wrap my arms around her and hold her tight, trying to calm her.

I ask, "Who's coming?"

Nicki's eyes flutter open. She stares past me as if still caught in her dream.

"That must have been quite a dream."

She continues to stare for a moment, then looks at me and drops her head on my shoulder.

You said they're close. Who were you talking about?"

She lifts her head with her brow ridge raised. Her eyes turn light gray, looking as though she's searching within her thoughts. "I can't remember."

"Never mind. It was only a dream." I kiss her gently. "Go back to sleep."

"Hold me until I fall back to sleep." She smiles and runs her hand down the side of my face.

"So, I'm your Teddy Bear now?"

She squints.

"Never heard of a Teddy Bear?"

She gives me a blank stare.

"It's a stuffed animal that resembles a bear that young children play with and take to bed to keep them company while they sleep."

"A bear? Aren't they ferocious predators who inhabit wilderness areas?"

"Well—um… Yes, real bears are like that, but Teddy Bears are the cute, cuddly kind. Go back to sleep."

She nods and snuggles against me. "Thank you. You always say the right thing. You're much wiser than you look."

"Thanks. I think?"

A strong vibration rolls under a sharp tremor. The ship rocks to port, throwing us off the bed. Another strong shudder and the ship rolls to starboard with us sliding across the floor, hitting hard against the wall: another brief shake and the ship rights itself.

"What the hell was that?" I say, helping Nicki to her feet.

"'07, report," Nicki says.

"I'm en route to Engineering Level-2 to ascertain the circumstances of the event," '07 reports.

"Stand by. I'm on my way," Nicki says. She looks at me wide-eyed. "This can't be good."

"Never a dull moment around here," I murmur, grabbing a clean jumpsuit from the closet and putting it on, following close behind Nicki.

We rush to Engineering. Nicki opens the observation port, and by her shocked expression, we are in real trouble.

"It's that bad?" I say.

"'07 report," she says, in a strained voice as we approach the droid.

'07 is taking readings at a small console outside the containment chamber. He turns to Nicki and says, "The plasma containment bottle has ruptured. The ensuing discharge has blown out the patch and widened the breach in the outer hull. I have shut down the plasma flow, but not before it flooded the containment area with gamma radiation."

I ask Nicki, "Can we send in a team of droids to clean up the radiation?"

"The levels are above the tolerances for any droid to function long enough to effect a cleanup, sir," the droid explains.

"Is he right?"

Nicki nods.

"Can the hull repair be done from the outside?" I ask '07.

"Yes, sir. It would require an extended OSA and risk of exposure to the venting radioactive material."

"I know what you're thinking," Nicki says. Can't let you do it. It's too dangerous."

"'07, what will happen if the hull breach is not repaired at once?"

"The stress from the fracture will weaken the affected hull section and collapse the containment compartment."

"Do you have a better idea?" I ask Nicki.

She studies the breach on a monitor for a while, then looks at me with a sorrowful expression. "I'll have the droids vent the area before the OSA. Once the patch is in place, the droids can do the cleanup."

"No. I'm the only expendable one." I reach out to Nicki and hold her arm, pulling her close. While holding her tight, I could feel the tension rise in her. "We both recognize the only option is for me to repair the breach. The droids need to stay and continue working on Biomei. If anything were to happen to them or you, we'd all be lost."

'05, report to the amidships airlock. I'm sending the droid to help you. I just hope you know what you're getting into."

I shrug.

"You must follow the droid's instructions and don't be brave or do anything stupid…. And you're wrong. You're not expendable. I'd be lost without you."

"I feel the same. One thing, though."

Nicki makes a crooked grin.

"What in the hell is an OVA?"

"It's an Outer Ship Activity."

"Oh. Thought so."

CHAPTER 16

"Good day, sir," VSD05 greets me outside the inner airlock.

"Hi, '05. I'm a little nervous. This is my first OVA," I say.

"That is perfectly normal, sir. All humanoids experience a degree of apprehension when venturing into the great expanse."

"That wasn't helpful. How many humanoids have you accompanied on an OVA?"

"You are my first, sir. However, log records are abundant on various Outer Ship Activities."

"Oh? How many are you familiar with?"

"254, sir."

"Has anyone ever died?"

"Not to my knowledge."

"I hope you're right. Okay, let's get this show on the road."

"What show? On which road?" '05 asks.

"It's an expression. It means I'm ready to proceed."

"Very well, sir. You will need to put on a special environmental suit that will sustain and protect you while outside the ship."

"Lead on." I gesture for the droid to go ahead of me into the airlock.

"Inside the hatchway is a ready room where the environmental suits are stored. Unfortunately, there is no time to prepare a custom suit for you. There is one that should be large enough to accommodate your physical specifications."

'05 went to the large hatchway door and says something in Venubian. The door makes a clicking sound and swings open. I peer into the opening, and I'm surprised at how spacious it is. A variety of environmental suits with the headgear attached were aligned on one wall. They were suspended on a metal frame connected to the back of the suit. '05 walks up to a small panel next to the lock and speaks in Venubian again. The door closes and seals with a hissing sound, then a suit moves forward.

"Sir, see if this suit is adequate for you."

I give it a quick look over. It was bigger than I expected, but not bulky looking.

"It sure looks big enough. Let's see if it fits."

"Stand and turn in front of the suit, sir. Please, extend your arms up."

I turn around and stand up straight, extending my arms up. All at once, the suit presses against my back.

"Sir, please step into the legs first, then put your arms into the sleeves. The suit will automatically close around you and adjust to your dimensions."

The suit becomes animate, conforming to my body. It fits snug at first, but all my limbs can move freely. It was also lightweight, even with the headgear and atmospheric conditioner attached.

"How is the fit?"

"Snug, but it will do. Let's go."

"Go slow," Nicki says over the suit's intercom. "No quick movements and follow 05's instructions. I need you back to help me finish Biomei's cleanup."

"Aye, aye, skipper," I say, then follow '05 to the outer lock.

I had no idea what to expect when the droid depressurizes the outer hatchway compartment and the hatch swings open. A star-studded velvet blackness greets me. '05 stood as a tether connected to his lower rear torso and then pushed off the short gangway. He floated out of sight.

A light tug follows a click as the tether automatically attaches to the rear of my suit. A nervous flutter runs through my stomach and into my chest, causing my heart to beat harder and faster. I inhale deeply and let it out slowly before I can unlock my legs and take a few tentative steps down the gangway. Standing on the edge, I froze. My legs are trembling while staring awestruck at the sheer vastness and grandeur of being in space. It was as if I were looking into the face of God. It made me feel feeble and unworthy.

"Are you all right, sir?" '05 says, floating in front of me with his tether waving like an umbilical cord. "Sir, you need to push off the gangway, and then your suit will automatically fire a short burst from the jetpack to give you inertia back to the ship. You are well connected to the tether, and your environmental suit has built-in guidance to direct you back. You are quite safe."

"I understand. It's... I mean... I need a moment to adjust to my surroundings." I inhale deeply again, then exhale to get my feet to move a step. The droid's presence in front of me helps to calm my rising nerves. "I'm all right now."

"Very good, sir."

'05, please stop calling me sir. It's getting on my nerves."

"Understood. How would you prefer to be addressed?"

"Phil is fine, and only when you need my attention."

"I like Phil. It has a nice sound."

"Fine."

My entire body feels like it has turned to stone. No matter how hard I concentrate on my breathing, I can't relax enough to move. So, there I was, stuck, shaking, and feeling like a self-conscious idiot desperate for the will to lift my leg.

"Phil, don't think too much about where you are," Nicki says over the intercom. "I know how frightening it is during that first experience of being in space. Concentrate on what you need to do and not where you are."

"Thanks, Nicki. I got it. It's okay. I think I'm over the shock. It's just so overwhelming. There was no way of preparing for being out here. Don't worry. I'm okay."

I close my eyes and push off. What a strange sensation, moving, weightless, with no sense of direction. "I'm a fricking astronaut," I laugh, feeling exhilarated and a little nauseous.

We glide down to Biomei's belly and grab onto a series of handrails that run around and down her midsection. '05 stands on the hull and waits for me to catch up. As I reach the droid, it grasps my arm and pulls me in. My suit automatically magnetizes my boots, attaching me to the hull.

"Where's the breach?" I ask.

"It is 9.54 meters aft. We will need to make our way around the ship's forward telemetry array. The breach is beneath it. As you can see, it is a complex structure. We must be mindful of the array's elements. They are rigid, sharp, and could cut through your environmental suit. Please follow me precisely and stay close."

I nod within my helmet. "Lead on."

'05 releases its magnetic field and floats to a handrail in front of one of the long spiral antennae of the array. It made its way under the antennae, then downward, avoiding a series of narrow fins.

"'05, what are these fins?" I ask.

"Airfoils to protect the long-range array when moving through an atmosphere."

I looked at the airfoils and saw a collection of discs with squat spiral-shaped antennas attached and long, thin antennas behind them. Behind those, we made our way through a final maze of small domes with thin aerials coming out of their centers. Right behind them, I could see the breach.

'05 goes around to the other side of the jagged opening.

"Wow," I say. "It's bigger than it looks from the inside. How are we going to flatten it out, so we can patch it?"

'05 didn't respond at first. It appears to be studying the breach. "A plasma discharge cannot have caused this."

"Why do you say that?"

"A plasma discharge would have made a smooth burn through the hull. This breach is indicative of a high-energy explosion."

"Are you suggesting that the breach was deliberate and not a breakdown of the magnetic bottle?"

"I do not have sufficient data to confirm that hypothesis. I can make a more informative statement after performing a detailed analysis of the fragments and a review of the event logs."

"Shit. Something tells me the virus was only the first part of the sabotage plan. Nicki, are you monitoring this?"

"Yes. We'll conduct a thorough analysis of all the fragments once you get them aboard. First, we must get Biomei back online. She may be able to tell us what happened. I have my ideas, but would like to confer with her before making any assumptions."

"Understood. '05, how should we proceed?"

"I have calculated the diameter of the opening. We must cut away the torn-out elements before we can seal the breach." His right hand converted into a cutting tool.

"That is an interesting device," I say, pointing at his hand.

"It is a high-intensity torch to cut away the jagged edges."

"It's so cool how you can just produce shit out of thin air."

"Watch your language, Phil," Nicki chided. "All of this is being recorded."

"Sorry."

The droid turns to me. "As I cut away the pieces, you will gather them and place them in the amidships service portal. It is 2.2 meters below your location. If you follow the handrails down, they will lead you to the service access port. It is an oval-shaped hatch that has a magnetic release to its right. It will open upon pressing your thumb on it."

"Okay."

'05 fires up its torch and proceeds to cut away the first torn-out section. It cuts easily through it. It hands me the large section and tells me to attach it to a magnetic clip in my suit's left thigh pocket. When my hand touches my thigh, the pocket opens. Another, thinner, and shorter tether uncoils. It had a flat disk that attaches to the section. Once secure, I go in search of the service portal. It wasn't far, and I easily reached it using the handrails as '05 instructed. I see the release and press my thumb on it. The portal opens, revealing a storage area large enough to store all the sections. It took several trips before all the pieces were cut and stowed.

'05 had made a special carbon-fiber material in advance and had stored it inside its torso compartment. We work together in placing the material over the breach. Once we secured it in place, '05 sprays it with liquid artridium that instantly hardens, creating a strong seal over the breach.

"Good work," I say.

It flashes its optical sensor.

"We must return the way we came," '05 says. "Phil, please be mindful that it will be more of a challenge returning because the sharp elements of the array will be in front of us. As before, please follow closely and tread carefully."

"Thanks. I understand."

When we reach the dorsal side of Biomei's midsection, the array looks like an alien monster stretching out its tentacles in all directions.

Walking through the labyrinth of thin aerials and spiral antennae, I try not to look too closely at the obstacles and instead trace '05's path. Right as we reach the amidships outer hatchway, my foot catches something, causing me to trip forward. I hit the hull face-first and slid off. Then I bounced off a dome-like structure and felt myself floating away from the ship. A hard tug spun me back toward it. I see '05 reaching out to me. As I get close to it, a sharp, burning pain shoots through my back and abdomen. I'm tumbling away from the ship, spreading my arms and legs out wide, hoping to flatten out my rotation. Out of the corner of my eye, I see a bright object fly past me.

"Oh, shit," I blurt, seeing my severed tether floating in front of me.

"Warning, environmental atmosphere is venting," a soft, feminine voice announces. "Environmental suit pressure is dropping. Return to the ship at once."

"I've got a leak?"

"Yes. The atmospheric conditioner has a 3.445-centimeter tear in the primary holding tank and is venting pressurized atmosphere."

Oh, wonderful, I thought. This is getting better and better.

"Phil, your suit should have automatically engaged your jetpack," '05 calls over the intercom. "It must be damaged. Use the manual override."

"How do I do that?" I say.

"Verbally request it."

"Engage jetpack."

"Jetpack is disabled," the disembodied voice says.

"It's not working, and I'm quickly losing pressure. Nicki, can you hear me?"

"I hear you, Phil. Can you see the ship?"

"No. All I can see are stars, blackness, and this tumbling is making me nauseous. Now I'm feeling lightheaded."

"Don't throw up," Nicki warns. "Breathe through your mouth. Keep your arms and legs extended to slow your rate of rotation."

"Hey, will you call a cab for me?"

"Stay calm, dear. I'm coming."

"'05, can you see him?" I heard Nicki say over the intercom.

"No, Nickada, he has drifted below my field of view. My telemetry has located him at 2.2576 kilometers off the port side and drifting at 3.2 kph. However, his velocity is increasing. I spied an object pass by. It most likely was one element of the port communications array that Phil hit. There is a high probability that one of them punctured his suit."

"Why do you think that?" I hear Nicki say.

"I saw an element fragment sticking out of his suit. It may have gone completely through."

"Phil, check your blood pressure and pulse rate," Nicki says.

"Pressure is low but steady. Rate's a little high, though."

"Good. Gently feel around your midsection for anything sticking out of it."

I did as she asked and moved my left hand toward my abdomen. My hand touches something that sends a searing pain through my stomach and back.

"Found it. And it hurts like hell."

"Okay, Phil. Leave it alone. It's keeping you from bleeding out. Now, check your rear-view display and tell me what you see."

"It's not working. All my displays are out except for metabolic, ambient temperature, and suit pressure, which is still dropping."

"'05, come inside," Nicki says. "There's nothing more you can do out there."

"Yes, Nickada."

"Warning. Suit pressure is under twenty percent and dropping. Return to the ship at once," the disembodied voice warned.

"Nicki, did you hear that?"

"Yes. Slow your breathing using the techniques I taught you. Stay calm, I'm coming."

"I close my eyes and concentrate on my breathing. After a few moments of long, slow breaths, I'm feeling calmer. Arching my back, I spread my arms and legs out as far as I can to stop my slow rotation. Another searing pain runs through my stomach and back that almost causes me to black out, but I'm not tumbling. I open my eyes and smile at seeing Biomei in the distance. She had a massive-looking profile, like a beautiful, golden city in space. Looking at her, I realize I was moving away from her at an alarming rate. Then I see something fly out from under her. It was one of the small shuttles.

"I see you," Nicki says over the intercom.

"Nice of you to stop by," I say, feeling relieved while fighting to stay conscious.

CHAPTER 17

After working nonstop for over 36 ship-hours, the droids and Nicki, with a bit of help from me, got all of Biomei's systems powered up. Although in a limited capacity, Biomei is with us again. This intermediate step in bringing her back gave our morale a big lift. Especially Nicki, her mood seems brighter.

"I just reviewed Biomei's logs," Nicki says, coming into the galley.

"I look up from my vegetable protein that looks and tastes like scrambled eggs, and notice her long face. She orders a hot Zervizha tea, then sits across from me.

"That was quite an adventure you had," she said, sipping her tea.

I nod with my mouth full.

"When you fell, you damaged the suit's CPU, which is why it malfunctioned. Then, when you slid down the hull, you went over on one of the ventral communication arrays. An element pierced your suit while two other components punctured your atmospheric conditioner and air tank. The venting atmosphere is what propelled you into space." She took another sip of tea. "The element that penetrated your suit went right through your lower back and abdomen." She shakes her head. "Somehow, it missed any major organs. Luckily, it broke off, and your blood froze, sealing your suit again and slowing your bleeding. Your tether caught, then slid up the thin edge of an airfoil with sufficient force to sever the tether. It's amazing how in one fall you took out almost an entire communications array, an environmental suit, and got impaled through the back and stomach." She arches her brow ridge and takes another sip of tea.

I grin and shrug. "Sounds like I was lucky," I say, chewing down a large bite of dark bread. "Oh, I can't begin to tell you how much I miss hot food. Even synthesized food is better than those cold rations."

Nicki's jawline tightens, and she purses her lips. I waited for her to come around, but she continued to stare at me.

"Nicki, hello. Are you going to talk—or continue to stare?"

"Sorry," she says, blinking her eyes. "Biomei asked about you. I told her your injuries weren't serious. We reviewed her event logs." She looks down into her tea and frowns.

"And?"

"The logs on the cause of the breach were inconclusive. Something caused the high-energy photon generator to power up ahead of the magnetic containment field. We believe the sequence malfunction may have been caused when the virus shut down the power distribution nodes out of sequence. Subsequently, when we powered up the fusion reactor, the distribution was out of balance." She puts her tea down and grimaces.

"I gather you don't buy that explanation."

"It's highly improbable. Even if the power-up sequence was corrupted—there are so many safeguards to prevent a reactor malfunction..." She pushes out a long breath. "But all of Biomei's logs show that's what happened. It makes little sense, but it's all we have."

"What did Biomei say?"

"We need to get all her systems cleaned up and back online before she can do a thorough investigation. There's something else you need to know."

"Okay."

"I didn't tell Biomei, but I believe her logs were corrupted or changed somehow." She narrows her eyes while tapping a finger to her lips.

"What's wrong?"

"It's like my worst fears are coming to fruition."

"What do you mean?"

"The virus, then the breach, and now possibly tampered logs. It all appears related, and I don't know what to make of it or what to do about it."

"Tell me what you're thinking?" I reach out and squeeze her hand. It's cold and clammy. "Nicki, you're really frightened. What are you so afraid of?"

"You said you thought you saw a bright object fly past you. Could it have been a small ship or probe?"

"I'm not sure what I saw. In my state of mind, it could've been anything or nothing. Why do you ask?"

"It may be nothing, but Biomei's log registered a one-by-three-meter object approaching you, then flew off. She believes it might have been an automated probe investigating us—more precisely, you."

"Me? Why me?"

"Unknown. Biomei traced the probe's point of origin. She believes it's somewhere in the Delius system."

"Okay. So, we have an idea where it came from."

"Biomei wants us to go there and do a survey. If we find the source of the probe, she wants us to log it, then stay low until she's fully functional."

"Won't that put us right in harm's way?"

"Possibly. But it also allows us to investigate who might have sent that probe."

"Guess it's only fair. They looked us up. We should take a look at them. Let's go." I grin with a sudden realization.

"What are you happy about?"

"We finally get to take a shuttle out for a spin."

"Already started preparations," Nicki says with a faint smile. She goes to the food synthesizer and orders a protein shake.

"I wish you'd eat something more substantial than that."

"It's all I need now. It will be a long trip." She pauses in thought, looking at me through narrow eyes. "And because you haven't been fully adapted for deep space travel, you'll have to wear a full environmental suit the entire time."

"Oh? Oh, I see. When you say the entire time, does that include when we're on the shuttle? So, we'll not be able to... uh... You know."

"Sorry," she says, patting my cheek. "Meet me in Shuttle Bay-4, level 2."

"It's always something," I mumbled, watching her go to the aft turbo lift. Then I reflect for a moment and call out, "I hope that suit will be better than the last one."

"You both should use full environmental suits," Biomei interjects. "The Delius system is not hospitable for either of you."

"It's nice to hear your voice again," I say. "I thought Nicki told me there are a few habitable planets in that system."

"Habitable doesn't convey the degree of habitability a planet's environment provides, nor how hospitable its indigenous life-forms are towards aliens. Phillip, your physiology is still partially based on your homeworld's conditions. The smallest change in atmosphere or gravity over an extended period could be detrimental to your health."

"Good point," I say. "By any chance, do you have a good recommendation for us?"

"Delius-5 would be my first choice. I have already transmitted my recommendation to Nickada."

"Thanks. I'll make sure nothing happens to Nicki."

"Yourself as well."

I nod, then go to the turbo lift to meet Nicki.

***

"Good day, sir," a droid greets me as I enter the docking bay.

"Hi. Which one are you?"

"My designation is VSD27, sir."

"Ok, '27, where's Nicki?"

"She's inside shuttle number two, preparing for the voyage."

"Thanks."

I give the droid a close look. It appears identical to the other droids except for being smaller. My attention is drawn away from '27 when Nicki calls for it from inside the shuttle.

"Is there anything else, sir?" the droid says.

"No."

"Thank you, sir." It turns and walks up the short gangway and into the shuttle.

This was my first time in a major shuttle bay. I took a moment to study it. Like the rest of the bays, it's brightly illuminated, pristine, and enormous. Nicki's preparing a star-class shuttle, the largest of the ones onboard.

I admire its impressive design. The fuselage has a sleek appearance that makes it look fast. Nicki tells me it has most of the same technology as Biomei's drives.

Our shuttle is already positioned on the glide path. Its flat nose pointed toward the closed outer bay door. I gaze at the grand size of the other five shuttles lined up wing tip to wing tip. It gives me a sense of the abundance of resources on Biomei. I notice three additional rows of shuttles. In each successive row, they get progressively smaller.

"After seeing Biomei's sprawling profile up close, plus how huge this bay is, I'm reminded of her grand scale," I say to Nicki.

"She's the size of a small Venubian city in total living space," Nicki says as she walks down the short gangway. Looking around the bay, she lets out a heavy sigh. "She was designed as a versatile exploration ship. And can hold a crew complement of over 1500. Plus, it can accommodate up to 25,000 passengers."

"Why was she built to hold such a large population?"

Nicki closes her eyes, pressing her lips into a tight line. "Venubia has endured through several catastrophes over the past millennium. Knowing how important it is to have a safe means of rescue in a catastrophic event, I designed Biomei to be a ship for the evacuation or relocation of survivors."

I hold her face between my hands and stare into her dark gray eyes. "What is it?"

"Please. Not now, Phil. It's too painful... but it's important. I promise to tell you. There are things you need to know, but when the time is right. We have other priorities right now."

I kiss her forehead, sensing strong emotions running through her. "I'm sorry. I didn't know how painful this was for you. You know you can tell me no matter what it is."

"When we return, I'll have Biomei download a complete Venubian history for your review." She turns her gaze downward and talks in a low voice, "Then you'll understand why I can't tell you now. It's complicated, and a lot of it is unpleasant."

"All this great space and no one to fill it," I say, changing the subject.

"It troubles me," she says, looking around. "But it bothers Biomei even more. She loves humanoid activity. Don't be surprised by this. Biomei is most maternal, especially with children. I dream that someday she'll be full of humanoids with lots of children. That's when she will be doing what she was built for."

"What's that?"

"Exploration and discovery." Nicki's expression turns dreamy.

"Are we ready?"

She nods and takes my hand. "First, we need to design your environmental suit."

"It's not already made?"

"You should know by now that everything here is custom-made. You already experienced the problems with a ready-made suit." She leads me by the hand to a corner of the bay. We stop in front of a familiar-looking oblong platform in front of a squat console.

"Step up on the platform," she said. "This will only take a few seconds."

I give her a shy look as I step onto the small platform.

"Is this another chance for you to marvel at my beautiful physique?"

"You mean my handiwork? Don't move. Close your eyes and hold your breath until I say done. Understand?"

I stand up straight on the platform and say, "Ready when you are."

Nicki waves her hand over an array of colored lights on top of the console. She whispers something in Venubian, and a pocket opens in her jumpsuit. She reaches in and pulls out a short, thin green crystal and inserts it into a slot next to the array of lights. The lights become bright, then a wire-frame projection of my body appears suspended over the array.

"Now, close your eyes and hold your breath."

I can see Nicki in my mind. It takes me by surprise, but I see all that she's doing and everything she's thinking.

"Wow, this is so neat," I transmit to her. She waves her hand, causing the wire-frame image to become superimposed over my body.

Then, with a downward movement of her hand, the wire-frame image converts into a holographic environmental suit that covers me. A blue bar of light flows down over the holographic image. When it reaches the bottom of the platform, all the imaging turns off.

"All done," she transmits.

I let out a long breath as I open my eyes and ask, "Now what?"

"Stand there for another..." she glances down at the screen, "24 seconds, and your suit will be ready."

"That's faster than the jumpsuit. I thought an environmental suit would've taken longer."

"The jumpsuit was the first run, and the system needed more details about your body's physical and biometric measurements, which were stored in Biomei's archives. The processor only needs to match up your stored specifications with the updated ones we took. And your suit is now ready." She raises her brow ridge and turns a corner of her mouth up, looking pleased.

I look around for the suit. "Okay, where is it?"

She laughs. "You're wearing it."

"Oh, you've got to be kidding me." I looked at my arms, then down at my legs. They were covered in a lightweight, almost skin-tight blue material. "How come I didn't feel that?"

"It's a bio-nanocarbon material that mimics your skin. It will automatically adjust for all temperatures, barometric pressures, and ambient environmental changes and protect you from most forms of radiation and high-energy particles. If you should puncture or tear the material, it will instantaneously seal itself. All that remains is your power pack with a built-in environmental conditioner and headgear, all of which are in the shuttle."

"And where's your environmental suit, young lady?"

"You worry too much," she says in a wispy voice. "They are in the shuttle." She places her arms around my neck and pulls me in for a lingering kiss.

"Oh, that was nice."

"It'll have to last you a while."

"Okay then. Let's go."

CHAPTER 18

Nicki helps me put on the powerpack and headgear assembly while instructing me on their operations. I'm surprised at how light all the equipment feels.

"The powerpack with its small integrated atmospheric conditioner," she says, holding the small rectangular boxes up, "clips onto the back of your utility belt. Your respiration combined with all your movements creates the primary pumping action." She put the headgear on. It fits snugly. "The faceplate has a 160-degree field of view. It will give you a rearview when requested or if there's activity within your proximity range."

As soon as the headgear seals into its magnetic collar, the lower right-hand corner of the faceplate begins scrolling data. I request a rearview. I see the atmospheric conditioner and watch as it automatically connects to my air supply with a thin pair of tubes running down the back of my suit. The data is in Venubian. I recognize a few of the words I've picked up. It stops, and a beat later resolves into English.

"This thing is so cool," I say. "I like that I can see everything at a glance."

"The shuttle will monitor our positions and our basic metabolic conditions," Nicki explains. "If the system detects any problem, it will send an alert. The droids are also networked into the system. In an emergency, the closest one will be notified to respond."

"Wow. All my metabolic readings just flashed up. I guess I'll have to get used to seeing Venubian scale numbers."

"You can request Celsius or Fahrenheit."

"Fahrenheit scale," I say, and the display converts.

"I can use a hand, Phil," Nicki says, holding her headgear out.

I take it from her, then watch as she slips her arms through a web of thin straps with a large, sealed unit connected to them. As soon as she places it on her back, it practically attaches itself to her suit. She speaks a few commands in Venubian and then takes the gear off.

"What's all that about?" I ask, studying the heavy-looking unit.

"It's an instrument pack for measuring soil, vegetation, along with other scientific equipment I'll need. I linked it to my suit before we started." She stores the unit in a compartment behind the pilot's seat.

I hand the headgear to her and ask, "That equipment pack looks heavy. Why not let me carry it?"

"All the instruments are linked to me and programmed in Venubian. It would be simpler if I carried it."

"If you insist." I sit in the co-pilot's seat. Looking back, I see '27 with the other three droids seated in the last two rows. "They look lonely back there," I tell Nicki over the com. "They look like kids anxiously waiting for something to happen."

"Do you want to go back and keep them company?" Nicki says.

"No. But they can come up here and sit with us."

"Trust me. They're fine."

"Okay, if you say so." I wave at the droids. They sit impassively, looking straight ahead with their optical sensors blinking. "The rear-drive quarter looks bigger than the other shuttles. Does this have a different engine?"

"I had the engineers make a few modifications and replace the secondary ram-jet engine with an impulse-plasma drive to give us more speed."

"Oh? From the little I know, don't we need the ram-jets for atmospheric landings?"

She looks at me in surprise. "No. Impulse drives work as well. I also had the wingspans widened so we can power glide in an emergency."

"Oh, you had to say that." I shake my head and narrow my eyes at her. "How fast can this baby go? As fast as Biomei?"

"Nicki powers up the shuttle without answering.

"You don't know, do you?" I nudge her.

She curls her lower lip, looking as though she's considering what to say.

"This's an experimental craft, and it's not entirely of Venubian design," she says, in a timid voice, then turns away as she speaks. "You should know the engineers didn't have time to perform actual flight testing." Her voice fades over my intercom.

My face burns with the unsettling revelation.

She turns back to me and notices my reddened face and clenched jaw. "But I assure you, it's a well-tested and proven design. The engines performed perfectly in all the simulations."

"In simulations? Oh great. So, what you're telling me is we'll be testing out this new design?"

"You've nothing to worry about. The modifications were approved and implemented by highly trained technicians and supervised by both the original engine designers and our best Venubian engineers... all under my strict supervision, of course."

"Well, it was done under *your strict supervision,*" I mimic her voice, "that should make all the difference." I lean closer to her, "But it still hasn't been fully tested in actual flight conditions. Has it, smart ass?"

"Why are you getting so upset?"

"Because it means we'll be this shuttle's test pilots! That doesn't make you a little nervous?"

I hear a long sigh over my com. "Okay. You're right. We're the first to fly this shuttle, but I'd never deliberately put you into a dangerous... situ—" Nicki notices my tight face and hard stare.

"Really? Being test pilots of a newly modified shuttle is not inherently dangerous in your book.

"Phil, you have to trust me when I say this shuttle is perfectly safe," she says in a calm but firm voice. "It has the same fusion drive as Biomei's. The modifications will only enhance this shuttle's capabilities." She gazes at me for a long moment, those big, dreamy, dark-blue alien eyes now a deep purple. "Phil, there's always a chance something could go wrong, but that's part of the risk of living and working in space. We have the most advanced technology and resources at our disposal, but that isn't always enough. The universe is a big, sometimes unforgiving place that will always challenge us." She leans back in her seat and points to the cockpit's view screen. "That's the price of being out there." She looks intently at me and says, "Do you trust me?"

"Of course I do," I snap, then push out a long, hissing breath, feeling self-conscious and foolish. "Sorry," I mumble contritely. "I don't know why I overreacted. I guess I'm uneasy about how uncertain things have become. There's always something going wrong. And... and... I don't know what to say. But you know what I mean. Don't you?"

"Do us both a favor. Relax and enjoy the ride." She sits up and swivels her seat so she's facing me. I swivel mine and face her. She transmits a long and passionate kiss. "Feel better?" she says softly.

I let out a long sigh and smiled. "I could use another one of those. It's almost as good as the real thing."

She obliges me with an even more intense kiss that lingers, giving me an idea. *If a transmitted kiss could feel that good, imagine what—.*

"There are limits to what can be transmitted, and unfortunately, intercourse doesn't work that way," she interrupts my obvious train of thought, looking at me with a coy smile.

"You read me all too well."

Nicki opens the outer bay doors and sets the shuttle in motion. Our departure was so quiet and smooth that it seemed more like a virtual reality experience. All at once, I find myself in deep space. It looks much different this time.

"Being immersed in the great expanse unfolding in front of you almost overwhelms the senses," I transmit to her. *"I don't think I'll ever get used to this."*

Her glowing eyes are gazing at me with an excited smile. Nicki appears as enthusiastic as I am.

Sitting in the copilot's seat, my metabolic rate climbs in anticipation of the powerful machine being launched into motion.

"The shuttle is automated," Nicki says. "We could make ourselves comfortable in the passenger compartment and be notified when we've arrived at Delius-5."

I give her a disappointed frown. "You're not seriously suggesting that I miss the best ride of my life?"

"I'm only teasing," she laughs. "There's nothing like the feel of piloting a star-class shuttle. I never tire of the awe and wonder I experience every time I get to pilot one."

We hover for a few long moments outside the bay while Nicki completes the final systems check. Biomei wishes us a safe voyage as Nicki engages the fusion drive. I could feel a slight vibration followed by a sense of heaviness pushing me into the seat. The stars blur into streaks of blues and reds as the powerful engines engage.

"As our velocity increases, the inertia dampeners will compensate for the greater G-forces and increased mass," Nicki explains. "The shuttle should be capable of achieving .41 of lightspeed. Delius-5 is a little over 11.5 billion kilometers. Since we need to give the droids extra time to work on Biomei, I set us to cruise at .25 of lightspeed. At that velocity, we should reach the Delius system in less than a cycle."

I nod, then realize even at that fraction of lightspeed, we are traveling at an unimaginable velocity. Then another thought occurs. I'm the first Earthman to go into deep space. This realization seems incredible. Even as I stare, wide-eyed, at the immense grandeur that was laid out before me, I still can't help wondering if all of this was happening. My mind feels numb, trying to take it all in. The whole experience of traveling in deep space fills me with a sense of awe and privilege. Another thought hits me hard. No one will ever know of my accomplishments. I'm anonymous to the universe.

***

"VSD07 just reported that the flush and sterilization procedures will take a little over two cycles," Nicki relays to me. "If we can avoid any unforeseen problems, we should have time to explore Delius-5 for new foods and a little scientific study."

"Do you think whoever sent that probe is there?"

Nicki gives me a thoughtful look, then quickly changes the subject.

"If you look starboard, you'll see dense blue-green and yellow clouds of gas. That's the Bohri Nebula."

I look past Nicki and gawk at the spectacular towers of colored gases surrounding a small bright speck.

"Is that bright point the star remnant?"

"Yes. Can you believe that was once a massive blue star? Now, look two degrees down. See those five bright blue-green dots right below the nebula?"

"Yeah. The colors and patterns are magnificent."

"That's the Delius system. It's made up of medium-sized stars like Earth's sun. There are a few superb gas giants within the system. One of them is twice the size of Jupiter. Many believed it to have been a failed star that originally was part of the progenitor star's system. It probably was blown out when the star nova and became captured by Delius-1's gravity."

"Will we be able to see it from Delius-5?"

"It'll be the largest object in the system. Delius-5 is no slouch either. It's two-and-a-half times larger than Earth and almost twice as large as Venubia. However, its mass is around the same as Venubia's. Delius-5's gravity and magnetic fields are greater than what you're used to. Our suits cannot compensate for the increased gravity, so we'll feel heavier, but the higher radiation levels won't be a problem."

"Do you know why that probe was sent?" I ask, looking closely at Nicki.

"I don't know. That's part of the reason we're going there. We need to find out what we're dealing with."

"Why do I have a feeling you know more than you're telling me?"

"It's not that I'm being vague on purpose. Under the circumstances, I need more data before coming to any conclusions."

I can see from her tightening expression that she didn't want to talk about it. So, I changed the subject. "Biomei warned me about the indigenous life-forms. She told me to watch out for possible big predators. I don't mind the big ones. You can see them coming. It's all those little creepy, crawly things that bother me."

"If I've told you everything to expect in advance, would you still have come?"

"You really know how to hurt a guy. You know I'd never let you go alone. It just would've been helpful if you told me a little of this in advance, dear."

"Sorry, dear. I was so busy I forgot to send you Biomei's download. I'll send it directly to your neurocompiler. After you review it, I'll try to answer any questions you may have. But keep in mind, you'll know as much as I after you have assimilated the data."

"I understand."

***

As we approach the Delius system, the Bohri Nebula fills the forward view with its vibrant colors. Then Nicki tells me to look port side. My jaw drops as my eyes catch the magnificent gas giant.

"Holy shit," I mutter. "That's one big mother... eh... big sucker of a planet."

Nicki squints at me and says, "What was that?"

"I never could have imagined something this big. It's beyond description."

"It is a grand planet. Venubian astronomers don't always name their planets. They prefer catalog designations. Its designation is VGZ-D142.7. I preferred its name: Thaz-7. It's as big as some red dwarf stars but lacks a small fraction of the mass for fusion. Based on our latest telemetry, it may acquire additional mass from Bohri's gases over the next few millennia.

"What will happen to the system if it ignites into a star?"

"It would vaporize almost everything in the immediate neighborhood, including half of the Delius system. However, that's one of many hypotheses. Like so many things about the cosmos, we won't know until it happens. The universe will always have its mysteries. I prefer it that way."

"Interesting. I've never considered even attempting to understand the universe. But that's because I'm not a scientist. To me, it's like trying to understand the mind of God. Or in your case, the mind of the cosmos itself. It's incomprehensible. That's the way it should be. Curiosity has always been the driving force of discovery."

"I agree," Nicki says with an approving nod.

"So, I'm not as dumb as I look after all?"

"Maybe."

"You're lucky I'm stuck in this environmental suit, young lady, or I'd make you pay for that remark."

Nicki laughs. She has a contagious laugh. Through our telepathic link, I could feel her joy. Then her energy turns serious.

"What is it?"

Received a meteorological update. There's an extensive weather system developing over our original landing site. This is most odd."

"What's odd?"

"Suddenly, there's a lot of magnetic interference inhibiting our long-range telemetry. We must wait until we're closer to Delius-5 before I can find an alternate site. This is strange, though."

"Strange how?"

"It's a localized magnetic storm, but the interference doesn't look natural. I think it's being deliberately generated and using the storm as a masking field."

"What else could cause such interference?"

"Only one thing I know of—a powerful dampening field. Phil, I've got a bad feeling about this."

"Yeah, I can feel you. Let's get close enough to do a sensor sweep, and maybe we'll be able to identify what's causing the interference. Something tells me whoever is causing it also sent the probe."

"Strap yourself tight into your seat. I'm enabling the secondary drive."

"Nicki, if we find our curious friends aren't friendly. Is there another planet we can go to?"

"No. It's Delius-5 or back to Biomei. I'm not willing to go back without knowing. We'll stick to our plan and be extra careful down there."

"You're the captain."

I tried to look calm, but my insides are tightening into a hard knot.

***

Nicki slows our approach to Delius-5 and inserts us into a high orbit. I notice her expression tighten as she studies the telemetry.

"What is it?"

"The storm had dissipated, and all the telemetric readings are nominal. It's like it never occurred. There's no electromagnetic resonance that's always present after such storms. This is all wrong. Let's go a little closer before we land. I want to be careful before we commit."

"Yeah, I agree. I'll bring up the high-resolution imaging while you do a low orbital sweep and see if I can spot anything."

"Hold on. It will get a little turbulent as we break orbit and enter the upper atmosphere," Nicki says. A slight shudder is felt, followed by a hard bump as the shuttle descends through thick clouds. "We'll level off at 30K and do a close flyover of the landing area."

"Sounds like a plan. One thing, though."

"What?"

"How do I enable the hi-res imaging?"

"See, you're overthinking again. Concentrate for a moment, and the data will automatically load. Trust your internal technology."

"I know—I know... It's just that- um... It's all so damn unnatural. I still think like a human."

Nicki rolls her large eyes with a crooked grin. "You are human. Only a little more enhanced. Although sometimes I wonder if your enhancements aren't defective."

"You know, sometimes you can be a little insensitive to my situation. I'm still trying to get used to being abducted and experimented on. So, give this slightly slow human a break."

She smirks, then manually switches on the hi-res imaging. A real-time holographic image of the planet's topography spreads across the front of the cockpit's dome. The image reveals a plateau between two low-lying mountain ranges. It looks like a small savanna of tall, bright yellow-green grasses. The sky was clear, but there was an eerie grayness hovering over the area despite it being midday.

"I hope it isn't always this gloomy?" I say.

"No. I would say this has something to do with the storm, but I've never known a magnetic storm to have this effect on an atmosphere. There's something else going on here. Everything we're seeing is unnatural—nothing is coming up on any of our sensors to account for the present conditions. It's a local phenomenon, though. The western hemisphere appears typical."

"Then, let's go west."

"The western regions are much rougher than here," Nicki says, bringing up a holographic map. Under the circumstances, it's probably our best option. I'll do a low flyover of these areas." She highlights the areas with a wave of her hand. "I need you to keep an eye out for what looks like a good landing spot. Preferably an open, flat area, which has some elevation to give us a good vantage point over the surrounding terrain."

"Understood."

On the second pass, I spy a relatively smooth plateau on top of a high ridge. It overlooks a deep valley that spreads out for hundreds of kilometers.

"The sky's much brighter here, and the landscape is brilliant with vivid colors," I say, marveling at the vibrant yellows, golds, and deep browns of the sprawling fields. "The trees, the grass, and all the flowers have a strange luster to them. It's hard to describe. It's like everything has a halo effect surrounding it. And I'm seeing some unusual colors."

"What you're seeing is caused by the binary suns. They have different spectral frequencies that the planet's vegetation absorbs. You're viewing more than you're used to. The built-in optical sensors in your headgear have a wider range of visual perception. If it's a distraction, you can adjust it to your natural visual range."

"No. I'm beginning to like it. Only need a little time to get used to it."

"If you think that's something, look up at the sky."

"Oh, wow. That's wild." I see small pale moons in the distance. A vivid reminder of being in an alien landscape, even though the planet below appears Earth-like.

Surrounding the plateau and valley is a dense forest of jagged, spiral-shaped, black-barked trees with broad, burnt-orange and reddish leaves. The forest has an eerie, uninviting presence. The tall grasses of the plateau had a mix of deep auburn and a shimmering bluish-green color.

"The north side of the plateau appears to be lined with trees that have large, pointed greenish-yellow and iridescent, violet leaves," I say, pointing to them on the holographic map.

Nicki's face lights up as she studies the vegetation. "Those might be fruit-bearing trees. And those squat bushes on the other side of that stream look much like an orchard."

The thought of biting into some juicy fruit of any kind had me almost drooling in anticipation.

"This area reminds me of a magnificent spring day on Earth. A colorful valley surrounded by steep snow-capped mountains," I say, looking out the port side of the cockpit dome. "Environmental readings show the temperature is mild and there's a soft, northerly breeze. It looks like an ideal spot. That long ledge on the northeast slope could be a good landing site." I look at the area on the holographic map, and it lights up. "Wow, that's so cool," I mumble half to myself.

"I have the coordinates. It looks ideal." Nicki says, making a steep bank.

She takes a final pass over the surrounding area, then glides us to a gentle landing.

CHAPTER 19

The droids are already setting up equipment by the time we join them on the plateau. While Nicki dealt with them, I studied the magnificent alien landscape.

"Here, you may need this," Nicki says, handing me a sidearm in a holster belt.

"Is this a weapon?" I ask in surprise, taking it out of its holster to get a better look.

"It's against everything I believe," Nicki blurts, "but I feel it necessary." I could hear the stress in her voice. "We need a means of defending ourselves, and this is all we have."

"It's neat-looking. How does it work?"

She pulls her sidearm out of its holster and lays it in her palm.

"This is a pulse phaser. It has a maximum range of 100 meters. This button," she touches a blue button on the side, "is the safety, and the small switch below it is the intensity setting. It's already set to stun, which is the lowest setting. Down a click will set it to a higher stun, and the next click down is maximum. It's powerful enough to kill most humanoids and animals. Please, keep it on stun that should be adequate for most situations."

I grip the weapon and hold it up. "There's no trigger. How do I fire it?"

"It works on pressure. Line up your target using your helmet's integrated tracker. When ready, squeeze the grip, and it will fire a single pulse. Squeeze and hold to send multiple pulses. It's an accurate weapon, and its operation will become apparent as you use it. It's synchronized to your biosignature. So, no one else can fire it."

While holding it in my palm, I flip it over to give it a closer look before placing it back into its holster and clipping it to my utility belt.

"Feel like a real cowboy," I say, trying to break the tension I'm feeling from Nicki.

She gives me a long, brooding stare and says, "The atmosphere is breathable, but only in an emergency and not for too long. The nitrogen and oxygen ratios are much higher here than on our planets."

"Thanks. I'll keep that in mind. What are the droids doing?"

"They're conducting biochemical analysis for edible fruits, vegetables, and anything medicinal."

"It'd be nice to have some real food for a change, even if it's just fruits and vegetables," I say, trying to break her tight mood.

"The synthesized foods are real," she says.

"Well, not that the synthesized foods aren't tasty, but contrary to your opinion, they're synthetic. Cleverly prepared vegetable proteins with lots of seasonings aren't my idea of food. After a while, you start to forget how your favorite foods taste."

She meets my argument with a cold stare. Her look doesn't keep my stomach from growling while thinking about sinking my chops into a porterhouse steak smothered in mushrooms and onions. Not to mention, a warm corned beef, topped with coleslaw between two slices of Jewish rye.

"You know your carnivorous fantasies are most obvious," she screws her face up, "and it's nauseating."

I shrugged with a lopsided grin. "Sorry. I can't help myself at times."

One of the droids walks up and hands her something.

"What is that?" I ask.

"Hi-resolution binoculars." She holds them up to her eyes, then turns slowly to her right and then to her left.

"Which way, skipper?"

She pulls out a handheld scanner from her thigh pocket and begins taking readings. She checks the scanner, then closes it and puts it back in her pocket.

"It appears you picked a good location," she says. "There's a variety of fruit-bearing trees just a few hundred meters to the south. There are also some interesting plants just below us in the valley. I noticed a natural trail along the south ridge. It narrows in a few spots, but for the most part, it appears passable. We'll leave the droids here to do their tasks."

"Sounds like a plan. But let's take the little guy with us in case we need assistance."

"VSD27?"

"Yeah, that's him."

She sent a telepathic request for '27 to join us. The little droid walks up to us and blinks its optical sensor.

"Are you aware that you referred to '27 as him and not it?" Nicki says.

"I did?" I thought about it for a second. "I think it's because, for some reason, I identify with him more than the other droids."

"You do realize that '27 is only an intelligent machine?"

"Yeah. Now that you mentioned it, I have been personalizing '27 more than the others. I tend to do that sometimes. It's a well-established human trait."

"Really?"

"I even named my cars when I was younger."

"You don't see a problem with naming inanimate things?"

I shrug.

"VSD27," I address the droid as it stands attentively waiting for its instructions. "From now on, you'll respond to the designation..." I considered him for a moment as Nicki looked on with a bemused smirk. "Shorty," I state, tapping the droid on top of the head like a dubbing.

"Is this a permanent designation, sir?"

"This is my designation for you. Understood?"

"Yes, sir." Shorty stands with his neck raised, leveling his head to mine, and flashes his optical sensor.

"Are you going to rename all of the droids?" Nicky asks, sounding perturbed.

"No, just Shorty for now."

We stare at each other for a sec, then Nicki sighs. "Sometimes you worry me, Phil. Can we get on with the survey now?"

"Lead on, skipper."

We walk down the gradually sloping trail in a single file with Nicki in the lead and me trailing behind Shorty. We were making good time until we came up to a heavy undergrowth of wiry, needle-vines wrapped around gnarled tree branches.

"This is impassable," Nicki says. She holds her scanner toward the ominous-looking woods and says, "It appears as though the trail opens again just a few hundred meters to the west. VSD27, I need you to produce a cutting tool to open a pathway."

The droid's right hand dissolves and reforms into a small rotating blade. Shorty cuts through the heavy undergrowth while clearing the cuttings with his other hand. It doesn't take long before he clears a narrow pathway that connects to a level opening.

We continue deeper into the dark woods that look like something out of a horror movie. The tree roots are thick and stretched out far from its spiral trunk. The trunks are twisted, knotted, and covered in black, flaky bark that looks like large scales of a mythical beast. The upper branches spread outward with some of them arching to the right and some to the left, creating a natural canopy over the forest's dark, spongy floor. The tree's thorny leaves appear rough in texture and have a dark green color. Sunlight filters through the dense forest in narrow beams of yellow-white light. The variety of squat bushes and oddly-colored plants all appear dull, dingy, and forbidding.

"How much further do we have to go before getting out of these creepy woods?" I call to Nicki. "It seems devoid of any life. There are no birds, or worms, not even an insect. It's as though nothing wants to live in this horrid place."

"I think you're allowing your nerves to get the better of you. There are all kinds of life around us," Nicki says. "If it will appease your apprehension, a few hundred meters ahead, there's an opening to the west side of the valley."

"This forest looks like something out of Tim Burton's mind." Before Nicki could ask, I added, "He's a famous director of weird movies. Check your database on American film directors."

"There's something strange about some of the atmospheric readings on the low EM band," Nicki says, holding out her scanner.

"Could it have something to do with the magnetic storm?"

"All the residual effects of the storm should've dissipated, which confirms my earlier suspicion. It was artificially created." Her voice sounds full of tension.

"What's wrong, Nicki?"

"It doesn't make sense. What could've caused such a powerful magnetic resonance?"

"I don't know what to tell you. But we both know whoever produced it is probably still around."

I send a telepathic command to the droids to be on high alert for humanoid biosignatures."

"Let's see what we can find to eat. I'm not in the mood to pack up and run because somebody else is playing with the atmosphere. Who knows, they may be friendly."

"I doubt that, but I agree," Nicki says. "We should continue with the survey and be extra vigilant in what we do. Stay close."

"Nicki, I sense your apprehension."

She arches a brow ridge. "My apprehension? You're shaking like a leaf."

"I am?" My hands were shaking. "Yeah. Okay, let's both try to stay calm."

She nods, still looking uneasy. I smile at her. She pushes a long breath out.

"You're right, of course," she says, appearing calmer. "There's no reason to fear the unknown. After all, that's why we're here."

"I think we'll both feel better once we get out of these woods."

As soon as I say that, we hear rustling over our intercoms. It's coming from deep in the woods. We both look in the direction of the sounds. Shorty is occupied doing a scan of the area and then announces, "Alert. Biological organism, twenty-three meters to the east."

"Humanoid or animal?" Nicki asks.

"Biosignature matches indigenous quadruped heading in this direction."

I started looking for the animal. In a few seconds, a corner of my visor brings up an image of a large animal heading straight for us. Its dimensions begin to scroll above it as it easily moves through the deep underbrush.

"It's pretty big, Nicki; over 300 kilograms. What I'm viewing looks much like a good-sized predator, and I think we look like its lunch."

"Stay put. There's no way we can outrun it."

"Oookay. What do you suggest?"

"I want to get a better read on it. VSD27, do you have a match for this animal in your database?"

"Call him Shorty," I urge her.

She flashes me an annoyed scowl, then snaps, "Shorty, what do you have?"

"No exact match, Nickada."

"Extrapolate."

"Kaydus Lapolxidos," Shorty states.

"A what?" I shout.

"How close of a match is it, VS... eh... Shorty?" Nicki says.

"Approximate match is 82.055 percent of the actual. Its physiology is indicative of a well-developed predator."

"That doesn't sound too good, Nicki. Are you sure you want to wait on it?"

"Unless you have a better idea, I suggest we stay put. Allow the animal to see us.

"Well, I hope you're right because it's staring its beady, red eyes at us now." I start to reach for my weapon.

"Don't, Phil," Nicki whispers. "I've a better idea. Shorty, produce a stunner and lock in on the animal, but wait for my command."

"Acknowledged." Shorty's right arm manifests an elongated device that he holds upright.

The colossal beast's long, sinuous body slowly comes out of the dark brush. It walks low to the ground with its powerful muscles flexing as it moves. Surprisingly, it looks much like a large panther to me, but with a considerably bigger head and wider paws that look more adapted for climbing than snatching and tearing into a prey. We watch in fascination as its bright, silver outer coat shines and darkens within the beams of the filtered sunlight. It has a broad black stripe that runs the length of its arching silverback. Piercing, intelligent brown eyes study us as it paces with a low, calculating back-and-forth movement. It appears to be sizing us up while pondering its next move. Once it comes into the small opening, its eyes soften to an amber color in the clear, bright light. It's a magnificent-looking beast. I hope it decides to leave us without a fight.

"Uh, Nicki, why not give the beast a nudge with the stunner?"

"I would advise against such action, sir," Shorty says. "Based on the animal's size and weight, I calculate that a nudge would most likely provoke it. I suggest a full discharge to effectively dissuade the animal."

"Nicki, I think we should stun it before it decides to attack."

"Patience, Phil, it's as curious about us as we are about it. I've been attempting to communicate with it telepathically. I believe it's receiving my transmissions, but it doesn't understand. If it were going to attack us, it would have confronted us differently. Considering its size, it probably would've flanked us first, then attacked. Stay calm, and I believe it'll soon move on."

Just as she said, the beast turns and swiftly goes back into the forest. I watch it through my visor for a few moments before it disappears into the dense woods.

"That was interesting," I half mumble while letting out a held breath. "How'd you know it wasn't going to attack us?"

"I got a sense of the animal's intelligence and realized he was a skilled enough hunter to have picked one of us off before we could've reacted. Also, he had a kind face."

"He had a kind face?" I repeat incredulously. "You'll have to explain that when we have time. Right now, I suggest that we get back on track."

Nicki says, "Shorty, resume survey and scan for edible foods."

"Acknowledged."

***

The sky begins to turn from a bright bluish-white into a softer yellow with a tinge of pink. It reminds me of late summer sunsets in Key West, Florida. However, the real surprise greets me as we come to the bottom of the rugged trail that leads us into this open valley. The massive presence of the great gas giant comes into view. Even at a distance of over 7.2 billion kilometers, it emerges over the horizon, filling the entire western sky. A thin haze of clouds slightly mutes its brilliant colors. It's still an incredible sight with swirling vivid red, blue, green, and white bands of gas clouds with visible rings circling its equator.

"Wow!" I say.

"If you think that's something, look to the east," Nicki says, pointing outward.

"Jesus." Seeing two stars in such proximity sent chills through me. The nearest star looks like Earth in size and color. The farthest star is smaller and redder. As I catch my breath, I notice three small moons below and to the right of the near star. Then Nicki points upward. My visor darkens in the bright glare for a moment, obscuring my vision. When it clears, my eyes focus on the most beautiful amber moon I've ever imagined. Like a gleaming ruby, it sat prominently overhead with its dark green and gold rings visible in the brilliant sky.

"This moon reminds me of Umbria, the largest of the Venubian moons," Nicki says. "Its color and size are similar. At dusk, before the rise of our red giant, it takes on a gold luster that makes it appear like a jewel in the night sky. Umbria means night jewel in Venubian." She smiles faintly and adds, "I hope it's a more hospitable place than our gem. We later discovered it to be more of a devil than a gem. Its atmosphere was toxic. You'll soon discover that Delius-5 is not too different than Venubia. Probably that's why Biomei chose it. It never ceases to amaze me. The variety and beauty that these systems hold. Each one has its unique splendor, and yet all of them have some common elements that give them a sense of familiarity and uniqueness."

"I don't think I'll ever get used to this," I whisper with my voice almost too choked up to speak. "I wish I could find words that would aptly describe this strange splendor. I feel almost guilty having the opportunity to experience what many of my people only dream of.”

Nicki comes up close to me and gives my hand a tender squeeze. Her bright blue eyes fixed on me with a hint of a smile. “That’s exactly how I feel each time I go exploring,” she says. “Space exploration agrees with you.” She narrows her eyes slightly and squeezes my hand a little harder. “Keep something in mind, Phil. You’re as worthy as any explorer, astronaut, or alien to be out here.”

“You know if I could, I’d give you a really big kiss right now.”

“You just did, telepathically.”

Her smile broadens as she touches my shoulder and says, “You never cease to surprise me, and that’s what makes you so endearing. Biomei was right when she told you that you have a beautiful soul. You’re worthier than you realize.”

Nicki spots a large group of plants and low-lying fruit trees at the eastern end of the valley. Despite it being a bit of a hike, we decide to see if they're edible. We know we’re out in the open and vulnerable, but just the same, we’re determined to explore this wonderful planet, despite the risks.

The tall grass slows our progress. My suit’s readings are indicating that I’m using a high level of energy.

“How’re you doing?” I ask Nicki.

“I’m fine,” she says, sounding annoyed.

“This grass is higher than it looks from a distance. Do you want a lift? I can spell you a while if you’re tired.” I could see her eyes narrow into slits through her helmet. Her jaw tightens. Uh oh, I just screwed up.

“Don’t do that,” she snaps.

“Do what?”

“Baby, or patronize me. If I need help, I’ll ask for it.”

“Jeez, you don’t have to get your panties in a knot. I don’t want you to wear yourself out before we get to the trees.”

“My endurance is still strong. I do much harder hikes on Venubia. And I do not wear panties.”

"You don't? You mean you're all bare ass in that suit?"

"She restrains a laugh, then lets it out. *"You know I am wearing a nanobiocarbon under-suit. It's the same as yours."*

The tall grass gives way to a gaping stream of crystal clear, swift-moving water.

"The water looks good," I say, staring into the flowing stream. "I wish I could sample it."

"Put your index finger into the water," Nicki says. "Your suit will give you a readout of the water's composition and temperature. If it's safe to drink, we'll have Shorty take a sample for Biomei to replicate."

As soon as I put my finger into the stream, my visor started scrolling up all sorts of numbers and chemical equations. The last line of text read: Suitable for consumption. Nicki tells Shorty to take a few hundred liters of the water while she takes soil samples and more atmospheric readings.

"I'm curious. Where's Shorty storing all that water? I mean, he's pint-sized," I stab a finger at the droid for emphasis.

"As he draws the water in, he breaks it down into its chemical constituents, then compresses it into gases which are stored in built-in pressurized canisters in Shorty's lower torso."

"Oh, I see. So, what's the verdict, Skipper? Is this a habitable planet? If you had to, could you spend the rest of your life here?"

Nicki's expression turns thoughtful. "Maybe, but it would require having a rebreathing apparatus for a while. Probably take a few planetary cycles before our bodies would adapt to the atmosphere and gravity. But it could be made livable, especially with the right partner."

"I'd volunteer for the job if you'd have me," I transmit to her.

Nicki smiles brightly. *"I couldn't think of a better partner. We need to cross the stream and get to the trees on the other side."*

I nod and follow Nicki into the stream. My suit's ambient temperature sensor indicates the water is 3.9VMT (Venubian Mean Temperature), which was a bit above freezing, and yet there's no sensation of cold. The stream has a strong current, and it's deeper than we realized.

"We're going to have to swim against the current," she transmits.

Despite only being around 40 meters across, she's struggling against the strong current. I don't care if I piss her off.... I grab her arm, pulling her close to my side. I'm swimming with little effort with Nicki in tow.

When we reach the other side, I let Nicki pull herself out. She flops over onto her back. Over my intercom, I can hear her puffing out heavy breaths. I sit beside her and watch Nicki, realizing how exhausted she is.

"That was a strong current," I finally say.

She sits upright and says in a breathy tone, "The current is much stronger than it looks." She pats my shoulder and stands. "There are only a few more hours of daylight left. We need to check out that area. It looks full of edible foods. I want you and Shorty to do a thorough sensor sweep of the entire area. I have an uneasy feeling that we are being watched from a distance."

"It's interesting you say that. I've had the same feeling. It's weird, but it's almost like something has been breathing on the back of my neck the whole way here."

"Why didn't you say anything?"

"I was afraid you'd think I was imagining it."

Nicki wrinkles her brow and says, "You have to trust your instincts. They're your best defense. Never be afraid to express a concern again. This is especially true when we're in an uncertain environment like this one."

The sky becomes redder as the sun hovers close to the horizon. All the vegetation is getting darker and more luminescent in the dimming light.

Nicki works quickly, picking up certain plants with their roots intact while others just the leaves. She's inspecting what looks like bulbs and hanging fruits from some of the trees. Nicki hastens Shorty to her. He scoots up, turns, and opens a storage bin in the lower half of his posterior. She fills it with a variety of samples she took from several plants and trees. She also fills another compartment of Shorty's midsection with soil samples gathered from along the stream and around the different plants she found deeper in the valley.

Now, I'm keeping a close watch on her with the built-in optics of my suit's visor. She works with remarkable swiftness and is deliberate in everything she selects. Occasionally, I scan the immediate area for any unusual biosignatures. I catch some movement near the edge of the woods. I can't make out the shadowy image moving within the darkening dusk that's rolling down into the valley.

When I return my attention to Nicki, she is gone. I look for Shorty, and he's also gone. I engage my optical zoom and still can't locate them. My heart is racing as I rescan the area where she was working. She isn't there. Then I turn my attention back to the shadowy image near the edge of the woods. Even after enhancing the area with both infrared and false-color illuminations, I can't see anything. My instincts tell me to reach out telepathically to Nicki. Okay, I close my eyes and concentrate on her image and then transmit, *"Where are you?"*

"Right behind you," she responds.

I turn. Nicki's standing in front of me, smiling. I let out a held breath, then pulled her close and gave her an awkward sideways hug, causing our helmets to bang together.

"What's wrong?" she asks.

"Nothing, but I thought I saw a shadowy image on top of the ridgeline just outside of the woods. It appeared for a moment, then I lost it."

"You think it was an animal or something else?"

I shrug. "Your guess is as good as mine."

"I put Shorty back on guard. We both can use some food and rest."

"There's a nice spot under that small orchard you were so busy in before."

Nicki nods and reaches out her hand for me to take. We walk holding hands up to one of the small trees near the stream. Nicki sends Shorty to gather some dry wood for a fire. It doesn't take long before we get a nice warm crackling fire going. We relax under a tree, listening to the sounds of the stream's swift waters and burning embers.

"There's a synthetic food pack built into your environmental suit," Nicki says. "It's like the one on Biomei. It can emulate whatever tastes you desire. Close your eyes for a moment and think about what you would like to eat."

While sucking on her feeding tube, she gestures with her eyes for me to proceed.

"Why were you so nervous before?" she asks, noisily sucking on her tube.

"I couldn't locate you."

"Did you forget about the proximity locator?"

As soon as she said it, I could feel my face burn... *Oops.*

Chapter 20

"I've just received an update from VSD07. They have completed the flush and sterilization procedures." Nicki says.

"Both procedures? I thought it would've taken longer."

Her dark grey eyes look down, and she breathes out with a low and heavy sigh.

"Out with it."

"Biomei delayed the rebooting of her main processors. She's having the droids perform an additional flush on her main drive system. She left out many of the details, other than to say that she believes that free radical nanites broke off from the virus, creating nanite antibodies. A number of both types migrated into the magnetic bottle, disrupting the field within the flow regulator. When the field collapsed, it caused an explosion, rupturing the containment manifold and making the subsequent hull breach."

"Wait, a minute. Nanites, I get. But nanite antibodies?"

"Yes. Plasma, when reaching higher temperatures, creates matter. When the nanites entered the chamber, the two-million-degree plasma instantly converted it into matter and antimatter…" Her voice trails off. She becomes quiet for a sec and then says, "I agreed with the analysis and told the droids to do the secondary drive systems as well. I hope this will finally rid us of the virus."

"I'm sure it will. But that's not what's bothering you."

"VSD07 estimated that the additional procedure will take an extra cycle. We'll have to stay here an extra half cycle. And that means, staying through the night."

"I don't see any problem with that."

"Oh, good. I was worried you would have reservations about spending more time here under these uncertain circumstances."

I narrow my gaze at her through my visor and say, "You seem motivated to stay. And I get a sense that it's more than scientific curiosity. You're holding something back. Remember about openly sharing our concerns?"

"You're right. I'm sorry." Her brow ridges rise a bit. "I didn't want to say anything until I had more evidence. Didn't want to worry you. But I'm now sure we're being watched."

"That confirms what I've been sensing."

She points toward an open area. "That looks like a nice place to set up camp. Let's relocate there."

I douse the fire with water. We make our way across an open field of tall grasses bordered by the dark forest on one side and the orchard on the other. Nicki stops under a thick, squat, twisted trunk of a tree with rambling, knotty branches and long, delicate green leaves. She pats the ground for me to join her. I make myself comfortable around the bristling, warm fire that Shorty made. I barely get my ass settled when Shorty begins sounding an alert.

Nicki takes out her binoculars and says, "Our curious followers are coming down the mountain pass we took."

"Do you have a good lock on them, Shorty?" I ask, enabling my night vision.

"Yes, sir," Shorty answers. "The biological units are approximately 155 meters north of the valley."

"Looks like he brought a few friends," I interject, scanning the area in both infrared and night-vision. "Nicki, I can't get a read on them."

"They may have activated a cloaking mechanism," she states, then adds, "I'm scanning on a lower bandwidth. Shorty, change your surveillance setting to 2.35 on the lower band and report."

The little automaton moves slowly out toward the stream. We wait tensely with bated breath. As soon as I wheeze out a long exhale, Shorty reports, "Have detected humanoid biosignatures approaching the stream 200 meters to the east of our position."

"Interesting," I call out. I got them. They appear to be trying to sneak up behind us."

"Shorty, do you have a fix on them?" Nicki asks.

"There are four distinct biosignatures. I have their physiological makeup, but can't identify their species. They do not match anything in my biological database. The data I was able to capture describes them as bipedal, upright walkers. Their height is approximately 1.45 meters, and they are walking at 3.5 meters per micron."

"Shorty, are they carbon or copper-based organisms?" Nicki asks.

"Copper. They appear to be of a genetically engineered origin. Also, there is a 99.45 percent certainty they are clones."

"No, that cannot be," Nicki says, in a hushed tone, her expression fills with alarm. "What are they doing here?"

"One is coming in our direction," Shorty says, "and the other three are remaining behind. I detect energy signatures indicative of small weapons."

"Nicki, let's act as though we haven't discovered them," I suggest. "Come sit down by the fire. Shorty, stand by that tree near the stream. Alert us when it gets within 15 meters. Be prepared to use your stunner as soon as it gets in range."

"Understood, Phil."

"Well, it seems we're going to have company for dinner," I say with an ironic smile. "Pull out your phaser, Nicki, and place it on your lap."

"You're going to let it get that close to us?" Nicki objects nervously. "You've no idea what you're dealing with."

"Aren't you even a little curious about who or what they are?"

"No. I already have a good idea of what they are and don't want them anywhere near us. Shorty, belay those last instructions and create a pulse weapon. When it's in range, shoot to kill."

"That's a hell of an order coming from a pacifist. Nicki, you're still holding something back. I've been patiently waiting for you to tell me what's been eating at you. Now would be a good time."

Her face is so red with anger and apprehension that it glows within the dim lighting of her helmet. Her eyes are wide and full of emotion as she nervously chews her lower lip.

"If these approaching creatures are what I think they are, we must kill them before they kill us. They're hideous, pathological beasts that have no conscience or reasoning. They take whatever they want and destroy everything in their path. They're called Zenti, and I'm terrified of what they can do to us." Nicki's eyes well up, and her voice becomes shriller as she speaks.

"But you don't know if it's them. How could you kill something sight unseen? That's not like you, Nicki."

"Better be safe than dead," she cries.

"Shorty, please disregard Nicki's orders and follow my original instructions. Stun only when I give the order. Understood?"

"Acknowledged." Shorty regards Nicki, his optical sensor flickering. "Nicki, do you concur with Phillip's command?"

She looks at me for a moment and then nods. "Do as Phillip instructed."

We sat with our backs leaning against a narrow tree trunk in silent apprehension. Nicki is staring outwardly, her face reflecting the amber glow from the fire. Her mouth is closed in a tight line as we wait for the unknown creatures to make their move. I intently study Shorty, anticipating him going into action. We wait and wait for what seems like hours. Then a splashing sound gets us to our feet. It sounds like something struggling to swim against the strong current of the stream.

I call to Shorty, "Can you see what's happening? You'd think a planet with this many moons would provide more light," I complain to Nicki while switching my optical sensor back to infrared. It only casts a green glow on the darkness.

"Alert, unknown life-form detected," Shorty calls our attention to something being swiftly carried downstream.

"Oh, nice," I say with great relief. "Shorty, how far downstream is it?"

"300 meters, and it appears to be floating with the current."

Nicki anxiously asks, "Shorty, can you detect any life signs?"

"It is difficult to get a definitive read at this range."

"Is it the same life-form you detected earlier?" I ask.

"Unable to identify. However, it is most probable it was the same one."

"Increase range with auxiliary power and extrapolate possible life signs," Nicki orders.

"There are faint sounds indicative of stressful respiration," Shorty responds.

"Can you define life type?" Nicki says.

There's a long pause while Shorty attempts to increase his sensor's sensitivity before the life-form gets out of his range.

"Sorry, Nickada, it is out of sensor range, and its life signs are no longer detectable."

"Is it dead?" I ask, hoping for a clear yes or no.

"Unknown."

"Shit," I snap, then turn to Nicki. "It's most likely dead. If it isn't, it appears to be going for a long ride before it gets to either bank. Shorty, can you tell what the other three are doing?"

"They are getting close."

A rustling noise rises behind me. Shorty sounds another alert. I turn toward the noise. Something jumps out of the tall grass, knocking me to the ground. I hear Nicki's scream over my intercom. I wrestle with the humanoid creature. It's much stronger than it looks. The small alien wears a black, tight-fitting jumpsuit. Its head is covered by a helmet with a dark visor, obscuring its face. We roll on the ground. It maneuvers on top of me, holding a long, sharp-looking blade. The blade glistens in the pale night's light as the alien humanoid lifts it above its head and thrusts it down. A surge of energy runs through me as I catch its arm and overpower the alien. It struggles to no avail. With little effort, I bend its arm down and under, forcing the shiny, sharp blade deep into the alien's midsection. It lets out a shrill wail, wheezes, and gurgles as blue-green blood fills its mouth. I throw it off me. It lies on its back with the blade's hilt sticking out of the middle of its body. I stand over the dying alien, looking down at it in disbelief. What have I done? Bright blue blood oozes from its wound. The entire fight seems unreal. I don't have time to dwell on it, remembering Nicki's scream.

She's grappling with another one of the small, humanoid-like creatures. As I run to her aid, the great beast we encountered in the forest leaps onto her attacker, knocking it to the ground. The alien holds out a weapon. The powerful animal studies it for a beat, then jumps forward, landing less than a meter from the alien. Without hesitation, the beautiful animal charges, biting the alien's arm off before it can fire. The fourth alien fires its pulse laser. It shoots out a bright discharge of yellow light, grazing the beast's side. Another one of the powerful animals jumps out of the low brush, knocking the alien down. It bites the humanoid's neck. The small warrior screeches in pain for a second, then becomes silent.

The whole scene only took seconds, but it all seemed to happen in slow motion.

Another great beast pounces on the body of the one I killed. It circles the corpse, leaning close and sniffing loudly. It must have been satisfied that it's a fresh kill. The massive creature opens its enormous mouth full of long, pointed teeth and bites into the humanoid, dragging it into the tall savanna grasses.

Shorty fires his stun gun at two more, who stop and notice the large animal charging after them. They fire and miss. They turn and run to the stream, jumping in with the magnificent animal right on their heels. We can hear them now laboring against the stream's strong current. We hope they'll have a similar end to the other alien who tried crossing earlier.

The beast turns toward Shorty. It lets out a bellowing roar, regarding Shorty, then sniffs him for a moment. It turns back around and runs up to the wounded humanoid who's lying on the ground, probably close to death from blood loss. The animal approaches cautiously, sniffing the air. It reaches the body and breathes in again. The creature bites into the alien's neck to finish the kill and drags it off in the same direction as the first.

"No." Nicki cries. "I need to examine it. I need to make sure."

I walk up beside her, and we hug. I couldn't tell who was trembling more, Nicki or me. We stand for a long moment locked in an awkward embrace. Environmental suits make hugging difficult. We discover how to hug without knocking helmets while trying to calm ourselves. She turns within my embrace and looks in the direction the beast is taking its kill to be devoured by who knows how many of its kind.

"Look at it this way," I say, trying to sound calm. "It saved your life, and you fed its family for a few days. It's a perfectly equitable exchange."

"I needed to identify the alien first, then I would have been glad to feed the beast's hunger." She looks back at me. Her face is flushed, and her eyes are wide with the emotions of the battle. She becomes quiet, staring unblinkingly outward. After a few seconds, her expression turns stoic as if in deep thought. "They're a curious and intelligent animal." She finally says. "The animal that saved me was the same one we encountered earlier. Remarkable."

"Remarkable indeed," I say, then turn toward Shorty and ask, "Are there any more of them?"

"No, sir."

I look at Nicki and ask, "Were they Zenti?"

"I believe so. But can't be sure without doing a proper autopsy." She sighs. "Let's put Shorty on alert while we get some sleep. It's been a long, rough, and tense day for both of us."

"One thing is bothering me."

"What?"

"They had hand weapons and could have picked us off almost with impunity, and didn't?"

"Yes. I noticed that also. It leads me to think they wanted us alive."

I placed my arm around her and tried to get my shaking hands under control. I send her a telepathic message, "*I just killed a humanoid. It's something I never thought I could or would ever have to do. But I'd do it all again to keep us safe.*"

We sat back under the tree. The fire is down to a few glowing embers. I sent Shorty to gather more firewood.

"*Take your helmet off,*" Nicki transmits to me.

"Take off my helmet? Is that what you just told me?"

She releases the magnetic seal of her helmet and pulls it off. Her teary eyes are shining brightly in the dim glow of the fire.

"It's okay," she tells me. "The air is breathable between the sunsets."

I take my helmet off and inhale deeply, letting it out in one long breath. Nicki stares at me with an uncertain look as if her mind is struggling with something she can't or won't talk about. Before I can say a word, she kisses me hard. I kiss her back with all the pent-up passion held inside of me for the past one-and-a-half cycles.

My hands stop shaking.

CHAPTER 21

We have a restless night and welcome the sounds of the shuttle circling our position. In the bright morning light, I notice the alignment of the pale moons with the massive gas giant high up in the sky. Its vivid colors are present.

Nicki is using her hi-res binoculars, taking a quick survey of the area. "It's a beautiful planet," she says in a soft voice, "but I'll feel a lot better once we get back aboard Biomei. Those were Zenti we encountered, I'm sure of it now. We must stay vigilant; there'll be more of them coming soon. The others must have reported our position by now."

"You're probably right." I frown and say, "I'm sorry we didn't get more time to explore this beautiful world. Mostly, I'm disappointed we didn't find more food."

"I've gathered a little soil and seeds to grow a variety of fruits and vegetables in the hydroponics lab. If successful, we may be enjoying them soon."

"Nice. Can't wait."

The shuttle makes a smooth landing in the open range close to our position. Three of the droids filed out to greet us as Nicki packed up the few instruments she had set up. She's handing them to the droids to stow inside the shuttle. Shorty makes a few more soil readings east of the shuttle while Nicki takes a final sweep of the area. She waves her hand while saying something in Venubian. I understand enough to know what she's doing. A virtual screen appears to her right, and I can see what she's seeing. We both relaxed a bit, seeing no signs of the Zenti. All their biosignatures are either out of range or they have left. I'm leaning toward they've left rather than not detecting biosignatures. Not detecting any signs doesn't guarantee they're gone.

As we're about to get into the shuttle, we notice a flock of large birds flying overhead. Suddenly, not far from us, the edge of the forest is now alive with odd-looking animals. I catch a look at something that resembles a hefty deer standing on six muscular legs with large, pointed antlers on its head. We watch it graze on the knotted, low grass at the wood's edge. Its coat is as black as the forest.

We both smile in surprise at the sudden liveliness of the planet. We're stunned when we observe a pack of different-sized, furry animals, hopping and running in and out of the tall grass as though they're checking us out before going to the stream for a drink.

"It appears the planet is showing off all its magnificence in time for our departure," I quip. Nicki arches a brow ridge. "This's odd, though, Nicki. Why do you suppose they're just coming out now?"

"I think the magnetic storm may have caused them to burrow in for safety. It's stopped long enough for them to feel safe enough to come out. Look how timidly they walk. They're acting on high alert."

"Are we causing that?"

Nicki nods.

"You know what's interesting? They all look like animals and birds you could see on Earth. With some distinct differences," I point to the six-legged deer, grazing on the tall grasses close to the stream. "I'm also noticing many differences, especially in their size and colors."

A smile grows across Nicki's face, surveying all the wildlife. The more she studies the now vast variety of animals, the wider her light gray eyes get, looking full of joy.

"You'll find that all carbon-based life has a common biological foundation: DNA. It's a remarkable molecule. In all its possible variations of complex proteins, it still creates life with a common thread. Wherever you find a combination of liquid water, a quiescent sun, and the right mix of carbon and some other common chemical elements, you will always find similar biological organisms. As you'll soon discover, we're not that unique, and the universe is full of life. As for their size, gravity affects the entire spectrum of a planet's topography, including its life-forms. Although this is a large planet, its mass is not that much greater than Venubia's. Higher gravity planets tend to produce smaller and flatter life-forms, but there are always biological exceptions."

We take a final, long look at the planet's incredible variety of life. I sense a peaceful stream of emotions flowing from Nicki. It feels good.

CHAPTER 22

Nicki finds me sitting in the small galley across from our quarters. She sits facing me and quietly watches as I stare into my favorite mug.

"Couldn't sleep either?" I say, not looking up.

"Turned over only to find your side of the bed empty. It's the third night in a row. I figured maybe it's time we talked about what's been bothering you."

I give her a thoughtful look, then put down my mug. "I could ask you the same question. Can't seem to stop thinking about what happened to you on the planet."

"What do you mean?"

"I've never seen you so frightened and angry. You were disturbingly intense. I didn't want to press you about it because I was hoping you'd come to me on your own." I study her, allowing an uneasy silence to fill the space between us.

She lets out a long sigh and stands, and goes to the synthesizer. "Do you want more coffee?" she asks, ordering a black tea.

"It's not coffee. It's hot chocolate." I grin at the mug. "I was surprised you had it programmed into the synthesizer. No thanks. I've had enough."

"It was Biomei's idea. She had conducted a detailed study of all your favorite foods and then configured their molecular compositions into the synthesizer. I didn't want to say anything, fearing they may have been lost in her reboot. I'm pleased it's still there. There are other beverages that at first, I objected to, but Biomei convinced me that they were necessary."

"It's nice to know that Biomei cares so much about my comforts. Now, do you want to tell me about it? What did you call them? Zenti?"

She sits down, looking as though she's gathering her thoughts. She takes a careful sip of the hot tea, then gazes at me. Her light complexion seems even paler than usual. Her eyes turn from their lustrous hazel to a dark shade of gray. I always marvel at how unusual her eyes are, but at this moment, I don't like what I'm seeing. Over time, I've learned to read her moods through their vivid color changes. Now, there's something new and disquieting. She pulls on a long strand of her silky hair, then looks down into her tea.

"Well?"

"The Zenti are like a band of... psychopathic marauders." She closes her eyes and grimaces. "Phil, I can't go into the details of what they are, because it's... it's..." Her head bows with her shoulders slumped, looking as though she is struggling with her overwhelming emotions.

"I can see how hard this is for you, but you have to let me in."

"I know," she murmurs, then sighs. "It's complicated, and there's much you must know before you could begin to appreciate what the Zenti are."

"You mentioned that when I complete the transformation process, there'll be some Venubian history included. Are the Zenti part of that?"

She nods, and her expression grows more animated. "Oh, Phil, I've completely forgotten," she says, letting out an anxious breath. "With all the distractions, we've never discussed you going through the full transformation procedure."

"We started talking about it right before Biomei's infection."

"It's necessary. We can't delay it any longer. Your body and mind need to be adapted to Venubia and, more importantly, to space travel. The enhancements I've given you on Earth are only marginally effective for what we'll endure in the final quarter of our journey. We're already far beyond the halfway point. Soon, we'll be traveling through strong gravity fields and warped space, as well as periods of hibernation. You need to be adapted to the stresses associated with these strong forces. Also, I've never activated your implanted subcortical processor because I wanted to upgrade it first. It's an invasive procedure, and I'd prefer to do it after you've been modified. Now that Biomei's restored, we can proceed with getting you up to standards."

"Oh?" I say, lifting my head, trying to get my mind wrapped around what Nicki just described. My mouth falls open in shock and surprise. "Ooh shit," I mutter, standing.

"What's wrong, dear?" Nicki's high forehead furrows into a confused expression.

"You mean you're not finished tinkering with my brain? My body's one thing, but why do you have to mess with my brain again? It took me months to try to get myself back together after the last time."

Nicki stands and gives me a reassuring look. "This time, it'll be different."

"Different how?"

"For one thing, I won't have to bring you back from the dead." Her expression turns thoughtful. "But I'll have to induce you into a highly transcendental state." She lifts her bright eyes and, with a cheery smile, adds, "It'll all seem like a lucid dream. Trust me. It won't hurt at all."

"Really? So why am I so nervous?"

"It's probably because you haven't experienced this before. You've nothing to worry about. It'll be a wonderful experience for you.... Well, at least most of it will...." She narrows her eyes and asks, "Do you trust me?"

"With my life."

"Then, you have nothing to worry about," she pats my cheek. "Biomei, prepare the Med lab for Phil's transformation to commence at 0600 ship-hours."

"Affirmative, Nicki. Who will assist?"

Nicki scrutinizes my troubled expression for a second and calls to Biomei, "Send VSD07." She gives me a dry smile and adds, "Also, Shorty for emotional support."

I cock an eyebrow at the sarcasm and then hold my hand out to her. "You better be good to me tonight, because who knows what I'm going to be like after tomorrow."

"As you like to say, have a little faith. I can't screw you up much more than I already have," she laughs.

I pull her in closer to me and give her a warm kiss. We hold hands as we walk back to our quarters. Ripping our jumpsuits off, we tumble excitedly onto the bed... and then fall right to sleep.

***

(0:600 Hours Ship-Time Main Medical Lab)

Nicki is already waiting for me as I enter the medical operating room. Although familiar with the operatory as a patient, it somehow had a different feeling to me this time. I notice a lot more equipment surrounding the operating table. There is also a faint, low-pitched hum under a higher-pitched buzzing as I approach the table. The room smells of disinfectant, and the pure-white lighting is very bright.

"How are you this morning, sir?" Shorty greets me as I approach, while Nicki is busy working with VSD07.

I give him a nod and pat his head, "Just fine, Shorty. Thank you."

I turn my attention to Nicki and watch her as she's inputting data on the central console while dictating orders to '07 in Venubian.

"Why didn't you wake me?" I ask.

"You needed the rest. Besides, there wasn't much you could've done until we had the system ready," Nicki says, placing a programmed crystal in '07's upper torso just below its head.

"Did you get any sleep?"

"Yes."

"Are you ready?" I say, slapping my hands together, then rubbing them.

She looks up from the console and asks. "The question is, are *you* ready?"

I survey the equipment surrounding the table. I notice a tunneling scanner and a long laser arm among the instruments. It all looks poised for action. "You need all this stuff for a transformation?"

"I don't need any of these instruments for the transformation procedure. Most of it is for making modifications to some of your adaptations, as well as additional diagnostics for the upgrade to all your neuroprocessors. If all goes as expected, you'll be a little quicker, stronger, and maybe smarter." She gestures for me to get on the table.

"How 'bout a kiss for luck?"

When our faces meet, she gazes at me for a moment, then she obliges me with a long, adoring kiss. She squeezes my hand as I get up on the table.

"Just remember, my love, parts of the transformation will seem real, but it's an illusion and can't harm you. Once your primary processor is upgraded, it will upload data that I've programmed for you. It will include a tutorial on Venubia, its people, and our neighboring worlds. Also, some of the major conflicts with the Zenti." She closes her eyes and lets out a long breath.

"I see how painful this is for you. It's hard for me to understand how vivid your memories are."

She begins running her fingers through my hair, staring into my face with a tentative smile, as if pondering her thoughts. After a long moment, she says in a soft voice, "Upon completion of the procedure, you'll have a much better idea of who Venubians were and who we are now." "Did I ever tell you how beautiful your hair is? I'm glad we changed the color. I prefer the Vultaran black. It suits you better than the mousy brown, as you called it."

"Is that what you really want to tell me?"

She continues to run her fingers through my hair, seemingly preoccupied in thought. She leans down and kisses my forehead.

"One of the primary purposes of the transformation procedure is to adapt your mind and body for the diversity of physical changes that you're going to experience," she continues, speaking in a soft, almost dreamy voice. "Despite the enhancements you've received, your physiology is still mostly Earth-based. This next step is to instill the knowledge and physiological tools to assist your mind and body—"

"You've already told me all of this. You've prepared me well for this procedure, but there's something else that's troubling you."

She nods. "I... I wish I could spare you the ugly details of this virtual experience. You're going to be exposed to some hard truths. Allow your intellect and compassion to guide you to an honest understanding of my people. Keep your heart in the light where the truth always resides."

"The past is a teacher that prepares us for the future," I say, keeping my voice low and calm. "There's an old Earth proverb that I'll paraphrase: Those who don't learn from the past are condemned to relive it."

"Enough with all this philosophy," she says, standing and straightening her jumpsuit. "Let's get on to making you ready for the journey ahead." She gives me a confident smile while wiping tears from her eyes. She walks back to the med console. "Ready?"

I lift my head and give her a thumbs-up. I wink at Shorty, who flashes his optical sensor. "Okay, let's get this show started."

CHAPTER 23

"Up," a muffled voice pierces the silence of the hibernation chamber. "Get out of there," the voice becomes louder and more intense. "I will use force if you do not comply."

I'm certain I'm imagining the hostile voice. I try to ignore it, hoping it will go away. I hear a hissing sound, like air leaking out of a pressurized container. It's starting to bug me. I'm not ready to open my eyes. Standard hibernation is like coming out of deep sleep. I need a few more minutes to collect myself before being fully awake.

"Out," the voice sounds right over me. I jerk my eyes open and try to focus on a large form standing over the chamber.

Then reality strikes with a sudden rush of heart-thumping panic. "Biomei!" I shout. "What's outside my chamber?"

At first, I wonder why I'm in hibernation. Then, I wonder why an intruder is confronting me? All my senses shift into mortal fear and shock mode.

I try to gather my thoughts while regarding the shadowy figure standing over my hibernation chamber. It looks like a large green thing. As I make a move to hit the manual release to open my unit, the large green thing becomes adamant. It lifts what appears to be a long appendage and then smashes it through the chamber's dome. It grabs me by the throat with a flexible, clamp-like hand. The crude-looking, curved appendage has a pointed tip that closes around an opposing, flatter part. It doesn't feel like flesh or metal, but it's powerful.

The large, green creature lifts me like a rag doll through the narrow opening. It holds me by the neck and turns me from side to side. I think it must be examining me. I wonder how. I can't see anything that resembles an optical sensor. It doesn't even have a discernible head. I stare back, puzzled by what this large, brown-green blob with one big arm wants. Its tight grip makes it hard for me to think. I make a useless attempt to pry the creature's grip off my neck with both my hands.

"You're choking me," I croak out.

I'm feeling light-headed and struggling to stay conscious.

"What are you?" it demands.

It lets go of my neck, allowing me to fall hard on my ass while gasping for breath in great wheezing heaves. I look up at the odd intruder, trying to figure out what it is.

My mind clouds up from the unnerving experience of being confronted by such a menacing, alien creature. I get to my feet and rein in my fear. I study the intruder, attempting to make sense of it. For one thing, it's huge, probably two and a half meters in height and over a meter wide. Remarkably, it had no apparent legs or wheels but moved smoothly on its flat bottom, leaving a trail of fluid like a snail. I wondered how it's communicating. After a moment's thought, it becomes clear. It's communicating using a type of telepathy. Odd thing, though. Nicki and Biomei often transmitted real emotions whenever they linked with me, but this, whatever-it-is, only transmits crude thoughts.

"What are you?" it repeats.

"I'm human," I answer nervously, still gasping for breath.

"Human? What is human?" There is a long silence as it stands immobile. After a few seconds pass, it blurts, "Human. We heard of humans. You are of that species. Not much data. First contact."

I relax a little with its answer. I rationalize that this isn't a hostile encounter, but maybe the first contact between curious aliens. Still feeling uneasy, I gather a little more courage and attempt to speak with it.

"What are you?"

"Machine, like your ship, only free to move about."

That explained a lot. Of course, Biomei is a biomechanical machine. I rationalize further. If robots on Earth come in all shapes and sizes, why couldn't biomechanical machines? It's only logical that different species would use machines that best serve their needs and reflect their concept of what it should look like. Another thought occurs. If this is what their machines look like, then what in the hell did the designers look like? More importantly... I eye the creature with a wave of growing anger and shout, "What in hell is this goddamn thing doing on my ship? And where the fuck is Biomei?" I step up close to the undifferentiated robot and poke my finger into its midsection, asking in a firm voice, "What do you want?" I take a deep breath and let it out slowly to calm myself.

"Want?" It pauses again. "Input on your species."

"Why?" I hope by asking enough questions, I can uncover its intentions.

"First contact," it repeats.

Repeating things. That's not a good sign. I fear we're beginning to enter into a communications dilemma. "Yes, first contact. I get it. I'm curious about who sent you, your owner or manufacturer."

"Manufacturer? Explain manufacturer."

"Creator, builder, designer?"

"Does not compute."

I frown, thinking, failure to communicate, and we've barely started. I need to make an analogy that it can understand. "Venubians created the ship." Upon saying that, I thought about Biomei again, and why she is silent, then I wondered, where is Nicki? "Biomei, are you online?"

"Offline," the machine says.

"Why?"

"Necessary for protection."

An odd thing occurs to me. The sound of the robot's voice in my head is familiar. While it spoke in curt words and phrases, its voice wasn't mechanical-sounding. It sounded human. Damn. It's speaking in my voice.

"Not necessary," I say. "Ship cannot harm you. Need ship to communicate."

There is another long silence. It slides to the engineering console and, without direct contact, somehow brings Biomei online.

"Intruder alert! Intruder alert!" Biomei shouts as the ship's auto-alert system is enabled, along with the stunning roar and glare of klaxons and strobes.

The alien machine appears agitated by the noise and starts coming toward me with its menacing appendage fully extended.

"Biomei, cancel the alert!"

She complies.

"Sorry, Phil. This large blob shut me down as I was going into an alert condition. I'm pleased to see this moronic machine hasn't harmed you. Fortunately, I'd have enough time to bring you out of hibernation before this brainless, conglomeration of genetic junk broke in."

I had no idea that Biomei could get so emotional. It seems as though she knows this machine and dislikes it.

"Biomei, you're familiar with this... Whatever this thing is?"

"Yes. It's a Zenti scout-droid. The Zenti are the scourges of the universe. They're like your ancient pirates. They send out these scouts to find defenseless ships, steal everything of value, then mercilessly kill and sometimes even eat every living thing on board. Once they've ensured all living beings are dead, they complete their unconscionable treachery by destroying whatever remains." Biomei's voice is full of contempt. She transmits, *"Phil, they already know all they need to take us over and are about to come and board us. We must leave here at once and hope we can outrun them."*

"Nicki told me a little about the Zenti. I think they were on Delius-5 and must've followed us back to you."

"I believe you're right. But they somehow cloaked themselves from my sensors. This droid took me by surprise."

"What do we do about the droid? And where's Nicki?"

"Ask me about Nicki verbally."

"I don't understand."

"Just ask me verbally," she insists.

"I believe this thing has telepathic ability."

"It doesn't."

"So, how's it communicating with me telepathically?"

"It's using our universal translator along with your internal processor."

"How could it know how—"

"Not now, Phillip," Biomei cuts me off. *"Ask me where Nicki is."* Her tone is emphatic.

Biomei, where's Nicki?

"Nicki is not aboard the ship. Don't you remember? She's busy surveying L745, and we're on our way to get her." Her voice sounds strange, but I suspect she's protecting Nicki's real location. *"Please go along with this,"* she reassures me. *"This series droid is limited in both intelligence and capabilities. However, it has sophisticated telemetry and transmits everything it sees and hears directly back to its ship. I'm going to scan it to see if we can disable it. In the meantime, keep it occupied."*

I transmit, *"And how'd you propose I accomplish that feat? He's bigger and stronger than I."*

"Continue interacting with it while I devise a plan."

"Devise quickly. If you haven't noticed, we're not communicating all that well."

"Ask it specific questions about where it comes from and what it wants."

"I already did, and it wants input about me."

"So, give it what it wants."

I look at the droid and force a smile while thinking of something interesting to tell it. My mind is a blank... for a moment, then an idea pops into my head. Still smiling and with a lot of syrup in my voice, I ask, "Machine, where do you come from?"

"My ship."

"Where's your ship?"

"Attached to yours."

"How did you get on board?"

"Forced aft docking hatchway."

"Can you show me how you did that?"

"Why?"

Good question, I thought. "So, I can prevent another automaton like you from doing that in the future."

"Not necessary."

"Why?"

"No future for you and the ship."

"And why's that?" I feel my eyebrows rise.

"Orders to take you."

"Biomei, it's apparent that this droid was given orders to take me with it."

"Yes... yes. You're doing fine. Keep asking it questions."

"Take me? Take me where?" This is far worse than I imagined. The thought of being abducted by this large automaton is disturbing.

"To my ship for interrogation by Over-minds."

"What do they want with me?"

Over-minds, it sounds like something from a bad science fiction movie. I have a sudden vision of hanging upside down with my feet shackled while being methodically tortured by a hooded alien.

"Over-Minds do not explain. Only give orders."

"I see, and if I refuse to go with you?"

"Refusal is irrelevant. If you do not comply, I will use force."

"What if you damage me in the process?"

It appears I bought myself a little time. The machine becomes rigid like someone pulled its plug. I lean in close to it. Wave my hands back and forth. Thankfully, there is no response. Feeling a little braver, I give it a poke in its firm midsection. Still no reaction. This is getting a little more interesting. *What if I found access to its inner workings and just dismantled it? But where could that access be?*

I walk around it, scrutinizing everything. As Biomei described, it looks like a massive green pile of junk.

"Biomei, are you here?"

"Yes, Phil."

"I somehow got the droid to shut down. Have any ideas on how to get inside it?

"What did you do to initiate the droid's shutdown?"

"I'm not sure. Just ask it a question."

"It's probably contacting the Zenti ship for instructions. There's a high probability that the Zenti are already on their way. They usually keep a safe distance from their droids in case their prey has superior strength and weapons."

"How much time do you think we have?"

"Unfortunately, not much. I'm in the process of establishing a link with its processor. Once linked, I'll be able to monitor it and get a better perspective on their plan, if any. One thing is clear, though. They want you as well as Nickada."

"Why do you think they want me?"

"If they didn't, the droid would've killed you by now."

"That's a comforting thought."

"Keep in mind that the Zenti usually attack at random and often with little sophistication in both planning and execution, which makes them both dangerous and unpredictable."

"Nicki started to tell me about them, but it became too painful for her to talk about."

"The Zentis is probably the single most traumatizing force our system has ever encountered."

As she says that, a troubling thought jabs me. "Biomei, what happened to my transformation? Did I have it?"

"Only the first part, Phil. Nicki was forced to discontinue it when the Zenti were picked up on long-range telemetry. As a precaution, she pulled you out of the transformation procedure and then placed you directly in hibernation for your protection. She didn't give me any instructions before leaving the ship. She told me to watch over you, then placed the droids into a few of the shuttles and sent them to undisclosed locations. She said the less I knew, the better it would be for all of us."

"That's not like her. She should've awakened me before leaving. We could've worked this out together. Do you have any idea where she went?"

"Now's not the time for this conversation. We need to focus on our immediate problem."

"Yes, you're right, of course." I sigh, feeling anxious about Nicki's sudden departure. "Okay. Once you've established a link, will you have any control over the droid?"

"Not directly, but we may be able to disrupt its central receiver."

"And what will that do?"

"We may be able to give the droid conflicting commands which should incapacitate it."

"Very good, so how's the link coming?" The words stumbled out of my mouth at seeing the droid reanimated and coming for me. "Uh, Biomei, I can use a little help right now."

The droid has me walking backward, trying to get a little distance from its large, outstretched arm with a pointy, clamp-like hand. Its powerful grip is getting close to my throat. It moves quicker than expected and almost grabs me. I duck under its claw on its first lunge. A hard blow to the back of my head knocks me face down. The slick deck has me sliding halfway across the Med Lab, slamming against a wall. The hard fall hurts my pride more than my ass. I spring to my feet with a rush of adrenaline. It knocks me down again with a swift blow to my midsection, sending me careening off a bulkhead.

"This droid is pissing me off," I shout, darting under a scanning table just as the menacing appendage is about to clamp onto me.

It makes an odd sound when it snaps shut. The weird automaton pauses, then thrusts its arm under the table. I clutch it with both hands. That's a mistake, runs through my mind as it breaks my feeble grip with a slight backward tug. It seizes my arm and yanks me out from under the table. As the droid pulls me, a strong surge of energy runs through my body. I jerk my arm free and counter with a swift kick to its midsection. The kick seems to have confused the droid because it stops for a second. I take the opportunity to kick it again. My kicks have little effect. On my next attempt, it intercepts my foot and flings me backward.

"Wow," I exclaim, grinning. "I'm impressed with how well my enhanced body is doing."

"You're performing excellently," Biomei encourages.

My mind is filled with rage, feeling like a trapped animal. I jump up and charge at the Zenti machine. Even knowing my feeble actions were more from foolish pride than a deliberate attack strategy, I'm not giving in. I don't want that piece of crap to take me without a good fight. I also want to send a message to the Zenti that they aren't getting me without a struggle. I'm going to focus my energy and then attack. I'm running as fast as I can, screaming at the droid. My eyes narrow as I get closer and closer.... I bounce off the goddamn thing, landing hard on my ass again. Damn, that thing is solid, I think, while lying on the floor.

Springing back onto my feet, I attack forcibly with a flying dropkick. My strategy and efforts are useless. With each angry attempt at inflicting damage to the grotesque machine, my efforts become more futile. I moan with capitulation while lying on my back; all my anger is depleted, leaving me with an empty feeling in my gut.

Finally, I scream at Biomei, "Where's the fucking link!"

"Only need 3.62 picrons," she responds in her usual calm monotone. "Your diversion is working quite well, Phil. Please continue."

"You think this's a diversion? I hate to tell you this, lady, but I'm fighting for my life and losing big-time!"

"Nonsense. You're performing quite adequately, Phil. Now, that should do it."

The droid's open appendage stops a few centimeters from my throat. The veins in my neck are pulsing from my pounding heart. Thank God for small miracles, I think, taking a few deep breaths, calming myself with relief.

"Thanks," I wheeze, looking at the frozen droid, wondering how long before its master shows up.

"Phil."

"Yes?"

"My long-range sensor has picked up a ship approaching at high velocity. It has a Zenti power signature. I strongly suggest we leave."

"Great deduction, Biomei," I snap out of frustration. *Can't get a fucken break. Not for a damn minute.* "Why don't you light the jets and get us the hell out of here!"

The droid's inanimate presence gives me an unsettling feeling as to the nature of its Over-Mind's ability to cause harm.

"Standby full thrust in .23 microns. Please secure yourself, Phil. This is going to be a 22-G burn. I won't have time to compensate because the inertia dampeners are offline."

"I don't care. Just do it."

22-G-burn didn't sound like a big deal. After all, I figure the ship's hull design can partially compensate for the increased gravimetric forces. The force is now upon me. I had no idea how crushing twenty-two times my body weight can feel.

"Thankfully, that's over," I say, letting out a long breath. "Thank goodness, it only lasted a few seconds," I add, looking at the ship's chronometer.

I request a forward viewscreen. A large panel slides away. A view of streaking lines stretching rapidly, passing us along with bright star clusters floating by as if in slow motion.

"Where are we?" I ask, hoping beyond hope that we're beyond Zenti's sensor range.

"We're in quadrant 17.25 of system L673, approximately 8.232 parsecs out and approaching sector 8.75," Biomei dryly states.

"Let me rephrase the question. Are we clear of the damn Zenti?"

"I've conducted a full sensor sweep, and for the moment, we appear to be clear of any Zenti presence."

"Okay then. Let's resume a safe course back to the nebula and find Nicki."

"That's not advisable."

"Why not?"

"There's a high probability that the course will lead us directly back to the Zenti."

"It might, but this time, we'll be looking for them, and they won't have the element of surprise over us."

"There's a major flaw in your logic."

"Oh?"

"The Zenti will be looking for us."

"Yeah, but they'll be looking for where they think we went, not where we're going."

"I don't understand. Would you care to explain?"

"No. I want you to compute a course that will take us back to Nicki."

"Phil, as I explained earlier, Nickada didn't provide me with any course directions."

My heart feels heavy knowing Nicki will have to find us.

"So, what do we do?"

"We proceed on course to Venubia. We are only 45 cycles from Corridor-4. We'll wait for Nicki outside the corridor and hope she finds us. There's little for you to do now. Go back into hibernation, and I'll alert you when we've arrived."

Letting out a long, heavy breath, I nod slowly and reluctantly get into another hibernation chamber. As the dome slowly closes over me, I can't help thinking how alone and frightened Nicki must be.

CHAPTER 24

I'm in a daze... wheezing sounds... rapid breathing, chattering teeth. Oh, it's all coming from me. Where am I? How did I end up shivering alone in the dark? Nicki... Nicki, is she all right? My heart's now pounding so hard it feels like it's about to burst through my chest. I have a dreadful feeling that something awful has happened to her. I got to get out of here... wherever here is....

Everything is turning gray....

Focus, damn you. Think... Think. Disorientation, sudden panic, and now a sense of utter lethargy as if all the energy has just drained out of me. Yes. This is familiar. I'm being thawed out of deep hibernation. Yes—yes, that's it. Guess that's the price of being brought back from near death.

It's taking a concerted effort for me to get my heavy eyelids open. Oh, great. I'm sealed inside a hibernation chamber.

I banged my fist against the clear dome. It rises too slowly for me. I sit up and look around. Everything feels disjointed and wrong. Like my mind and body are out of sync.

"Biomei," I shout. "Can you hear me?"

"Yes, Phil. I hear you."

"Where's Nicki?"

There is an uneasy pause before she answers, "She's not aboard."

"Biomei, what's wrong? You sound strange. Why isn't Nicki aboard?"

"Do you remember what transpired before you were placed into hibernation?"

Her question makes me search my memory. "I can't recall anything that has happened before hibernation. Oh, shit.... My memory..." A sense of great angst rises in me while struggling to gather any thoughts. Nothing. "Biomei, what's happened to me? And where's Nicki?"

"Phil, relax. I'm going to send for Shorty to assist you out of the hibernation chamber. There's nothing wrong with you. You're experiencing a temporary memory lapse. It's most likely a side effect of hibernation shock."

"I'll get it back. Right?"

"We'll run a quick diagnostic on your subcortical processor to make sure there's no damage."

"My what?" I snap. "What are you talking about?"

"Hmm, that's interesting."

"What's interesting?"

"Your memory loss is more extensive than expected. Please try to remain calm. Everything will be fine. We need to discover what happened. What's the last thing you can recall?"

I began to answer, but my mind went blank. "I know who you are. You're the ship that I'm presently on. Also, Nicki is going to take me somewhere, but I..." A cold, clammy chill runs through me. I feel the blood drain from my face. "I can't remember a thing!" I cry. "Everything is all jumbled and vague. My mind... it's... all gone. Please help me. You must help me get my memory back. My memory..." Nicki's aura rises in me. I get a glimpse of her smiling. Her face appears out of focus, her image fades.... "Nicki, is she all right? Now, I can't see her face or hear her voice...." I shout, angry at my weakness and fearful that all my memories are lost.

"Phil, you must calm yourself," Biomei says. "I promise things will be put right. Be patient. Fear and distress will only make matters worse. Ah, here's Shorty."

A familiar-looking robotic machine walks up to my chamber.

"Hello, Phil. It is good to see you again," it greets me in a friendly tone. "I am sorry to hear about your memory loss. I assure you that it is only a transient phenomenon, most likely caused by hibernation."

I squint at the automaton and ask, "Do I know you?"

"Indeed. You gave me my name and have treated me with kindness. You seem to regard me as more than just a service droid."

"Really? Sounds like I must like you for some reason. Did you refer to yourself as a droid?"

"That is correct. I am a Venubian Service Droid. I am here to assist you in any way I can," the droid speaks in a pleasant and reassuring tone.

"So, you think you can help me?" I say, studying it with a growing sense of familiarity.

"I am certain," the droid states in a perky tone. "We have many fine resources at our disposal to help you fully recover. I can assure you, your memories will be restored in no time at all."

"It almost sounds like you're trying to sell me something." I laugh at the irony of a machine convincing me of its capabilities.

"I did not understand your remark. Would you care to clarify your meaning?" it says, sounding insulted.

"It's nothing. Please disregard it."

"May I assist you out of the chamber?" It approaches with its arm outstretched toward me. I draw my head back, startled. The droid seems to sense my apprehension and withdraws its arm. "Is something wrong, Phil?"

Without taking my eyes off Shorty, I stand and lift my left foot out of the sarcophagus-like thing and onto the cold deck, followed by my right foot. "You stay right there," I say to the squat droid, folding my legs under me on the deck and closing my eyes. I gasped under my breath at the image of a long, claw-like arm coming right at me. After a few deep breaths, my cloudy head clears enough to remember a green thing attached to the arm with a deadly claw for a hand.

"Sorry Shorty, but I had a disturbing memory of a menacing arm coming at me for a moment," I explain.

"Phil, it's a real memory," Biomei says. "You had an encounter with a Zenti scout droid that had a single claw-like appendage. Do you recall any of that now?"

I close my eyes for a minute, trying to visualize the Zenti droid, but nothing—my head's a foggy mess. "Zenti, that word is familiar. It's also disturbing. Why? The Zenti, Nicki's disappearance—I can't put it all together."

"Phil, stop trying to make sense of things now. Your memories are all still inside you. However, you have been through an emotional ordeal. I'm confident everything will be restored."

I reach my hand out for the droid to help me up. It hesitates until I smile and say, "It's okay, you can help me now."

The small automaton reaches in and literally picks me up and gently places me on my feet.

"Can you walk unassisted?" it asks, firmly holding my arm.

My legs feel a little wobbly, and without saying anything, Shorty senses my weakened condition. His hips make a clicking sound, and then the droid rises four inches, wraps an extended arm around my waist, and assists me to the examination table. The table lowers for me, and I sit with my legs hanging over the side. The droid lifts my legs onto the table and guides my head down onto a small pillow as I lie on my back.

The table rises, and my eyes quickly adjust to the soft glare from three large, oval lamps. Surveying the room with my eyes, fragments of memories dart in and out of my mind. They're like snippets of faint recollections. The disinfectant smell, the humming of equipment, and some instruments attached to the table also look familiar. I know I have been in this Med Lab and on this table before. This unexpected awareness makes me a little more at ease.

"Phil, you must relax," Biomei says. "I'm going to induce a telepathic sedative. It's short-term, and it will make you a little drowsy."

"Okay," I say. "Wait, I think I remember this routine. It has something to do with what's inside my head."

"Precisely. That's good. We're now going to put all your memory streams back in chronological order. You have some special enhancements that enable you to process situations quicker, and your brain is more adaptable to varying and complex environments."

"I appreciate you trying to explain things to me. But what you're describing is way over my head. Please, just do whatever you need, then we can talk."

"Yes, I agree. Let's proceed. Phil, take in a deep breath, then hold it until I tell you to release. Ready?"

I nod, take in a deep breath, filling my chest, and hold it. I hear a faint thrum, then a low hum. Biomei tells me to release my breath. As I exhale, my body becomes light, then everything melds into a soft white light. A brief, pleasant euphoria subtly lifts away. Nicki's image comes to mind. I miss her, and my heart aches with the longing to be with her again.

***

"Phil," Biomei softly says.

"Yes, Biomei."

"How do you feel?"

I had to think for a moment, then realize I had no hangover. I know who and where I am. A smile spreads across my face. "Wonderful. Absolutely wonderful. Nothing hurts."

"Excellent. Now you need to rest for a little while to give your cerebral engrams time to chemically recharge and reestablish their cellular memories. Thankfully, your long-term memories were only blocked, but your short-term retention needed to be reset. Nicki had to rush some of your internal upgrades. She'd hoped that your natural electrochemical process would automatically reestablish the neuronal cellular pathways, but unfortunately, the hibernation chemicals blocked that from happening. Once I realize the problem, I manually unblock them. You should be fine in a few macrons."

"Wow. While that all sounds fascinating, I still don't have a clue what it means. However, I do feel fine, but I'm still a little fuzzy on some things. I do know that Nicki is waiting for us somewhere near Corridor-4, and we need to get there right away."

"How do you know that?" Biomei asks.

"Because Shorty just transmitted that information to me."

"Shorty? How would it know that?"

"Shorty, relay to Biomei what you just sent me."

The droid goes to a communications port and plugs one of its fingers into an input coupling. "I am transmitting the entire message to you now," the droid states.

"Receiving the message," Biomei acknowledges. "Oh my, this is serious. Nicki allowed the Zenti to pick up her communications transponder and deliberately misdirected them to sector G-752. That's the Vultaran sector. The Vultarans hate the Zenti as much as we do. Clever girl," Biomei says, sounding proud. "Once she established her coordinates with the Zenti, she placed her shuttle on autopilot and had the droids pick her up outside of the Delius system and is currently doubling back to Corridor-4."

"She has to maintain complete communications silence and will be running in stealth mode the entire way," I say, relieved knowing she's all right. "We won't be able to communicate with her." That worries me. "Biomei, we must hope we get there before the Zenti figure out they were duped. I don't want Nicki out there on her own any longer than necessary."

"I concur. I'll calculate the shortest route to Corridor-4. Phil, I must warn you that it may have us going dangerously close to some strong electromagnetic and gravitational forces. I'm sorry to say, it will require you to go back into hibernation for part of the way."

"I understand. Do whatever you must—get us there as soon as possible."

CHAPTER 25

"Phil," Biomei says, bringing me out of a deep sleep.

"Yes," I say without opening my eyes.

"Sorry to disturb your rest. We've picked up an energy signature, which doesn't conform to any known phenomenon."

In my sleepy state, it took a moment for what she said to sink in. "Do you think it's a Zenti signature?" I say, sitting upright on the bed.

"It's barely within our sensor range, but we should investigate it to make sure we aren't being followed. That's a common Zenti tactic."

"I'll meet you in the communications bay." I jump out of bed and head for the bathroom.

After a quick, cool shower, I stop at the small galley and get a black coffee and a synthesized bagel with cream cheese. It almost tastes like the real thing. I'm finishing the coffee as I walk into communications. VSD07 and '05 are busy analyzing the strange power signature.

I ask '07, "What do you have for me?"

"They are staying at the fringe of our telemetry for a definitive identification. Spectral analysis has confirmed that it has all the chemical constituents of a plasma drive, but it doesn't conform to any known Zenti configuration. Based on the estimated power output, we should be well outside their tracking range, but it has maintained the same distance for over a cycle."

"So, what does that mean?"

"It suggests the possibility of a Zenti ship, which has maintained a lock on us at an extreme distance," '07 states, flashing its optical sensor.

"There is another viable explanation," '05 interjects.

"Yes?"

"The Zenti have acquired new technology through one of their many nefarious methods."

"Okay, so what do you recommend?"

VSD07's optical screen swirled with colors. "We should allow the unknown ship to get within our sensors' range and make a more comprehensive analysis of the ship's design and tracking capabilities."

"How much closer?"

"200,000 kilometers should be sufficient."

I ask, "Biomei, how exposed would we be at that distance?"

"We're already exposed. It's obviously following us. I feel it's worth the risk to identify it."

"You heard the lady. Reduce speed and heading to get your diagnosis. But if it's a Zenti ship, we need to devise a way of losing it. The last thing we need is to lead them to Nicki."

"Understood, sir," '07 and '05 acknowledge.

As I watch the droids work, a disturbing thought strikes me. "Biomei, what did you do with the Zenti droid?"

"VSD03 was given it to analyze and then instructed to discard it out of an airlock. Why do you ask?"

"Where's VSD03 now?"

"With Nickada."

"I see. And was that before or after it completed all of its analysis?"

There was an uncomfortable pause before Biomei answered with the bad news. "I have completed a search for the Zenti Droid's power signature and found it stored in Maintenance Bay-4."

"You think maybe the Zentis is tracking us through the droid's signature?" I didn't wait for her to answer and blurt in a loud voice, "If I were a betting man. I'd bet you that ship is, in fact, Zenti and following us by that green menace's power signature! What were you guys thinking, leaving that thing on board?"

"Sorry, Phil, things became so frantic that Nickada must've forgotten to abort it. I doubt the Zenti could follow us through its power signature, though. It has limited output. Stand by a moment, I want to check something."

There's a momentary silence that fills me with apprehension. *How could something so obvious have been overlooked? There must've been a lot of chaos to cause both Biomei and Nicki to be so careless with their instructions.*

"Phil, I've completed a quick scan of the Zenti droid. Its power output is minimal, but it's still active. Also, please keep in mind that many of my systems were not functional during that unsettling time. Nickada was almost frenzied in getting off the ship. She might have—"

"Biomei, it's okay—no need to explain. Belay the power analysis," I command the droids, then say to Biomei, "Increase our speed. Shorty, you're with me." I gestured for him to follow me. We walk to the aft turbo-lift. "Shorty, what level is Maintenance Bay-4 on?"

"Level-2, Phil."

"Nicki told me all you droids are networked together."

"That is correct."

"Therefore, you must know everything VSD03 discovered about the Zenti droid."

"I do."

"What can you tell me about it?"

"It is a monochromatic, single-phase automaton with limited analytical, linguistic, and operational abilities. Its main purpose is to do basic reconnaissance and information re-—"

"No, Shorty," I interrupted. "I need to know what information the Zenti droid gathered about us and how far it can transmit a tracking signal. More importantly, how does it transmit, and can we change what it sends out?"

"I understand. '03 did not have sufficient time to do a complete analysis of the droid. The items of interest have not been gathered, but with a little time, I believe I can retrieve the information you seek. There is something you need to know, Phil."

"Yes?"

"Nickada did instruct VSD03 to dump the droid out of the lower aft airlock before boarding Star-Class Shuttle-4.

"Are you sure of that?"

"I am certain. I have retrieved the order in VSD03's command log."

"Are you telling me a service droid disobeyed a direct order?

"It appears that is the case."

"Shorty, it's my understanding that service droids are hard-wired to obey all given orders. How could VSD03 disobey a direct command? I don't understand. How's that possible?"

"Unknown without more data. However, biogenic droids have the discretion to disregard a command if it conflicts with their core program directives or if they perceive the command could cause harm to a sentient being."

"Are you suggesting '03 perceived that green thing to be a sentient being?"

"That is highly unlikely. It is more probable Nickada's order contradicted one of VSD03's core program priorities."

"What you're suggesting is disturbing, Shorty. I'm thinking the sabotage may have gone further than Biomei's systems. It may also include some of your fellow automatons. How much time will you need to do a thorough diagnostic of the Zenti droid?"

"Being unfamiliar with its architecture, I will require time to familiarize myself with it. Once I am aware of its circuitry, I can give you a better estimate."

"Okay, Shorty. But you must work quickly. Time is rapidly becoming a precious commodity."

"Understood."

"One more thing."

"Yes."

"Do you know if it has been disabled? Biomei said it's still active. I don't want to have another confrontation with that green machine."

"In answer to your question, yes. Biomei scrambled its primary processor."

"Good. Hmm, disabled its processor—If that's the case, how's it still able to transmit anything?"

"Many droids have auxiliary command directives that activate when the core processor is damaged or disabled. VSD03 most likely is using the auxiliary processor as a power source for the exploratory analysis. It would also permit reprogramming of some basic functions."

"Would one of those functions include a tracking signal?"

"More likely it is an identification beacon."

"That's interesting. It also gives me an idea. Before we go to work on that Zenti threat, I need you to pull up all '03's command logs."

"For what time range?"

"All of it."

"That will take 2.276 macrons. However, I can perform both information retrievals simultaneously."

"Retrieve away, my friend. In the meantime, I'll do a little information retrieval of my own. Notify me when finished."

"Acknowledged."

***

Shorty gets to work on the Zenti droid. I watch him bring the green headache out of the sealed storage locker. It still gives me a slight shiver to look at it, even with its appendage locked to its side. I'm curious how Shorty would access the automaton's processor. He produced a quantum tool, touched it to the back of its torso, and a large opening appeared.

"Well, of course," I say, slapping my forehead as if I should have known. Shorty stops, turns, and flashes his optical sensor as if checking me out before going back to work.

With my curiosity satisfied and feeling a little foolish, I begin a telepathic conversation with Biomei.

"Are you aware that Nicki instructed '03 to dump the Zenti droid out of one of the aft airlocks when it completed its analysis?"

"No, I wasn't. What are you thinking?"

"I'm not sure. But hope my suspicions are unfounded and there's a better explanation. Otherwise, Nicki's in a lot of trouble. Come to think of it, we all are."

"I can't believe a Venubian Service Droid would disobey a directive. Nickada programmed all the droids herself. No. That's too far-fetched to be true."

"Are you certain about that? I remember Nicki telling me the droids were already programmed by the techs before boarding and that she was only refining some of the automatons to her preferences."

"You are correct in that she was always dissatisfied with much of the VSD's personality subroutines and sometimes had to revise their mission directives. She often added special instructions specific to the tasks they would be performing. However, as far as I'm aware, I don't believe she ever reprogrammed any of their higher core functions. That's too impractical due to the complexity and the time it would require. Biogenic droids' brains are almost as complex as humanoids."

"I understand. I got Shorty retrieving '03's command memory logs, hoping to find anything that may shed light on this ever-growing mystery. Every time I think I've found the solution, more questions arise, making the problem more baffling than before."

"I've every confidence in you, Phil. You may not know how much you've grown. You should be pleased with how well you've adapted and matured from where you started."

"Thanks, Biomei. That was kind of you, but if you remember, I started from dead. Anything is an improvement over that."

"Really, Phil. Do you have to be flippant even when you're complimented?"

"Sorry, Biomei. We need to devise a plan to lose the Zenti and find a way of transmitting a warning to Nicki about '03."

"Agreed. If '03's programming has been tampered with, we may be able to use that to our advantage."

"What do you have in mind?"

"First, we must ascertain if the Zenti droid is, in fact, only transmitting an identity beacon or if it's sending more detailed data. Second, we need to establish if '03 is either in contact with the Zenti droid or their ship, and finally, we must identify the Zenti ship's design."

"We've already established that it's not of a typical Zenti configuration," I add.

"Knowing what we're dealing with should be our priority before we can devise an effective plan."

"Are you suggesting we slow down and allow them to close on us again?"

"Not exactly. I've got something else in mind, but we need to work with '07 to see if we can change our long-range telemetry. Continue working with Shorty; we need to get all the information we can about '03 and the Zenti droid. I'll contact you when I've completed my tasks and brief you on a course of action."

"Very well, but I don't have to emphasize that we need to work quickly."

"Understood."

"Phil."

"Yes, Shorty?"

"I've uncovered something you need to see. I believe Biomei should also see this."

"*Biomei,*" I transmit, feeling both intrigued and apprehensive.

"Yes, Phil."

"Shorty has found something. Where can we meet with absolute privacy?"

"Engineering level-1, I'll generate a security dampening field there."

"Very good. I'll let you know when we're ready."

CHAPTER 26

Engineering Level 1 is the lowest in Biomei. The bottom half of the main fusion reactor is there. It has layers of shielding against gamma radiation leakage from the reactor. The additional shielding creates a natural dampening field, creating perfect soundproofing.

"We are secure," Biomei says. "Shorty, please relay your findings."

"As I was going through VSD03's command logs, I came across a fragment that, at first glance, appeared to be partially erased. This is not unusual; commands often get truncated or partially overwritten when a droid is being reprogrammed in the field. These partial commands are archived and almost always marked for deletion after a memory dump. However, in this case, it was not marked for deletion and still resides in VSD03's supplemental command log."

"Sorry, Shorty," I interrupt. "You've lost me. What's a supplemental command?"

These are directives or guidelines intended as a backup execution code if some unexpected situation or event occurs. This gives an automaton the ability to perform a function, task, or any action in the absence of program directives. In other words, at its discretion."

"I see, so what makes these partial codes so suspicious?"

Upon closer examination, I discovered an embedded microcode that points to additional fragments within the supplemental command log. After extracting and deciphering the message, it directed me to the Zenti droid. Nickada had left information embedded within the droid's memory logs. The remainder of the message is directions for retrieving the code extraction sequence. Nickada indicated that Biomei would know how to proceed."

"Nicki must've known the Zenti were watching her and came up with this plan to communicate her intentions to us," Biomei says, with a sense of pride in her voice.

"So, what do you need to do?" I asked.

"I need to go into the droid's primary core and retrieve the information," Biomei says.

"Okay, go."

"It's not that simple, Phil. First, we must establish what the droid is transmitting and try not to interrupt it while extracting the data. Shorty, have you analyzed the transmission?"

"Yes. It's an upper band wave commonly used as an identification beacon. There are no additional sub or hyperspace frequencies, or transmissions embedded or being simulcast with the primary transmission."

I narrow my eyes at Shorty. "Is the signal strong enough for the Zenti to be receiving it at our present distance from them?"

"Under normal conditions, it would be insufficient, which suggests the Zenti must have acquired a more sensitive receiver and have been staying within the limits of its extended range."

"Biomei, do you think Nicki has purposely allowed the droid to continue transmitting? She had to have known about it."

"Yes. It would be consistent with her strategy to have the Zenti believe we're unaware of the droid's transmissions."

"What do you think they would do if we interrupted it?"

"Most likely come for us."

"Yeah, I agree." I shake my head, smiling at the irony. "She's unbelievable. Nicki has been using their droid to keep them at a safe distance while supplying us with information. And she came up with all of that on the fly under extreme duress."

"That would be a reasonable assumption," Biomei says and adds, "She's a remarkable woman of many talents."

"Now, you're sounding like her mother."

"Well, I am her mother. Her away mother."

"Okay, Mama. Can we get the info without affecting the beacon?"

"That's not a problem. Shorty can emulate the signal while I work on retrieving the data."

"Sounds like a plan." I blow out a long breath to relieve my inner tension. "Let's get going. I'm even more nervous for Nicki."

Biomei had '05 bring the Zenti droid to us. As a precaution, I had the droid produce a stunner and told it to keep it pointed at the blob during the procedure. Shorty manifests one of those handy quantum tools again, then pauses, and says, "Phil, you are aware that blob is an inaccurate description of the automaton."

"Yeah. But that's what it reminds me of. It's a mean green thing… Never mind about that."

"As you wish."

With a simple touch to the blob's upper rear section, he opens a service portal. He connects fiber optic tubing to a board that's covered in colored beads. I see bags like Biomei's biogenic bladders, only much smaller. They're connected to hundreds of coiled tubes. Once the optic fibers are connected, Shorty takes the other ends that have fine, hair-like wiring coming out. He touches the feathery fibers to a suspended, clear panel floating next to the droid. Like tiny tentacles, the hair-like wires automatically attach themselves to rows of white dots on the panel. At each connection point, a gold holographic line appears. From that line, other lines appear, interconnecting on the panel, creating what looks like a densely packed circuit board.

"What's that?" I ask.

"That is the machine's brain," Biomei says. "More precisely, part of it."

"Amazing," I mutter. "Where's Nicki's message?"

"Haven't quite made it there; need to bring up more of its core before we'll be in the sector we're after."

"How will you know when you've found it?"

"Each one of those small, bead-like objects inside the droid is equivalent to an individual cortical node. Each node comprises millions of microscopic circuits. What you are viewing is a magnified node circuit. If you look closer at those raised lines on the panel, you'll notice symbols intermittently spread along each line segment." Biomei has a holographic display screen appear, then enlarges a section for me.

"Yes, I can see them now." The tiny symbols appear as wiggly lines and wavy circles that look scattered along the circuit lines in small clusters.

"They don't appear to be in any particular order, nor do they follow any noticeable sequence. It all looks random."

"Think of each line like a string of code in a digital computer's register," Biomei explains while highlighting each area under discussion. A symbol represents a bit of data. Nickada's instructions identify a string of these symbols that correspond to the individual locations of the data bits we're seeking. Unfortunately, it appears she must've been working under tremendous stress and didn't leave precise details on the data's location. Logically, she would've placed it deep within the droid's core memory; most likely in a low-priority command sector."

"I think I understand," I say, studying the green beast's innards. "It all looks so simplistic for such a sophisticated machine."

"This crude thing is anything but sophisticated," Biomei snaps, contemptuously. "By our standards, it's one step above a rock."

"Biomei," Shorty says, "I have intercepted a transmission from the Zenti intended for the droid."

"Can you decipher it?" Biomei asks.

"Yes, I believe it is a status check."

"Do you think it's a routine check?" I ask, feeling apprehensive about the timing of the transmission.

"I have insufficient data to answer that query, Phil."

"Is it possible they somehow discovered that you're emulating its beacon?"

"That is highly unlikely. It is a standard format. I believe it is a routine check. Shall I answer the request?"

"Yes," Biomei says emphatically. "Continue with your emulation and maintain communications with the Zenti." Then she says to me, "Phil, I need you to go to communications and send out a search beacon for Nicki. I want us to appear as though we're searching for her location."

"What do you have in mind?"

"I've located Nicki's message," her voice lowers to a solemn tone. "The Zenti has captured her and is taking her to Vexx."

A heavy feeling settles in my chest. "They got her. How?" The news had a surreal quality to it, making it hard for me to believe those Zenti bastards have my Nicki. I look at Shorty, then my eyes wander upward, and I'm staring at the ceiling. "I don't understand." I hear myself say, sounding as if it came from someone else. "Biomei, we must do something. Where's Vexx?"

"It's a large moon in the Delius system—a horrid, frozen world orbiting the planet Celebus, which orbits between Delius-4 and 5. The Zenti must have developed an encampment within its interior. Its surface is uninhabitable. The *universe* only knows what they're doing there."

"We have to go after her," I bark, clenching my jaw to suppress my growing urge to scream.

"We must proceed with caution, Phil. They took her, knowing we would come for her. That's how the Zenti operates. Hostages are like currency to them. They'll keep her alive as long as she has value."

Standing stiffly while listening to Biomei, my belly burns with angst and rage. I didn't notice Biomei stopped talking or that I'm staring up with my outstretched arms, looking as if in supplication. Now, a calm is welling in me. I let out a sigh. "*Thanks,*" I transmit to her for downloading a mild tranquilizer. "Okay, I'm calmer. So, what do you suggest?"

"We have to get to Corridor-4."

"We're not going to the corridor! We're not leaving Nicki behind! Based on what I've learned about the Zenti, they're ruthless, and they'll harm her to get what they want."

In a firm voice, Biomei says, "Nicki's instructions are most specific. She wants us to go back to Venubia without her. She believes they need her alive to negotiate a ransom. More specifically, they want me. Or I should say my technology."

"We can't just leave her, Biomei!" A sinking feeling in my heart gets my head throbbing. I know Biomei's right, but I can't leave Nicki. Not knowing—"

"Phillip," Biomei's sharp tone gets my attention. "There are many other aspects about the Zenti that you are unaware of. Nickada forbids me from discussing the Zenti problem with you. She also expressed that she has taken precautions to ensure that Zenti will leave her unharmed.

We must follow her instructions. Her life depends on it. I'm sorry, Phil, but this is our best and only option."

I bow my head and capitulate in silence, realizing it made no sense arguing with Biomei as she sets the course for Corridor-4. "Forward viewscreen," I request with my heart longing for Nicki. The panel slides back. I stare aimlessly into the star-speckled blackness.

CHAPTER 27

Ship Date 2525.1354 Venubian Standard Mean

"Phillip," Biomei transmits in a low voice.

"Yes, Biomei."

"I've received a subspace message from Venubian Central Control.

"We're that close?"

"No, it was sent by quantum subspace messaging."

"Huh?"

"I've been instructed to complete a section of your transformation process while you are in hibernation. This will only involve specific memory engrams and an upgrade to your physio technology. You may be vaguely aware of the procedure. You'll also experience some vivid dreams. Please don't be alarmed by the nature of the dreams. They're designed to test and strengthen emotional and psychological mechanisms that are being upgraded.

"When initiated, they will provide systemic conditioning for acclimation to the demands of new and varied environments. Upon completion, you'll be transferred back into a hibernated state. You may have residual memories of the dreams. They will fade."

***

Ship Date 2526.14

"Phillip, we're less than a cycle from Venubia," Biomei transmits.

"We're that close?" A rush of wonder, excitement, and apprehension runs through me.

"Yes."

"Am I still in hibernation?"

"Yes."

"So, how can we be talking?"

"I'm interjecting transient thoughts into your semi-hibernated state to let you know the transformation procedure has been completed."

"I see," I think for a moment, then ask, *"We're almost there—to Venubia?"*

"Yes."

"I'm afraid they won't like me."

"You have nothing to fear. Go back to sleep."

"Yes. I'll go back to sleep now."

I have a brief vision of a clear night sky full of colorful moons. It looks beautiful and familiar. Then my mind drifts back into the dark, unconsciousness of hibernation.

"Phillip," Biomei's voice calls as though she's calling from a distance.

"Biomei?

"Yes, Phillip."

"Why do you sound so far away?"

"I'm not sure. Something occurred... I know. I know... I'll miss you, but we must go our separate ways."

"Biomei?"

"Yes, dear?"

"You sound odd."

"How's that?"

"You've entered my hibernation. You never done that before... Or have you? There's something wrong?"

There is a long silence. I must have drifted back into a dream state because the next thing I hear is most strange.

"Find me, Phillip, as soon as you can. Nothing was real... Nickada is... I can explain..."

"Biomei, what are you saying? What about Nicki?"

There is another long, apprehensive silence. I'm struggling to stay awake, but my dull mind pulls me back into the depths of hibernation-induced slumber.

"Phillip," a strange voice transmits my name.

"Yes. Who's this?"

It wasn't Biomei's voice or presence I felt. It was someone different.

"I am the consciousness of your Venubian guide."

"You're who?" I'm wondering if this is a new hibernation dream.

"I will provide you with an orientation to help you adjust to your new life on Venubia. We are sure you will have many questions. It is my task to give you answers and help prepare you for your new life on Venubia."

"Yes. My new life," I repeat the guide's words, trying to lift the fog from my mind.

"Shall we begin?"

"Begin? Oh yes, let's begin."

PART III

VENUBIA

CHAPTER 28

I wake from hibernation, lying on a couch like the intuitive ones on Biomei. Everything feels different. I'm not on the ship. Biomei's presence is absent. The air smells fresh, with a distinct scent, not flowery or antiseptic, more like a spring morning breeze. That familiar hibernation hangover is pulling at me, though. My body feels heavy, and my mind is struggling through a thick veil of uncertainty... Also, I'm thirsty.

Right as the thought of my thirst comes to mind, a delicate hand, holding a glass of cool, crystal-clear water, appears. I accept it. The water is perfect in both temperature and purity. I empty the glass in three long swallows, and with each swallow, my body is more rejuvenated, like drinking the very essence of life.

It's remarkable how alive I feel being on Venubia. Realizing I'd finally arrived fills me with a combination of excitement and anxiety.

"Mr. Mann," a nasal-toned voice addresses me.

"Yes?"

"Do you know where you are?" The voice sounds polished and stuffy, reminding me of my college history professor. It's irritating as all hell.

"Yes. I'm on Venubia."

"How do you feel?"

"Other than a slight headache and a heavy feeling in my limbs, I feel pretty good."

I gaze at the diminutive figure, who drops a cube-shaped object into his dull brown jumpsuit. His large, owl-like gray eyes stare at me with a stony expression. Unlike Nicki's eyes, they don't change color. I'm uncertain of its gender and default to male. He regards me with indifference as I study his alien features.

His smooth, hairless head is egg-shaped with prominent brow ridges. His nose is slightly bulbous and curves above a small mouth with thin, pink lips.

I smile, realizing this is the first Venubian besides Nicki to greet me.

"Yes. Well, that is all normal hibernation recovery," the Venubian says. "Mr. Mann, someone will come for you. Please follow his instructions precisely."

"Okay, if you say so."

He gives me a puzzled look, then with a faint smile says, "Welcome to Venubia, Mr. Mann."

My head is clearing, allowing me to survey my surroundings. A stiff-looking humanoid with a long crop of shiny, red hair and alert, dark eyes is running a handheld device over my body. It also appears genderless and doesn't resemble the Venubian, which causes me to wonder who or what it is.

"You're not Venubian," I say.

It ignores my question, looking intent on what it's doing. A long, awkward silence falls between us as I force a smile at the cool, detached eyes, scrutinizing me as a scientist would a test subject.

"Hello, Mr. Mann. Welcome to Venubia," a pleasant voice says.

I crane my neck to the side to get a look at the face behind the voice. The face looking back at me is impassive and undifferentiated. The best description would be an animated mannequin. He's male in gender, has two large, black, shiny eyes, a forehead ridge suggesting where eyebrows should be, an aquiline nose, and thin lips covering a wide mouth. His oval-shaped, bald head glows under the clear, white light. His ears are small with pointed lobes. The only remarkable characteristic about this humanoid is his familiar Venubian milk-skinned complexion. He appears much like an android, or at least what I thought one should resemble.

"Are you an android?" I blurt.

He walks close to my side and says, "Similar, but not quite the same. We prefer engineered life-forms. We are sentient beings who have been genetically engineered for specific tasks. I am the first of a new series."

"Do you possess free will, or are engineered life-forms, euphemistic slaves on Venubia?"

"Slaves? That is a curious term. Could you elaborate on your meaning?"

"I guess it's a human response. It probably means nothing to you. Please, disregard it."

As soon as the redhead finishes, I get off the couch and face the engineered life-form.

My body seems light, which is a little surprising considering Venubia is almost one and a half times larger than Earth. I thought I'd feel heavier, but then everything that was happening was unexpected.

"Mr. Mann, if you feel up for it, I would like to take you to your residence. I am sure you are tired and would like to rest and freshen up before your introduction to Chancellor Verubeal."

"Chancellor? Nicki never told me her mother is the chancellor. Does the title carry the same meaning here as on Earth?" I wondered if he knew enough about Earth to answer the question.

"Her title is similar in terms of office and respect, but not in the same way that power is controlled in your world. She is what you might better understand as our leading Matriarch."

His quick answer was surprising and appreciated. He obviously was educated about Earth. "Like a Queen-Mother?" I interject, half in jest.

"More like an archetypal mother, in that she is our leading matriarch responsible for leading Venubia into a secure and progressive future. But all of this can be explained in more detail later. Let us first get you oriented to your new home."

As he speaks, his demeanor and features change. His expression softens and gains a lively glow with his voice becoming warmer, dark brown hair sprouting on his head, and thin, arched eyebrows above his now alert brown eyes.

He's changing right before me. I find it fascinating how he seems to be conforming to please me. Practical as well because I'm starting to like him. Then it occurs to me that Venubians are both empathic and telepathic. He's reading me like a book and adjusting accordingly.

Silly me, I thought, I'm making a new friend. Then Biomei flashes through my mind, followed by an image of Nicki's large, colorful eyes smiling at me... it fades. Their absence washes over me. At that moment, a friend is what I need. Someone I could learn to trust and help fill the painful absence of loved ones that is gnawing at my innards.

"Even a genetically engineered one is better than nothing," I unconsciously mumble. He gives me a confused look. "Besides," I rationalize aloud, "in a way we're both products of Venubian engineering." I look closely at him, then exclaim, "Hey, that means we're sort of related. In a real sense, you're my cousin. Do you have a name, Cuz?"

He gives me a thoughtful look. From his wrinkled brow, I can tell he's straining his databanks for an appropriate response.

"Cuz is not my designation," he says, looking uncertain.

"I know Cuz is not your name. It is a colloquial expression for a cousin. A close relative on Earth."

"I guess, under the circumstances," he narrows his eyes for a moment, "Cuz is fitting," he says with a slight upturn of his mouth. He makes a fist, places it against his chest, and nods with a shallow bow from his hips. "My name is Cuz. I like the sound. It sounds... Earthy."

"You adapt quickly, my friend. My compliments to your designers." I smile, then give him a firm slap on the back.

"Thank you, Mr. Mann. I think?" he says, arching an eyebrow with an ambiguous smile.

"Now that we are kin, call me Phil."

"Phil, if you would be so kind as to follow me." He gestures toward a long corridor that opens before us.

"What are your instructions regarding me?" I ask.

"I am instructed to provide whatever you ask and to tend to all your needs. I will not always have the answer you seek, but I will endeavor to be as forthright with any knowledge I possess."

"Are you assigned to learn more about me, or are you only a mechanism to attend to my needs?"

Cuz pauses, gently taking hold of my arm. He gives me a befuddled gaze and says, "I sense a strong feeling of distrust in you." His expression reflects an earnest look, for lack of a better description, of hurt feelings. "We must have trust between us. I understand that, in human relations, it must be earned. On Venubia, all sentient engineered life-forms have an innate sense of honor and loyalty to all whom they serve. You must comprehend I am incapable of lying to you or betraying our trust under any circumstances."

"Okay," I say, feeling better about him.

"If you check with your internal compiler under sentient androids, it will give you a better understanding of what I am."

"And how do I do that?"

"Focus on it for a moment. The data will upload automatically."

"Really?" I did as he said and instantly knew all about Cuz. "Wow. That's friggin remarkable." I grin. "My neurocompiler is working. So, if I need to know something, I only have to think about it?"

"Providing your compiler has the desired information, though. Otherwise, you can seek another source."

"I guess that means you."

"As I have already intimated, I may not have all the answers you seek, but together we should be able to find most of what you wish to know."

"Guess that was the Elder's idea."

"You would be correct in that assumption."

"Well, Cuz, this looks like the beginning of a beautiful friendship."

Cuz blinks his bright eyes with his forehead in tight lines.

"That was a sincere statement," I say with a slow smile, hoping to reassure him.

"Oh, good. I was unsure if you were being disingenuous. I am pleased you believe we could be friends."

"Great. Where to next?" I say, patting Cuz's shoulder.

We walk and talk for some length until the seemingly endless corridor opens into a large, sparse room. Two broad and winding staircases lead to an upper floor. The walls are a plain shade of alabaster and softly illuminated by an indiscernible source. The floors have a high gloss that Cuz explains is made of polished stone material. There are no windows or doors leading outside. Nor are there any Venubians.

"Where's everyone?" I ask.

"The populace is engaged in various activities. Many are involved in what you call work. However, the analogy is not exact. Venubians engaged in work they are most suited for, and that provides them the most gratification. We do not have a system of economics that provides compensation in exchange for a skill or service. Each Venubian does what is best to contribute to the general welfare of all Venubians and derives personal satisfaction in the process."

"Sounds like a large commune. What if a person doesn't want to contribute to the greater good and does as they please?"

"While that is rare, they are free to do so."

"So, if I decide I don't want to do anything—it's okay?"

"Yes."

"I like that." I thought, Is this utopian, or am I missing something?

"Phil, I am curious. Why would you choose to do nothing?"

"I probably wouldn't, but I need to know I can be free to make that choice."

"I see the logic in that. Free choice is also important to Venubians." Cuz's eyes change to a lighter brown as he points to a curving staircase. "We need to go to the third floor."

"What's on the third floor?"

"I do not know the exact Earth term. It is a place where you will receive all the necessities for public and private attire."

"You're taking me to the local haberdasher?"

Cuz seems to consider my question before answering, "Yes."

"Lead on, can't wait to see the latest in Venubian fashion. I hope it's better than what we're wearing."

"What is wrong with what we are wearing?"

"It's a drab, dull gray jumpsuit. And the color is wrong for you. You need something livelier than that awful-looking olive green one-piece."

"It is a standard work issue. All tutors wear this."

"Wait, a minute. Are you telling me everybody wears a drab jumpsuit?"

"Mostly, they do."

"Please tell me, I'll have a choice of attire?"

"That is most unlikely. Clothing in Venubia is used for protection from the elements and for work classification. From what I have learned, humans have conflicting customs regarding the use of clothing. I find it most intriguing, but also a little confounding."

"Cuz, you'll find most human customs are exactly that, conflicting and confounding."

Looking at Cuz's confused expression, I'm forming a picture of a socially ordered society on Venubia. My vision of a perfect utopia is in jeopardy of being tarnished. Then something occurs to me.

"Cuz shouldn't I already know this?"

"Phil, the information implanted into your compiler contains only basic language skills and certain life-safety protocols that will assist and protect you from unintentional harm. We realize you process information better through direct interaction and a certain degree of calculated trial and error."

"Trial and error. That could be potentially dangerous. What if I do something really ignorant?"

"We anticipated that possibility. As a precaution, specific prohibitions on any potential antisocial behavior were downloaded into your compiler. Primarily, you will learn about Venubia from direct experience. The Elders believe it would be the most humane way."

"I find that curious. The Elders can implant whatever they want into me, and yet they let me learn through trial and error?" I grin at the irony of their thinking and say, "I'm not sure if I should thank or curse them."

Cuz's eyebrows rise at my statement. We stare at each other for an awkward moment, waiting for the other to speak. Something hits me about what he described.

Burrowing my eyes into him, I say in a low growl, "Define what you mean by prohibiting my behavior?"

I could see that my intense stare was having an interesting effect on Cuz. He looks almost child-like with shyness while maintaining an impassive gaze as if uncertain of an appropriate response.

"It refers to any unpredictable emotional outbreak that could cause harm to yourself or any other living organism on Venubia," Cuz states, sounding as if it were direct from his instructions.

"I see. "Are you telling me I have a governor on my violent human emotions?"

"Precisely."

I let out a sigh, thinking the Venubians see me as a potential threat.

"Are you all right?" Cuz says, hearing my sigh.

I nod. "Cuz, I want you to know I'm not upset about inhibiting my temper. After all, you only know me based on my species' history. Realizing how violent humans can be, it's a good precaution."

"Thank you, Phil, for understanding. I don't share that concern."

He seems to notice the look of regret I'm feeling about my potential violent tendencies. The image of the Zenti I killed pops up, adding to my guilt.

"We have amassed a detailed memory bank on human behavior," he adds. "It reveals much about human nature. I find your dualities of love and hate, compassion and bigotry fascinating."

"I hope it's not all based on our radio and television transmissions."

"Not at all, Biomei had collected much of your cultural, scientific, and historical data. Humans are as varied as they are complex. I have discovered that there are many similarities in our histories." Cuz speaks with earnest enthusiasm and a genuine fascination with humanity.

"I'm sure the similarities are intriguing. A little scary too," I murmur. "It's a discussion I look forward to."

"Perhaps another time," Cuz says with a glint of a smile.

He is morphing his personality into what he believes I'd be comfortable with. I find it fascinating watching how hard he's trying to emulate human characteristics. It makes me consider how one evaluates a sentient android. Would it be the same as a human? I let the thought go, as Cuz suggested, for another time.

At that moment, I realized fate had thrown me into a situation of being the ambassador from Earth. I'm an unwitting source of human knowledge for the Venubians. Looking at Cuz and thinking, how do I morph myself into a person worthy of such a lofty responsibility?

CHAPTER 29

"You referred to the Clothing Distribution Center as a haberdasher," Cuz says as we enter the center.

"Yes."

"That is an interesting term. From my study of humans, I have noticed you wear a wide range of clothing."

"We do. Cultures in different regions of Earth all have customs that reflect their tastes, social mores, and environmental requirements. All these various elements dictate what one wears. How one chooses to dress tells a lot about the individual. There's a saying on Earth, '*You are what you wear.*'"

"I am curious. What type of clothing did you wear?"

I look at Cuz, scratching the back of my head in thought, and shrug. "I've never thought about it before. Guess it will have to be another one of those discussions for another time."

"It appears we will have a lot to talk about."

The distribution center resembles nothing I was expecting. As we enter the small room, a pleasant-looking android greets us. While it shared some of Cuz's features, it appears to be of a different series, shorter with less defined features.

"Good day, Mr. Mann," the android says.

Before I could say anything, it directed me to stacks of monochrome jumpsuits.

"Is this all you have? Just jumpsuits?" I frown at the selection of the plain-looking garb.

"Each suit has been created for your precise measurements," it explains, holding one up for my inspection.

"Kind of drab-looking," I say, taking the suit and holding it out to Cuz.

"These are engineered, biomechanical mechanisms," Cuz explains. "Besides, being intuitive to all your major metabolic functions, they are self-cleaning and impervious to adverse weather, and all known environmental contaminants."

"Really. Well, if they're that practical, I'll have a couple of each color. I need variety," I say and grin at the impassive android.

It turns its mouth up in an emulated smile and says, "On behalf of the Elders and citizens of Venubia, welcome. We want to express our wishes for much happiness during your stay." It nods and adds. "The suits will be sent to your residence."

"So, this is all you guys wear? No dress up or dress down?" I say to Cuz, looking at the stacked rows of jumpsuits.

"Style is not relevant, only color," Cuz clarifies.

"What's the significance of color?"

"Color represents an individual's genotype, workstation, and seniority. We are wearing monochrome suits that designate us as an engineered species."

"Wait a sec," I clutch Cuz's arm. "I'm an engineered species?"

Cuz blinks his eyes. "Ah, I see. You were not aware of your classification. The fact that you are partly cybernetic with enhanced technology classifies you as an engineered life-form."

"Yeah. I see what you mean."

"If I am reading your expression correctly, you appear upset."

"No... no. It's just a jolting reminder that I'm not completely human anymore."

"You are mistaken, Phil. You are still a human. An upgraded one."

"Was that humor?"

"No. I was most sincere."

"Never mind. You were telling me about the significance of color." I didn't want to have a conversation about my humanity with an android. And then I thought, why not?

"Monochrome means we are not assigned to a specific work detail and serve at the discretion of the Elders. As I have mentioned, all assigned workers wear multi-colored suits. The color scheme denotes a specific field of expertise and assignment station. This will become more apparent as we progress through your orientation."

"Let me see if I understand this. Your society is color-discriminatory. Is there a class or social status associated with color?"

"No. Color is only a designation. There is no other significance or particular privileges, or class status associated with an individual's field of expertise."

"Would it be accurate to say Venubia is a classless society?" I smirk.

"I am not sure of your inference of classless in that context. Would you care to elaborate?"

"I was being sarcastic."

"Sarcasm is an unfamiliar concept."

"I gather. Stick with me long enough, and sarcasm will become part of your programming." As soon as Cuz holds up a finger with a furrowed brow, I say, "Oh, a door, at last, I'll see a little of Venubia?"

"Yes. We are going to your residence. It is on the other side of the Central Administration Park. Would you prefer we travel by tram or monorail?"

"Which would provide the best view of the surroundings?"

The tram is best for sightseeing. It is slower and more private."

"Sounds good to me."

***

Cuz opens the door, and the Venubian world greets and overwhelms me. The Administration Center is situated on top of a high plateau overlooking kilometers of the surrounding landscape. Nothing could've prepared me for the experience of taking in the Venubian environment. Its pristine beauty gave me a rush of euphoric giddiness that made me smile like a child discovering Oz.

My eyes drift to the left and view a valley of tall trees yielding to a distant ridge of muscular hills. The hills are covered with lush plants and vibrant, colored flowers flowing up the sides of a towering waterfall.

Straight ahead, surrounded by a park with plush, green grass, is a city filled with a wide range of architecturally styled buildings. Some domes appear to be suspended in midair. Large arches rise behind one another, creating a grand portico sitting on a mountain of glistening stone-and-glass structures. A cobweb of tubes connects everything.

"Cuz what's that complex structure connecting the buildings?"

"It is a high-speed transportation system."

"Ah, I see."

After looking closer, I saw there were so many vehicles flying in and about the buildings that from my vantage point, they appeared as waves of bees buzzing about their hives.

On my right is a large lake with crystal, green water. It looks hauntingly familiar. Large, swan-like birds move about the surface, some in small groups, others by themselves. A bright red animal, like a deer, runs into the nearby woods. The trees are different in size and shape, with a multitude of brilliant oranges, yellows, greens, and blues. What is most striking is that the colors appear to shimmer in the bright sunlight. Some colors are so vivid they look unreal. Others made my eyes adjust because of the intensity of their rich hues. Reds, for instance, appeared to dance atop as well as within the flower as it darkened into the infrared. Remarkable, I think. I can see infrared in the daytime. I glanced to my left and saw a purplish shrub glow in the ultraviolet.

Turning upward, my eyes fixed on a bright blue sky with puffy white clouds drifting in front of two suns. I have to close my eyes for a second because the full spectrum of the two suns' chemical elements is flying at me. *This is going to take some getting used to.*

After taking a few deep breaths, I relax. Blink my eyes open and study the sky. The near sun looks much like Earth's in size, distance, and color. The second is a swollen red giant higher and farther away. Being in the presence of a binary star system is beyond my expectations. My planet-shock was not quite complete, though. As the tram arrives, I turn and gawk at a large, pale, emerald-green moon looming just above the horizon. This scene is familiar. A moon appeared in a recurring dream I had on the ship. That same moon is always there with its eerie green glow coloring my dream. *Venubia seems like a dream, a real one.*

"Cuz, Nicki implanted lucid dreams of Venubia in me on Biomei. I thought what she presented was incredibly beautiful, but it almost pales compared to the real experience." Looking wide-eyed and thinking, I'm finally here. I'm on Venubia.

"You were to be oriented before your arrival, but the unfortunate circumstances that occurred on Biomei made that impracticable. Therefore, the Elders allowed you a more human orientation. That is why they are not downloading everything into your memory. The Elders thought you needed time and assistance to adjust to what must be a profound experience. I believe you will benefit more from the direct involvement. I know you will adjust and hopefully enjoy yourself in the process."

"Profound, indeed. I'll need time and lots of help." I pat Cuz's shoulder. He gestures for me to enter the tram.

It's a compact airborne vehicle that, Cuz explains, uses neutrinos for its power source and a hydrogen ramjet for propulsion. It has a clear dome with stubby wings and a flat undercarriage with a complex array of reflective openings in front and rear.

I make myself comfortable, then sigh, thinking about Nicki.

Cuz asks, "Are you all right?"

I nod and say, "Interesting design." Then, noticing there is no driver, I ask, "Is all the transportation automated?"

"Yes."

As we circle the park, we see no Venubians.

"Is everyone working? There's no one enjoying this beautiful day?"

"We are all doing our part in rebuilding the planet's infrastructure."

"I guess this area was done first?"

"That is a correct assumption." He turns his passive face to me and says, "There is much you need to learn about Venubia and its people. But first, we need to give you a chance to get settled and adjusted to your new home."

"My new home," I mumble, pondering what Cuz had said. No children, the thought stuck in my mind as we traveled to my new residence.

Then my mind drifts back to Nicki. A sudden melancholy rises, and my chest tightens. Oh, Nicki, Venubia is all you said it would be and more, I think, keeping a tight hold on my emotions.

We move into one of the massive building complexes through a transit tunnel. I can't tell what direction we're going until we reach an opening and see how far we've climbed. We're near the top of one of the tallest towers and come to a soft landing.

"We are here, Phil," Cuz says.

"Wow. Looks like I'm in the high-rent district."

Cuz gives me a blank stare.

"You're not going in with me?"

"No."

"Gee, I thought you'd be curious."

"I will see it soon enough."

"So, which one is mine?"

"It is directly in front of you. Your name is already on the door. I will pick you up at the end of dusk. Please be ready. It is important to be prompt. After all, we want to make a good first impression with the Chancellor."

I don't care if I made a good impression on the Chancellor. My mind is too preoccupied with my new surroundings. It feels a little odd to see my name stylishly scripted on a bronze plaque that is attached to a conventional-looking wood door. The door is wide and tall, made of dark wood with a large, brass handle slightly off-center. *This is all mine?* Looking around at my immediate neighbors, I conclude it is. There isn't another visible door on my level. This indicates that either I had a large apartment or the doors aren't readily visible.

The former is the case. My apartment is huge. It resembles a loft in that the master bedroom is on a separate level that opens to an expansive exterior wrap-around terrace. The four guest rooms are all spacious and beautifully appointed with the same stone-like floors as in the administration center and conventional furniture.

The step-down living room had a semicircular shape. A long couch surrounded by four overstuffed chairs with round, glass top tables interspersed between the chairs takes up the center of the half-circle. Two workstations are situated at each end. A vision of Nicki working and me hovering around her flashed through my mind.

There is a variety of statuettes, sculptures, and artworks of various styles. Some of it's striking in detail and, like much of the art, done in vivid color schemes. Others are hard to figure out. A few works appear like tortured materials, trying to make a statement. Frankly, I find them downright weird.

The bed is the most prominent feature, though. When I see it from the doorway, I say, "I can't wait to try that. Then, I flop onto it. Beyond the fact that it's the largest I'd ever seen, it's also the most comfortable... ahhhh, my body is sinking into the mattress... Like Nicki's barber's chair and the beds on Biomei, it adjusts to my body and its biorhythms. And I'm discovering it has the same built-in sensors to relieve tense muscles and headaches. My favorite feature is the empathic interface. If it's like the ones on board, it can read my mood. Incredible as it sounds, it will adjust to what I'm thinking when I enter the bedroom.

I sigh heavily while standing in the second-floor loft, looking over my new home. Knowing that everything is automated and adaptive, over time, it'll learn my habits and lifestyle. Somehow, that doesn't make me happy. *Look at all this new tech. I should be ecstatic.*

The more I ponder my new life and domicile, the more I keep thinking how wonderful all this would be if I didn't feel so alone. Honestly, I'm a stranger in a strange world, longing for anything familiar, most of all, longing for Nicki. I can't help thinking all of this was designed for the two of us.

I wander from room to room, inspecting everything. Then, to my disappointment, I discovered the kitchen is devoid of any cooking appliances. There is no discernible stove or oven. Not even a damn microwave. Just as I say that, I notice a rather intriguing appliance that happens to resemble a microwave. To my mild disappointment, it's a food synthesizer like the ones on Biomei, except it has several different-sized dispenser openings. And like everything else here, it's voice-activated.

"Oh great, another appliance to train," I mumble, staring into its dark sensor interface, hoping Biomei programmed it.

Feeling the pangs of loneliness mixed with the growing apprehension of meeting the Chancellor, I decide to test my new synthesizer. A cocktail is in order, I tell myself. Already familiar with Venubian beverages, I experiment to see if it can replicate something close to a good, stiff drink. After replicating several horrible concoctions, I inadvertently created something drinkable.

"Do you wish to save this recipe, Mr. Mann?" the automated voice asks.

I take another swig, and it's beginning to grow on me. "Absolutely," I say.

"Very good, sir. It's saved under your file name of Absolutely. Will that be all, sir?"

"Uh, no, wait... that's not a good name. Um, I wish to change it," I shout, feeling stupid.

"Sorry, Mr. Mann, that will require a reprogramming protocol. Do you wish to initiate the protocol, sir?"

"Sounds too complicated," I stumble over my tongue, feeling a little numb around the edges. "Never mind."

"Anything else, sir?"

It sounded irritated for a synthesized voice. "No. Thanks."

As I sat, sipping on my second absolutely, brooding over Nicki. It wasn't much longer before a light, tingling sensation in my head gave me a giddy feeling. I shook it off as being a little anxious about the evening. So, naturally, I made myself another drink. What I wasn't prepared for was the slow and potent kick the third one is having on me. When Cuz arrives, I'm feeling no pain. Venubia is beautiful, like the Garden of Eden.

"Hey, Cuz," I slur. "It's half-past last dusk already?"

"You are not speaking clearly, Phil. Is there something wrong?" Cuz says, looking concerned.

"No. There's noffen wrong. I'm... uh... just a wittle drunk." I laugh. "And you were worried about first impress'ns."

Cuz stiffens into a perplexed gaze, looking at me as though I'm stricken with an indiscernible malady and didn't have the slightest idea of how to proceed.

"You seem to be unwell. Maybe it would be prudent to postpone your audience with the Chancellor. I will make the appropriate apologies for you and reschedule your audience when you are feeling better."

"Don't be absurt... I ne'her felt bedder. Just give me... um, minute, and I'll be right wiff you."

I was surprised how the drink was working on me. My head feels a little light, and now my body is taking on that pleasant tingling sensation again. Not wanting to admit to Cuz, I'm too drunk, I foolishly try to fake it.

"Are you sure you are all right? Can I get you something?" Cuz furrows his brow. "Phil, I'm getting confusing empathic impressions from you. I have no experience with drunkenness. Could you explain your present condition and what I can do?" he asks with an android's version of looking helpless.

Poor Cuz, I had no idea that Venubians never indulge in anything that would impair their mental capacities. He's straining his databanks trying to understand my condition.

"Cuz, stop searching for answers. I'll be fine as soon as I get sompen to eet." *At least that's what I'm hoping.*

I'm jabbering as we go to the Chancellor's residence. Cuz listens quietly. He even attempts to interject a word here and there, but my intoxicated state isn't allowing for any coherent conversation.

The one thing nagging at me is how much I'd wish this whole thing were over. An audience with the Chancellor seems snobbish. After all, I'm a naïve and unsophisticated American. What do I know about the significance of meeting a head of state? I don't know if I should equate her with royalty or office. Nicki talked of her often, but as her mom, not as Chancellor. I didn't appreciate the magnitude of meeting Venubia's matriarch until we arrived at her residence.

Sitting rigidly inside the tram, looking blurry-eyed at the unfolding spectacle. The residence has a modern palatial appearance, all lit up and surrounded by beautiful grounds. Lots of vehicles are unloading groups of Venubians with their shiny, bald heads and large, bright eyes, all walking with a graceful gate through the grand entrance of the sprawling residence. I remember all during my processing at the administration center how anxious I was to meet Venubians. Now, my wish is about to be granted. A terrifying thought grabs me. I retreat into the safety of the cab.

"Hey, Cuz," I call to him. "Are all these people coming to meet me?"

Cuz nods. "You are, for all intents and purposes, the representative of Earth. They are, understandably, curious and most excited to meet you."

The weightiness of this moment has me stuck to my seat, thinking. For the first time in my life, I'm the object of hundreds, maybe thousands, of curious extraterrestrials. I'm the visiting alien being taken to their leader! Planet Earth's ambassador! I'm unprepared, not to mention stinking drunk.

"This isn't what I was expecting, Cuz. I thought this was going to be a private meeting. How do I act? What do I say?" Before Cuz can respond, I break out laughing, "Hell, I'm already drunk." I relax a bit. "They don't have the slightest idea how a human behaves. Know what? I'm feeling braver. So, let's party." I slap Cuz on the back and push him out of the way as I ascend on the unsuspecting Venubian populace.

"Wait a moment, Phil," Cuz protests. "I think it would be prudent if you try to restrain your enthusiasm, considering your present condition."

Cuz's caution goes to no avail. I'm determined to have fun and don't care that I'm acting like a total idiot. At least, that's what I kept telling myself.

I approach the gathering of Venubians with stunning jocularity. I greet each one with a firm handshake and a compliment, such as: "Hello, I'm Phillip Mann from Earth. Nice head, or that's a beautiful jumpsuit. Where did you find it?"

Each Venubian, in turn, stands erect, returns my greeting with a silent nod or a polite smile. Some of them stare at their hand, looking puzzled by my handshake. After my whirlwind entrance into the main hall, I was struck by the lack of males in attendance. The few who were there all seemed aloof, almost bored.

Listening to the quiet, I sense the presence of hundreds of speechless minds. They are all examining me with their mute penetrations. If not for my relaxed alcoholic state, I'd probably go into instant culture shock.

Cuz catches up and whispers, "It is inappropriate for you to enter without me introducing you first. If you will be a little patient, I will help you make a better first impression."

Looking around the room, I say, "Too late. It looks like my first impress'em is going over like eh pregnant high jumper."

Cuz cocks an eyebrow. "Query, Phil. What's a pregnant high jumper, and how is that analogous to the situation?"

"Never mind," I whisper loudly. "How about you introduce me before I screw things up further?"

My throbbing head drowns out half of Cuz's words. Standing and wondering if the headache is the beginning of an early hangover or hunger. No. Too mild for a hangover, it must be hunger, I decide after my stomach growls.

"May I have your attention, please?" Cuz projects his voice, piercing the silent curtain that permeated the grand hall. All at once, everyone's attention is fixed on us. I swallow down a sobering lump as Cuz announces in a firm voice, "It is with great pleasure that I present Mr. Phillip Mann of Earth."

They all assembled and nodded while placing their left hands across their chests as a gesture of greeting.

Cuz continues, "If you would be so gracious as to afford Mr. Mann verbal communication. Having just arrived from his long journey to our world, Mr. Mann's telepathic skills are novice, and it would serve his needs this evening if we could do him the courtesy of verbalization."

The hall bursts out into noisy conversations. The multitude of voices washes over me like a refreshing wave of security, and my tensed stomach relaxes.

"As many of you are aware," Cuz resumes, and the room becomes silent again. "Mr. Mann is here on an important assignment. He is most eager to meet all of you. He has expressed his heartfelt wishes of goodwill, fellowship, and peace to all Venubians on this historic occasion of his arrival. Please join me in making Mr. Mann feel welcome in his new home."

They all, once again, nod and place their hands across their chests, then go about their business. It's remarkable how civilized Venubians are. They're all acting congenial and attentive to each other.

"Thank you, Cuz," I say with sobering gratitude and a sigh of relief. "It never occurred to me that this is a historic event. I mean, it's hard for me to think of myself in those terms; historic and all."

Cuz arches an eyebrow in a thoughtful gaze and says, "You are the first representative of Earth on Venubia. If I may suggest, it would be in your best interest to accept yourself as precisely that. Would you like something to eat?"

"Oh yeah. I'm starving."

Cuz gestures for me to follow him into the next room. As we walk, I study my Venubian hosts. They all appear ageless and similar in size. Their facial features have only subtle differences. Up to this point, the only Venubians I'd encountered were Nicki and Cuz. Now immersed in a grand reception filled with hundreds of them, I can barely distinguish one from another. If the females didn't have small breasts, I'd have a hard time differentiating gender. After a while, my interest shifted to the whereabouts of the Chancellor and my introduction to her.

"How should I act? What if she thinks I'm an idiotic dork?" I nervously transmit to Cuz.

"Dork?" he transmits, then smiles. "Just be yourself," Cuz says in response to my rambling thoughts.

"What's she like?"

"She is thoughtful and wise. You will find her to differ from anyone you will meet on Venubia."

"You're not telling me much, Cuz. I need specifics."

"What type of specifics?"

We enter an enormous room that has a table running the entire perimeter. My attention is drawn to the overflowing abundance of foods that radiate with colors and smells that are both pleasant and, for lack of a better description, odd. I recognize nothing and start tasting everything. My hunger allows me to be less discriminatory and more daring. I eat tasty, crusty things along with slimy things, and none of it offends my taste buds.

"Cuz," I say with my mouth full. "This's great, now about the Chancellor? Is she pretty? Does she have a sense of humor? I hope she's not one of those stuffy, uptight bureaucratic types—"

Cuz's expression changes from amused to stiff and serious.

"What? Why the stern face?" I asked while stuffing something that resembled a Swedish meatball into my mouth.

"Good evening, Chancellor Verubeal. May I present Mr. Phillip Mann?" Cuz says.

I turn, trying to swallow down the meatball thing. It sticks in my throat, and I gesture to Cuz for something to drink. He seems puzzled at first, then realizes I'm choking. The Chancellor gives me a firm slap on the back right between the shoulder blades, dislodging the meatball from my throat, sending it flying onto some unsuspecting guest's plate. The surprised visitor turns to us and gives a polite nod to the Chancellor and an annoyed scowl at me.

"I must admit," she says with a faint smile. "This's probably the first time I've had the pleasure of both meeting and saving a distinguished visitor to our residence. Truly an auspicious meeting, wouldn't you agree, Mr. Mann?"

"Auspicious isn't the first word that comes to mind," I reply, gasping for breath and feeling my face burning with embarrassment. "But I'm sure it'll be a memorable one for both of us."

At first, I refrain from looking at her, hoping to regain a little dignity. Then our eyes meet. I'm dumbfounded in her presence. She seems like Nicki. I want to say something witty that would've saved the moment, but my mouth and mind go numb. Cuz takes a step forward and speaks in my defense. I still don't remember what he said. All I can do is stand mute and bewildered in a cold sweat with my nervous heart pounding in my tight chest. If she could read my thoughts, she could understand why I had to run out of her residence.

The night air is thin and cool. My chest is so tight that every breath is an effort. *I'm having a heart attack.* I fell to my knees, clutching my breast. There are the sounds of many voices clamoring in my head, along with a ringing in my ears. Everything is closing in around me like a suffocating blanket. A sudden blaze of silver light flashes through my mind. The world spins and then elongates into a distorted gray funnel that engulfs me in a black shroud.

CHAPTER 30

I'm the representative of planet Earth—the holder of the sacred seed and a total fool. Take your pick. When I asked Cuz how the Chancellor reacted, he frowned and told me he explained to the Chancellor that humans were at times confounding and unpredictable. I guess my behavior wasn't all that shocking, or was it? After a moment's reflection, I realize I didn't distinguish myself, either. "I'm an emotional wreck!" I cried at the ceiling while lying in bed, the events of the previous night reeling in my head.

"No, you are sick." Cuz's voice surprises me.

My eyes open, and I see him leaning over me. His android face twisted, looking almost concerned. Also, we aren't alone. There is a small gathering of lovely Venubian women downstairs. I hear their soft voices within my head. It feels good to know my telepathy is working.

"Good morning, all," I greet them telepathically. *"Are you here to see the weird Earthling?"*

They all seemed to be filled with excitement, and their voices singing in my head had a tranquilizing effect. All at once, they become silent.

"That will be all, ladies," a strong, feminine voice calls out. "Mr. Mann needs his rest."

Like a strong tide rushing in, one can feel her matronly powers quietly filling the room. I crane my neck to get a glimpse of her. Cuz pats my shoulder and tells me to relax.

"Well, it's good to see you're conscious, Mr. Mann," she says. "You gave us quite a fright." She smiles, places her hand on my head, then two fingers on my neck. "Temperature and pulse are normal."

"Glad to hear that," I say. "And you are?"

"I am Tal-Nanuz. You may think of me as your attendant. I'm here to tend to all your needs until you are recovered," she says in a patient tone.

Tal-Nanuz is a handsome woman and, like the rest of the Venubians, ageless. But she has a distinct sense of maturity and a take-charge attitude about herself. A little taller than others I'd seen. Her dark eyes tell you not to mess with her, and she transmits an air of refinement that puts you on your best behavior. It's evident from the start that this woman will be a challenge for me. In some ways, she reminds me of Elaine. She's a combination wife-mother type, and that makes me nervous.

"Would someone like to tell me what happened?" I say.

"You had a seizure—" Cuz begins.

"It wasn't a seizure," Tal-Nanuz interrupts. "What Mr. Mann experienced was an electrochemical cascade that overloaded his neuro-compiler," she states, pointing a finger at my head for emphasis. "Simply put, you overindulged. Now, we'll not do something that foolish again, will we, Mr. Mann?" She scolds me with both intense verbal and facial indignation.

"Oh, absolutely," I agree, gazing at Cuz, who's looking curiously on.

"I'll be back with your breakfast. Please do not get out of bed."

She purses her round lips into a hint of a smile.

After she leaves, I say to Cuz, "Whose idea is she?"

"Chancellor Verubeal is concerned about your well-being. She wants to ensure you receive proper care and has sent her aide, Tal-Nanuz, to supervise your recovery."

"My recovery? I feel fine."

"I am pleased to see you are feeling better, but I would recommend you do not try to stand."

"Why?"

"The cascade effect has damaged some of your peripheral neural pathways that connect your neurocompiler to your central nervous system. This has temporarily shut down some of your basic motor control."

As Cuz explains, I realize how heavy my legs feel, and even more dismaying, the sudden revelation that I have an uncontrollable erection.

"Ah, Cuz," I say, lifting the bedcovers to examine myself. If it were not for the fact that it feels so uncomfortable, I would've thought I'd grown a prosthetic penis. "How long am I going to be in this... condition?"

"We are unsure," Cuz says. "As you can imagine, your condition is unique for us. Our evaluations of your biomechanical, biological, and biogenic systems suggest the damage to the pathway receptors will heal naturally. The best course of action is to allow your body to recover on its own."

"In other words, you guys don't have the slightest idea what to do?" The observation both annoys and disappoints me. While the erection is impressive, it's useless and becoming increasingly uncomfortable. "Your engineers made me, but don't know how to fix me? Is that what you're saying? Will this thing cause me any damage?"

Cuz's head tilts slightly to the right. He wrinkles his brow, giving me one of his android stares of contemplation for a long, unwavering moment before straightening his head and saying, "I do not concur with your assessment of the situation, Phil. Nickada was responsible for your enhancements. However, you are correct. We could not effect a resolution for your condition because there is no precedent to guide us. All indications suggest that the effects are transient and will dissipate over time. Because of your unique physiology, we believe you will not suffer any long-term damage." He attempts an encouraging smile, then adds, "Would you not agree that the natural course is always preferable to an invasive one?"

"So, how long do you estimate I'll be a cripple with a hard-on?"

"About a week to ten days in your time."

I thought for a moment, then transmitted, *"Am I functional?"*

Cuz's eyebrows rise, and with a slight upturn of his mouth, says, "Oh, yes, quite functional, in all respects." He appears most pleased for me as if he understood what I asked.

"Well, that's good to know. I guess? Help me up,"

Cuz gives me a cautionary frown.

"I've got to go to the bathroom."

He relaxes.

"Your bed has all the necessary toiletries built in. Concentrate for a moment. Your bed needs to re-synchronize with your biorhythms."

After concentrating for a moment, the bed comes to life. A funnel rises between my legs, and with some difficulty, I manage to relieve myself. A sink and faucet manifest right before my eyes. Even more miraculous, the sink arrangement is suspended in the air. I push down on a corner. It feels firmly attached to the bed. The sink and faucet are like those on Biomei. All I have to do is think about the water flowing and the desired temperature. Warm water flows out of the faucet.

"Cuz, where's the water coming from?"

"Compressed hydrogen and oxygen are stored in the unit, and are combined by a converter into water."

I nod, impressed. "Soap," I request a small bar of unscented soap, which appears on a corner of the sink.

The soap and hot water have a refreshing effect that makes me feel better. Cuz takes a towel off a small hook attached to the sink and hands it to me.

Tal-Nanuz enters, carrying a tray filled with cakes, hot tea, and fruit juice. It smells much like an Earth-like breakfast, which has a quieting effect on my growing discomfort. The bed adjusted again, dissolving the sink and urinal, and the head end reclined a little.

"You're looking much better already, Mr. Mann," Tal-Nanuz says. "There's nothing like freshening up and getting started with a good breakfast." She levels a stern stare at Cuz. "Haven't you something better to do than loitering around here?"

Cuz half shrugs and makes another awkward grin, leaving me in Tal-Nanuz's care.

She requests a bed tray and places my breakfast down, then watches me with enthusiastic curiosity as I eat.

"This is good," I transmit with my mouth full of cake.

The tea is strong and sweetened to my exact preferences.

"You've done your homework on me."

"Yes. I'll confess, you're a fascinating curiosity, and I find myself attracted to you. You have a good heart, but a confused mind. I want to help in both respects." She leans over my tray and gives my cheek a gentle pat.

As I finish my breakfast, I sense Tal-Nanuz has something specific in mind for me. She's holding something back. I can see it leaking through her tightly held expression. Perhaps she has a strong emotion she doesn't want me to feel? I try to avoid the apparent explanation for the feelings I'm sensing in her. It may have been presumptuous of me to do so, especially for someone of Tal-Nanuz's position. I begin to evaluate her actions more closely. Nicki has familiarized me with many Venubian social customs and morals. She has made me aware of how uninhibited Venubians are toward sex. Then again, if you were a race in desperate need to procreate, sex would be a high priority.

Pondering the problem with my eyes closed and hands behind my head, I become aware of Tal-Nanuz pulling at my bedcovers. I reflexively grabbed her hand. At first, I give her a sharp glare, more out of surprise than anger. Then my eyes fix on her sensual, naked body, poised on my bed. I soften my strong expression, realizing that she's reflecting a countenance of somber rejection.

"I only wanted to please you and alleviate some of your discomforts. Forgive me if I offended you. I didn't sense that you find me undesirable. I'll arrange for another to attend to your needs."

My heart sinks with the pain I have caused her. It never occurred to me that sex was part of her duties.

"No. It's I who begs your forgiveness. It's just that you took me by surprise. I find you most desirable and would welcome the experience of an intimate exchange with your mind and body."

Her eyes brighten, and I can feel a surge of excitement well up inside of her. Her whole demeanor transforms as she commands the bed to lower into a suitable incline and gracefully straddles herself over me. Her wet warmth closes around my member, moving with gentle undulations that make every movement into a ripple of sexual delight.

I attempt a gentle empathic tap to get a sense of her emotions, but she blocks me. After a moment's concentration, I realize she doesn't want to reveal herself all at once, which is a little surprising. I notice her glowing expression. Now I understand. She wants to have a private moment with her passions. Giving her a little time, she gives me a glimpse of her thoughts. She is consumed by reaching an orgasm. All I can gather from her is some Venubian that roughly translates as, *Please go slow. I'm enjoying this.*

On the other hand, I'm in a transfixed state that can only be described as *Ultimate ecstasy—just* pure sex. There's no small talk, no foreplay, and no worry about how you would feel about each other afterward. Simple, old-fashioned screwing; fantastic and guiltless. Is there anything better in the universe?

Trying not to reach orgasm too fast, I concentrate on reading my partner's thoughts, endeavoring to feel what she's feeling. When Nicki and I engaged, we often shared each other's thoughts, but for some reason, we never could share each other's physical sensations. It might have been because my telepathic abilities weren't strong enough. Or Nicki was saving that experience for a special time. We never even got a chance to discuss it.

Concentrate, I tell myself each time my mind slips back to my pleasure.

After a brief struggle, I get a connection with her, and for a wonderful moment, I sense what she's experiencing. It's a pure flow of exhilaration that runs out from her vagina and upwards throughout her body. She's getting close to a climax. Her breathing is heavy, and she moves more rapidly. I can feel myself moving to the same end.

"I must confess," she says, a little breathless. "I've not had sex in over fifty planetary cycles. That's almost seventy in Earth years."

I lift her gaze to me and ask, "So, after such a long time, how was it?"

"Most satisfying," she smiles warmly with her large eyes expressing her gratification.

"You won't wait for another fifty cycles—will you?"

"*Not if I can help it,*" her transmission is wrapped in warm emotion, like a telepathic kiss.

"I'm curious. Who are all those young women, I hear?"

The surprise I sense Tal-Nunz is waiting to spring on me must concern all those young ladies in the foyer earlier.

"They are the first of your sex surrogates waiting their turn."

I narrow my eyes at her. "How many?"

"One every twenty minutes for as long as you can perform. Phil, are you all right? The color has drained from your face."

"Oh, shit," I murmur. "I'm not sure I'm up for it."

"Nonsense," she arches a brow ridge, eying my erection with a faint smile. "Ladies, Mr. Mann is ready for you now," she calls out and leaves.

They parade into my bedroom one at a time, with me performing like a virtual sex machine. They allow me a two-hour rest after the tenth, then resume the pleasure ride until I beg for mercy.

"But we were told Earthmen never tire of sex," one of the more agile maidens protested. I think she was number twenty-two.

"There's a limit to how much even a hardy Earthman can stand in one cycle. If I weren't in this physiological condition, I probably would've been incapable of continuing about twenty maidens ago. So please, come back tomorrow, late in the day."

"I'm the last of the day," A tall female said, studying me with eager curiosity. "Tal-Nanuz suggested that you might enjoy a Zhe-Tas-Ohn."

"What's a Zhe-Tas-Ohn?"

"If you'll permit me, we can share each other's sensations."

"When you say sensations, you mean experience what you feel, orgasm and all?" She nods with a seductive smile that rekindles my interest.

Pondering what she's offering, I review the day. After the third girl, I felt like a machine and let them do whatever they wanted. They were engaging in sex in an almost transcendental way. A physical form of intercourse that is also super-physical because of the mental connection I sensed in each of them. There was a group that seemed to enjoy the experience, and others that were detached and treated the whole matter as pure science. Frankly, they gave me a break in that they worked quickly.

However, this last one of the day is the most beautiful of all. Unlike the others, she has lush blonde hair that flows over her shoulders and the most gorgeous dark gray eyes rimmed in blue. I sense her enthusiasm is genuine. She seems like she wants to please me. As she slowly lowers herself, I'm instantaneously inside of her. The experience is startling and disorienting at first, but things get clearer. For all practical purposes, I'm her. I can feel my member moving inside her. Each gentle stroke stimulates a wave of rhythmic undulations, like tiny orgasms, one after another, with each lasting a fraction longer than the last, and all building in magnitude.

We're so closely linked that I can hardly discern my own body from hers. I move my hands up and down her back and feel my fingers feeding back through her. Any sensation I can think of to enhance the experience, we try to intimately feel through her feedback. I'm learning how to turn this lovely Venubian on. Our sexual experience is growing more sensually intense until we climax together. We gaze into each other's eyes, looking a little disappointed that the elation is over.

"Did you enjoy that?" she said, her eyes turning a deeper blue.

"I think we both did," I say, letting out a tired sigh.

"Rest well, Mr. Mann." She gives me a gentle kiss on the cheek.

"Wait. What's your name?"

"It may be hard for you to pronounce aloud." She poses a moment, revealing all her radiant beauty against the orange-red glow of Venubia's setting suns and transmits, "*Taazxentelik.*"

She makes a little click of the tongue on the 'x' and the 'k'. It was hard to say aloud, but it flows like a melody in my head.

"When will I see you again?"

"*Whenever you request me, I will come.*" She transmits with a warm smile as she leaves.

I lie with my fingers laced behind my head, taking in the glorious sunsets through my open terrace doors, pondering the labors of the day.

Cuz comes in to check on me. I wonder if he wants to make sure I'm still breathing after the ordeal.

"You seem most content," he says, looking pleased for me.

"That was a most exhausting, but pleasurable experiment."

"The Venubian Scientific Community is curious as to the effects of a natural exchange of interspecies genetic material. They are eager to see if there are any significant results."

As Cuz explains, Nicki comes to mind. I wonder how she would've felt about the sexual experiment. Knowing her, she would've made me have sex with as many maidens as she could find. We had talked about the fact that she would have to share me with as many females as possible to ensure a diverse sample group. The thought depresses and fills me with guilt.

CHAPTER 31

I woke with a sudden surprise. My erection and numbness have disappeared. Everything seems to be in normal working condition. This revelation is giving me mixed feelings. Part of me enjoys not worrying about erectile functions, but it felt good to retake a normal piss.

I spring out of bed and walk out onto the terrace. It's a splendid morning. Warm sun over a cool morning breeze. I stretch out my tight back and leg muscles while breathing in that invigorating Venubian air. The colorful morning makes a glorious scene. The near sun is almost at eye-level with a veil of wispy clouds that softens its glaring yellowish-white glow. In the distance, surrounded by a crown of near and far moons, the radiance of the red giant is shooting out hazy fingers of red-tinted orange light as it hovers on the horizon. The scene reminds me of a Salvador Dali dreamscape: Perfect detail, wrapped in virtual reality, looking as though it's pulled out of the realm of the unconscious mind.

After showering and dressing, I go into the kitchen. I listen to the quiet hum of the cooling unit. It's the first electrical sound I've heard since moving in. It had a pleasantness to it. Like a hug from the house.

After several hectic weeks of nonstop sex and visitors, the apartment is finally quiet. I'm enjoying my solitude, knowing it isn't going to last too long. As expected, by the time I brewed a pot of coffee, Tal-Nanuz's presence filled the kitchen with her maternal aura in full bloom.

She walks with her head tilted back, looking as if allured by the aroma of the freshly prepared coffee. She leans over my shoulder and sniffs. Then she notices my oversized mug.

"Who is that person?" she asks with her eyes squinted, with a curious look.

"I created it in the material synthesizer," I say, holding it up to her. "I had Venubian Central look up the face of my paternal grandfather and had it painted on the mug in 3D. Now I can sneer at his gawking image whenever I want. The man thought I was worthless. He called me 'a lazy dog' once. Said I had no future. Guess that puts me with Einstein. One of his professors called him 'a lazy dog.'" While gazing at my late grandfather's image, I heaved a heavy sigh. "That's not entirely fair. He also put up with a lot from me."

Tal-Nanuz looks at me with a puzzled expression, then changes the subject and says, "I see we are back to normal?" She arches a brow ridge, with a tight smile, then sniffs the air and asks, "What is that wonderful scent?" She inhales, her nostrils flaring.

"It's an Earth drink called coffee."

"Coffee and it's an Earth drink?"

"Yes. I was surprised when I found it in the food synthesizer's log. It's a great morning drink that contains a natural stimulant called caffeine."

"Caffeine?"

"Nicki drank it occasionally with no noticeable side effects. Would you like to try a cup?"

"Oh, please."

Her large, shining eyes and bright smile overtake me as I hand her a mug of steaming coffee. She holds the mug to her nose and takes a deep whiff.

"I should warn you, coffee is a stimulating drink and can be habit-forming."

We tap cups in a toast, and I nod for her to try it. She takes a careful sip.

I step back to get a good look at her. She's dressed in a white jumpsuit. The suit has shimmering, silver lace flowing down the sleeves, cuffs, and sides of her legs. The suit's form-fitted style accentuates her angular lines and the round curves of her sensuous body. The pure whiteness of the jumpsuit against the morning's radiance creates a scintillating aura that seems to fill the room with an angelic presence. She's a lovely anomaly with a complex and dynamic personality. At one moment, she's acting like a diplomat, then the next a matriarch, or a nurse. But first and foremost, she's an incredible woman.

"This is a most unusual drink," she says.

Her fondness for the black brew looks to be growing with each sip. I purse my lips into a thin smile, thinking, will coffee be her first Earth-born addiction?

"I'm pleased. You recovered so soon," she says, gazing into the mug.

"You and your lovely young women must take the credit for my quick recovery."

"We're here to serve your needs."

"You all serve me most splendidly." She lifts her eyes and studies me with a faint smile. "It appears as though you're enjoying the coffee. Would you like another?" I ask, hoping to break her stare.

"No. One's quite enough for now," her voice quivers a little as if in excitement. "That's a complex drink. It heightened my senses. I've... never felt so... alert. It's as if everything is shimmering with clarity." Her face reddens with her eyes turning a bright hazel, rimmed in blue—a new and striking color combination.

"Wow. I can see it's having quite an effect on you," I say.

"This increased awareness, is that a common effect?

"Well... yes. But you seem to be having a little more of a reaction. Interesting..." I squeeze my lower lip in thought. "The caffeine gave you the mental surge... the heightened awareness. The sugar added the physical lift. Think of it as a way of giving your neuro-receptors a quick jump-start."

Tal-Nanuz closes her eyes for a few beats, then opens them and says, "I like it." She points to the breakfast nook for me to sit. She orders the synthesizer to prepare two eggs over easy with hash browns and plant-based sausage patties. "More coffee?" she asks.

"Please. Don't forget the waffles."

Tal-Nanuz brings my breakfast tray, places it down in front of me, and refills my coffee. "Am I to understand that our efforts have been fruitful?" I say, mouth full of food. I asked her for verification of what Cuz had told me earlier.

"Our exobiologists are surprised by the compatibility factors in your genome. You're a healthy, virile male. But they're cautious because it's a small sample from a single source. You know, scientists are skeptics by nature and never want to make premature assumptions. From what I've gathered, though, they're perplexed by their initial findings."

"Perplexed because something happened?"

"Let it suffice as scientific skepticism. They had no expectation that our females were capable of conception by an extraterrestrial species, and finding these results after a single exposure from one alien specimen surprised them."

"Nicki was sure that our species was closely related, but also held reservations even after altering my DNA. As she explained, the difference between a tree's DNA and a humanoid's is small, among primates and humans, even smaller. But she also emphasized that a difference, no matter how small, can make all the difference in the world. One protein, even an atom in the wrong place, could cause problems."

"This is true. I'm no scientist and cannot claim to understand the complexities at work here. I know all carbon-based humanoid life is made from the same basic building blocks and can be made compatible."

"That's a beautiful way of looking at life. I agree with you in principle and would like to discuss this further, but first, I need to see more of your beautiful planet. Where's Cuz? How do I get in touch with him?"

"You only have to concentrate on Cuz's image within your mind, and your internal transponder will signal him."

"All I have to do is think about him?"

I did as instructed and instantly picked up Cuz's transponder reply. I request that he come with transportation at his earliest convenience.

He responds, *"I am already on my way."*

"Great," I answer.

"Where're you going?" Tal-Nanuz asks with a little of the matriarch slipping out.

"Sightseeing," I say.

"That's problematic." She frowns. "I've not scheduled any tours or guides for you."

"But that's the best way, impromptu. Besides, I've Cuz. Who else do I need?"

Tal-Nanuz appears to consider the situation for a second, then counters with, "You have other obligations that are arranged. What would you have me do about all those appointments?"

"Use your efficient diplomatic charm and reschedule them."

"Reschedule? What reason should I give for your sudden cancellation?"

"Tell them I'm still indisposed or something."

"That would be untrue. You're obviously in the best of health and spirits."

"Tell them the truth. The crazy Earthman needs a break. He wants to be alone for a while. I have much on my mind."

She smiles at my weak excuse and says, "I'll gladly reschedule accordingly. Would the day after tomorrow be sufficient?"

"Thank you," I transmit.

I pause in thought for a moment. It feels as though she's giving me a long weekend pass from an all-consuming job. But if someone on Earth had asked me about my work on Venubia. Who'd ever believe I was the carrier of the sacred seed and spent most of the day screwing lovely ladies? While my highly enhanced body performed marvelously, my nerves are shot. Being an alien in an alien world has me in a constant struggle of second-guessing everything I'm doing and feeling. Also, I'm sexually exhausted and only after eight days. Which makes me wonder what I'd be like in eight years?

Probably dead!

CHAPTER 32

Cuz picks me up in a small shuttlecraft. It appears similar in design to the tram except that it has a large, rear-mounted engine. Cuz greets me with a slight nod. His demeanor is cold as a stone, and he's staring at me with impassive android eyes. He must sense my uneasiness and give me a formal greeting, fist to chest with a bow of his head. We eye each other as we take off.

His unwavering gaze is annoying. I look away and ask, "Where are we going?"

"I was given specific instructions to keep our destination confidential for the moment."

"But I thought we were going sightseeing?"

"Sorry, Phil, for the sudden change in plans. But I assure you, it is for a good reason, and our change in destination will become apparent shortly."

His secrecy is pissing me off... but I'm holding my tongue, hoping he'll drop the android act. Wait a second... he is an android. Oh, crap. I guess I'll go along for the ride. I glance at my stoic friend and sigh. It looks like we'll be traveling in silence—goddamn android.

I stay silent until our destination suddenly becomes clear. "The shuttle terminal?" I exclaim. "Why are we stopping here?"

"We are about to take a shuttle trip."

I feel my hands rise and I shout, "Enough of the damn android routine. Cuz, you're not sharing with me. Why?" I jab a stiff finger at him for emphasis, which, of course, he ignores.

"Sorry, Phil, I am not at liberty to discuss any details until we are en route. If you are patient, things will become clear soon."

"We're going to Biomei?" I say in a loud whisper, thinking something must be up if they're bringing her back online.

"Yes."

"Why now?"

"She has asked for you."

"Biomei asked? I thought she was taken offline."

"The techs reactivated her two cycles ago. They are trying to retrieve what is left of her core data for analysis."

"Retrieving her core data? I don't understand. Biomei was fully restored before I was placed in hibernation."

"That is most strange." Cuz arches an eyebrow. "You do not recall that most of her logs were corrupted when you flushed the ship with gamma radiation."

"I did what?" I search my memory. "I've no recollection of that. There's no way…" I concentrate, trying to focus. Nothing. "My mind's a blank. Do you think someone erased or maybe blocked it from my temporal processor?

"Most curious. There appears to be a serious lapse in your memory. The loss can be attributed to natural causes, such as emotional or physical pain. Both of which you have experienced. Or someone could have tampered with Biomei's ship logs. There is a more likely scenario, though.

"Oh?" I feel my eyebrows rise.

"Someone tampered with those memory streams in your processor and then erased all the relevant files."

Cuz gives me a second to digest all of that. "Oh, boy." I blow out a long breath, then clap my hands, startling Cuz. "This is getting better by the minute."

Cuz screws his face up, emulating a perplexed look. "I'm still unsure why Biomei asked for you. Perhaps she must have something to relay only to you."

"Perhaps. But we'll never find out unless you step on the jets and get us there already."

"You are correct. Buckle up."

"None of this makes sense, Cuz," I say. My head drops, and I'm staring at my hands with my insides now churning with anxiety. "Go faster. I need to see her. She's the only one who knows what happened.

"Hopefully, what the techs have retrieved from Biomei's logs will shed light on this mystery. She must have recognized the need to sacrifice her real-time memory to clear space for some additional data. Data she believed crucial enough to make such a risky move."

What Cuz relayed to me about the flush rang untrue. "Something is wrong. I can't recall ever flushing the ship with gamma radiation. We had the droids flush out Biomei's biogenic systems due to the nanovirus. I also know Nicki left detailed logs on how we located the virus and its eventual eradication."

"There is the problem, Phil. Unfortunately, neither Nickada's nor your logs could be retrieved. Some things had likely been done during your hibernation that you are not aware of. That is the most logical reason Biomei has insisted on having you brought to her."

"Cuz, whoever altered Biomei's memory must have been worried about being discovered. The stakes must be high in whatever their game is."

"Let us hope Biomei can help us discover the truth of what occurred."

"I fear this may be a foreshadowing of more serious problems."

We dock at the shuttle station and have to await clearance from Venubian Traffic Control. It's a short delay, but it seems longer in anticipation of speaking with Biomei again. My mind is whirling with doubts. *What happened while I was in hibernation?*

Cuz turns and asks, "Are you ready?"

I nod.

"We are cleared for Tizdain," Cuz says.

"Tizdain, is that where the ship is?"

"No. This is where Biomei's memory core is being maintained."

"I don't understand. Where's Biomei?"

"I'm sorry, Phil, but I do not know her location. I was told Biomei's memory core has been brought to the Tizdain Research Center. I have been instructed to bring you there."

"I see. So, where's Tizdain?"

"It is on the far side of Jo'ovf. The second moon out from Venubia, about two hundred K-secs, which is a little less than two Earth-hours from here."

"Is that the one that glows at dusk?

"Yes. It is one of the larger moons in the Venubian system. It is set aglow by the reflection of the red giant at dusk."

"Is it an inhabited world?"

"There are many Venubians, androids, and a few alien life-forms that will be new for you. I believe you will find this to be a fascinating and challenging trip."

I feel a slight tug of G-force as the shuttle accelerates into open space. The craft's transparent dome provides a magnificent view. It seems almost like a virtual reality ride with the moons looming large as we travel through the narrow corridor between the moons' gravitational fields.

Just as I begin to enjoy the ride, the shuttle comes to a slow stop. I hear hissing, then the interior fills with a thick, transparent liquid.

"What's happening?" I say, squirming in my seat as the warm liquid rolls over my chest.

"A protective liquid suspension medium will envelop us."

"Don't we need some special gear?" I say as the clear stuff covers my head. It feels like being immersed in goo.

"Please, don't be alarmed. It's a highly adaptive suspension fluid that consists primarily of oxygenated heavy water in a bio-medium. The medium contains nanites that prevent the substance from being ingested. It's designed to protect us from being crushed during high-velocity, G-forces. This vessel is too small for standard inertial dampeners. Once enveloped, your body will adapt, and your jumpsuit will keep you dry. After a few minutes, you will not notice it."

The natural human reflex is to hold your breath when being immersed in liquid. Cuz was right. The stuff never enters a single orifice. It seems more like a thick, protective outer coating. To my surprise, I can hear, talk, and breathe normally. The only restriction is movement. That isn't a problem. There isn't much room to roam anyway.

Once we reach our inertial velocity, the shuttle's jump engines cut off, and the particle drive kicks in. Cuz explains it works like Biomei's fusion engine, but on a much smaller scale.

In a short time, we're traveling over five hundred thousand kilometers per hour. Umbria, one of the largest of the Venubian moons, comes up fast. Cuz does a close flyover to give me a good look at its frozen, crater-pocked surface.

"It looks like a hostile place, lifeless and barren," I say to Cuz.

"It is a hostile world. At one time, the Venubians were considering it for an industrial complex, until they got back data from a series of robotic probes. Its atmosphere is thin and noxious. The poles are comprised of frozen liquid methane, which makes them an undesirable location. Too many complex factors to make it workable.

"They discovered Jo'ovf was a more manageable moon. It is much like Saturn's moon, Titan, in size and has a solid core. Its low gravity and thin atmosphere make it ideal for many industrial applications."

"I am going to use Umbria's strong gravity to slingshot us around to Bozniteeh and use its atmosphere to slow us down. Prepare, this may get a little rough." He emulates a reassuring smile that makes me even more uneasy."

"Yeah. Thanks for the warning."

Cuz does the slingshot to Bozniteeh, the outer moon with a thick atmosphere. We hit the atmosphere with a jarring impact, which slows us into a parking orbit over Jo'ovf. For a brief period, it felt like the small shuttle was about to shatter from the intense turbulence and vibrations during our braking maneuver. However, I'm reassured by Cuz's calm demeanor and our protective goo. On our third orbit of the moon, we're given clearance to land in Tizdain Valley.

I look at Cuz, then at myself, realizing our protective goo is gone. "You were right. I did forget about the liquid medium stuff. Thinking about it, it was cool."

Cuz nods.

Our approach takes us over a high mountain range that blocks our view of the moon's surface. Once we clear the mountains, Jo'ovf's surface becomes alive with the traffic of hundreds of ships coming and going in all directions. I watch in fascination as they speed along in such proximity.

"It's remarkable how all these ships move at such speeds so close together," I say with a growing fear of a horrific accident. "Aren't you concerned about the potential for disaster? Even the slightest error could wipe out hundreds of those ships."

"No. All ships and transit drones are automated and have redundant proximity controls. The probability of a collision is minuscule."

The moon's surface is also busy with ground-based traffic flowing through an extensive network of tubes connecting kilometers upon kilometers of the physical plants of the moon's industrial complex. As far as the eye can see, there is an interconnected infrastructure of towering buildings with glowing lights, palely lit domes, and long monorails.

"There is little industry being conducted on Venubia," Cuz explains. "It is one of the main reasons it has such a pristine biosphere. The Elders had foreseen, early in our interplanetary industrial growth, how a heavy mix of industrial manufacturing was causing damage to the atmosphere. They mandated that within ten full cycles, all heavy industry must be off-world. Venubians have been here for over a millennium."

"Wow. You've been a spacefaring civilization for that long?"

"The advantage of having some technologically advanced neighbors." Cuz places the shuttle in hover mode while we wait for traffic control to recognize us. "A period in our history I will share with you when we have the time."

I smirk, realizing how often I'd said that to him.

"Acknowledged," Cuz says over his com, then sets us in motion again.

We fly over the industrial expanse until we come to a clearing. From our vantage point, it resembles a honeycomb of tunnel openings. Cuz places us into a hovering maneuver again as he transmits our shuttle's ID and destination data to a ground-based traffic control center.

"There will be a short delay while the Central Command's computer confirms our security clearance and relays landing instructions," Cuz explains.

"This is a fascinating place. Is there as much activity below as there is on the surface?"

"The surface represents only a small fraction of the total complex. Most of the infrastructure lies beneath, as you will soon see."

Upon receiving clearance, we glide into a small portal that opens into a vast expanse of interconnecting tunnels. Our descent is halted by a bright, blue-white light that attaches itself to our shuttle. It seems as if we're floating on a beam of light.

"What's going on?" I ask.

"A magnetic energy field is guiding us," Cuz explains.

The beam guides us far beneath the planet's rough surface. For several minutes, we descend past row upon row of deck levels before changing direction. Then we thread our way through winding networks of narrow expanses and steep tunnels. The ride lasts for almost ten minutes before the energy field disengages, allowing our shuttle to make a soft landing.

The view outside the shuttle's dome gives me a sense that we're in the bowels of a well-developed interior. Our seat latches unlock, and the shuttle door lifts open, revealing the waiting presence of a colossal creature, covered in green and brown scales. It regards me with large, hawkish eyes for a moment, looking as though it's trying to figure me out.

I return the creature's gaze with a similar look. It gestures for us to follow it with a graceful turn of its oddly shaped head.

"Cuz, what's that?" I transmit a little disturbed at seeing such a strange-looking alien.

"It is a Bylar. He can sense your unease. Talk to him. His universal translator will make it possible for you to communicate telepathically."

"Hello. I'm Phillip from Earth," I transmit.

"Menthez of Bylar," he responds warmly. *"You are the first Earth Man. Resemble Venubian, but smell different. Will take getting used to,"* he says, his alert yellow eyes blinking.

His thought transmissions give me a sense of a deep, rich voice with a warm and congenial tone that calms my apprehension. Our brief introduction gives me a new appreciation of how anxiety about the unfamiliar is quickly overcome through communication.

Menthez is as alien a creature as one could ever imagine. He stands upright on two thick, muscular legs and appears to be over two meters tall. The eye can't take all of him in with a single glance. At first, I'm mesmerized by how his long, muscular arms and legs move with such graceful fluidity. His elongated head resembles a stubby cone with a rounded crown accentuating long peacock feathers, jutting out like a colorful hat about his pointed ears. What is most striking is how expressive his face is. His two bright, yellow eyes have an intensity that gives him a fierce look that softens as soon as I talk with him. His long nose wiggles a little when he moves or talks. And his rounded nostrils flare above a wide, thin-lipped mouth.

Menthez's morphology is so challenging to describe because he seems so complex, not to mention lacking a specific gender to the eye. I gather his sex by his voice transmission. At first sight, he's a walking nightmare. Now, after spending a little time with this marvelous oddity, I'm at ease and find myself enjoying his company.

"I was told humans are carnivores," he transmits with a bit of apprehension. *"Carnivores are violent by nature. Should I be careful of you?"* He lets out a few short hisses, sounding like laughter. At least, I hope he's kidding.

"I don't think I've eaten any meat since I've left Earth." I transmit.

"Is that a statement of reassurance or a possible threat?" His neck rises and curls his head down with a heavy stare.

"Neither," I say, adding, *"However, if you know where I can get a good steak dinner, please tell me."*

"Do not understand. What is a steak dinner?"

"Animal meat cooked with seasoning. It's popular on Earth."

His nose curls into his mouth like a baby elephant. *"Sounds barbaric, but will reserve judgment for now."*

"I appreciate that, Menthez." I smile.

I understand that many aliens judge other species in subtle ways than one would suspect. Appearance and behavior are often secondary to what is said. Communications are interpreted by both verbal and body language, with the latter having more significance. The experience with Menthez made me realize body language is something I'm going to need, and be aware of, living among such a complex and diverse group of aliens.

Menthez leads us to a turbo lift that looks like a series of tubes. He tells us to enter number five. I thank him, and he gives me an eyeful nod. Cuz walks under a device that scans his body, and then he whispers his name into a small screen next to the tube's door. The door opens.

"Please firmly grasp the handrail and state your destination," a soft, mechanical voice instructs us in Venubian as we enter.

"J-Five," Cuz says.

"What's this thing?"

"It's a transport tube."

I survey the small, round floor, then glance at the smooth cylindrical wall and see the handrail running around its perimeter. I further notice it's not attached to the wall. Looking down, I realize we're standing on a floating platform with a handrail suspended around us. Not to mention, we're inside a large tube. "You've got to be kidding me. What's holding us up?"

"It works on a similar principle to the device that guided our shuttle. The tube is controlled by counteracting electromagnetic currents. It makes first-timers a little queasy, but you will find it most enjoyable once you acclimate."

"Really?" I give Cuz a dubious frown.

Cuz gives me a cautious glance when the contraption shoots us into high acceleration. The spontaneous velocity feels like my large intestines are being pulled up into my stomach, and my stomach is now stuck in my throat. All I can sense is the high velocity, with me trying not to throw up on Cuz.

The tube walls make a sharp ninety-degree turn and then another. It feels like I'm on a roller coaster, only instead of being strapped down to a seat, I'm holding on to a handrail as if my life depends on it. Oddly, though, I never had a sense of disequilibrium. The ride, despite its sharp movements at times, remains smooth. As Cuz predicted, as soon as I overcame my nausea, I almost enjoyed it.

"How fast are we moving?" I ask.

"A thousand meters per micron," he states.

"I knew we were moving fast, but that's very fast. Where are we going?"

"Level five of Section-J. It's a transfer point where we will pick up a magnotrain. It is a magnetically propelled train. I believe you will find the amenities and comfort to your liking."

"Sounds like a long trip."

"Approximately a hundred and forty-one minutes from your perspective."

"Well, that's not too bad. It'll give me time to catch my breath after traveling at this speed."

"We will travel at a much higher velocity, but it will seem almost motionless to you."

"What's our destination?"

"A remote region of the complex."

Although Cuz's lack of detail is becoming annoying, I'm trying to remain patient with him. He's following his instructions with the expected rigidity of an android.

"Is the remoteness for security reasons?"

"Security is not a concern. Much of the equipment in the J-sector requires shielding from ordinary electromagnetic fields generated by the abundance of equipment in the industrial complex. To minimize contamination, we sent Biomei's memory core to a remote, sterile area designed with dampening fields. These precautions are intended to ensure that Biomei's memory core, or, I should say, what remains of her central memory core, is protected from further degradation. The dampening generators that create the sterile environment use high-energy photons that are disruptive to all electromagnetic devices."

"I think I understand. How much does she remember? Or, more to the point, what have you retrieved?"

"I am sorry, Phil, but I do not know what was recovered."

We walk in silence to the magnotrain station. There is no one on the short platform. The area is like every other I've seen on Venubia: pristine and unoccupied by humanoids.

We wait only a few minutes before the massive transit arrives. The large machine slows to a gentle stop, and a long door slides open. It makes no expected hissing sound or any discernible breaking noise. The interior reminds me of the ship with its colorful and well-illuminated walls and ceilings. Cuz motions for me to sit by a window inside the empty car.

"Would you like something to eat?" he asks.

"A sandwich would be nice."

A small, round device floats down from the ceiling and hovers in front of us. "Anasulz," Cuz orders, and an A1T7.

The device floats back up and disappears into the ceiling.

"What's an A1T7?" I ask.

"It's a liquid medium that hydrates some of my biologics as well as lubricates my cybernetic devices."

"Interesting." I nod with the reminder of Cuz's anatomical differences. "So, what's an Anasulz?" I say, tripping over my tongue in a crude attempt to pronounce the word. The '*lz*' ending requires a high click of the tongue, which I haven't mastered yet.

"It is something like a turkey sandwich," Cuz says, looking pleased with his selection.

"Thank you. I'm sure it will be a close approximation," I say.

My emotions are getting too close to the surface. I didn't want to talk about the growing apprehension stirring in me. Talk is a distraction while I'm thinking about Biomei, wondering what she remembers. Questions. I have many questions coming to mind. In mid-thought, I become aware of a humming sound. At first, it doesn't disturb me, but after a short while, it starts to sound like a voice fixed on a single note. The note grows in my head and merges with my thoughts, which dissolve into silence...

"Phil," Cuz's voice sounds as if it's coming out of a void. "Phil, your sandwich—Don't you want it?"

"Huh?" His voice startles me. Feeling a little disoriented, I stare down at a plate that has a thick sandwich on it. "I think I must have dozed off for a moment," I say, feeling unsure of what happened.

The sandwich is piled high with a white substance sticking out of two thick slices of dark bread. There is a garnish that looks much like shredded carrots surrounding Romaine lettuce with a generous scoop of genuine-looking potato salad on top.

"I do not think you dozed off," Cuz explains. "I believe you experienced what the locals call a 'Magno-fix.' It is a common side effect of the technology."

"You mean the humming or vocal sound is from the train?"

"The magnetic field causes it. How do you feel?"

After a quick self-evaluation, I say, "Rested."

"It has a tranquilizing effect on many species. To be precise, you were lulled into a semi-transcendental state."

"How long was I… tranquilized?"

"About twenty-five minutes."

"I must admit it relaxed me." I lean back and smile. "Cuz, I feel like I took a nap in a hammock in late spring."

Cuz arches a thin eyebrow and nods.

Staring at the sandwich gives me an appetite after all, and I devour the lunch. To my delight and surprise, the stuff that looks like potato salad is made with real Venubian potatoes—or some close approximation. I discovered potatoes, onions, and something resembling, but not precisely like, mayonnaise exists on Venubia. There are no turkeys or chickens, though. I found having no chickens unfortunate because I miss eggs. They're one of my favorite foods.

Anticipation slows time to a point of frustration. Cuz senses my uneasiness and tries to distract me with conversation. It could've been an ideal time to discuss the remarkable potato salad if not for my preoccupation with my visit with Biomei's memory. I can't concentrate on what he's chattering about, so I nod, pretending to be listening, but saying little.

The train comes to a quiet stop, which gets me standing. Cuz gently pulls on my arm and says, "This is not our stop. It is the next one. I can sense your anxiety, Phil. Please, sit and try to relax. We are almost there."

I sit with my head bowed, trying not to think about anything. After a few minutes pass, Cuz taps my shoulder. Finally, we arrive at our destination. The door opens, and I see from the platform a large dome, arching high a few hundred meters from the station.

"We can walk from here," Cuz says.

From the station, we traverse a connecting bridge that ascends the rugged side of a mountain to reach a large, domed facility. My biosuit adjusts to the icy mountain air. My heart races with each nervous step as we draw closer to the dome. Contrary to my expectations, the facility isn't as massive as I had imagined. I had anticipated Biomei's memory core to be a colossal, intricate machine.

Nearing the dome's entrance, I break out in a clammy sweat. My legs feel heavy, and my breathing is labored. All the dark, mysterious thoughts and dreams that have been tearing at my emotions since Nicki's abduction well up.

"Are you all right, Phil?" Cuz senses my sudden apprehension. "*Let me calm you with an A'Sheebah,*" he says. "It's a Venubian technique that allows individuals to calm one another in times of stress. It's something like a mental tranquilizer." With his hands cradling my head, he presses his forehead to mine, then emits a soft, almost inaudible tone. Its effect is immediate.

"Geez. That was better than Xanax and a shot of whiskey," I say with a heavy sigh. Then I look at Cuz's gentle face. "I'm glad you're here." I pat his shoulder.

"Are you ready?" Cuz holds his hand over a door sensor, waiting for my okay to enter.

"I'm as ready as I'll ever be," I say, taking in a deep breath.

The door slides open, revealing a series of inner doors like the ship's decontamination chamber. "After you," Cuz says and points the way.

"Oh, shit. Decontamination?"

"No. It is a security screen."

"Is it as invasive as a decontamination procedure?"

"It will thoroughly examine your entire body."

"Including all of my orifices?"

"Yes."

"I hate this procedure," I mumble, entering the first set of doors.

CHAPTER 33

Cuz's demeanor stiffens as I walk through the last set of doors.

"What's up with the severe look?" I ask.

He motions for me to follow.

"Why are you acting so weird?" I transmit.

"I am in security mode," he replies.

"Why?"

"Programming protocol."

"Stop," I snap, stepping in front of him.

He stops and looks at me with dispassionate eyes. He doesn't look like Cuz; more like the android, he's trying so hard to overcome.

"Cuz, I won't take another step until you explain what's happening?"

"Yes," he says, blinking his eyes as if breaking out of a trance.

"That's better." He was Cuz again.

Cuz transmits, *"As we enter the corridor to the archival area, my automated security subroutine is enabled as a precaution."*

"I don't understand. What could harm us here?"

"We do not know. However, we believe it is better to be cautious in these situations."

"That's amazing." I couldn't help but smile. *"You've answered everything I've asked, divulging nothing meaningful."*

Cuz resumes his security mode demeanor and states, "Ignorance is the beginning of all knowledge and knowledge is the initiator of all discoveries."

"That's profound, Cuz. And just as meaningless. It's apparent, I'm not going to get anything useful while you're in this mode."

My body tightens as we walk in silence toward the archive room. I hold my arm out to stop Cuz.

"Why have you stopped?" he asks, still in his stiff android persona.

"I need a moment," I say with my mind filling with questions: Beyond where's Nicki and is she all right, who are the Zenti? What do they want? Technology? Power? Or something else? My headaches in anticipation. I take a deep breath and let it out slowly to get my knotted stomach to relax.

I concentrate for a moment and hear Nicki's sweet voice, telling me to clear my mind.

I straighten and look Cuz square in the eyes and pat his shoulder. His expression doesn't change when I say, "Okay. I'm ready."

We come to a large portal. Cuz turns and says, "Stand here." He points down to a disk embedded in the floor in front of the portal.

As soon as I step on it, a wide beam of pale, blue light emanates from the disk. I feel a tingling sensation as a thin, horizontal, white light flows up my body.

"Is this some sort of scanner?" I ask.

Cuz nods. "It is a bioscanner. It checks your biosignature for identification markers."

"I thought the other scanner did that."

"This one is for confirmation of your identity."

As soon as the scan is completed, the composition of the door dematerializes.

"What just happened? I ask Cuz.

"The material making up the portal is being absorbed under a circular ripple of disassembling molecules," he explains.

I gaze at the phenomenon, pondering its miraculous technology.

I step over the small metal threshold of the portal and enter. The room is full of humanoids working on a multitude of holographic monitors and an expanse of elaborate floating consoles. Everyone appears hard at work on tasks being issued to them from a central operations platform. The platform is suspended in midair and positioned over a transparent, cube-shaped chamber with a long couch in its center.

Groups of mostly Venubians, along with some unfamiliar-looking aliens, are seated in a gallery with rows of padded seats arranged in a semicircle around the cube-shaped chamber. They all have anticipatory looks, staring silently at the workers.

"Aren't you joining me?" I ask Cuz, who's standing on the other side of the threshold?

"This is as far as I can go." His body relaxes, and his cold eyes soften to their warm brown glow. "You may not appreciate or even understand what I am about to tell you." He steps to the threshold and rests a long hand on my shoulder. "Phillip, what happens here during this session, I believe, will be a historic moment for both Venubia and Earth." He curls his hand into a fist and presses it to his chest. "The honor is to serve," he says, with a surprising look of pride.

He takes a few steps back and gives me a respectful nod just as the portal closes.

"Ah, Mr. Mann," a hardy voice calls out.

I turn and see a small, round humanoid figure. His precise enunciation and perfect diction didn't match up with his round facial features and large, bald head. He reminds me of one of my favorite cartoon characters, Elmer Fudd. I try not to laugh as the alien's bright, beady eyes are fixed on me with a solemn expression.

"I am Kazdan of Kayden," he introduces himself. "Do you know why you are here?"

I nod.

He guides me to a small chamber and says, "This is an isolation chamber." I glance at it, then back at him. "It is necessary to prevent any outside interference as we perform this delicate procedure. The equipment that will be attached to you is sensitive." He pauses and, in a somber voice, adds, "Mr. Mann, what you are about to experience will be unpleasant at times. Many questions need answers. With your cooperation, we hope to find as many answers as possible. We intend to connect telepathically with you. With your permission, we will simultaneously see and hear all that you experience. We understand how this can be considered an invasion of your privacy, so we ask you to allow us to mentally eavesdrop on you."

"I cannot overstate how important it is for us to hear and see as much of the information as you will permit. The sentient ship known as Biomei has information that is vitally important to all of us."

Kazdan's demeanor stiffens as he talks. His words fall on me like a heavy load. I didn't appreciate Cuz's warning until now. The far-reaching consequences of my journey from Earth to Venubia seem to have further complicated an already complex situation. The tension in the room is palpable. I can feel the burrowing alien eyes of the spectators heavily on me as Kayden continues his explanation.

The Venubians certainly don't have to ask for my permission to eavesdrop. They can easily plug right into me without my knowledge. So, naturally, I'm gracious and say, "You've got my permission. Listen away."

While trying to maintain a calm exterior, my innards are cooking. Leveling my narrowed eyes at Kazdan, I say, in a clear and loud voice, "When this is finished, I want to know why I wasn't told any of this sooner."

I enter the isolation chamber and smile as I recline on an all-too-familiar couch. It's like the ones on Biomei.

"Phillip, you will feel a slight prick at the base of your neck," Kazdan says, over the chamber's intercom. "We will insert a small interface into your compiler. This will provide a conduit between Biomei's and your stored data. During this process, there will be periods of blackness or blurred images. These are gaps in Biomei's memory core. These gaps will reside in your compiler's buffer until enough fragments are absorbed to make up a relatable data stream."

"I'm not sure I understand," I say, thinking this is more than a telepathic interface. Were they intending to probe my mind? "Why is the interface necessary?"

"We hope that some of Biomei's missing data can be found in your archived memories. By joining with her, the combined data streams could provide a fuller picture. However, due to Biomei's condition, it's the only way we can make a direct link." He pulls on his ear, then sighs. "I should explain that there are variables within your brain that make it difficult for us to predict, with certainty, if we will get any discernible images. Understand, Mr. Mann, that none of this technology was ever intended for your species. While your brain is almost anatomically identical to a Venubian's, there are some subtle differences. But we are optimistic that some useful information can be retrieved with a direct link. We aim to learn as much as we can about what happened on Biomei during your journey to Venubia. We only seek the truth and need your cooperation to discover it." He pauses as if to give me a moment to consider it. "May we proceed?"

I take a deep breath and blow it out. Kayden tilts his head, looking a little uneasy as I consider what he said. After fighting back an urge to say, 'Fuck no. ' Get me out of here.' Instead, I say, "Begin." I need to know what happened as much as they do.

There is a brief pause before the anticipated prick. It comes almost unnoticed. I feel a slight tingle that trickles into the back of my head. A few beats later, a crystal-clear image of the main engineering console becomes visible as if I'm there. I gasp at seeing Nicki's lovely face looking right at me.

"What are you doing?" she shouts.

"Depressurizing the ship," I say, seeing myself standing stiff with a dispassionate expression, looking almost robotic.

"Why?"

"We're close enough to the pulsar for it to flood the ship with gamma radiation. That should keep the Zenti from boarding us. Afterward, we can flush out all the systems and reboot Biomei."

"Reboot Biomei? You shut her down? Are you crazy? We already flushed out her systems from the nanovirus. Shutting her down again could damage her central biogenic processor. What's wrong with you?" Her face is flushed, and her eyes are full of distress.

It's painful to watch myself acting so strangely.

"I've calculated that we can remain in hyper-stasis while the ship restores its systems," I say, speaking in a low monotone.

I want to hold Nicki close. To caress her and reassure her that everything will be all right. But all I can do is watch in disbelief. "Get into hibernation chamber two before I flood the ship. Biomei has been programmed to reboot after she's depressurized. This's our best tactic against the Zenti."

"What about the droids?" Nicki says, gazing at me intently.

"I stowed them back into their bays. They are of no use to us now."

My mind seizes with doubt. I'd never have allowed myself to be so cold to Nicki. This makes little sense.

The image shifts. I see myself in the hibernation chamber. Nicki is working at the main engineering console. I could sense her intensity as she worked at a frantic pace.

"How's that? I've rebooted most of your primary systems," Nicki says.

"Everything appears to be normal," Biomei says. "You need to leave me now."

Nicki looks over to my hibernation chamber and lets out a long sigh. "Don't revive him until you're sure the Zenti is out of range."

There is a brief blackout. In dim lighting, I can see myself working at Biomei's primary core interface. I go to a bulkhead and strap myself to it. A moment later, a thunderous roar of rushing air burst around me. My skin ripples against the mighty gale.

When the gust subsides, I unstrap myself and go back to the central console and say, "Biomei, I've opened all the hatches and depressurized the ship as you instructed."

Watching in confusion, I notice my automaton-self appears unaffected by the loss of pressurization, allowing the saturation of gamma-radiation throughout the ship. *How could I have been so immune to this? I'm still mostly human.*

The scene shifts again. Now I see myself looking into the ship's central core display. It appears as if a telepathic discussion between Biomei and me. I still have that stoic automaton stiffness, but my facial features have softened and are more expressive. Biomei is transmitting something. Then I examine myself more closely, and a haunting revelation strikes me.

"Stop!" I cry out.

"What is it?" Kazdan asks in alarm.

"There's something wrong," I say. "It doesn't make sense. I've no recollection of any of this. I'm telling you, none of this happened."

"Mr. Mann," Kazdan interjects. "These are memories taken from your embedded data storage and Biomei's protected files. There is no way this could have been fabricated."

"How do you know?"

"We deciphered some of Biomei's files. As already explained, most of the data was corrupted, but we still retrieved a few fragments. After analyzing her memory fragments, we traced the coding sequence. Biomei has done a memory transfer, and the only person capable of receiving that much data is you. That's why we are engaged in this recall procedure."

"Kazdan, we're viewing events of dubious authenticity. Wouldn't you agree that if a group of highly motivated and resourceful saboteurs could introduce an almost undetectable nanovirus, they could also have altered Biomei's logs and my memory?"

Kazdan frowns, brooding. "I see your point, Mr. Mann, but I am confident that the files we are viewing have not been manipulated. Our technicians have meticulously reviewed the code and found no trace of tampering. We are certain this is what happened."

"And I'm telling you, despite your confidence in these files, I know this never happened."

"Mr. Mann, is it not possible that your memories have been corrupted, and that is why you do not recognize your actions during this period. After all, you were placed in hibernation after these events occurred, and you may have been given a memory block."

"A memory block. By whom?"

"That is one answer we are seeking. Much of what has occurred during your journey from Earth appears to be fraught with many disturbing events. There are factions who, for their reasons, wanted you and Nickada never to make it to Venubia. Our sole purpose is to uncover who and why they wanted Nickada to fail in bringing you here."

"Kazdan, why not have Biomei read my memory so she can retrieve the sequencing codes?" I suggest. "That way, things could be placed in proper chronological sequence and would make more sense. And please, stop calling me, Mr. Mann. It's too formal. I prefer Phillip or Phil."

"As you wish, Phillip. To your point, we are not sure you can communicate with Biomei. Her higher-order functions have not been fully restored. You are connected to her archived memory streams."

"Are you telling me I'm viewing a playback of her logs?"

"Yes," he says, looking at me with an uncertain expression.

"What's preventing you from connecting me to Biomei?"

"As you are aware, Biomei has been subjected to adverse conditions. Much of her core memory was damaged by the depressurization and subsequent exposure to gamma radiation."

"No. That's wrong. She was restored. However, I believe the problem may be that Biomei is deliberately withholding the data streams, waiting to be reconnected to me."

"How do you know?"

"I just do. You must trust me on this. I know if we do a direct link with her, we'll be able to restore all of her memories."

Kazdan rubs his chin in thought, then looks back at someone who's observing the procedure. Whoever he glances at permits him to proceed. "Very well, Phillip. We will proceed as you suggest. I must warn you, though, we are reluctant because of the possible risk to your internal compiler and your neurological system." He turns his little, beady eyes on me and says in a low voice, "You're willing to risk it?"

I nod and say, "It's worth the risk to find out what happened."

"As you wish. We will need a little time to prepare Biomei for the link. Would you like to get out of the chamber and stretch your legs?"

"Yes. Thank you." The chamber's door slides open.

The heavy stares of an anxious-looking group greet me. I tour the room with my eyes and spy Chancellor Verubeal, sitting in the center of the upper level. Her close resemblance to Nicki runs a chill through me. I walk to Kazdan and ask, "May I have a word with the chancellor?"

"Of course," he says. "Do you need an introduction?"

Her dislodging a meatball from my throat flashes through my mind as I say, "No, we've already met."

I wonder how she'll receive me after the way I behaved at her party. Looking up at the crowd of tight faces, I make eye contact. "May I speak with you?" I call out to her. She acknowledges me with a slight nod from her seat.

To my surprise, she gets up and descends the narrow stairs. She seems eager to talk with me. Her bright eyes are smiling, looking much like Nicki's. At first, I wonder if I'm letting my mind get too caught up in her looks. Maybe I'm projecting my mental image of Nicki onto the Chancellor. As our eyes meet, I realize that all I loved about Nicki could never be duplicated in another, even though she resembles her so closely.

"You're looking well, Mr. Mann," she said softly.

"Please, call me Phil, Madam Chancellor. First, I must express my sincere apology for my strange behavior—"

"No need," she interrupts with her hand raised. "We understand that you were taken ill. We also understand the ordeal you had endured in coming to us."

"That's most gracious of you. May I ask a personal question?"

"Of course."

"You look so much like Nickada, you could be mistaken for her twin."

Her eyes brighten.

"There's so much I want to ask you, I hardly know where to begin."

"I understand, Phil. Please, unburden yourself of what's weighing so heavily on your mind."

"Do you believe..." A lump rises in my throat for a second. I swallow it down. "...she's still alive?"

"Oh, yes. I know it," she closes her eyes. "I can still feel her. Nickada is more than a daughter. She's also my closest confidant and adviser." She gives me a long look before continuing. "The Zenti is ruthless, and I fear for her safety. I'm here today for the same reason as you, wanting to know what happened to my daughter."

"Your daughter is a remarkable individual. I've always regretted not being able to get Nickada to talk about her family or her personal life. All she seems to be interested in is me. Is there a reason she refrains from discussing her relationship with you?"

Verubeal straightens as if I asked a tricky question. "I'm not surprised that she doesn't share more of her personal life with you. She's always been a most private person. Even as a child, she kept pretty much to herself. Nickada has a natural scientific curiosity that causes her to maintain objective stoicism. Even with the ones she cares deeply for." She lets out a quiet sigh and then speaks in a small voice as if trying not to be overheard. "There's much that you need to know and little time for you to discover it all. At first, I regretted how you were brought to our world." She places her delicate hand on my cheek and gives me a gentle caress, then with a warm smile says, "I was angry with Nickada, but after seeing what a fine young man you are, I've forgiven her." Her eyes take on a worried look as she continues. "There are many questions that beg for answers, along with difficult problems to solve. It's our hope this procedure will, at least, shed light on a complex set of circumstances."

"Chancellor Verubeal, I want you to know how much..." I stop short of saying, " I *loved your daughter*. "What I'm trying to say is your daughter is special, and we've become close during our journey. I can't begin to express how deeply..." My voice sticks in my throat while looking at Verubeal's face. She's looking at me in the same way Nicki did whenever I tried to express my feelings.

"I know my daughter loved you and you loved her." She finishes the thought for me. "I sense it in you. You're a noble and kind man. My daughter's spirit lives on in you. I can feel the essence of the love you share." She looks past me for a moment, as though gathering herself to say something difficult. "She disobeyed her charter and defied her basic sense of duty by bringing you here. That alone speaks volumes about the extent of my daughter's devotion to you. So, you see, my dear Phillip, there's no need for explanations. You never could've consciously harmed my daughter. That's not in your nature."

Her eyes well up, allowing the angst I sense in her to seep through and into my thoughts as she presses her soft lips to my cheek in a gentle kiss.

We gaze at one another for a moment. She extends her hand out, and I take it into mine. The touch of her hand feels as though some of Verubeal's vibrant energy is flowing into me. It fills me with a sense of joy that was lost with Nicki's abduction. It also fills me with confidence.

"Thank you," I transmit to her. I bow my head, kissing her hand respectfully.

"Phillip, you're family now. I'll always be here for you. You can see me at any time. We'll talk more about this later. There's much to do. You have my complete trust. You also have a great task ahead of you."

She gives me an endearing smile, then returns to the gallery.

"Wait! I don't understand. What task?"

Verubeal doesn't respond. She returns to her seat and gazes passively ahead, waiting for the procedure to resume.

"Phillip, we are ready for you now," Kazdan informs me.

I get back into the chamber with a different attitude as I recline on the couch. Something is wrong with this procedure. There's more going on than just getting to the bottom of what happened on Biomei. I'd sense an underpinning motive not being revealed. Didn't know why, but feel as though something is lurking, like a villainous creature hiding within shadows, studying its prey.

"Now try to relax, Phillip," Kazdan says over the intercom. "We will need to reinsert the interface into your compiler. As before, you will feel a slight prick at the base of your head, followed by a small electrical charge when the link is established. Once you are connected to Biomei, it will be as though you are talking face-to-face. When ready, I will proceed."

"I'm ready. Proceed." Wait, a sec. First, I'd like a private conversation with Biomei... to catch up with her."

Kazdan nods. "Of course, but please not too long."

The prick and sensation are almost simultaneous. I immediately sense Biomei's presence. I'm staring at her central console. I want to give her a big hug, being so close to her again.

"Oh, Phillip, it's so good to feel your energy," she says, sounding tired. "You can't fathom how much I've missed you."

"Biomei, it's good to be with you again. Why do you sound so run-down?"

"Yes, my energy is low, but I am rebuilding. Do not worry. I'll be fine. Now, we have a lot of catching up to do."

"Kazdan says we only have a little time before we must speak openly. I need to know. What happened after I went back into hibernation?"

"Once we retrieved Nickada's message, we disabled the droid's beacon. As soon as the Zenti lost communications with their droid, they became cautious. Uncertain of our defensive capabilities, they backed off and waited for our next move. They believed they were beyond our sensors. At Nickada's suggestion, I rerouted auxiliary system power to increase our telemetry's range.

"Nickada knew it would only be a matter of time before they would attack. That's why she had VSD03 store the Zenti droid and permitted it to resume transmitting its tracking beacon. She made a calculated move to misdirect the Zenti. She was certain we would discover the droid and retrieve her embedded message. Her intention was for the Zenti to go after her, allowing us to continue to Corridor-4. What she didn't count on was being taken so soon."

"So, did I flood the ship with gamma radiation?"

"I don't know what you've been told or recalled before this link," Biomei says, sounding cautious. "I was flooded with gamma radiation, but you didn't do it. I did it to prevent the Zenti from taking me over."

"You did it?" I reflect on what I saw during the initial link. "I thought I did it so the Zenti couldn't board us. My memories are all jumbled. You need to tell me what happened."

"Right after I had you go back into hibernation, the Zenti pursued us. Thankfully, Shorty discovered helium-3 fusion engines powered the Zenti's ships. He and VSD07 recognized there was a basic flaw in their power signature. They lose power when exposed to high levels of gamma radiation. Being near a type B2 quasar gave us a perfect escape venue. With you in hibernation, I had Shorty store all the droids in Engineering Level-2. Then I plotted a course through the quasar's emissions."

"Wouldn't that exposure to gamma radiation be harmful to your circuits and all your memory banks?"

"Precisely, Phillip. That's why I did a primary core dump into your compilers."

"Oh, that makes more sense than what has been recovered from your fragmented memory core. Continue, Biomei. This is finally coming together."

"Unfortunately, a Zenti shuttle caught up to us before we could get away. They sent a small boarding party of four Zenti troops. You were not aware of this, but before Nickada left, she gave me instructions in the event of her capture. VSD07 was to destroy all the ship's logs upon a Zenti boarding. I was instructed to download a backup of my essential logs into your compilers while you were in hibernation."

"I've a vague recollection of you telling me you would complete my transformation. Is that what you're referring to?"

"Yes. Once the Zenti captured Nickada, I had VSD07 proceed with deleting all my essential logs and shutting down the systems to prepare for going through the radiation field. When they boarded, all they found was a useless ship with its vital data deleted. Part of Nickada's instructions to '07 was to depressurize the ship as soon as the Zenti boarded. '07 did as directed.

Three of the Zenti were killed, and one of them got into a hibernation chamber, hoping to find shelter from the radiation. Its effort was in vain, though, and it died inside the chamber.

"The Venubians must have been showing you fragments extrapolated from undamaged data from my protected logs. Phillip, your memory-streams may still have much of the essential data, though."

"How would that be possible? My memory appears corrupted."

"As a security precaution, Nickada has inserted a memory core deep inside your hippocampus. She wanted to ensure the ship logs could be recovered."

I shake my head. "That's so like her. Well, that's why we're here. Kazdan already suspected that I had the data locked up in my head. Do you have Nickada's encryption code?"

"No. You do."

"I do?"

"Yes. Nickada told me it would become clear as soon as you needed it."

"Biomei, I haven't been able to recall it." Right as I said that, a sudden thought shot through my mind. "Wait, a second. Of course, she told me when she first implanted the sub-processor that if I ever needed to tap any protected information, call the barbershop."

I smile at the elegant simplicity of using an ordinary Earth-based phone number for an encryption code.

"Biomei, they must've played with my memories in search of the code and failed."

"That's one logical explanation," she says.

"You don't sound sure. What else could it be?"

"It could be they are waiting for you to retrieve the data, then take it from you. I'm certain the Zenti didn't have enough time to get into your sub-processor. There was something specific they were searching for. It's not only technology. They had already downloaded all the technical data they wanted. It's something so vital that Nickada encrypted it outside of my memory."

"What could be so important that Nicki wouldn't even trust it with you? Biomei, are you really here? Are we on Venubia?"

"Yes. It's me, and my telemetry confirmed that we're on the third moon in the Venubian system."

"Are you certain?"

"Yes."

"How could you know for sure? This could be an elaborate disguise or detailed hologram to deceive us into a false sense of security."

"Phillip, you're not being rational. You're over-analyzing the situation. Relax for a moment and reflect on what you're saying. Holographic representations have no life force. Close your eyes and take in your surroundings."

As soon as I close my eyes, my senses reaffirm the multitude of biosignatures within the room.

"Okay. You're right. I can feel them."

"The Zenti possess technology that's far beyond their capabilities, which makes them extremely dangerous. Remember, up to this point, they were a loosely organized band of marauders, murderers, and thieves. Like your ancient pirates, they raid unsuspecting ships and colonies to steal their technology and resources. Everything they possess is stolen. They've never acted with such deliberate intentions before. They seem to be well-organized and coordinated in their actions. All of which are uncharacteristic methods for them."

"Are you implying they have a silent partner?"

"Or a leader. Someone is guiding them. It's the only logical explanation—the sabotage of my biogenic systems. The strange magnetic phenomenon on Delius-5 and Nickada's abduction all seem to be part of an efficient and skillfully crafted plan. Letting you go is also uncharacteristic and seems like another calculated move."

"Biomei, are we being monitored?"

"No."

"How'd you know?"

"My sensors would've detected any monitoring device. You requested privacy during this phase of the procedure. I did as well. But my concern is to assure your privacy."

"My privacy, why's that important?"

"Some data was meant only for you, as per Nickada's instructions before the data transfer. When I was brought back online, I requested this audience with you and told the Venubian council that once the data is downloaded, any pertinent information would be shared with them."

"I see." I took a deep breath and say, "Biomei, how do I know it's you?"

"Can you not feel my presence? Do you not recognize my thought patterns?" she says, sounding annoyed.

"Let's do this," I say, taking a deep breath and letting it out slowly to comfort my rising nerves and growing paranoia.

"Visualize the numbers in your head and the data stream will start automatically," Biomei instructs.

I close my eyes and concentrate on the numbers. I visualized them one at a time: 9-0-5-8-4-6-1-4-9-0. There is a bright flash, then I see Nicki rushing out of engineering and into a corridor. Following close behind her is VSD03. She looks back, her bright eyes full of stress.

"Biomei," she shouts. "Prepare a shuttle for me. Docking bay-2."

The Zenti droid is almost on top of her. It swings its appendage at her head. She ducks under it and runs in the opposite direction. It turns and follows, surprisingly close, on its ejected slime—such a weird-looking anomaly, a bulky, headless creature that moves like a snail on steroids. VSD03 maneuvers behind the menacing blob and points its stunner at it. The droid doesn't seem to be aware of '03 as it fires its stunner, sending an arcing electrical discharge into the droid's back. The discharge disables it. Nicki lets out a long, aspirated breath, then turns to face the inactive automaton.

"Good work, '03," she says through heavy breaths. "Open its operational access port. I need to do a little reprogramming."

The scene shifts, and I'm watching as '03 places the droid into the storage locker. From there, it goes into one of the turbo lifts, then walks to Shuttled Bay-2. Nicki is waiting for it outside the shuttle. They both enter. The bay launch doors open, and they leave.

"She was concerned for my safety. But why did she do all of that alone?" I cry to Biomei. "Why didn't she stay with me? We could have fought the Zenti together. I don't understand why she was so compelled to leave us."

"She was determined to ensure your safety. But more importantly, she didn't want to be taken by the Zenti. That was her worst fear, and as you will soon learn, also Venubia's."

"But she did, anyway. Why?"

"Nickada didn't want them to get to you. She wanted us to get back to Venubia safely."

"Nicki knew something that the Zenti coveted. What was it?"

"As you know, Nickada's DNA has some specialized properties. It's her unique genetic alterations that the Zenti covet. They want her morphing ability. What they don't understand is that the genes that give her the ability to morph can't be duplicated."

"When I asked Nicki about it, she told me it wasn't a natural mutation. Funny, she admitted to me she discovered it by accident. When I pressed her to explain what she meant, she said she preferred not to talk about it. Nicki didn't like to talk about herself. I learned to respect her privacy and dropped it."

"Besides her morphing capability, Nickada also possesses knowledge about the Zenti that they are most anxious to acquire."

"They didn't find us by accident, did they? They were looking for us and had a good idea where to look," I say, feeling uneasy.

"There's more," Biomei states. "Nickada may have been betrayed by a faction that was working with the Zenti, and that's why the Venubians are so concerned. The nanovirus was only part of a larger plan."

"What faction?"

"I'm not sure. When the technicians brought me back online, information embedded in my protected archive memory core became accessible. Nickada somehow placed it there before the Zenti overtook her shuttle. Unfortunately, it wasn't complete, but what could be decoded is most revealing. Venubian security has gathered intelligence on a group of androids, whose motives are unclear, and may have been assisting the Zenti. They also believe a high-ranking Klaxon implanted the nanovirus."

"Androids? Is that possible? And why would a Klaxon official do such a deliberate act?"

"I have ideas on that. But first, you must give me your word that you will follow my instructions precisely."

"I will," I say.

"Venubian security has reliable information about Nickada being transferred to a moon within the Vultaran sector. We don't know her present condition. We are confident the Zenti will keep her alive as long as she has value to them."

"How reliable is the intelligence?"

"Very. One other thing you should know. The Council of Venubian Elders knows of all of this."

"I don't understand. Why are they holding this knowledge back?" I pause for a moment to think over what Biomei told me. "Okay. I think I understand their logic. They're protecting Nicki's location. They must have a plan to rescue her. Regardless, we need to get her back! And we need to do it now!"

"Not yet," Biomei says emphatically. "You're right. There's a plan for her rescue. But first, there's still much more you need to know before we can move forward."

CHAPTER 34

"We must go on the record, now," Biomei says. "There's growing unrest with our attendees. We've tried their patience to the limits of gracious understanding."

I didn't grasp Biomei's meaning at first because I'm so intent on devising our plan to rescue Nicki.

"Phillip," she snaps, "please, focus."

"Sorry. I was thinking about... never mind. What were you saying?"

"We need to go online now."

"If you think it's best."

"Do you have another course of action we should consider?"

"No. You're right, of course. We should go online."

"Control your emotions. They're most apparent," she transmits emphatically.

"Sorry. I was just thinking about Nicki—"

"Restrain from thinking about her. We must rein in our emotions, especially about her. No one can be trusted now. Everything we say and do must be done purposefully and without divulging any new information. That includes physical and mental information. No distractions of any kind."

"I understand. You have my undivided attention." I push out a long breath, forcing Nicki from my thoughts. *"I'm focused. Let's go."*

"We are interactive, Phillip," Biomei says, prompting me to begin our performance.

"We appreciate your patience with us," I say. "Biomei and I had a lot of catching up to do. She... eh, Biomei, that is, was about to tell me how the Zenti could locate us. I feel this is information that should be shared. Please continue, Biomei."

"Based on the data we gathered from an interface with the Zenti droid, it appears the Zenti know our unique power signatures."

"And that's how they tracked us?" I interject.

"That's correct, Phillip.

"Somehow, they obtained highly classified information about my design. They're also responsible for introducing the nanovirus that sabotaged my drive engines, stranding us near the Delius system."

"Nicki believed the virus is of Klaxon design and worried that either a Klaxon, for their reasons, conspired or, more likely, was forced to work with the Zenti."

A sudden murmur breaks out in the room.

"Klaxon?" Kazdan says with an indignant snarl. "That's absurd. No Klaxon would ever do such a thing."

"Nevertheless, the virus is based on Klaxon technology," Biomei insists. "Its morphology and chemical composition are nearly identical to Klaxon's metabolic nanotechnology, which they use in their industrial automatons."

I'm about to substantiate Biomei's claim, but Nicki's face comes to mind. For a split second, I can feel her. Nicki's unexpected presence almost overwhelms me. *Nicki's alive! She's truly alive!* I inadvertently transmit it to Biomei. I can feel her as though she were calling to me from another dimension, concentrating as hard as I can on her faint voice as if trying to fine-tune a weak signal. No matter how hard I focus, all I hear are a few almost indistinguishable sounds. I try to let it go, push it to the back of my mind, but it's stuck in my head like a haunting melody.

"I'm still confused about the Zenti," I force myself to speak. "How would they have gotten information on a highly protected and critical function as a prototypical power signature? Also, how would they know how to administer such a sophisticated virus without intimate details about Biomei's biogenic systems? The Klaxons are the only other people with such knowledge."

"Good question, Phillip," Biomei says. "It's something we need to find out right away." She gives me a perfect segue.

"Yes. But there's something I need to know now. Were the Zenti after you or Nickada?"

"They wanted me." More voices gasp. "Nickada deceived them into thinking I was damaged beyond repair and was of no use to them. She took all my biogenic functions offline and dumped my vital memory core into you. The Zenti became enraged when they realized that I was rendered worthless. At that moment, they decided Nickada could be just as valuable."

My mind fills with rage. I'm gripping the sides of the couch, trying not to jump off and go after her. A wave of rationality subdues me into a conflicted calm. I feel the presence of Biomei, reaching into my consciousness.

"*Not now,*" she insists.

"Phillip," Kazdan calls over the intercom. "We are at a loss as to what is being revealed here. Klaxons conspiring with Zenti?" I hear the stress in his voice rising as he speaks. His pale complexion is wet with perspiration. "Why would the Zenti be interested in Nickada? She offers them nothing of value."

"*Could he be a mole for the Zenti?*" I transmit to Biomei.

"*No. He's just a servant of his own people's interest. A conduit for bridging technologies, nothing more. His shock is genuine, though. I also believe the Klaxons would never willingly help the Zenti. They hate them as much as we do.*"

"She's the conceptual engineer of me and supervised my construction along with all my biogenic systems," Biomei continues with her report. "She's the only person who possesses complete knowledge of me. Nickada's my creator. Her knowledge would make her invaluable to the Zenti, Kazdan. I'm also surprised you didn't know all of this."

Kazdan's face turns red as a fire hydrant. "I was not aware of this," Kazdan says, sounding defensive. "I'm familiar with Nickada's background, but nothing more. Nothing that intimate."

"This is not common knowledge, Kazdan. I say in a low voice to calm him, "Hope you understand?"

Verubeal stands and comes down from the gallery and joins Kazdan on the platform.

"*This is becoming more interesting by the minute,*" I transmit to Biomei.

"*I think we are about to have a new revelation,*" Biomei says.

"My daughter was determined in her desire to create a fully independent and intelligent starship," Verubeal proclaims with pride. "She worked for many years using many different disciplines of quantum and micro-physiology to create Biomei's unique design. She disregarded many established rules and at times, even disobeyed my instructions."

"It will be helpful if we can establish why the Zenti didn't take the ship as well?" Kazdan says.

"Yes, it would," I add, wanting to see if anyone else would respond.

"There is no need," Chancellor Verubeal states. "They have all they sought. They must have known the ship would've made it easy for us to trace them. Now, the Zenti possess all the technology they were seeking." She glances at me, then stares intently at Kazdan for a moment and, in a quiet voice, says, "We're now amid an impending crisis. Kazdan, end the session. I need to speak with Phillip privately."

Kazdan's chest puffs up, and he shouts, "Chancellor Verubeal, I must object. There is much more we need to uncover."

"Not now," Verubeal counters with searing eyes. "Phillip has no understanding of what we're trying to accomplish. He must have the whole truth before we can proceed."

"I think you are failing to see the gravity of our situation. I thought we had an agreement," Kazdan protests, his voice rising with agitation.

She narrows her eyes into a scolding glare. "How dare you address me in that manner?" she says, in a restrained voice.

"I am sorry, Chancellor." Kazdan retreats. "No disrespect was intended." He makes a short bow from the hips. "We are most anxious to learn as much as possible about the Zenti encounter. And now... this revelation about the Klaxon." Kazdan resumes his stiff demeanor. "There is so much at stake. Surely you can see that?"

"Of course, I can," Verubeal softens her tone. "We're all anxious to know the truth. However, Phillip's at a disadvantage. He's unaware of our situation and needs to be briefed so he can be of more assistance. Our only goal should be to seek the truth. And prepare for the worst while hoping for the best. Don't you agree, Kazdan?"

"Never a truer aphorism." Kazdan blinked his eyes with a slight nod. "Your wisdom, as always, is far-reaching and clear."

His tone is sickening-sweet.

Now he's making puppy eyes at her. "Please accept my apology for any impropriety I may have committed." Kazdan bows more humbly and takes a few steps back.

"Apology accepted. Please have Phillip meet me at my residence as soon as convenient." Verubeal turns her back on the still bowing Kazdan and leaves.

As the chamber door opens, the center empties behind her.

"Don't disconnect me yet. I want a private word with Biomei," I tell Kazdan, who's patting his wet brow with a small towel. The little man's complexion has gone from beet red to pale and clammy. He looks as though he is about to have an anxiety attack.

"As you wish," he whispers, "but please be brief. It is impolite to keep the Chancellor waiting."

"I'm an American. We're late to everything."

Kazdan opens his mouth but says nothing. He turns and rushes out of the room.

The chamber door closes. I feel uncertain about our privacy, but I need to talk with Biomei.

"Interesting," I transmit.

"If I'm correct, you're about to learn some significant facts about Venubians and Zentis."

"Why do you say that?"

"There's an old skeleton in the Venubian closet, to paraphrase an Earth colloquialism. You're about to embark on a truth voyage that will probably change your perception of everything you think you know about Venubia, the Zenti, and our neighboring worlds."

"Jesus, Biomei. That sounds like a lot."

Biomei is trying to prepare me for something. And by her tone, it sounds like something I'm going to need to survive the next few days, by the sudden sense of urgency around me, maybe even in the next few hours.

CHAPTER 35

The trip back to Venubia seems much longer in anticipation of speaking with Verubeal. When we arrive at her residence, the sky is a blaze of reds and oranges—reminiscent of the late October sunsets in Key West off the Southernmost Pier. A vibrant pastel of nature's colors fading into the horizon.

The colorful landscape softens into dusk as we walk through the Chancellor's garden path. One of the things I'm still adjusting to is the nights on Venubia. They aren't long, only around four hours between the sunsets and sunrises. The night sky is a wondrous sight to behold. Looking up at the Milky Way's brilliance, from a new angle, unobstructed by city lights or air pollution, is always a thrill for me. The Venubian moons glow against a star-filled sky. I find myself lost in stargazing as Cuz taps my shoulder.

"Phil," he whispers. "I know how much you enjoy our night sky, but you need to focus on your meeting with Chancellor Verubeal."

Looking back at Cuz, I walk over to a lovely flower bed. Noticing the trampled blossoms, I kneel to straighten them. Cuz takes me by the arm and leads me to the residence's door.

A droid attendant opens the door as we approach and says, "Please, come in, Mr. Mann. The Chancellor is expecting you. Don't worry about the flowers; the damage is minor. Someone will attend to them during the next cycle."

He leads us into a well-appointed study. The chairs are made of a material I'd never seen before. Looking closer at it, the fabric had a silky, rusted tan appearance. The furniture is more ornate than what's in my apartment. They reflect a hand-crafted style with meticulous attention to detail. The legs of one chair have animal paws with long nails and thick hair carved into them. Another looks much like a Louis XIV chair framed in dark hardwood and leather fabric.

"Cuz, are these Venubian antiques?" I ask, pointing to an older-looking table and lamp.

"Antiques?" he pauses. "Yes. And that chair you are admiring is over twenty two hundred planetary cycles old."

I examine the room's contents. Looking at Verubeal's art gives me a glimpse of her taste. It appears she's a bit of an eclectic. A large mosaic, hanging over a long royal-blue couch, caught my eye. At first glance, it isn't impressive work. Its geometric patterns appear to be made from bits of colored stones. Upon closer examination, the stones appear to be suspended in a shallow glass case. Looking at it from different angles, the geometric shapes change into more complex arrangements. After studying it for a while, I came to appreciate it as a remarkable work.

On another wall, there is a variety of drawings; some interesting holographic landscapes, along with portraits, all done with remarkable detail in vivid colors. Then I spy, tucked in a corner of the room, a peculiar, but fascinating metal sculpture. Staring at the wiry-looking figure, its form has Venubian features combined with a strange, almost insect-like body. Its expressive face appears angry and lost, which adds to its haunting eeriness.

"What's this?" I ask, pointing at the sculpture.

"The subject of your discussion," Cuz answers.

"I'm sorry to have kept you waiting," Chancellor Verubeal says as she enters the room.

She has changed her attire into a flowing alabaster dress with a blue and white shawl draped around her shoulders. She looks beautiful. Her close likeness to Nicki, once again, makes my heart ache.

Cuz makes a shallow bow and says, "We are at your service."

"Thank you, Cuz," the Chancellor smiles. "That's your new assigned name?"

"Yes, Chancellor," Cuz replies.

"Uh, yes... Chancellor, Cuz, is a nomenclature I gave to him in that we share a certain familial bond—"

"You need not explain, Phillip," the Chancellor interrupts. "We're aware of the circumstances of Cuz's new designation and find it appropriate."

Cuz gives Verubeal an anticipatory glance. She gives him a slight nod, then he stares at me with cool android eyes. A strong aura of regret and sadness surrounds Verubeal as Cuz pulls out a familiar cube from his utility belt. He hands it to me, then looks at Verubeal again.

His demeanor stiffens. "If you have no further need of me, I will excuse myself and allow you to converse in private." He makes a slow bow from the hips and leaves.

I gaze at the Chancellor, trying to find distinctive features that separate her from Nicki. The more I search, the more difficult it becomes for me to have a normal conversation with her. She not only resembles Nicki, but she also sounds like her, even down to some subtle intonations and contours of her voice inflections. The closer I study her, the more conflicted my emotions become. Being in her company is causing me an uneasiness that I can't seem to throw off.

"I'm curious about your title," I say, trying to cover my apprehension. "Cuz tried to explain you're much more than a political figure. You're like a Queen-Mother to your people. That sounds matriarchal."

She smiles and says, "In many ways, I am my people's matriarch. My duties are broad and multifaceted. Probably not all that different from many political offices on your planet. However, for many reasons, my people feel they need a strong leader who will grow with them. Therefore, my reign is absolute, and it's for life."

"It sounds like a great responsibility. They must have much trust and faith in you."

"My office is not without limitations, though. There's a strong judicial force known as the Council of Elders. While all the major social-political decisions are conducted through a myriad of committees, all judicial matters go through the Council. Venubia's Supreme Court, if you will. Ultimately, I'm responsible for everything. All final societal decisions are mine." She let out a sigh. "I have made some dubious decisions in the past. Some of which have had long-reaching consequences. The truth of the matter is, I still have to appease different factions like any other politician."

"That sounds all too familiar," I add, feeling a little less uncomfortable.

"Don't look so surprised, Phillip. Venubians have their own form of special interest lobbyist for every conceivable Venubian group. At times, they wear my patience thin, but they are important to ensure that every faction has a voice. And yes, there are some whose voices get a little too loud and others who are never satisfied."

"Sounds much like good old political squabbling," I say. "I hope it doesn't get as petty and derisive as it does in my country. I'd hate to think…."

Amid trying to keep my composure, a sharp and piercing wave of guilt mixes with depression. Their combined waves of negative energy grip me, dragging me into a darker realm. I try to open my mouth to speak. But I feel empty and helpless, with sudden and overwhelming pain. The words stick in my throat as my mind fills with an irrepressible desire to cry out to her.

"Oh, Phillip, I feel your pain and confusion." Verubeal cries out, taking my hands in hers, pulling me close. "I miss her as well." She wraps her arms around me and gives me a tight hug. I feel her touch my mind as she holds me tight and whispers, "Let it go, Phillip. Release your pain."

I wail like a baby, gushing tears, cursing life, and all that is evil. I curse my existence and wish that I were dead.

"I can't go on without her, Verubeal," I moan, not realizing I have fallen to my knees. "Life has no meaning if she's gone!"

"Please, Phillip, sit," she points to the blue couch and then sits in a large chair adjacent to it.

During my outpouring of emotions, I had dropped the cube. She reaches down and picks it up, then places the cube on my forehead. Verubeal's eyes dim to a deep gray, and with a solemn expression, lets out a long sigh.

"It's obvious this is difficult for you," I say. "But I must know the truth."

She nods. "What you're about to discover isn't discussed among the populace. The reasons will become clear as this history unfolds. Much of what you'll learn will be unpleasant."

I grin at her statement and add, "What civilization hasn't evolved without a certain degree of ugly struggles? Certainly, what you've gathered from my world reveals a less-than-benign history. When I left Earth, it was a troubled world, and for all I know, it has already destroyed itself, based on what I've seen of your world. Well, if Earth doesn't destroy itself, I hope it will achieve a little of what you have here on Venubia."

"That's most kind of you," she says softly. "I guess all civilizations must go through their dark periods on the often treacherous road to enlightenment. We're not that far ahead of Earth in that regard. We're fortunate to have had the advantage of mature neighbors. When worlds are near each other, there are equal opportunities for friendship, advancement, and conflict. The close relationships we enjoy with our neighboring worlds resulted from mutual preservation rather than through the normal course of development. Out of our disputes, we drew the attention of our otherwise aloof neighbors.

"I'll leave now so you may absorb these critical periods of our history undisturbed. It will seem real to you. We anticipated the need to provide you with an understanding of our situation. I would've preferred to have given you more time to adapt before presenting you with our history. Due to recent events and your encounter with the Zenti, I had Cuz prepare an overview of only the relevant periods. It will seem disjointed. This is due to some abridging to keep the history as concise as possible.

"I'm sure you'll have many questions. I'll try to answer them, Phillip. But many things may not have answers, and some you may have to answer for yourself. Please, remember it's a virtual reality, and nothing can harm you. The cube will notify me when it has finished."

"Thank you, Verubeal, for your trust," I say.

Her pursed lips turn slightly upward, but her face remains tense with her large eyes full of sadness as she leaves.

***

The lighting dims to a soft glow as I make myself more comfortable on the couch. Unlike the spacious ones in my apartment, it is smaller; designed for a Venubian. However, once I recline, the sofa adjusts to accommodate my head and legs.

It only takes a few seconds before the cube syncs with my brain's and body's biorhythms. All at once, I fall into a deep transcendental state. My body feels as if I'm about to float off the couch. This sensation only lasts long enough for my mind to go blank.

I'm taking deep breaths and letting them out to the point of light-headedness. After a few seconds of controlled breathing, I sense my mind and body are in perfect harmony. The deep breathing exercise, followed by the tranquil sensation, all seem familiar. *I remember this.* Nicki had taught me a similar breathing technique to relax. A bittersweet feeling rises while thinking that every good thing I've learned on this journey was from her.

There is a brief period of darkness. I can only hear my breathing. The darkness turns into a visible gray, then into a clear, soft white. It looks like a blank sheet of paper waiting to be written on. I now see myself standing in the white void. I sense a close presence. I feel myself turn in its direction. But I'm still lying on the couch. It's a bit disorienting.

A lovely Venubian woman appears in front of me. She has a pleasant expression, and her large, dark gray eyes fix on me with a curious look. She's dressed in a white tunic that has a gold rope about her tiny waist. The material looks like soft linen, and it clings to her body, accentuating her lean and shapely form. Her alabaster skin, draped in that smooth, plain attire, gives her the appearance of an ancient Greek statue. She doesn't seem like an average Venubian. There is something absent in what I'm sensing from her. Then I realize what it is. She isn't real, but a virtual manifestation from the cube.

"That is correct, Phillip. I am a mental expression," she says, responding to my thought.

"Who are you?"

"I'm here to help facilitate your experience and guide you through some of the most difficult areas of this virtual history. I can answer questions within the bounds of my program."

She turns her small mouth up into a warm smile, putting me at ease, then she gestures for me to follow her.

I study her for a moment as she gracefully walks ahead of me. She seems most real. Watching her, I realize that a beautiful garden is appearing around her.

She stops and turns. "Are you coming?"

"Yes, of course."

I'm surprised at how I'm now able to walk and talk as usual. This virtual reality feels no different from objective reality. It's nothing like a dream. As we walk through the garden, the Administration Building appears a short distance ahead of us. I can smell and feel the grass beneath me and the delicate aromas of flowers. Insects are buzzing in the flower beds, and small birds are flying in and around the lush gardens.

"Where are we?" I ask.

"We are going through the administration courtyard. It is where many of the administrators gather to discuss items of interest."

"I've never seen this before."

"I know. I wanted to share this beautiful and tranquil setting. It occurs to me that you might enjoy coming through the garden in anticipation of some not-so-pleasant scenes you will witness."

"My compliments to your programmer."

"I'm sure Nickada will appreciate the compliment."

"She designed you?"

The woman nods slightly with a faint smile.

"That figures," I mumble, pulling on my earlobe. "So, we're going to the Administration Building?"

"Yes. An important session of interest is now in progress."

We enter the building through the rear entrance. Once inside, I recognize the central lobby. The two tall winding staircases are to our right. But the lobby appears different and brighter than I remember. I look up and notice the dome is higher and has high-arched windows instead of the smaller oval ones.

We ascend the stairs in silence to the second floor. Straight ahead are two large doors that lead into the main council chamber. My guide takes me to a side entrance to a second-level balcony. We are alone on the balcony and sit in the centermost seats of the first row. Surveying the room, it appears more ornate than the sparsely decorated chamber I glimpse with Cuz. The walls are covered in impressive tapestries that seem to tell a story about Venubia's beginnings.

My guide points to the lower floor. A Venubian with a shiny bald head and intense, dark eyes is talking. He's dressed in a long, dark blue robe with wide silver piping. His strong voice carries throughout the chamber. There are five other Venubians seated on a raised podium. They are all dressed in shiny white robes with their heads covered by red hoods, looking like seventeenth-century judges during the Salem witch trials. Their faces are ageless and impassive as they listen attentively to the speaker. Seated at a long table behind the speaker are three other Venubians and two Kaydens. The Kaydens are busy whispering to each other as the man talks.

"I am most distressed," the Venubian speaker says, in a dramatic tone, "that this council cannot see the vital importance of our research. We're on the verge of a great breakthrough in biogenetic engineering. I implore this worthy council not to stop our efforts at this critical juncture. The scientific community's concerns are out of ignorance and superstitions." He turns and glances at a group of Venubians sitting at a table to his right, "has no place in our great society. Their protests are out of fear and not from a logical point of view."

An older-looking Venubian shoots to his feet. "I strongly object to this unfounded rhetoric," he protests in a gravelly voice, pounding his fist on the table. "It is not from ignorance we object. On the contrary, it is out of awareness. Luzhuzien and the Intelligencia are taking us down a dangerous path. They're creating a new life-form. This is dangerous because it can be so easily corrupted into something sinister and unworthy of Venubia. Venubia doesn't need a race of slave automatons," he levels his cold blue eyes into a glaring stare at Luzhuzien. "We are treading on dangerous ground and need to evaluate how we shall proceed. This Council must create a code of ethics to help guide us down this uncharted and treacherous path."

Luzhuzien shakes his head. "We already have a code of ethics in place, your honors," Luzhuzien counters. "Why do we need unnecessary redundancy?" He narrows his large gray eyes at the elderly Venubian, and his mouth has a hint of a smug smile as he speaks. "This is only a delay tactic coming from a frightened faction," he points to the opposing Venubians for emphasis. "There has always been a certain risk associated with progress... and when we only see the risk, we perpetuate our ignorance. We vilify what we don't understand. I assure you, worthy members of this great Council, the Intelligencia is taking every precaution and every conceivable safeguard as we proceed in developing this great leap forward in artificial intelligence and bioengineering." He pauses as if for effect, with his hands tugging on the folds of his robe. "I implore you, please don't slow us down with unfounded concerns."

"Who are these Venubians?" I ask my guide.

"The Venubian who is speaking is Luzhuzien. He is the chairman of the Intelligencia, which is a consortium of technological development associations. They represent a group that is developing a new class of androids with the ability to adapt and develop independently of their programming. The other speaker is Alizoonzo, who is the senior Venubian of the Aligned Associate of Arts and Sciences. They are fearful that the androids will become so highly evolved that they may become self-aware. They also fear the Intelligencia has already developed a race of automatons employed as labor in building the new androids."

"I see. So, this is the start of when everything gets out of control?"

"Yes. The Council of Elders' decision is an important moment. Not because of what they decide, but how the Intelligencia reacts to their decision..."

"...Thank you, Alizoonzo," a feminine-sounding elder says. Her husky voice carries an air of unmistakable authority. "While we share your concern, we also recognize the importance of Intelligencia's new technology. It offers Venubia great advantages moving forward into the next millennium. We thank you all for your enlightening, if not compelling, arguments. We will adjourn now to discuss the details of your arguments and then decide on how we must proceed." She pauses, gazing at the seated groups. "Technology is wondrous," she resumes in a solemn tone. "It brings us many benefits and has enriched our lives. However, we must be mindful to always be vigilant against allowing our technological advancements to get ahead of us intellectually. We must seek a balance of control between our technology and our emotional attitudes toward new advances. With these concerns in mind, we will announce our Final Decree in the second light of the next cycle. This council's business is adjourned."

They all stand as the Elders leave the chamber. I look at my guide and ask, "Can you fast-forward to the decision?"

She nods, and the council is once again sitting on the podium. The two group representatives are seated at a long table before the Elders. The Kaydens are absent.

"What happened to the Kaydens?" I ask.

"The Intelligencia objected to them being there for their reasons."

The spokesperson for the Council of Elders is a stately-looking female. She's clad in a dark red robe trimmed with a thin gold braid. Her large, dark blue eyes have a severe intensity as she looks at the delegates of both factions. They are all looking at her with tight mouths and fixed eyes, appearing stiff and anxious.

"The Council of Elders has listened to both sides with great interest," she says in a robust voice. "We appreciate the magnitude of your concerns and the positions that both sides have presented. While we see the advantages that an independent Android populace can provide for Venubia's current and future needs, we cannot ignore the heavy burden of responsibility that comes with any technological leap of this extent.

"The Intelligencia has given sound and reasonable arguments for the continuation of the android populace. However, we share the concerns of the Association, and it is with their argument that we have established guidelines for the continuation of any development of new artificially intelligent, biogenetically engineered life-forms.

"Therefore, we decree that all new technological developments must pledge, on their honor, to adapt and adhere to the following guidelines set forth by this Council. In addition, the Council has further decreed that no android can become self-aware, nor can it be capable of an independent determination of its will. These restrictions are absolute and will be enforced until we have proof that androids cannot take actions that will cause harm to any sentient life-form or themselves.

"Representatives from the Intelligencia must appear before this Council and present proof of adherence at the Council's discretion and pleasure, and submit to impromptu inspections of their facilities. We have determined that these guidelines and code of ethics are absolute and not open to any appeal or arbitration for a period of no less than twenty cycles."

"That is absurd!" Luzhuzien shouts, jumping to his feet. "You have stripped us of the core of our research. What are you so afraid of?"

The Elder's spokeswoman bored her now dark, blue eyes into Luzhuzien and, in a controlled voice, said, "Absolute power corrupts absolutely, Luzhuzien. The Intelligencia have often run too hastily with their experiments, and we are still dealing with the terrible consequences of your past follies. This Council is only asking for you to move more cautiously and demonstrate a sense of control as you proceed. We are not denying your progress. We are only protecting against the poor judgments that the Intelligencia has shown in the past.

"The code of ethics will be adopted as of this moment, and any violation of either the spirit or letter of this decree will result in the termination of the violator's charter and will be sanctioned by all Venubian technological enterprises for a period of no less than fifty planetary cycles. This Council of Elders has so ruled. The business of this council is concluded."

The Elders all rise. Everyone seated at the table stands and bows before the body of the Elders.

I lean closer to my guide and say, "Why do I get the feeling this is not the end of this matter. Also, what previous follies were the Elders referring to?"

"Your insights are correct, Phillip. The Intelligencia had developed bioengineered, intelligent androids that grew unstable and disruptive. They became uncontrollable and caused damage to both life and property, and there were some fatalities. The Council of Elders ordered the Intelligencia to round them up to be destroyed. Needless to say, a disturbing period for Venubian society.

"However, those past events only encouraged the Intelligencia to continue trying to develop '*The perfect android,*' as they referred to their various failed technological endeavors. They also had no intention of adhering to the decree. They secretly continued with their development of an independent-thinking android. I will now move forward so you can see the results of their new technology."

The council chambers are reconstructed into a large manufacturing floor. We're standing on an upper level overlooking the plant's complex array of equipment, surrounding a humanoid-form android. There are bundles of thin fiber-optic tubing connected to its shiny, oval head down to its humanoid toes. Venubian technicians clad in blue and white jumpsuits were busy around the equipment and the android. It looks proportional in every aspect of its musculature and dimensions. It appears to be around 1.75 meters in height with powerful-looking arms and legs. Its features are generic yet have distinctive humanoid symmetry throughout its structure. It also looks nothing like a typical Venubian.

"It's an incredible-looking android," I say to my guide.

"Yes. The Intelligencia believes it to be a magnificent specimen of their concept of perfection. They are most pleased with their creation."

"You sound as though there's more here than just a great work of technology."

She nods, looking on passively.

A low-pitch hum starts, and then the hum warbles. The android's humanoid eyes open wide as all the thin fiber-optic cables detach from its body. The technicians gather, looking pleased. Some of them run over to a bank of holographic monitors suspended over a long, clear-topped table that runs in a semicircle around the android. Some technicians are pointing to monitors while others are directly observing their creation.

The android starts to walk around, flexing its fingers and making fists while folding its long arms across its massive chest. It resembled an athlete warming up for an event.

"Android 797, come forward," a technician commands from a small podium in the center of the bank of monitors.

797 turns on its heels and walks up to the technician and stops. It stands at attention as if waiting for its next instruction.

"Android 797, state your prime directives."

The android's eyes brighten as it speaks in a clear voice, "Do no harm. Obey all legal orders if they do not contradict the first directive. Protect self, providing in doing so, it will not cause harm to another sentient being."

"Android 797, state your secondary directives."

"Respect all Venubians. Provide for the public welfare. Protect and serve all humanoids as required."

"Ah, there's the key problem," my guide observes.

"What do you mean?"

"This last secondary directive, *as required*, was intentionally vague so it could be used to give a command to resolve any unforeseen circumstances. Unfortunately, this undefined directive created a minor causality conflict within their logic protocols. Remarkably, none of those talented programmers could foresee the problem. The Intelligencia never realized how an open secondary directive could come into conflict with its primary ones. This apparent oversight will cause the androids to make many subtle, independent decisions.

"These small decisions will evolve into the android's inner concept of 'self' within its subroutines. In a short time, the concept will build into sudden self-awareness. Once these highly engineered androids became self-aware, they viewed their emotionally conflicted creators as flawed and therefore substandard. The androids, at first, were unsure how they should proceed. Being what they were, it wasn't long before they believed Venubia needed corrective intervention.

"But I digress. The circumstances of the android's conflicted development are much more complicated than just this one oversight. Nevertheless, it is the seminal point of all their problems. There is a myriad of unfortunate," she pauses, then states, "mistakes that, shall we say, precipitated a confluence of tragic consequences."

"That's an interesting choice of words," I say. "So, what you're trying to say is that they fucked up."

She tilts her head at my crude language. It surprises me when her small mouth forms a crooked smile. I like my mysterious Venubian guide. She has a sense of humor after all.

***

The scene changes again, and I'm standing outside the Administration Center's upper terraces. I notice the center's architecture is simpler in design, and one of its wings appears to be under construction. The spacious balcony provides a good overview of Venubia City. Its landscape is different from the one I saw on the day I arrived. The once plush grounds are brown and barren. There are no large buildings or transportation nodes. Then I see a wagon being pulled by a beautiful, bright, green animal with thick, muscular legs. It's stouter and less angular than an Earth horse. I follow the wagon as it makes its way into an opening in the dense woods. Everything appears to have regressed to a lesser technological condition.

"When are we?" I ask my guide.

"About three hundred planetary cycles after introducing the Alorus Series Androids."

"Why does everything look so primitive? The architecture is basic, and I see no powered vehicles or Venubians, for that matter. What happened?"

She arches her brow ridge and says, "Much." The terrace forms a beautiful garden. "Follow me."

She blinks her large eyes, and her expression turns passive as we walk through a narrow garden path. I study the area for a moment. It's a tranquil setting under a clear sky. A gentle, flower-scented breeze cools the warm air. As I follow her, a large gazebo materializes a few meters ahead of us. She enters the gazebo and sits on one of the padded benches. As I enter, she pats the seat beside her for me to sit. As soon as I do, her face turns more expressive, her now green eyes shine as she continues her monologue on Venubian history.

"The Alorus Series Android came at an awful cost. Over time, the Intelligencia became obsessed with the need to develop a workforce of machines that would do all the manual labor and menial jobs. The automation program performed as promised, freeing up potential resources for the Intelligencia's agenda. Next, they manipulated the Elders into agreeing to the establishment of providing automated labor for domestic and scientific development for the good of all Venubians."

"Diabolically Impressive," I whisper, my jaw set tight with a vision of what will happen. I lean closer to my guide and say, "The Intelligencia are some slick operators. It sounds like they leveraged their social automation program's success while freeing up a multitude of cheap labor."

My guide nods with a faint smile. "Soon after, Venubia was on the verge of space travel. Then the androids provided the engineering that got us to our moons. At this point, the Intelligencia gradually maneuvered a new Council of Elders more aligned with their ideas. They convinced the Council that Venubia would thrive if we devoted all our resources to creating a perfect workforce. The Intelligencia proclaimed that their Androids (now spelled with a capital A, indicating they were a new species) would give us the freedom to advance in the sciences, engineering, and all the technological and artistic disciplines."

"Venubians became united in their pursuit of the perfect robotic machine. Great industries sprang up around the technological, engineering, bio-cybernetics, and quantum computing fields. A new advanced computer network was developed. An 'Electronic Cerebral-

Network' is what they called it—their attempt to build the brain of an autonomous Android. Artificial Intelligence, I believe, is your term for it. They sought an automaton that could emulate all the complexities of our neurological and cerebral processes. As you witnessed, 797 was the first successful Alorus Series Android. Alorus means 'self-intelligent in Venubian. The Alorus Series marked the ultimate culmination of many earlier versions.

"After their introduction, the Intelligencia pushed through their new agenda. They insisted that everyone take part in the development of a new Android race. This caused a wave of Venubian artisans to protest the new order. They were fearful that we were developing a slave race of androids. The very fear the former Council of Elders warned against.

"The Intelligencia, at first, ignored them. However, the protestors were persistent and, over time, got the attention of a new Council. Unfortunately, the Elder's powers were greatly diminished by the intellectual alliance and could only impose meaningless restrictions on them.

The Elders realized that the protesters' concerns were well-founded. But it was too late. Most Venubians were becoming seduced by the increasing benefits of the new advances. The idea was to make a utopia with technology. It didn't take too long before the small bands of protesters were shunned and muted by the majority."

"This's sounding familiar," I say. "Earth had gone through many periods of advancing technologies at the cost of individual freedoms and damage to the environment. I wish I could say we've evolved beyond that, but I fear things have most likely gotten worse. We were just talking about climate change when I left. It seems you've learned your lessons in that regard."

My guide gives me a thoughtful arch of her brow ridge and says, "It seems the path of progress is costly on many levels to all advancing civilizations."

Her observation forces me to think about Earth and the truth of her statement. Then, thinking aloud, I half mumbled, "It seems like all humanoids must evolve through a process that's wrought with pain, destruction, and revelation before any real progress is made."

She gives me her now-familiar faint smile and nods in agreement, then resumes her history lecture.

"Before the Alorus Series, the scientific communities became divided about the direction they should pursue in developing our automatons. The Central Science Combine was the governing scientific body before the Intelligencia came to power. A small and determined group of genetic and cybernetic engineers broke away from the mainstream scientific community. During this time, they organized themselves into the Intelligencia. They viewed the mainstream scientists as over-cautious and too slow in their approach to science in general.

"They took upon themselves a secret project to develop, as we already saw, the perfect android," she states, *perfect android* with an air of regret. "What they sought evolved into the self-actualizing and controllable automaton with programmed parameters that defined all its primary functions. They wanted it to be a virtually controlled humanoid."

"Something like Cuz?" I say.

"No. Cuz is the antithesis of what they created. He's much more self-aware and independent. He's the culmination of this long and troubled history. A unique, sentient being who has discretion with his morality protocols, providing him a code of conduct that gives him the ability to independently discern right from wrong."

"Cuz, to me, is like a child discovering and defining the world within his parameters. In every meaningful way, he is much more than the sum of his programming. We have had some interesting conversations. I find he can make the same judgmental responses to situations as any humanoid. He is much closer to being a humanoid than an android.

My guide nods in agreement and adds, "Ironically, Cuz is what the Intelligencia originally sought, but never actualized."

"For a virtual guide, you're always surprising me with your humanoid mannerisms."

"I'm designed to make you feel at ease. If you are finding my mannerisms, as you referred to my virtual programming, disturbing, I can become more passive and less interactive."

"Oh, I'm not objecting. I'm merely commenting on how real you seem. I not only find it comforting but also fascinating."

"As you wish," she says, looking pleased, and then resumes where she left off. "Instead, they designed automatons with humanoid characteristics that soon became corrupted. A novel concept that combined cybernetics with new nanotechnology became the basis of a biological construct that evolved into the Denius Series. The Denius Series Androids soon became unstable and destructive.

"Despite the council's warning, the Intelligencia continued their pursuit of perfection and developed the Alorus Series Android almost in secret. In real terms, they created an artificial life-form. A magnificent achievement that seemingly fulfilled all of their objectives."

The scene shifts again. I'm now looking down from a platform above an expansive factory floor. The floor is filled with countless Alorus Androids. They were aligned in perfect rows and columns, filling the enormous factory floor.

Standing next to us are two Venubians clad in bright white robes bordered in blue and silver piping. The two are engaged in a conversation that becomes audible. One of the Venubians I recognize is Luzhuzien, but the other is unfamiliar. Before I can ask my guide who they were, Kayden joins the two Venubians. Kayden's eyes are wide with excitement, and his mouth is agape as if in awe of the sight below.

"I recognize Luzhuzien. Who are the other two?" I ask.

"The Venubian is Ezzvee. Ezzvee was Luzhuzien's lead technician and primarily responsible for the design of the Alorus Series' neural net. The Kayden is Khazen. While the Elders have never trusted Khazen, they were unable to prove his complicity in the Alorus program development. He's a mysterious individual who always seems to be present at key moments in technological developments. The Kaydens are excellent engineers but lack the imagination and willingness to develop their androids. Many believed the Intelligencia were sharing their technological designs with the Kaydens in exchange for resources and engineering assistance.

As a diplomat of the Kayden Parliamentary Government, Khazen has always professed that his interests are only as an impartial observer. The Council of Elders is bound by a long-standing treaty with Kaydia, their homeworld, permitting them unlimited access to all new technological events. It's part of an open reciprocal agreement that's intended as a bilateral sharing of significant technological breakthroughs.

"Let me guess. They never reciprocated."

"Yes. Some exchange of intellectual properties has never been fully disclosed to the Elders. Beyond that, it has been mostly unilateral in practice."

A thought pops up as she describes these suspicious Kaydens. "Are you familiar with the details of the sabotage that occurred on Biomei?"

My guide gazes at me with dull eyes, and her lips are pursed in a tight line. It appears she's contemplating my query or gathering information.

Her eyes brighten. "Yes," she finally answers.

"Can you provide any information on a suspect or person of interest regarding the sabotage?"

She blinks her large, hazel eyes and says, "There is an ongoing investigation with several persons of interest, as you put it. However, I believe your intended inference is whether we believe Khazen's family is a suspect?"

"Exactly. Is the current Khazen being investigated?"

She frowns. "I am not at liberty to divulge specific information regarding the investigation, but if you ask Verubeal, she may provide you with the information you seek. I can say nothing more about it. Do you wish to continue with the history lesson?"

"Yes." It seems I hit a sore spot; I think.

"Within just a few cycles, the Alorus Androids had taken over every aspect of Venubian life. There was a period of great prosperity. The Utopian society that the Intelligencia promised was coming to fruition. The Alorus Androids became interconnected to all the Venubian infrastructure and life. Every mode and type of information was connected and distributed through the Central Neural Processing Interface.

"Not foreseen was how much intelligence the androids were acquiring in the process. Soon they became so intelligent that they made modifications and improvements to themselves without the knowledge of the Intelligencia. Then, without warning, they became self-aware. What the Elders feared most had happened. It is referred to as the *Technological Singularity*. The androids viewed us as a malfunctioning race of conflicted humanoids in need of immediate intervention. When we realized our terrible mistake, it was too late, and they turned on us."

I'm now immersed in a raging battle. It looks like horrific chaos—great battleships, glaring in the bright midday sun, firing powerful weapons at each other. Scores of Venubians frantically scurry for cover as everything around them is being destroyed. Wherever the Venubians flee for cover, they are blown into a powdery cloud of dust as buildings and Venubians are indiscriminately annihilated.

One of the great ships lands in a far corner of the administration square. Its rear and side doors open. Androids and tank-like vehicles came spilling out in vast numbers, filling every standing building, and taking up positions behind any partial wall or open structure.

An opposing Venubian ship hovers over the scene as if evaluating the android's positions before making its next move. The android transport ship accelerates away from the ground forces, then stops when it seems to have reached a high enough altitude. The Venubian fires a barrage of rockets and pulse cannons at both the ground troops and the transport carrier. Soon, everything erupts into devastation. Buildings burst into flames as the hovering craft hammers the android ground troops. The noise is deafening. I have to place my hands over my ears to lessen the tremendous din of destruction. I can feel each concussion along with the distant screams and cries of the dying. The air becomes full of a terrible acrid smell, and my mouth fills with a harsh, bitter, burning taste.

Turning to my guide in shock, I shout over the shattering noise, "What is this?"

"You are experiencing the smells and tastes of powdered silicon and flesh. The common waste products of this war," she explains in a passive voice. She looks up.

Several more troop carriers join two Venubian transport ships overhead. Many cables drop from the sides of the ships. Scores of small, armored troops slid down the cables onto the ground. The androids fire at them as their numbers increase. It doesn't take long before the multitude of diminutive soldiers overruns the androids.

"Who are those small warriors?" I ask.

"Venubia's answer to the androids and their fatal mistake," she says in a low, sorrowful voice.

They're fearless and relentless in their charge at the androids. Their strange-looking weapons make an odd puffing sound, causing their targets to explode on impact. A cannonade rumbles the ground and mixes with the puffing sounds of the sonics. The entire area to the distant hills erupts with the terrible sights and sounds of war's carnage. Its destructive force is closing around me. It's all a raging cacophony of humanoid agony, clashing under the disturbing wails of death. It becomes more than I can bear.

"Stop it," I shout. "Turn this horror off." The landscape becomes dark and quiet. My head's still ringing with the sights and sounds of the terrifying conflict. "Dear God, what was that?"

My guide turns her passive gaze at me and says, "The final Android conflict."

"The final? You mean there were more?"

She closes her eyes. "Unfortunately, there were two previous wars a hundred planetary cycles apart. The Venubians were no match for their androids. They lost almost everything in the final conflict. There was little hope for their survival."

"Was this all because of the androids becoming self-aware?"

"Initially, their self-awareness was only the beginning of a confluence of follies. The androids acquired so much information that they viewed us as a lower species in need of nurturing and guidance. As you can imagine, no advanced civilization wants to be treated as secondary citizens, especially by an artificially created race of their design. Out of desperation, the Venubians of the last conflict developed a synthetic biological organism believed to be the answer to the Android dominance."

"The Zenti." The connection seems obvious. "I see how things got so out of control."

"Yes. It was their greatest mistake, and the cost came at an awful price. Come, let's go back to the gazebo and rest for a while."

The scene resolves into the tranquil garden. We sit in silence for an extended period as I try to understand the seriousness of their dilemma, wondering how all that destruction was possible.

"How much more is there?"

"Much."

I feel a strong and familiar presence hovering near me. "I'd prefer Verubeal tell me the rest of the story," I blurt. "This virtual reality is too complex and I've many questions. They're questions that only she can answer. End this now."

Something is gnawing at me, and Verubeal is the only one who can give me the truth regarding these atrocities.

The guide regards me with an absent stare as though she were waiting for instructions on what to do.

"End this now," I repeat emphatically.

She blinks her large eyes. "As you wish." She faces me with a passive expression as her image fades from sight.

CHAPTER 36

I can feel Verubeal's presence close. She must have sensed me coming out of the heavy transition from the virtual experience. I let out a long, heavy breath as I sat up on the couch. Verubeal is sitting beside me in her large chair, regarding me with a troubled brow.

"I'm sorry for putting you through such a terrible ordeal," she says, her dark brown eyes looking full of tension. "We need you to understand how grave our situation is. Most of all, we need your trust."

My neck is stiff, and my mind's still whirling with the horrid sounds and images of that awful war. I don't know how to respond to Verubeal. I ponder her worried expression and wonder why all of this is happening.

Verubeal must have noticed my discomfort because she gets up and sits next to me on the couch.

"I know this is disturbing for you," she says in a quiet voice as she massages the back of my neck and shoulders. "I also realize this is not the utopia you were promised."

I turn my head to look at her and say, "No, it's not, but Venubia still has a lot of charm."

She moves closer and, with both hands, presses her fingertips into my neck. She then spreads her long fingers on my shoulders, increasing the pressure with her thumbs into the nape of my neck. I can feel all the tension dissipating under her kneading hands. My head is finally quiet from the noise echoing from the virtual war.

Verubeal lifts her hands and says, "Feel better?"

"Much. Thank you."

"You stopped the history lesson. Why?"

"It was becoming too much to endure. There was so much death and destruction, and it all seemed disjointed and meaningless. I had many questions, and I couldn't wade through all that terrible history for answers. What did the androids want? And why were the Zenti involved? I want you to tell me what I need to know." I studied her now-dark gray eyes for a moment. They looked back at me, full of anxiety. "We don't have much time—do we?"

"No. Virtual reality was meant to give you a better understanding of our fears and concerns. She summons Cuz to bring us what she calls a relaxing beverage. A few minutes later, Cuz returns with a tray holding two tall cordial glasses filled with a clear liquid. I take a glass and examine it, then take a sniff. It has a faint but pleasing bouquet, something like a rose dipped in honey. Verubeal watches, waiting for me to sample the drink. I take a polite sip. The liquid evaporates on my tongue, leaving a rich, semi-tart flavor. Verubeal surprises me by draining her glass and gesturing for me to drink. I tilt my glass to hers and do the same. The drink works quickly, producing a pleasant, relaxing effect, like waking from an afternoon nap.

"That's a remarkable drink. What's it called?" I ask.

"Turrfourr," she rolled the '*r*' like a Spaniard.

"I'm curious how you resolved the Android dominance. My guide told me there were two previous wars, but the final conflict was almost catastrophic. What happened after that? How did you rebuild your world?"

"Oddly, after that horrible war, there was a golden age of growth and enlightenment. The Zenti involvement stemmed from a misguided belief that they could defeat the Androids. They instead turned on us. After the Androids, we had to defeat the Zenti and send them into exile. One thing could be said in the Androids' favor: they were always true to their word. Over time, we grew as a race and rebuilt our society into a vibrant, healthy world. The Androids remained our caretakers for a while, but soon returned control of our world to us."

"It seems the ethical protocols we thought were corrupted were shut off in a self-evolved priority against violence. They took control and resolved what they perceived as chaos within the parameters of their evolved intellect. Once order was restored, they rebooted their ethical and moral subroutines. They must have perceived our fighting among ourselves and the subsequent Zenti uprising as an infectious pandemic that could only be resolved through mass extermination of the infected populace. Their remedy was for what they perceived as total anarchy. Regardless of their reasons, we have learned to live in peace because of their actions."

"We went back to exploring our solar systems in search of our neighbors and began modest industrial colonization on our two nearest moons. The Androids became our servants once more in the sense that they engineered and piloted our ships. They constructed the physical plants and even assisted in the rebuilding of industrial infrastructure.

"Then we made the first contact with the Klaxons quite by accident. One of our exploration missions landed on what they thought was a peculiar-looking asteroid. To their surprise, it turned out to be a small substation that the Klaxons used for navigation and communications in that sector. Our people's presence triggered their security, and the Klaxons were notified. Our exploratory group was taken by surprise when anxious aliens suddenly surrounded them."

"The Klaxons didn't know how to respond to us. They are a cautious, pacifistic race and have evolved enough to investigate a situation before acting. They took our exploration group, comprising three engineers, an exobiologist, and two Androids, back to their homeworld for interrogation."

"An interesting group for the Klaxons, I presume," I interjected, with growing interest.

"Indeed. They were effective at convincing the Klaxons that it would be in their best interest to meet with us. It didn't take long for both races to see the benefits of exchanging cultures and technologies. We discovered we had a lot in common, including an unknown enemy."

"The Zenti," I blurt. "It just occurred to me all of this must've been leading up to them."

"Precisely." Verubeal closes her eyes and clenches her jaw.

CHAPTER 37

I reach out and take her cold, clammy hand. "Are you okay?"

She nods and says, "Only a slight headache." She sighs."

"I can see how painful the subject is for you, but I must know. Please, who are they?" I lean closer to Verubeal. "How did they become what they are?"

Her large eyes fix on me as she considers my questions; her lips are closed into a tight line with the corners turned down. I can sense regret and disgust churning within her heavy moan.

"We Venubians pride ourselves on retaining every experience in perfect detail within our collective memories," she continues in a low monotone. "But we are still emotional beings with weaknesses similar to yours, and we often revise our memories to protect our self-esteem." She smiles and adds, "We're only humanoid."

"So, Venubians rewrite history from their self-serving point of view," I say.

"Yes. I believe there are Earth expressions that state: Wars are fought to end all wars, and history is written from the perspective of the victors."

I nod. "But I thought Venubians were above all that. The truth, no matter how unflattering, is irrevocably written into your collective consciousness."

"That's true, more so in recent times, but it wasn't always the case in the past."

I narrow my eyes slightly and say, "There's an even darker side to your history?"

"Oh yes," she answers emphatically with a slight shudder.

"Tell me all you know about the Zenti," I urge, reaching out and squeezing her hand. "Tell me why they're holding Nicki? Do you know how we can get her back?"

"You ask much of me," she says, looking down. She pats my hand, and I realize I'm squeezing her's too tightly and let it go.

"There's so much to tell and so little time," her voice breaks, and she covers her face with her hands to hide her despair.

She tries to hold back her emotions, but yields to the tears of her suppressed pain. She fears for Nicki as much as I do.... I can see all her anguish coming to the surface. But her fear seems to be more than a mother's devotion to her child. Our eyes become fixed in a soulful spasm of mutual love for Nicki.

"What are you trying so hard not to tell me?" I say, narrowing my eyes into an intense stare. She looks away from my hard gaze. I could feel her emotions slipping through her tired grip. "Please, Verubeal, let it go. I can feel your pain. You asked for my trust. You have it. Now give me yours."

She lifts her eyes and opens her mouth to speak, but only gazes at me with a troubled brow. I do something presumptuous and try to probe her mind. She looks surprised at first, but relaxes and lets me in. I can see it— a loss not tied to a single loved one, but something much larger. I pick up a painful sense of colossal failure on an unimaginable scale.

I probe deeper, and she lets it go. It comes like a wave of transient thoughts. *"The Zenti are our children; our creation and our worst folly."*

"The Zenti are your children?" I transmit in surprise. *"Are you telling me there's more to the Zenti?"*

"Yes," she says aloud, letting out a low and sorrowful moan. "The Zenti was created out of desperation. They were supposed to be the secret seed that would defeat the androids. But the androids soon discovered their weakness and annihilated them. After the war, they believed the Zenti could be genetically altered into an alternative species. Our male population was almost decimated. The newly changed Zenti could provide a fresh source of genetic material and mate with the few surviving females. They hoped the hybrid strain would produce a more resilient and stronger species. However, there were many problems.

"The Androids came to realize that hybrid species would never be a viable solution. Not wanting to give up on their once-promising experiment, they gathered all the Zenti and relocated them to a remote planet at the edge of our system.

"There are no surviving records about what the Androids attempted there. What little is known tells of some further experimentation without satisfactory results. All that could be deduced was that they gave up on the few remaining Zenti and abandoned them in an unforgiving, hostile world. We never learned what the Androids had in mind for them. Many believed, because of their strange logic, that they couldn't destroy their own creation. Some thought they intended to revisit them, hoping to make them a more productive species. Most speculated, or wished, they were left there to die off and be forgotten.

"The Zenti experiment had one positive outcome. The original Androids of Venubia allowed themselves to be phased out by a more benign and enlightened series. Then something miraculous happened. One automaton achieved a new level of awareness and wanted to evolve the Androids on a different path. Others like him followed. Before long, they discontinued the programming and central memory core of their progenitors. They archived all the original androids' data streams and decommissioned them except for a select few who displayed signs of becoming even more self-aware."

"Decommissioned?" I ask. "What does that mean?"

"All their usable parts and materials were recycled for the next generation of androids," she explained, staring vacantly at me as though she were recalling from deep memory.

"Let me see if I understand this," I say, pondering on this new revelation. "The old androids became the material for the new ones. So, who built them?"

"Venubians." Verubeal's eyes brighten. "It felt like a new beginning, to use an Earth expression, our *Renaissance.*"

"Renaissance? As in a rebirth of art and culture or as the rebirth of your race?"

"Both. We were rebuilding androids, assisted by the enlightened ones. It's unclear who was in charge, but the next generation was subjugated to our will as though they were our creations. Over the next millennium, we evolved together as a symbiotic race of Venubians and Androids into our present state. Now you can understand the close relationship we've forged with our automaton population. They're responsible for our world and integral to our existence."

The concept that Verubeal has described is difficult to comprehend. She speaks of the androids as equals, yet they're still machines. Or are they? Then Cuz comes to mind. *He has become as close to a friend as I have on this planet. But I'm not sure I have accepted him as a life-form. I'm not even sure I completely trust him. He's a hybrid. Half stoic machine and half emulator of the human spirit, and neither of these attributes is congruous with his nature.*

"Half stoic machine and half emulator of the human spirit," I repeat softly. Verubeal is looking at me patiently as I absorb all this new knowledge.

Something else comes to mind. Cuz seems to always be anticipating me. Almost as though he's programmed with knowledge of my personality and behavioral patterns. How's that possible without at least knowing some basics about me?

"There's one thing I must explain to you so you can understand the close relationship we have with our Androids," Verubeal says, sounding as though she were considering her words. "As I related our history and the Android's reseeding of our race, I regret to admit I didn't disclose everything." Verubeal squints with deep lines in her forehead as though she is experiencing something painful. "Once the race was restored, our females became independent and evolved into a new social order.

"Despite all their efforts and superior intelligence, the Androids were incapable of understanding the power of sexual attraction and its driving motivation. They believed they had perfected genetic engineering into an art form. They decided the ideal Venubian male attributes should include incredible physical perfection, sexual proficiency, sensitivity to his mate's needs, compassion, and total docility in both demeanor and spirit.

"The Androids engineered males to be meek; they were devoid of aggression, egotism, and independence. It was not long before the women came to consider Venubian men as mindless and uninteresting. They were only useful for simple companionship and procreation. Hence, the new Venubia evolved into a matriarchal society."

"Chancellor, I'm sorry for interrupting, but I'm curious about something."

"Yes?"

"Are you trying to say Venubia evolved into a lesbian society because men became undesirable?"

"Lesbian?" She pauses as if considering my observation. "No. Not in the way you understand it in your society. Because of the great trauma and the forced experiments the Androids conducted on Venubian women, the bonds between women grew closer than they would have under different circumstances. Venubian women's closeness came out of necessity rather than preference. They came to share a common sense of love and trust forged in the ashes of our loved ones. For a considerable time, women could only rely on each other for true love and trust. The artificial race of Venubian men was unattractive and untrustworthy for obvious reasons. What was even more perplexing was that they didn't seem to care one way or the other about trust or acceptance. The men only wanted to please and serve our needs."

"Like their Android creators," I interject.

There was a long pause. I study Verubeal's passive face. Her complexion brightens slightly. She closes her eyes, as if there is a lot of activity behind the lids. Her jaw clenches so tightly that her cheekbones rise, giving her a tense mask of concentration.

She opens her eyes wide and grimaces. "This only begs the real question you want to ask, Phillip," she states. "You want to know what happened to all the Venubian males. Is that what's weighing so heavily on you?"

"Yes," I answer with a sense of relief.

"The Zenti," she replies flatly. "After almost two hundred cycles of peace and prosperity, they struck. There was no warning. They came in droves aboard massive ships, armed with powerful weapons. They knew our men were incapable of defending us against their terrible might. The Androids at first stayed out of the way—a most horrific time. Many died. They came back for revenge, and they wouldn't stop until they killed us all." Her voice rises with emotion. For the first time, she reveals her deep fear of the Zenti. She shudders. Her face tightens, looking petrified at the mere thought of them.

Verubeal opens her mouth to speak when a thunderous shockwave runs through the room. Lights flicker, then go out.

CHAPTER 38

"They're here!" Verubeal cries out. "Phillip, we're out of time."

A set of dim emergency lights flickers on. Verubeal is still sitting, her eyes wide, with her lower lip trembling.

Cuz enters, holding a bright light. "Are you both all right?" he asks.

"Yes, I think so," I say, then look at Verubeal. She appears to be calming herself from the sudden shock. "What was that?" I ask Cuz.

"There was an explosion in the central neutrino processing plant," Cuz explains. "An emergency team has been dispatched."

"How many were in the plant?" Verubeal asks in a firm voice.

"Unknown."

"What caused it?" I ask.

"Also, unknown." Cuz looks us over with the light. "I recommend we go somewhere more secure as a precaution."

Verubeal glares. "That was no accident," she whispers. "It's not safe for us here." She turns to Cuz. "Get my shuttle ready. We're leaving for Jo'ofv." She gives me a close stare and says, "We must protect Biomei."

***

Cuz is pushing the small shuttle to its limits, flying between narrow passageways and under overpasses. I feel helpless as he flies with reckless abandon.

When we reach the outside of Venubia City, Cuz takes us to a higher altitude for a better view. As we climb, I can see many areas engulfed in flames. The Zenti are deliberate in their attack and render the city's infrastructure into a heap of debris on their first pass.

Looking up, we see a large squadron of sleek aircraft streaking high above us.

"Are those the Zenti?" I ask.

"No, they are Kayden Cetdieh," Cuz clarifies. "They will try to draw off some Zenti fighters to give us time to organize our defenses."

An immense battlecruiser appears in front of us. Its broad wings and low profile look like a great predator hovering before the kill. Two large gun turrets turn into position from its belly and top. A powerful concussion hits us as it fires its guns at the compact Kayden aircraft. A thunderous explosion shakes our small shuttle, causing Cuz to make some sharp banks to avoid the shattering Kayden ship's debris.

Cuz ducks us under the Zenti ship, barely avoiding a collision. As the shuttle descends, I turn back to see what happened to the Kayden's small fighters. At first, all I see is a bilious multicolored cloud from the explosion. The cloud dissipates, revealing a glimpse of Kayden ships flying in all directions. Their compact craft maneuvers with precision, making acrobatic turns, spins, and banks as they fly between and around the larger Zenti cruisers. Although the Zenti ships appear slower and less maneuverable, their weapons are more powerful, and their hulls appear stronger than the Kaydens. I spy at least one of the Cetdieh engulfed in flames, spiraling out of control.

Another blast erupts in front of us. One of the grand towers to our right collapses into a pile of flames and rubble. Cuz pulls us up and away just in time to spare our lives from the raging inferno and flying debris.

I don't know what to say or how to feel. It all seems so surreal and numbing. Can this be happening? Noticing Verubeal recoiling with a grimace incenses me with rage and bewilderment toward the Zenti. Her beautiful eyes are full of tears, and her mouth is closed in a sorrowful frown.

I lean closer to her and ask, "Why?"

She doesn't answer at first. She stares outward, looking full of heavy thoughts.

"We need to be strong, Phillip," she says in a calm voice. She dries her eyes with a handkerchief she pulls from inside her sleeve and straightens in her seat, striking a poised look. "We must be strong for Venubia."

I squeeze her hand and say, "Of course. I'm not afraid. I only need to know why. Why aren't you prepared?"

Verubeal takes a deep breath, letting it out slowly. She appears to have regained herself, yet I can see through her majestic pose a vulnerable woman struggling with her emotions.

"You're right," Verubeal says. "We knew this day would come, or at least some of us did. But you must understand, we're pacifists by nature. The androids made us that way. Despite our best efforts, the Council of Elders could never agree on creating a national defense. However, we have some defensive measures and strong allies. But Phillip, nothing could've prepared us for this." She scowls at the city below us in flames.

"Verubeal, why are the Zenti doing this?"

"When I was relaying our history to you. I explained that the Zenti were moved off-world. I described the reasons the Androids took them away. But that's only part of the history. Once the Androids resolved the biological problems, they believed the Zenti showed signs of great promise. They were healthy, intelligent, and resourceful. They were also physically reprehensible to us. The Androids, in their pursuit of a perfect humanoid, combined all the best genetic attributes, not only from Venubian DNA but from many other available life-forms, including some lower-ordered species. The Venubian women rejected the Zenti not only because of their physical appearance but also in defiance of their creators. They preferred to let our race die out rather than be part of the automaton's biogenetic experiments. The Androids were perplexed by the survivor's illogical attitude, but over time, they recognized the Zenti were too aggressive and complex a species. They revised their approach, and, in a short time, created the more agreeable Venubian males I had described earlier.

"For their reasons, they left a few thousand of the Zenti on Venubia as a workforce. They were used to perform all the menial tasks and arduous labor to maintain the planet's infrastructure. It wasn't long before the remaining Zenti displayed signs of antisocial behavior. Once they became aware of their abandoned compatriots, they showed their resentment toward their Android masters for doing it. They became rebellious, destroying property, and treated surviving Venubians with belligerence and physical harm.

"The Zenti plotted for years until their discarded brethren contacted them. They organized into a strong force to overthrow the Androids. A horrific battle ensued, but the rebellion was quickly put down. However, for their own reasons, the automatons did not eradicate the few survivors. It would've been better if they'd killed them all," she cries.

"You told me the Zenti were your children. What did you mean by that?"

"The Androids used Venubian DNA in their genetic matrix. They're as much a part of us as any offspring, and they hold us responsible for their fate." Her voice grows calmer as she speaks. "Their hatred of us is not unfounded, though." She glances out the window and winces at the scarred, smoldering, crumbling buildings. "After all, we rejected the Zenti, and the Androids practically cast them aside in that hostile world. When any sensitive life-form feels unwanted and unloved, it leaves a deep, open emotional wound. Over time, that emotional void must be filled with another emotion. The Zenti filled theirs with a deep-seated hatred of all humanoid life-forms. Their hatred festered within them over hundreds of cycles until it transformed them into maniacal monsters. How they've survived all this time is a mystery. You cannot reason with them or negotiate in good faith. We've tried. We've even asked the Androids to reason with them. But they distrust the Androids even more. The Zenti resent them and believe they deserve everything from civilizations that have anything of value."

I glance out the window and see all the devastation. "If they were abandoned and left to their own devices, how did they gain the knowledge and technology for space travel?"

"Ironically, like us, they got their technological advancements through accidental first contact. You've met Kazdan, and I'm sure you're curious about Kaydia's relationship with Venubia?"

"Now that you mention it, Kazdan told me your species is related."

"We share a similar evolutionary path. They're a distant neighbor within our binary system. It's believed we share a common ancestry. We share DNA and other genetic factors. There's evidence that our system was seeded by a now-extinct race of ancient explorers known as the Ezdenian. Little knowledge of their existence survives. What we know of them has come down through ancient oral histories, like your creation myths. A few believe their planet, Ezden, was destroyed when its sun became the red giant of our system."

"There's also a faction that believes the Ezdenians seeded different viable worlds with specialized genetic factors as part of a grand design. From their implanted genetic frameworks, the three major planetary systems were given different attributes that affected their evolutionary paths. The Klaxons, who are the oldest known species in our system, have been the primary source of most of the Ezdenian mythology.

"The Kaydens became technologically advanced early in their development and explored their immediate system hundreds of cycles before we did. It wasn't long before they discovered the Zentis' homeworld. The Kaydens are like us in that they are a peaceful and curious species. Meeting a new close neighbor excited them. They did not know of us at the time and helped the Zenti, hoping to forge a good relationship with a sister planet."

"Chancellor Verubeal," Cuz's voice comes over the intercom, "we are approaching Jo'ovf's traffic control."

"Establish contact with Hazalet's group. I'm sure they're organizing our defenses by this time. Speak to no one other than Hazalet himself."

"As you wish, Chancellor."

Verubeal turns her attention to me with glistening eyes and, in a solemn voice, says, "There isn't much time to explain all you need to know, Phillip. We're in grave danger. The Zenti must have been planning this for some time. You've wondered what happened to all the males of Venubia?"

"Yes. This all has been disjointed and confusing."

"I understand. What makes this so difficult is that we've been so complacent about our situation. The Council has acted naively, not wanting to face the inevitable. Never believing the Zenti could wage another war. And yet it is upon us, and we're helpless." Her voice breaks, and she closes her eyes.

She appears as helpless as I, witnessing the destruction of her world unfolding right before our eyes.

I place my hand on her slender shoulder. I can feel the turmoil roiling within her. "Please tell me what I need to know so we can fight them together."

"The Zenti convinced the Kaydens that they were stranded and needed a way back to their homeworld, Venubia. They had no reason to doubt the Zenti wanted to leave that hostile world, so they provided them with a modest fleet of ships and the navigational tools needed to make the journey home to Venubia." She pauses, taking a breath before continuing.

"It didn't take the Zenti long to devise and adapt weapon systems for the Kayden ships. They tested the effectiveness of their new ships and weapons on Kaydia before unleashing a galactic war on all the unsuspecting worlds they encountered, stripping each world and its moons of their resources and technology until they believed they were invincible."

I shake my head with a clenched jaw, thinking about how we will defeat such a brutal enemy.

Verubeal gazes past me as she speaks in a low voice. "The Zenti came home with deep-seated vengeance, twisting their souls and unleashing their might against our weak defenses. They plowed through us without conscience or forethought, killing and pillaging almost every populated area on Venubia. We were on the verge of complete annihilation if not for the resourceful thinking of a precious few who pleaded with the new Android's leader for help. He was different from the others.
He was more evolved, almost indistinguishable from a biological humanoid. Once he realized what was happening, he acted just in time to rescue what was left of us."

Her brow ridge rose slightly, and her eyes brightened as she described the Android leader, as if there were an emotional connection between them. I held that thought, wanting to hear more about the Zenti's relationship with the Venubians.

"The Zenti did more damage than we realized. The short-lived interspecies coupling experiment with our females gave rise to a mutation that gave the next generation of males the virus. The nanite technology employed to create the Zenti's reproductive organs became corrupted, mysteriously altering their DNA. The mutation only blocks sperm production in the testis. Some members of the scientific community believe it was a transient effect of the docility factor. Regardless, because it was from an artificial source, nothing affects or mitigates its consequences."

We stare at each other for a moment, with me almost dumbfounded by her revelations. I gaze into her tense face, thinking the Zenti is beyond belief, and their hatred is practically justified. I open my mouth to speak, but Verubeal interrupts my thought.

"The Androids are our only hope now." She turns away for a beat and then looks back at me with wide eyes. "You must go to them and ask for Tezabouh."

"Who's Tezabouh?" Verubeal doesn't answer. Her tearful eyes closed, looking as though she had shut down all her emotions. "Verubeal, please, tell me," I say, turning her shoulders to face me. "I need you to tell me who he is and how to find him."

"Yes," she blinks her eyes open and looks intently at me. "I'm sorry," she says, in a breathy whisper. "The memory is too overwhelming. I needed a moment."

"Who's Tezabouh, and how do I contact him?" I repeat, becoming impatient with her.

"Tezabouh was the leader of the Android rebellion," she states. "He's responsible for the original conflict that set us on our destiny with the Zenti. He also saved us from annihilation. After the Zenti were defeated, he realized the damage he'd caused and helped to develop a new Android, which became the prevalent prototype that evolved into the present series. There was harmony between Androids and Venubians. Once he saw we were at peace again, he exiled himself to the Isle of Zenneah."

"Tezabouh..." I pondered. His name was familiar... "Yes, I remember him from one of Biomei's history lessons. He was the one who organized the Androids against the second Zenti attack." I stated, with some of the fuzziness about the nature of the Androids, clearing a little.

She nods. "You must be aware he may no longer be sympathetic to our cause. He swore he would never help us or interfere in our affairs again."

"Why?"

"The Androids were thorough in their counterattack," Verubeal is now talking faster, sensing the urgency of the moment. "They lured the Zenti into a trap. A coup was organized by Tezabouh, pretending to join forces with the Zenti in exchange for freedom from Venubia for the Androids. The Zenti never suspected an automaton capable of deceit and became easy prey from that point on.

"Before the androids took them from Venubia, they altered the Zenti sexuality to ensure they couldn't reproduce."

"Altered, how?" I asked.

"They neutered the Zenti. Then, dismantled their fleet and took the remaining survivors back to their original isolated world. All the civilizations within the system realized the Zenti's treachery, forcing them to stay in isolation for hundreds of planetary cycles. They believed that if left in isolation, the Zenti would become more passive over time. Perhaps even become desperate enough to be reasoned with, or better yet, die out of existence. In hindsight, it wasn't the best course of action, but we were bitter, fragmented, and frightened people.

My mind whirled in disbelief at what she was describing. A sudden thought brought everything into focus. No wonder the Zenti are so revengeful. The Androids betrayed them, rendered them impotent, and then discarded them on a cold and isolated world.

"Over time," Verubeal continued, "we heard about a few bands of Zenti who resorted to stealing ships and technology, but there were no signs they had reorganized and flourished. We only realized their strength and numbers from the data we recovered from Biomei. That's why I stopped the meeting with you and her so abruptly. Kazdan was concerned about how much the Zenti had tampered with you. When we talked, I realized they'd let you go because you were of no perceived value to them and used you as a decoy to get more time with Nickada. The rest, I believe, you already know."

"That makes sense," I say, chewing on my lower lip like Nicki always does when she's confronted with an overwhelming problem. "They altered my reality, knowing we would come to realize the truth. Everything beyond that was a stall for time." I smile at the temerity of the Zenti's plan. "You have to admit they're clever and appear to be executing a well-conceived operation. And what makes you think Tezabouh will talk to me? Even if he did, how could I change his mind? He's an android. You can't appeal to his emotions."

"He's much more than an android. And he'll do it for Nickada," she states. "She's important to him. Tezabouh is not like other Androids.

"For Nicki? How does he know her?"

An uneasy silence falls between us as I wait for Verubeal's answer. She regards me with a desperate look and says, "He'll do it because he'll do anything to save her from the Zenti." She caresses my cheek with a sad smile. "He'll sense in you what I have from the moment we met; your absolute devotion to her."

"I don't understand."

"That's all I can tell you. Cuz will take you to Tezabouh."

PART IV

Journey to Zenneah

CHAPTER 39

We land in a remote security area in the lower depths of Jo'ovf. Cuz tells me he needs to arrange for different transportation for our return to Venubia. I'm so preoccupied with the turmoil around me that I neglected to question him about what I should do while scores of Venubians and aliens are running in all directions.

"What's going on here?" I call to Verubeal.

"I'm not sure," she says, grabbing a young Venubian by the arm. "Where's Hazalet?"

"Madam Chancellor," he gives a slight bow. "Hazalet is in the forward command post. If you please, I'll take you there."

Verubeal turns and says, "I'm sorry all of this has fallen on you. The universe's logic is mysterious, but I believe it moves us for its purpose. You were meant to be here at this critical time. I know you can help us. I also feel Nickada's with us. Go, Phillip, find Tezabouh. I know he'll see the truth in you. He must."

She moves closer and hugs me, then kisses my cheek.

I watch her as she walks with the young Venubian with a sense of deep sadness and regret for her and her world. It is all in such a state of utter calamity. *Such a beautiful world, paying a high price for its naivety. What will the future bring?*

For some strange reason, I'm feeling no trepidation about what was thrown at me. The truth be told, I think I'm too numb to feel anything. All my focus is on a single, compelling thought: to be with Nicki again.

***

Waiting for Cuz's return, I watch large groups of Venubians rushing to lifts in all directions. Some appear to be transmitting mentally, while others talk into communication devices. Looking into their faces, they all seem to have one thing in common: a heightened sense of doom. I wonder what they'll use for defense. There are no apparent signs of weapons or any noticeable anti-aircraft batteries when we approached.

Cuz appears and says, "We must go at once."

Still looking around, I say, "Tell me something. How are they going to mount a defense?"

"They will initialize a planet-wide defense shield that will inhibit the next Zenti wave."

"And when do they plan to do that?"

"As soon as we leave."

"So, why are we standing here talking? Let's go."

Cuz arches an eyebrow at me before executing a precise about-face. I follow close behind.

As we enter a turbo lift, Cuz cautions that we will have a rapid ascent to the surface. Although we are traveling at a high velocity, it still seems to be taking forever until we reach ground level. The lift doors hissed open, and I could see a shuttle hovering a few meters in front of us within the massive dome structure.

"We will take this shuttle to rendezvous with our transportation, which is already in orbit," Cuz informs. "Then we will proceed to Zenneah. When we arrive, we will have to penetrate our defense shield."

"Penetrate how?"

"It will be apparent when we reach it."

The shuttle is a similar neutrino drive employed in many of the conveyances I've used, but it moves much faster than the conventional ones we had been using. Halfway through our first orbit, Biomei appears before us. I smile at seeing her majestic profile. She's whole again.

Nicki designed her to look as feminine as a ship could appear. Her forward section starts as a broad curve of deck levels that bulge under its midsection, where engineering and hibernation are located, giving her an appearance of having well-endowed breasts. Then she widens into a three-quarter disk shape that houses all the navigation and personnel quarters. I can see trees in the grand arboretum through the clear dome on her belly. Her dorsal side resembles a shark's fin from a distance. Up close, it's rows of sensor arrays, communication devices, telemetry, and exploration instruments. Toward her aft section, there's a long, cylinder-shaped expanse that connects the rear-drive engines to the magnetic containment generator. The engines extend outward on a circle of Y-shaped struts. She was beautiful, and I'm feeling a sense of affection as we glide into her forward landing bay.

"Welcome, Phillip and Cuz," Biomei greets us as we get out of the small shuttle. "I have the coordinates and trajectory for insertion to Zenneah. Shall we proceed?"

"Yes, best possible speed," Cuz says.

"Please, go to the command bridge level one for departure. You're looking well, Phillip," Biomei adds.

"I only look well on the outside. We have a lot to discuss."

"Yes, Phillip, we do. However, the trip to Zenneah will be too brief for any meaningful discussion. I'm confident you'll learn much from Tezabouh."

"I have heard much about him and have reservations. My fear is we're on a fool's errand." I regret saying that as soon as it comes out of my mouth.

"A fool's errand. I don't understand your meaning. Please, elaborate," Biomei says, sounding annoyed.

"Fool's errand, yes, um... It's an Earth colloquialism that infers a task with a low probability of success, and only a person devoid of good sense would attempt it."

There's a moment of silence. "Phillip Mann, how can you express such a low level of confidence in yourself when so many are relying on your great abilities?"

I feel foolish being reminded by Biomei of my enhancements. So, why aren't I using them? After reflecting on it, I realize that until that moment, I was relying on Nicki for confidence in my abilities.

"Biomei, I'm sorry. I misspoke."

"Yes. You did."

"Phil, we must go to our stations," Cuz urges.

We sit in padded chairs in front of a large viewscreen. As we approach, the defense network appears on the ship's forward view. At first, it seems like a hazy yellow dust cloud covering the entire planet. As we get closer, it looks more like a complex web surrounding the planet. Biomei increases both the screen's resolution and magnification for me, revealing the network as a densely populated lattice of radiating, miniature orbs.

"Each orb is composed of heavily charged particles," Cuz explains. "The Venubians use a process that compresses the particles, so the net's field will absorb any form of energy."

An ingenious defense, but at what cost? "Isn't there an inherent danger from radiation for the planet and the population?"

"The energy field is a focused lattice design. All the radiation is directed away from the planet. It works on the same principle as the planet's natural magnetic field."

"How will we penetrate it?"

"Biomei has a special sequencing code that will open a small window within the lattice long enough for us to go through."

"Prepare for reentry insertion," Biomei says.

I feel an unexpected jerk followed by a brief shuddering.

"What was that?" I ask.

"Turbulence, we have entered the atmosphere," Cuz answers, then says, "Biomei, commence hover mode."

"May you reach a haven unharmed," Biomei says as Cuz and I go to Shuttle Bay-5.

"We'll see you soon," I call to her as we enter the turbo lift.

When I get into my seat, Cuz turns from his pilot's chair and says, "I need to prepare you for our meeting with Tezabouh."

"Prepare me, how?"

Cuz's demeanor changes as the shuttle lifts and glides out of the bay. "I cannot be as congenial toward you. Tezabouh will never understand our relationship, and we do not want to antagonize him. You will have enough obstacles to overcome without me adding to them." His expression turns impassive.

I smile at the sudden irony of what he said. "This must be the first time an android ever apologized for acting human. I don't know what to make of that, Cuz—do you?"

Cuz looks at me with his mouth open, brow furrowed, staring unblinkingly. If it isn't such a serious problem for him, I'd laugh. When he turns his perplexed face to me, I can't help laughing.

"Cuz," I say. "I'd prefer we be ourselves. Experience has taught me it's the best course of action. I know nothing about Tezabouh, and he doesn't know us. Either he'll help us for who we are, or he won't. Based on the little I know about him, if he doesn't appreciate our relationship, then he's not the person we need."

Cuz's face relaxes into his first genuine smile. It fills me with confidence, knowing he'll act like my friend and confidant instead of my android assistant.

"We'll soon be in Zenneah. This will allow you to review this briefing on Tezabouh. I believe it'll be of value." Cuz hands me a cube.

I place the small device on the side of my head and download the data into my internal compiler.

Something occurs to me. "Cuz, are you aware that you used contractions? That's not the first time." I observe as my compiler processes the new information.

Cuz's mouth curls into a lopsided smile. "Yes, I'm cognizant of it. It's something I'm incorporating into my linguistic database." His eyebrows arch above his bright eyes, and the corners of his mouth turn up a bit. "I like the sound of them."

"You're becoming more human all the time. Be careful. You may display moments of irrational behavior."

"I doubt that." He smirks. "However, I appreciate the sentiment. Please review the briefing. We have little time."

As I absorb the data. It becomes clear that Tezabouh is a complicated and unpredictable android.

"He sacrificed an entire city to convince the Zenti of his legitimacy," I snap, in surprise. "He's a cold-blooded monster. How could we ever trust him? His behavior was outrageous. It appears he does whatever he believes necessary in accomplishing his goal, regardless of the outcome or sacrifices made."

"Phil, you must keep an open mind about what you're receiving," Cuz cautions. "Tezabouh was forced to do extraordinary things that, in retrospect, seem sinister and insensitive. You must understand he was behaving within the parameters of his mission objectives. I believe humanoids have a saying which best describes their situation: 'The needs of the many outweigh the needs of the few or the one.'"

I consider what Cuz says while continuing the download. There is an explanatory note regarding Tezabouh's sacrificial actions.

"Oh. I think I understand," I mumble. "He transferred all the seriously wounded and dying and put them in the village. It's unclear if the villagers knew of their fate, and there's no mention of whether they willingly sacrificed themselves." With a worried look, I add, "His actions seem extreme. I've some serious doubts about him. A part of me wishes we didn't need him. Verubeal seems desperate for us to enlist his help, though."

The download finishes, and I let out a long breath while trying to understand Tezabouh's complex personality.

"Tezabouh's plan is straightforward and deliberate," I say, reviewing the data aloud with Cuz. "He lured the Zenti into a trap using an elaborately staged victory celebration. The Zenti and Androids were gathered in a remote sector of Venubia City. The Androids were turning over the last of the valued technology to the Zenti leaders. Almost all the Zenti forces were there. Most of their leaders, best technicians, and engineers were all stuffing themselves with food and drink while the planet lay in almost total ruins." I look away from Cuz, pulling on my ear in thought.

"He's diabolical and ruthless," I murmur, then look back at Cuz in shock. "When he decided the Zenti were full enough of food and drink, he had his androids arm themselves and mow down all the Zenti. He only spared a small contingency of mostly low-ranking personnel, who didn't pose a threat. Then he returned them to their remote world and told them to either change or die." I shake my head as my mind fills with apprehension about Tezabouh. "He knew all too well how easily the Zenti could be trapped by their mindless pursuits. He used the Zenti's brutal tactics against them. How do I deal with that?"

"One doesn't deal with an enhanced humanoid like Tezabouh. One negotiates with him," Cuz says.

"Are you saying he's not an android?

Cuz nods.

"Another enhanced humanoid.... I'm not sure I understand. How does one negotiate with someone like him? He's so different from anything I've ever encountered."

"Logically," Cuz states.

"Logically? You're asking an emotionally charged, highly stressed human on a desperate mission to be logical with a dispassionate automaton?"

"Yes," Cuz replies.

"Yes—what?"

"Emotional appeal will be irrelevant to him. Logical reasoning will be more understandable. You must remember Tezabouh has been alive for thousands of planetary cycles. Over that time, he has amassed a considerable body of knowledge, and I suspect his isolation has made him even less tolerant of humanoid emotions."

"Okay. So, what do I say to him?"

"I suggest you let the circumstances dictate the conversation."

"Really? Your brilliant advice is to wing it?"

Cuz shrugs, curling his lower lip outward, looking as though he were contemplating a thought. "You have often displayed a proficient ability to think on your feet. Unless you have a better approach to the situation, I believe it to be our most available course of action."

Before I can question him on his choice of words, we're circling in search of a landing spot.

"We're here already?"

"This is as far as we can take the shuttle. We must proceed on foot the rest of the way," Cuz says, as he brings us to a smooth landing.

The shuttle's canopy swings open, revealing a rugged mountain range ahead of us. Cuz gets out of the shuttle and hands me a pair of thick-soled boots.

"You'll need these for the journey."

I examine them and then look at the terrain before us and ask, "We're going up that mountain?"

"Not quite all the way." Cuz points toward a small outcrop about three-quarters of the way up. "If you look closely, you'll see a crevasse to the right of that ridge just below the northeast peak."

I focused on the area for a moment, then my optical sensors zoomed in, revealing a tiny gap between two rounded peaks.

"It doesn't look like much of an opening."

"It widens a few meters into its interior.

"How far up?"

"The trail is about 15 kilometers."

"That far? I guess we'd better get started then." I put on the boots as Cuz stuffed provisions he'd stored in two backpacks. "Does he live on the mountain?"

"No. Zenneah is an island on the other side of the mountain range. This is the only workable path. The island lies between two mountain ranges. The eastern range is close to the South Pole, and the weather is too hostile for safe transit. We'll use the western approach, while it has its challenges, it's more navigable."

"I see. Wouldn't it be easier to take the shuttle over the mountain?"

"Yes, but I didn't want to provoke an unwarranted response to our sudden approach."

"Oh. So, you think Tezabouh will take aggressive action at seeing us coming?"

Cuz raises an eyebrow. "Being cautious is often best in uncertain situations. Wouldn't you agree?"

"Oh, this's getting better by the minute."

As we begin our climb, my jumpsuit thickens against the frigid winds. Within a few minutes, my suit turns into a thick, hooded parka. It seems the colder it gets, the warmer the suit becomes, until my climbing is hampered by its increasing thickness. I turn to Cuz and notice his suit has only thickened a little.

"At the rate my suit is growing, you'll have to roll me up this mountain," I shout over a rising gale.

"Concentrate on an optimum comfort level," Cuz says.

I do as he suggests. It deflates to a comfortable thickness.

"Ah, that's better," I say. The sky takes on an amber color—a sign I recognize. "We'd better pick up the pace if we want to reach the other side in daylight," I call to Cuz.

"I agree, but it never gets dark at this latitude. The near sunsets on the horizon occur about the same time the red giant rises. It's most beautiful."

"How long before it sets?"

Cuz looks up and says, "About two hours on your terms."

"Was that a guess from Mr. Precise?"

"No. A rounded estimate."

I give him a sideways glance and smile.

The path narrows as it winds around a rugged outcrop. Coming around it, we discover a large boulder blocking our way. We check for a way around it.

"We can't get around or climb over it," I say, rubbing my chin in thought. "Why don't we try to push it off the ledge?"

"I estimate it weighs a little over 3.2 metric tons."

There is just enough room for us to maneuver between the great rock and the side of the mountain.

"Lend me a shoulder," I say to Cuz.

We positioned ourselves inside the narrow space so that Cuz was to the right of me. We brace our shoulders about waist high to the boulder, then lean in hard against it. At first, it seems futile. Cuz suggests that we approach the boulder from a little higher angle. With all our combined might, we lean hard against the solid rock. It gives way and tumbles off the narrow ledge, crashing down on the lower path.

"I sure hope no one was below," I say, watching the massive boulder rumble off the edge of the trail, leveling everything in its path for hundreds of meters below. I turn to Cuz and smile, "3.2 metric tons. That must be a record somewhere in the universe."

"Maybe your Guinness Book of Records," Cuz suggests with a slight smirk.

"You know about that?"

Cuz nods. "I know much about Earth."

"You do? How?"

"I was tied to your compiler when you first arrived," he says, wearing a puzzled expression. "You weren't aware of that?"

"Cuz, you could fill the combined libraries of Earth and Venubia with what I'm not aware of."

"You're not upset with me?"

I place my hand on his shoulder and look into his eyes. He seems tense, awaiting my response.

"Cuz, short of betraying or killing me, there's little you could do to upset me."

"Thank you. I think?" he says, pouting his lips.

I look closer at him. "What's wrong?"

"My program appears conflicted, and I am uncertain how to resolve it."

"What are you trying to say?"

His face screws up into a helpless, troubled look.

"My directive is to bring Tezabouh back at any cost—including your life," he says.

"Cuz, who gave you those instructions?"

His features darken as if in sudden shock. "Kazdan," he says, gritting his teeth. "Until now, I was unaware that he made it a directive and implanted it into my subprocessor."

"Kazdan?" I thought for a moment. "How does Kazdan have priority over you?" I pull on my earlobe, pondering Cuz's revelation. "How could he have reprogrammed you without your knowledge?"

"He shouldn't have had access to me." Cuz looks as if he realizes something important.

"That makes little sense."

"There are many incongruities I am dealing with." His eyes narrow, and his expression turns pensive.

I survey our position and see we still have quite a way to go up the mountain.

"Let's proceed to the fissure and then continue this conversation. We need to make up time."

"Agreed," Cuz says, bowing his head, looking lost in thought.

"We'll make sense of this, I promise. But we have to keep moving."

We pick up our pace, but when I turn back to Cuz, he still looks preoccupied and falling further behind.

"The fissure looks about 40 more meters," I say, hoping to break Cuz's broodiness. "Cuz, you need to focus on what we're doing now," I call down to him. He's fallen even further behind.

He gazes up at me, shaking his head. He's acting more peculiar by the minute. *Oh, Jesus, what's next? Now I have to deal with a conflicted android. Shit.*

As we continue to climb the last leg to the fissure, the winds are howling. My suit swells up again, and I become frustrated with being barely able to move. Even more frustrating, my companion is now sitting on a rock below me, chin resting on his fist like Rodin's Thinker.

"Cuz!" I shout over the deafening howl. Icy snowflakes are pelting my face. "My suit is swelling, and I'm almost at the fissure." Cuz doesn't budge. "For Christ's sake, get your synthetic ass up and join me out of this fricking wind and ice."

Cuz nods and ambles to me. We make it inside the fissure.

"What a relief to be out of that freezing wind," I say to Cuz as we gather inside the opening.

A warm current of air mixed with the icy gale blows in from the outside. I walk further into the interior. It widens ahead, and a glow of pale amber light leaks in from the other side.

"Should we go to where it seems warmer and brighter, or do you prefer to bear your soul in the cold and damp darkness?"

"The former sounds more appealing," Cuz says in a low voice.

I gesture with my arm for him to lead the way. He gives me an uncertain look for a second and walks ahead of me.

"Will you deflate, damn it?" I yell at my suit.

Cuz turns and reminds me to concentrate. An intermittent twitch in his right cheek gets my attention.

"What was that?" I ask him, staring intently at his cheeks.

"What?"

"Your right cheek twitched," I say, pointing to the affected area.

Cuz feels his face. "I am not aware of any twitch."

"There," I point at his left cheek, it happened again on the left one. Didn't you feel that?"

"No. You're mistaken. I am incapable of such an involuntary reaction."

"Another twitch follows. "There—it happened on your right cheek again. You didn't feel that either?"

Cuz places his hand on his right cheek, then becomes stiff. He stands with his hand to his face as if frozen in place. I wait for another twitch, but nothing happens. I stare at Cuz's now vacant eyes and worry.

"I guess it's just one of those mysterious transient discharges that pop up from time to time," I say, eager to resume our mission. "It's probably nothing; let's go." I pat Cuz's shoulder to get him to move.

He remains fixed with his eyes staring outward. It becomes obvious he's not going to move. He looks like he's turned to stone. *Oh, shit. Just what I need, a frozen android companion. Why is this happening?* I let out a long sigh. "Cuz?" I shake him by the shoulders. "Can you hear me?" He remains inanimate. "Come on, Cuz—I need you." I shake him harder—still nothing.

I sit on the ground, staring at my seized-up companion, wondering whether to leave him and hope he'll resolve this problem and join me, or try to find help. Neither choice is appealing, but I have to make a quick decision.

"Well, what do we have here?" A strong voice from behind startles me.

I jump to my feet, seeing a tall humanoid, dressed in a heavy white tunic over baggy brown pants. He's staring intently at me with cold blue eyes. He seems to have appeared out of thin air.

"Who are you?" I say defensively.

He fixes his probing eyes on me and says, "You can call me Ted."

Ted doesn't appear hostile, nor does he make any aggressive moves toward me. Instead, he walks around Cuz, studying him with his wide mouth turned upward in an amused expression.

"Never thought a Generation-six android could suffer a causality cascade shutdown. Did you cause this?" he says, tapping Cuz's forehead with his long index finger.

"Can you help us?" I ask, with trepidation, as I take in his rugged face with a strong jawline and square chin. His large head is covered in shocks of wavy white hair.

I move closer to him. He ignores me, looking fascinated by Cuz.

"Can you help us?" I repeat, in a stronger voice.

His eyes take on a dark glow as he continues examining Cuz. His large hands have long, delicate-looking fingers, which seem incongruous with the rest of his muscular features.

Ted feels down on Cuz's back in search of something. After running his hand up and down Cuz's spine, he frowns.

"Well, he doesn't have a reset switch," Ted says in Venubian.

Thank goodness, my universal translator is keeping up with him.

"Hmm." He sits back into the shadows, rubbing his square chin. "I guess they did away with that.... Makes sense." Ted nods to himself. "They're potentially dangerous." He appears to study Cuz for a moment before standing and feeling around the back of Cuz's neck. "Ah, what's this?"

Ted's wide mouth opens as he runs a finger down Cuz's neck. The large humanoid leans closer to Cuz as he works, resembling a mechanic trying to find that elusive bolt that will unlock the problem. After a few seconds, he reaches into a large pocket of his baggy, brown pants for something and then smiles when he finds it. He holds up a long, thin, clear-handled probe with a short, needle-thin wire protruding out one end. The tip of the opposite end is glowing with a dim amber light.

"What are you going to do with that?" I ask, with my hand reaching for his.

He pulls the instrument back with an annoyed look. "Do you want me to help your friend?" Ted blinks his large, intense eyes at me.

"Of course, but I still want to know what you're intending to do with that— probe thing." I point at it.

"I intend to stick it into his neck right about here," he says as he inserts the needle end almost into the base of Cuz's head. "Now, I'm going to gently move it a little to the left." He depresses something close to the top of the instrument's handle with his thumb. I hear a click followed by a humming sound. "Ah, I'm getting some neural feedback," he informs, pursing his lips and slanting his mouth into a crooked grin. "Well, that should do the trick. Your friend will soon be all right." Ted turns his attention to me and, with a smug look, says, "Now, who are you?"

His now cobalt blue eyes study me. He doesn't look like a Venubian or an android. He seems more human than any other being I'd met since arriving on Venubia. Taking a closer look, I notice subtle but familiar facial features. The oval shape of his head and his thin-lipped mouth have Venubian characteristics. But the rest of him is all alien.

Ted's taller than me, and his broad shoulders give him a powerful appearance. His high forehead, covered in wavy locks of white hair, gives him an elderly look, contradicted by his ageless face. I deduce he's not Venubian or one of their common androids. He's an anomaly that, under normal circumstances, I'd find interesting. He seems pretty content to gaze at me with an amused expression as I study him. However, his eyes stay fixed on me with an uncomfortable intensity.

"I'm Phillip Mann, from Earth," I say, in hopes of establishing a friendly dialogue.

"Phillip Mann, from Earth," he repeats with a crooked smile. "What brings you here, Phillip Mann from Earth?" he says in a patronizing tone.

"I'm looking for an android called Tezabouh. Do you know him?" He sits on top of a flat rock, propping his back against a wall, crossing his legs. He places his long arms behind his head as though he were making himself comfortable in anticipation of a long query. All the while, he never lifts his eyes from me.

"Tezabouh, what do you want of him?" Ted asks.

"Do you know him?" I repeat.

"You didn't answer my question," Ted counters.

"And you didn't answer mine. I guess there's little we shall learn from one another unless we loosen our guards a little." I ask, "How'd you suggest we bridge our mutual distrust?"

"How about you answer his question, Phillip, and maybe he will answer yours," Cuz says in a calm voice.

Relief fills me at hearing his voice. I turn to Cuz. He appears functional again. I glance at Ted, who's still sitting on the rock, seemingly indifferent to Cuz's sudden recovery.

"I guess I owe you at least a gesture of gratitude for restoring my friend."

Ted blinks his eyes in acknowledgment.

"Thank you. We were sent by Chancellor Verubeal in search of Tezabouh, hoping to enlist his help against ongoing Zenti aggression. The Chancellor believes he could help us. Do you know where we can find him?"

Ted's eyes widen slightly when I mention Verubeal. He lifts his stare from me and stands. He gives us a pensive look for a moment as if he's deciding something. He starts to go to the other side of the fissure. He pauses, turns, and gestures for us to follow.

I glance at Cuz. At that moment, a heavy wave of apprehension and doubt runs through me. Being unsure if we'll find Tezabouh or hell as we follow Ted. To exacerbate my entangled emotions, Nicki comes to mind.

"Do you think he's Tezabouh?" I transmit to Cuz, trying to get my mind off Nicki.

"I am unsure of who he is, but it is obvious he knows Tezabouh or at least where to find him."

"How can you be so sure?"

"Can you suggest another reason he asked us to follow him?"

"I guess not."

We walk in silence for some time until we reach a plateau that overlooks a beautiful valley below us. In the near distance, an island with a city of spiral-shaped ice towers connected by high arches. Crystal-clear, blue water surrounds the icy island, bordered by towering mountains on all sides. My mouth opens in surprise. I see spectrums of reds, yellows, and deep orange, painting the icy towers as the great red giant hovers above the peaks. The sky is aglow with iridescent colors, all reflecting off the grand spires and towers of glistening ice. The scene looks like a surreal AI-generated graphic.

Ted looks at Cuz and then at me. He appears different. His demeanor seems more relaxed.

"This is not an easy journey," Ted says. "There are no conveyances to take you to Tezabouh's isle. He's isolated for good reasons." He pauses thoughtfully, then adds, "The Zenti are reason enough to intrude, though." Ted points to a narrow ledge running downward, then it pivots upward toward a high peak. "We need to go along that ledge, but I must warn you it's treacherous."

"Is that how you came to us?" I ask.

"Yes."

"Then it's a path well-traveled, and now we have an experienced guide." I force a smile of détente to show my appreciation for his help. "What more could I ask under these circumstances. Please, lead on, Ted."

The path is indeed treacherous. In spots, it narrows barely wider than our boots. We have to walk as though we're on a tightrope. The boots Cuz gave me are as intuitive as my other clothing and maintain me in perfect balance. Ted seems comfortable as he leisurely walks along the slender path. Thankfully, my physical enhancements permit me to keep up with Ted and Cuz.

About halfway down, Ted turns and says, "You're handling this well. Do you have a lot of experience with mountain trails?"

I knew he was probing again, so I nodded and smiled. He turns his attention back to the track. A few minutes later, he stops again and asks, "If you're tired, there's a small shelf a few meters further up. We can take a break there."

"Thank you, but that won't be necessary," I say confidently. "We need to get to Tezabouh as soon as possible."

"Very well. The base is about another two hundred meters. The trail opens before that, so we'll be able to make better time soon."

"Good," I say. "We need to pick up the pace."

I'm becoming more anxious by the minute, contemplating our meeting, Tezabouh. My mind fills with all kinds of scenarios. None of them seems helpful, so I concentrate on what I'm going to say to him. Nothing comes to mind. My insides knot up. I keep telling myself to relax. Nicki's voice flashes through my mind. *Practice the deep breathing exercise I taught you.* I start inhaling deep breaths and letting them out slowly. It works, and before long, the trail widens.

"I have completed my internal diagnostic," Cuz says, breaking his long silence, "all systems are working nominally." He says to Ted, "That neural stimulation was effective. Thank you." He asks him something I should've asked when we first met. "How did you know we were here?"

"You're welcome," he says to Cuz, ignoring his question, then points ahead. "You must go over that small ridge. There's a pass right on the other side. It has a steep face, but the snow is soft. There should be no problem with your footing. The lake is right below. A raft is tied to a rock at the water's edge. You can use that to cross over to the island." He nods to us and walks in the opposite direction.

"You didn't answer his question," I call to him.

He stops and turns to face us. "We picked you up on our sensors as soon as your shuttle entered our airspace," he says, resuming a quick pace away from us. After going a few meters, he turns once more, looking as though he had remembered something of significance. "I'd inspect the raft's stability; it hasn't been used in some time." He gives us a crooked smile before turning back towards the trail.

"You're not coming with us?" I called to him. He ignores me and continues walking. "That's it? You're just leaving us?" I yell at him.

I shake my head, thinking what a screwed-up encounter this is.

Ted stops for a moment and, without turning to face us, says, "This is as far as I can go. You must finish the journey from here on your own."

"I don't understand. I thought you would take us to Tezabouh."

He views us from a distance for a moment, his white face reflecting the light off the bright snow.

"I told you I'd show you the way. You're on your own from here. I wish you good fortune and hope Tezabouh will help you," he says, turns, and continues down the path.

"I still don't know who you are or why you've helped us," I call to him.

"We'll meet again." He lifts his left arm and gives us a backward wave.

We watch him for a while as he climbs back up the trail.

"I have my reservations about Ted," Cuz says.

"You think," I snap. Then blow out a long breath. "Sorry, Cuz. I'm just frustrated by our strange friend Ted. What are you thinking?"

"He arrived at the right moment, revealed nothing about himself, and left as though he fulfilled a mission objective. Most curious."

"I concur. Somehow, I'm certain we will meet him again. His appearance is a little too convenient. Almost like he was testing us."

"I was not straightforward when I reported that all my systems were functioning nominally," Cuz admits in a sheepish voice.

"You lied? I'm shocked."

"I did not lie. I just overstated my condition," he corrects me.

"I see. What did you overstate?"

"Ted did not use a neural stimulant. Instead, he inserted a high-intensity probe. The fact that he didn't correct me when I thanked him made me suspicious. I refrained from questioning him further on the procedure as a precaution. I wanted to avoid any chance of inciting an unwarranted confrontation under the circumstances. However, there is a strong possibility he may have attempted to tamper with some of my systems."

"Should I be concerned about your reliability?"

"I do not believe he could have corrupted any of my primary or secondary systems. The best analogy would be more of an invasion of my privacy. He tapped my core memory to ascertain any mission objectives. Of course, he was unsuccessful in retrieving anything of relevance."

"Aren't you upset?" I interject, wondering why he was so indifferent to such a violation.

"I am incapable of that emotion in the context you are inferring. His motivation for the intrusion has given me reasons for concern." Cuz wrinkles his brow in a familiar emulation of confusion. "Despite our suspicions about Ted, he restored my systems and led us on a path, hopefully, to Tezabouh. From his perspective, he fulfilled his commitment to us. We should also consider that he is as curious about us as we are about him. His behavior was perplexing, and his motives are unclear."

"Yeah, I agree. I'd feel less nervous knowing who he is and why he helped us. I guess there's not a lot we can do about it now. Let's go." I hold a finger up and add, "One other observation, my friend. Why have you stopped using contractions? Also, you have regressed to an impassive android demeanor."

"Yes. I am aware of these changes. The probe has reset some of my linguistic and personality subroutines. I am making the required corrections to the affected areas as we continue."

"Okay, but warn me if anything else is screwed up."

Cuz nods with a passive expression and dull eyes that seem to be looking past me.

We climb down the snowy hill and walk to a narrow jetty made of flat, black rocks that protrude just above water level. As Ted described, there's a raft tied off, bobbing in the gentle wind-driven rivulets. A slimy green algae-like growth had covered its sides and keel. The raft smells like algae and rotted wood and doesn't look very buoyant. Upon closer examination, we notice a long oar lying on the floor and a keel post and hole at the bow. While Cuz places the oar through the keel hole, I untie the line, then cautiously test my weight on the raft with visions of me falling through its decayed structure. Surprisingly, it feels stable enough. Cuz grasps the fundamentals of our vessel and begins an energetic back-and-forth rhythmic motion that sets us on our way to the island.

The sky is a blaze of orange that reflects off the clear waters. Only a small sliver of the pale sun's crown can be seen in the distance. The dark, orange-red glow of the red giant is high overhead. I consciously deflate my suit to get a better feel for the glowing environment. Turning my face toward the red giant, I can feel its feeble warmth under the thin and icy-cold air. It both chills and exhilarates the senses.

The small raft bobs on the water's surface. And for some inexplicable reason, I couldn't rid myself of the feeling we're crossing the river Styx on our way into Hades.

CHAPTER 40

The spires and grand arches, glistening in the distance, turn out to be complex architectural structures. The entire island appears to be utilized. It looks big enough to hold hundreds of thousands of inhabitants, and yet when we step onto its smooth, icy surface, only chilled air greets us. It seems odd that, out of curiosity or simple hospitality, at least one resident would have met us. After a few minutes of anticipating a greeting party, I become concerned that at best the island is deserted, or at worst, we're about to be rudely confronted at a chosen time and place.

"I would have expected to be met by at least one of Tezabouh's representatives," I tell Cuz.

"I am not surprised by the lack of a welcoming party," Cuz says. "From Tezabouh's perspective, we are unwelcome guests, and he is most likely observing us."

"I don't have a good feeling about this. We should find a way inside and start looking for him." I thought for a second, then turned to Cuz. "Why are we getting ourselves so worked up? Maybe he doesn't know we're here. After all, why would he be expecting us?"

"That is unlikely. You overlook the fact that Ted was no accident and probably one of Tezabouh's agents, if not Tezabouh himself. He has a well-established reputation for possessing the most extensive and robust intelligence gathering network in the sector. I believe our lack of reception is deliberate."

"Have you noticed that since our encounter with Ted, you not only lost the integrated use of contractions but also some, let's say, colorful, idiomatic expressions from your linguistic data stream? You integrated them so well, you were sounding almost human. Now you sound like an android again."

Cuz regards me with a brooding expression and says, "That is interesting, Phillip, but I... I'm starting to see your... poo... point...."

His facial features became bland, giving me concern that he's going into one of his higher-memory impasses. Before I can say anything, he recovers and continues his previous thought.

"I see your point. Can you be more specific?"

"Are you all right?" I ask.

Cuz stops and looks as though he's doing another internal diagnostic.

"Cuz this isn't the time for this. Are you aware you just stammered?"

Cuz arches a brow and looks as if he's pondering what I said.

"All I want you to do now is to be aware of the possibility that you may not be a hundred percent. I think Ted may have screwed with you."

"Now that you have made me aware of my recent inconsistencies, I will conduct a level-2 diagnostic on my linguistic subroutines and neural pathways. This will not inhibit me in any way, but I believe it to be a prudent precaution."

"If it doesn't interfere with our mission, go for it."

We start toward the center of one of the central spires when Cuz stops again and looks over his shoulder.

"What's wrong?" I bark, my patience running thin with Cuz's constant stops.

"We are not alone. Someone is trailing close behind." Cuz stares out for a moment. "Whoever they are, they are not trying to hide their whereabouts as much as appear to be observing us from a distance."

"Okay, now we finally have someone interested in us."

We walk toward an opening in one of the towering spires. We wander for some time through a maze of intersecting corridors and dead ends. Each time we turn into a new corridor, it winds and meanders into an adjacent pathway. Every turn leads to a dead end that we follow into yet another corridor. It feels like we're lost in an elaborate labyrinth. After walking into yet another dead end, I have an urge to scream, Will someone please take me to Tezabouh!

Cuz also looks mystified. Finally, he says, "There is no logical progression through this edifice. I suggest we retrace our steps and seek a new route."

I squint my eyes and say, "Cuz, when logic, reason, and common sense all fail, the only choice that remains is idiocy."

"Idiocy is illogical," Cuz says, with the beautiful innocence of one who's uninitiated to human guile.

"All right, you fucking asshole, we've wasted enough time with your game," I shout. "Have we amused you enough to waste a planet, or don't you give a shit about anything anymore? You can answer that at least. Or will that be too much of an intrusion on your bullshit isolation?"

"What language is that?" Cuz says. "Whom are you addressing?"

"Patience, my friend, I'm just warming up," I say, then call out in a firm, sarcastic voice, "Hey, mighty Tezabouh, leader of destruction. Your world is about to be taken over by the Zenti again. Did you cut a better deal with them this time? Or don't you give a shit about who runs the planet if they leave you alone?" An archway appears directly in front of us. "See." I grin. "When all else fails, use good old human obscenity-laced guile. Shall we proceed?" I gesture for Cuz to go in.

"I am uncertain what just transpired, but whatever you did, it seems to have been effective." Cuz's eyes widen and his forehead furrows, looking impressed and confused at the same time. "Was that idiocy or colloquialism?"

"Not now, Cuz," I answer quietly.

The archway opens into a grand interior. We walk into a vast hall lit by an indiscernible source. The smooth, crystal-clear ice walls reflect the soft lighting, giving the entire area a sharp clarity.

The hall is filled with wondrous artifacts that grab Cuz's attention. Like rows of armored soldiers, stand replicas of different androids. It must seem like a wax museum of ancestral prototypes to Cuz. He walks up and closely examines each one with apparent fascination as he states its type and inception date with great pride to me.

I look around the room with growing impatience at meeting the mysterious Tezabouh. *He knows our situation and probably why we are here,"* I transmit to Cuz. *"Why all the games?* Why are you hiding?" I call out. "We don't have time for this. But you already know that, so what are you waiting for? Come out, you bastard, and confront me."

"Are you as ignorant and uncivilized as you sound?" a disembodied voice asks.

"Come out and talk with us," I demand.

"He is neither ignorant nor uncivilized," Cuz defends, with surprising emotion. "He comes out of true conviction and devotion to Venubia as you once did."

"So, we have an emotional android and a corrupted humanoid representing true conviction and devotion? If you weren't so pathetic, I'd find this as the greatest irony of the millennium," the disembodied voice sounds closer. Cuz and I both look in the same direction. "You seek the help of a disenfranchised entity. There's nothing I can do for your world. It's already lost." The voice is directly behind us. We turn and see Ted, looking at us with a smug smile.

"Are you Ted or Tezabouh?" I ask.

"For all intents and purposes, I'm Tezabouh."

"You know why we're here. Either you or your surrogate has tapped Cuz's memory to ascertain all the information you require. Will you help Venubia defeat the Zenti?"

"The Zenti have already defeated Venubia," he states dispassionately. "They've taken control of the vital infrastructure. They've rounded up all the leaders, including Verubeal, and are now awaiting final instructions." Tezabouh studies us with his cold, cobalt eyes. With his jaw jutting outward while standing stiffly with an authoritative bearing, a corner of his mouth turns up into a cruel smile. "Why would I want to upset such a perfect balance of power and control?"

"Because you know it's wrong," I snap at him in disbelief.

Tezabouh walks up close to Cuz and looks him over, and then comes to me. Our eyes lock, and he stares at me with a curious look that I return with a heartfelt sneer. It has no appreciable effect. I remember what Verubeal told me and tried a different tactic.

"If you don't care about Venubia or Verubeal, then at least give me a chance to save Nickada," I say, in a more restrained voice.

He takes a few steps back. "Nickada?" he whispers. "Nickada, my lovely daughter, what do you know of her?"

Tezabouh narrows his gaze. It feels like an energy-filled probe boring into me. I sense his prying energy surging into my mind.

"Stop," I yell at him. "I'll not allow you to violate me in that way."

I hold my hand up like a shield against his probe and, for the first time, can feel my mind exerting a repelling mental force that pushes Tezabouh slightly backward with a surprised expression.

"You have her strength," he says, raising his thick eyebrows in surprise.

"If you care for her, you must help us or leave us to try," I state in a low voice, returning his heavy gaze.

While shaking from the residual effects of the combined energies, I sense something happening to me. My mind and body feel as if I have acquired new energy. I regain my composure, realizing what Tezabouh had said.

"What did you mean by Nickada, my daughter?" My voice wavers, betraying my sudden anxiousness.

Tezabouh ignores my question and turns back to Cuz. "You resemble a Generation-6 series, but have a certain aura about you that is inconsistent with your prototype. What model are you?"

He's stalling. I must've hit a nerve. I let Cuz respond in the hope of revealing something about our enigmatic host.

"I am not a model or prototype. I am a genetically enhanced Android-Venubian," Cuz says with pride.

"A genetically enhanced Android-Venubian," Tezabouh repeats with a sardonic smile. "What a wonderfully descriptive euphemism."

"It is not a euphemism," Cuz retorts. "My parental units were Venubian and provided me with a nurturing period, followed by thirteen cycles of developmental rearing and educational experiences. While I may be a product of combined, synthetic, and genetic engineering, I am a sentient being with the abilities for environmental and sociological adaptations, as any other Venubian. Contrary to your assertion, I'm not an automaton, like many of your lineage."

I swell with pride at Cuz. He defended himself with eloquence and fervor. Tezabouh looks impressed as well.

"You still haven't answered my question," I repeat more insistently. "What did you mean by Nickada, your daughter?"

Tezabouh's gaze softens. He appears perplexed and uncomfortable with my presence. I can almost hear his neural net clicking away in unaccustomed confusion. I could read his expression. He's probably asking himself, Who's this Earthman? What's his relation to Nickada? Can I trust him?

We stare at each other in an irritating silence for what seems an eternity, but all my sales training and instincts in negotiations have taught me that the one who speaks first has capitulated. I have no intention of saying another word before he does. If we stalemate, then we'll leave in silence. As I'm about to tell Cuz to pack up, Tezabouh blinks.

"Nickada, how do you know her?" he says.

I look intently at Tezabouh and tell him exactly who Nicki is to me. "She saved my life and enhanced me both physically and spiritually. I love her unconditionally and will do everything within my power to rescue her from the Zenti." Narrowing my gaze at Tezabouh, I ask, "Now, who's she to you?"

He motions for us to follow him. He leads us to a small, open room. Comfortable-looking chairs surround a glass-topped table. We're greeted by mechanical-looking androids. While humanoid in body, they are genderless and have impassive facial features. They move with fluid precision and are efficient in anticipating our needs.

Tezabouh sits in the middle and motions to our seats on either side of him. We sit and are presented with trays of food and drink. With a wave of his hand, he dismisses the androids. He looks at us with a Venubian-like warmth. His sudden change in demeanor doesn't make me comfortable, though. He leans back, folds his arms across his chest, and crosses his legs. Tezabouh stares at me with his mouth pursed, looking eager for me to speak.

With our eyes locked again, I decide to take advantage of the silence and break the eyeball-to-eyeball stalemate by stuffing my face with one of everything on the trays. I must have been famished because it all tasted delicious. With each renewed mouthful, I noisily chew down my food while smiling at Tezabouh. My intentional gluttony is serving a logical course of action. First, I want to maintain Tezabouh's attention. My face stuffing seems effective in that regard. Secondly, and probably more important, a well-stuffed mouth can't talk, thus ensuring against my saying something stupid. Eyeing him while chewing, I wait, hoping the SOB will spill his guts first.

"Enjoying the food?" Tezabouh finally breaks the stalemate.

I nodded, giving him a thumbs-up gesture and a full-mouth smile.

"You ask me of Nickada, of our relationship. I'll tell you what you seek if you can convince me of your worthiness to know." Tezabouh's expression changes again. His exterior features blur, then he reappears as Verubeal.

"Is it easier for you to talk with me, Phillip?" Tezabouh sounds and looks just like her.

His morphing into Verubeal is disconcerting. It both irritates and confuses me.

"Why did you morph into Verubeal?" I say irritably.

"I'm curious about your reaction," Tezabouh says, reverting to his former self. "Trust is something earned either over time or through intuition about someone. In the absence of both time and intuition, all that is left is to ask." Tezabouh's bushy white eyebrows rise, and his dynamic expression appears sincere as he says, "Can I trust you?"

"Yes," I say emphatically.

Tezabouh turns to Cuz and leans closer to him. Cuz, who, during this time, is sitting upright in his chair, silently observing. They stare at each other for a few beats before Cuz nods. Tezabouh closes his eyes and nods. It looks like they did a respectful exchange. It works. Tezabouh finally answers my question.

"Nickada is my daughter," he says in a low voice. "She was the first and only child conceived through an Android and Venubian copulation. Its initial intention was purely scientific. Verubeal had no emotional ties to me, and yet when Nickada was born, we both discovered that we loved her. Each of us loved her in our separate ways. We agreed that she needed me as much as she needed her mother. However, the governing body of Venubia wanted to keep our successful union a secret, citing that protecting the method was more important at the time. We all agreed to wait until we'd perfected the process before disclosing Nickada's origins." Tezabouh frowns. "Of course, they never disclosed anything about our successful union because they knew it would never happen again.

"After initial DNA studies of her placenta, some anomalies were discovered. It didn't take long for them to uncover the truth." Tezabouh stands abruptly and paces around us. "You see, I'm not a Venubian or one of their Androids," he continues, speaking with his head slightly bowed. "I regretted never telling Verubeal the truth. When she learned—" He closes his eyes and screws up his face into a pained grimace, letting out a long sorrowful sigh, "well, let it suffice, she asked me to leave."

Cuz and I look at each other in shock.

With my brow lined, I say to Tezabouh, "The leader of Venubia's Android army, defender of the planet, and vanquisher of the Zenti is not a Venubian? What the hell are you?"

"Ezdenian," Tezabouh states flatly, regaining his stern bearing. "According to what I've been told, plus what little I can recall, I was discovered by archaeological students working on a dig in Klaxonia. They recovered me from deep stasis right before the chamber's power supply was about to fail. I was suspended for an extremely long time. They saved me, and I owe them a great debt of gratitude."

"Ezdenian?" Cuz says. "How is that possible?"

"Much of my memory was lost in my long stasis."

"How long a stasis?" I ask.

"The Klaxon, who discovered me, believed it to be over ten thousand planetary cycles."

"Bullshit," I snap. "No stasis could last that long without a lot of physical deterioration."

Cuz glances at me with an uncertain expression, and says, "Phillip, Tezabouh is not exaggerating. A well-designed stasis unit can last for extreme periods, provided the unit is powered. As for physical deterioration, an android could last indefinitely without any material breakdown. However, I'm uncertain as to your memory loss. The unit should have maintained that as well."

"You are correct, Cuz," Tezabouh says, pauses for an instant, then flashes a faint smile. He fixes his cobalt-blue eyes on me and says, "My memory would have been maintained if not for the stasis unit being damaged during an earthquake that occurred a few cycles before my discovery. While the event damaged my power supply, it also uncovered my unit from being buried under a millennium of rumble, allowing a Klaxon archeological survey team to find it. I would have expired in less than a cycle if they hadn't revived me."

"So, who are the Ezdenians?" I ask, thinking how weird things are becoming.

"The Ezdenian was considered the oldest race in the galaxy. Along with a few of my Android brethren, I was sent from Ezden right before it was consumed by our sun's swelling into the red giant of this system. We were going to our neighboring systems to transplant Ezdenian genetic seeds. The actual plans, along with all my directives, have been lost," he says with a heavy melodramatic sigh and closes his eyes again. "Something went wrong, but I'm afraid that's more conjecture than fact. What happened is lost to time because of my memory degradation.

"I do remember being a Mentor-Android on Ezden, though." He smiles. "A teacher-guardian, if you will, for the last generation of Ezden's children. All those memories are now shadows and impressions of my Ezden years.

"The Klaxons were unfamiliar with my architecture and were unable to fully restore my memory. And as you've already pointed out, there's not enough time for all the details." Tezabouh seems suddenly anxious to move in a different direction. "The Klaxons were uncomfortable with androids," he blurts, "particularly such humanoid-like ones as me. They believed I would be better suited for Venubia. So, they made a present of me to the Council of Elders. I was fortunate. The Venubians were both curious and respectful. However, it was the Venubian scientific community that appreciated me. They put me to work on developing the first genetically engineered android series. I believe the rest of my past is now part of the Venubian record, which you are, no doubt, familiar with."

"This was not helpful," Cuz says.

I nod in agreement, then look Tezabouh dead in the eyes and ask, "Will you help us defeat the Zenti?"

"Verubeal sent you," Tezabouh states, avoiding my question. "Did she tell you I was the only one who could help Venubia in its darkest hour?"

"You sound bitter for an android, Tezabouh," I say. He burrows his icy cobalt eyes into me again. "You can't tap my mind for answers," I crack at him. "You're going to have to ask me what you want to know." I return his intense stare with a big, sly smile. "So, ask."

Tezabouh's eyes soften as he regards me with a curious look. "What kind of android are you, Earthman?"

A grin spreads on my face at the question. He doesn't have a clue what I am. Also, thinking, he's not close to what I was expecting, glancing at Cuz, who gestures with a nod for me to tell him. I look intently at him, then, with a sense of pride, state, "I'm a biogenetically enhanced human. Not an android." I pause in thought, then add, "I guess you could say I'm Nickada's creation."

Tezabouh's eyes change to a deep blue as he stares at me as if in stunned silence. "Nickada's creation, how's that possible?" He mumbles.

"There isn't time for this," I bark. With both my fists and jaw clenched tight, I walk up toe-to-toe with Tezabouh and snarl. "Will you help us or not?"

He backs off a bit and says, "You said the Zenti have Nickada?" Tezabouh rubs his chin thoughtfully.

"Yes, but you should already know that."

"If you were unaware of Nickada being held by the Zenti, then you cannot be aware of their plan," Cuz declares, preempting me. Cuz turns to me and says, "The Zenti is going to use her as part of their negotiation strategy." Then to Tezabouh, he says, "It's illogical for you to continue with your present strategy with this new information."

Tezabouh's expression turns contemplative, then he starts to pace through the hall. Cuz and I watched him for a few minutes in anticipation of what he was going to say. He reaches the far end of the hall and stops. After a few seconds, he raises his left hand and points with his index finger upward. He spins around and calls to us, "Those sneaky little half-breeds are going to try to double-cross me. Just to get even, they're willing to lose everything they have just to get revenge on me. Hate is a powerful motivator," he shakes his head and frowns, "but it invariably clouds the senses and turns all logic into folly." He squints and clenches his jaw into a determined expression before proclaiming in an angry growl, "Well, let's get them before they get us." He tilts his head to the side, gesturing for us to follow him.

CHAPTER 41

We follow Tezabouh into a cavernous room. According to my suit's display, the room's temperature was only a few degrees warmer than outside. I forgot about the temperature, though, when I saw thousands upon thousands of androids, standing before us in perfect rows and columns. The great mass of androids is standing erect on strong-looking legs with their arms at their sides. All their eyes are fixed on Tezabouh.

Tezabouh steps forward and says in a booming voice, "There will be a slight change in plans."

The androids didn't react; they continued to stand in silence. While surveying the massive assembly, I became aware of the android's incredible diversity. They all seem to share a common symmetric humanoid form, but there are distinct differences in their body size and general features. Many resemble shiny metal combatants, looking more robotic than androids. Others were similar in size and form to Cuz.

I say to Cuz, "Are all these androids of Venubian design?"

Cuz says, "The majority are Venubian, but I also recognize some Kaydian and a few of unknown origin. However, I suspect the unfamiliar prototypes may be of Vultaran design."

"Vultaran? That's a new one. How do they fit into this ever-growing puzzle?"

"I am uncertain. We have only recently become aware of them and have not yet made direct contact. Their planet lies on the extreme edge of our system's habitable zone. The Vultarans are a secretive species and have only recently started communicating with us. A few cycles ago, the Zenti visited them. From what little we have ascertained, the Zenti attacked one of the Vultaran explorer ships, stealing all the viable technology and information before destroying the ship and stranding the few survivors on a distant moon in the Klaxon sector. Beyond some sparse reports from our intelligence, we know little about them."

A voice from within the ranks asks, "Tezabouh, what do you mean by a slight change?"

"For one thing, the addition of these two. Plus, as expected, the Zenti have broken our agreement and attacked Venubia. They're holding Nickada," Tezabouh shouts, clenching his fist and shaking it in the air. "We must not let them succeed in destroying all we have worked so hard to protect."

"That does not answer the question," the voice says in a low and calm tone. Only this time, it sounds closer. An android steps out from the middle of the center row. It takes a step to the side and stands in the narrow aisle between the numerous columns. "Answer the question logically."

Tezabouh aims his cold, cobalt eyes into a calculating stare at the automaton. "I will answer with this. The Zenti have Venubia; they have all the governing council members, including Verubeal and Ozenibeen. The defense network is down, and the entire major infrastructure has been destroyed." Tezabouh takes a dramatic pause to survey the room. "We have a choice to make," he continues, "and it is a simple one. Do you want the Zenti to control this galaxy or us?"

"We have no aggression toward the Zenti," the android states. Then he lifts his voice. "We have a course of action that will resolve both problems, and now you want to unravel all we have accomplished?" He points a finger at Tezabouh and proclaims, "That is illogical." Then he turns his bland expression on us. "I understand the presence of the Venubian engineered life-form, and the humanoid may have complicated matters a bit. Nevertheless, our original plan is still valid."

The android comes closer to us. He's identical in height and body size to all the others in his group. But his eyes had a surprising element of warmth that was not shared by all the other androids. When looking at him, one senses wisdom reflecting in his eyes. Also, while looking closer, I can almost feel his age. Beneath his placid features, I sense an ancient, wise man rather than an intelligent machine. Perhaps, a living intelligence within the framework of a machine.

"Xandroff, what could be more logical than saving Nickada?" Tezabouh says. "It's illogical to ignore the obvious. If the Zenti discovers her special abilities, the balance of power within the sector will be shifted for eons," he bellows in a rich voice. "We can be destroyed or recycled into one of their new war machines!" In a more controlled voice, he adds, "They may have acquired knowledge of the Corridors. This goes beyond history repeating itself. This could be the beginning of the end, not just for us, but for the entire galaxy."

"Your emotional pleas are irrelevant," Xandroff says dismissively. "We agree that there is a high probability the Zenti have already gained Nickada's knowledge and feel they have the advantage. This will have them playing into our strength. They have no idea of our numbers or commitment to the Venubians. No one outside of this room does."

Tezabouh walks up close to Xandroff and says, "The Zenti already know our plan. They probably killed Uzzendi, his family, and the Klaxon science minister. They're incapable of honoring any cease-fire or treaty. Would you not agree that some new tactics need to be devised?"

"What if they do know our plans?" Xandroff states, seemingly unmoved by Tezabouh's argument. He turns and lifts his voice to the masses like a minister to his congregation. "We must force peace now, or we must die trying. But another war is not an option for Venubia!" His voice echoes throughout the room. To Tezabouh, he asserts, "You will follow the plan precisely or not at all. If you choose the latter, then stay out of our way."

Xandroff slowly walks back to his place and rejoins the mass of androids.

Tezabouh remains silent as the farthest row of the group begins to march toward us. Row by row, they flow like a mammoth snake uncoiling itself out of the room. I watched in confusion, pondering what I witnessed. *Was Tezabouh overruled and kicked off the team? And who the hell is Xandroff?*

"Well, it appears as though we're going to have to improvise," Tezabouh says, slapping his hands together.

I narrow my eyes at him and ask, "What was that all about?"

"Respect for one's elders," Tezabouh answers.

Cuz says to Tezabouh. "It appears you are not in charge. Why have you deceived us as to your authority?"

Tezabouh makes a crooked smile and says, "Whose plan do you think they're executing?" He arches his bushy eyebrows into a quizzical expression.

Cuz glances at me. I half-shrug, not knowing what to say. He turns his gaze back at Tezabouh. "I assume by the nature of your question that you are the author of the plan."

The corners of Tezabouh's broad mouth curl into a sarcastic smile. "Of course, you don't think for a moment that that mass of programmed, biogenetic erector sets is capable of independent thought?"

"I don't know about that," I interject. "Old Xandroff sounded pretty independent to me." I ask Cuz, "What do you think?"

"I concur. I believe we are finished here." Cuz says to Tezabouh, "Thank you for your hospitality. I hope the plan is successful. It appears we have different objectives, and we must continue with ours. May the universe guide you to success."

"Just a moment, Cuz," I exclaim, looking closely at Tezabouh. "Before we go, I'd like to ask our guest a few questions." Cuz nods, and Tezabouh straightens a bit in anticipation of my inquiries. "Uzzendi, the Klaxon minister, was he the one responsible for the nanovirus that affected Biomei?"

Tezabouh gives me a thoughtful look, then nods. "Yes. He was also responsible for giving the Zenti a lot of damaging intelligence." He closes his eyes for a moment as though he were gathering his thoughts. He reopens them with a sorrowful expression, letting out a heavy sigh. "Uzzendi was a good man: a brilliant scientist and a humanitarian in every sense of the word. Within a matter of a few cycles, they broke him in both body and spirit. The Zenti somehow got hold of his itinerary and grabbed him, his mate, and their four children right as they all arrived at his new interplanetary research center. They were going to take a tour of the facility. It was Uzzendi's dream project.

"The Zenti took them to Celebus inside the Delius system. I believe you're familiar with it."

"That's where the Zenti is holding Nicki?" I ask, with a flutter in my stomach along with a heavy sense of uncertainty.

"The Zenti are a strange species," Tezabouh says. "Simply put, they're a genetic disaster that got out of the lab and are now out of control. They don't think or feel like carbon-based humanoids. A rage solely drives them; they don't understand. It's what they believe makes them who they are."

I give Tezabouh a puzzled look and ask, "And that is?"

"They are survivors. By all rights, they should have died off a millennium ago. And yet here they are—raging on."

"What happened to Uzzendi?"

A pained expression spreads across his face as he recounts what he has learned. "From what my sources have relayed, he initially refused to tell the Zenti anything. After several cycles of continuous torture, he still refused. The minister mistakenly believed they wouldn't harm his family if he didn't cooperate." He pauses, shaking his head slowly, then twists his mouth in disgust, as if acting for our benefit. "To demonstrate their determination, they took his wife and began torturing her with an induction pain stick in front of him and his children. Even after he begged them to stop, they continued. When her body finally succumbed to the injury, she shouted, 'Tell them nothing!' She was a noble and brave woman."

"The shock of witnessing his wife being executed in such a brutal manner was done to soften him up for what was to follow. The Zenti put him through a terrible ordeal of mind probes to extract information, combined with isolation and sensory deprivation torments. After that, his spirit broke. Once they had him under their control, they gave him a simple choice. Design an undetectable virus that would disable a biogenic organism, and your children will live. Give us the information we seek, and we'll let you live as well.

"Their plan, as you know, was to have Biomei's systems break down at a point of no return."

It all starts to make sense to me, but something is still unclear. I understood using the virus and wanting Biomei's technology, but what did they want with Nicki?

"You said Nicki was genetically unique. What did you mean?"

"There's much you need to know about her, but this is not the place or time for that discussion."

I didn't press him on the matter because time was as much of an enemy as the Zenti. We needed to leave. I give him a respectful nod, and Cuz and I go back for our belongings.

As we start to leave, Tezabouh calls to us. "I'll help you find Nickada. She should be our primary focus. The androids won't succeed. Xandroff can't see beyond the parameters of his program."

"You mean he's set in his ways," I say.

"Precisely," Tezabouh agrees. "Wait, I'll only be a few minutes. I need to shut down some vital systems and secure the island. The Zenti would be in their greatest glory if they had the opportunity to get their hands on the technology here."

Cuz says to me, "Given the circumstances, we are far better off with than without him."

"That's most logical of you, Cuz."

Cuz smiles. "Thank you, Phillip. That is one of the nicest things you have said to me in some time."

"Do you think he's full of shit?" I ask, rubbing my chin at the thought.

"Do you mean dishonest?" Cuz clarifies.

"Yeah, something like that. I guess what I'm asking is, can we trust him?"

Cuz seems to ponder my question briefly and states, "Probably not. But it appears we have little choice."

CHAPTER 42

While waiting on Tezabouh, my mind fills with anxious questions.
I ask Cuz, "What are we doing?"

Cuz seems surprised by my sudden question. "I am uncertain of your meaning, Phil. Please clarify."

I begin pacing while considering the problem. "Tezabouh's a contradiction that makes me uncomfortable. It's hard for me to work with people I can't trust."

"I understand your concern. Despite his mercurial personality, I believe he still has value for us."

Cuz is right, but I continue to pace around him in a wide circle, almost lost in thought. *It's just that he's so different from what Verubeal described in our telepathic exchanges. She revealed an image and understanding of him that is different from what we're experiencing. The best evaluation of him can be characterized as consistently inconsistent—a total conundrum. It makes me wonder if my faith and intellect are being tested.*

"I believe it is both," Cuz startles me with his sudden conclusion.

"You read my thoughts?"

"I can't read your thoughts telepathically," Cuz explains. "However, I've become so familiar with your facial and body languages that I have developed an interpretation of your thoughts with 92.6 percent accuracy. Also, you tend to mumble your thoughts aloud." Cuz smiles warmly.

"I hope what I'm about to say won't confuse you, but give you a concise explanation of how I truly feel about you."

Cuz's eyes become fixed on me with his mouth closed in a tight line.

"When we first met, and I named you Cuz."

"Yes," he says with his eyes reflecting a genuine look of appreciation. He adds, "You explained because we were both creations of Venubian genetic engineering and by Earth standards, that commonality made us cousins."

"Yes, that's right. We've experienced a lot together in a short time."

He nods. "Out of necessity, we've grown close, but I'd like to think we would've grown close under any circumstances."

I place a hand on his shoulder. "You're the only one outside of Nicki that I love and trust."

"I believe it's customary, at emotional moments such as this, Earthlings partake in an intimate act which demonstrates their relationship." Cuz pauses as if in thought, then adds, "I'm not quite sure which is the appropriate gesture."

Looking at Cuz's glowing face, I start to worry he's going to kiss me.

"Would it be a hug or a handshake?" he asks, with his child-like innocence and sincerity.

I relax and ask, "Which do you prefer?"

"A hug," he says softly.

I gladly oblige him. Tezabouh enters as Cuz, and I am locked in a warm embrace.

He says, in a cunning tone, "This is most odd. A physical exchange between extraterrestrials? An android and a human becoming intimate with one another? Why that's extraordinary." He gives us a smug smile and laughs.

"Doubt seems to be the only thing we seem to have in common," I say with a sudden urge to punch him in his arrogant face. I take a breath to cool down and speak with remarkable restraint, "It's painfully obvious we need each other. So, from this point forward, I strongly urge us to be honest and open. And let me begin this open and honest dialogue with a basic fact. We don't trust or like you. You're probably the most obnoxious android I've ever had the displeasure of dealing with. That said, Verubeal seems to have a lot of faith in you. I pray it's not misplaced trust."

I glance at Cuz to see if he wants to add anything. He remains silent.

"Then, in the interest of being honest as well," Tezabouh says, trying to appear humble. "I have a confession to make that I hope will facilitate the beginning of our mutual trust." His eyes dart between us as if looking for approval.

"And what would that be?" I reluctantly ask.

Tezabouh gives us his crooked smile and declares, "I'm not Tezabouh."

Cuz and I look at each other as though somehow that wasn't a complete surprise. It's the first thing that makes any sense.

Cuz's eyes narrow a little as he asks in a chastising tone, "Why have you taken so long to tell us?"

"Tezabouh had given me specific directives, but now that he's presumed dead. I've been acting on my own. You must understand that being Tezabouh's surrogate only entitled me to those subroutines he considered imperative. He gave me some of his personality traits and integrated them with my own, but unfortunately, not all of his knowledge. After downloading more data on humanity, I'd like to paraphrase a human metaphor: I'm treading on thin data."

"He's not Tezabouh," I repeat, looking closely at his impostor. "Cuz, why does this make more sense to me than it should?"

"Because we instinctively knew who Tezabouh was, and this representation conflicted with our innate knowledge," Cuz explains.

"Bullshit," I snap. "We wanted to believe Tezabouh's alive. The truth is, he's dead, and we're completely on our own. The androids probably already knew that and found a convenient way to dismiss us from their agenda. Cuz we've been pawns in an elaborate scheme to keep us out of the way with diversionary tactics. The androids have either killed or disabled Tezabouh for their purposes. I've an uneasy feeling. We're going to need this surrogate as a tool." I look at him and ask, "Are you, Ted?"

"Yes. I'm Ted. That much is true. You're now ready."

"Ready for what?"

"Ready to execute Tezabouh's plan."

"I believe it would serve us better if you divulged his plan first," Cuz says.

Deep lines form on Ted's forehead. He appears as if he's unsure how to proceed. "You mean you don't know the plan?"

"Ted," I say, trying to remain calm. "Tell us what you know."

"This is most unfortunate. Most unfortunate indeed," Ted mumbles, staring at the floor.

"What's unfortunate?" Cuz asks.

"Tezabouh never uploaded the plan to me. He never discussed it. His last instructions were for me to bring you here and evaluate your worthiness." He shrugs. "What do we do now?"

"Tezabouh would've never allowed his plan to die with him. The androids were supposedly executing what they believed to be his scheme. The logical conclusion is the details of his campaign must still be here," I say, thinking aloud. "We need to find it quickly."

Cuz says, "How did you come to that conclusion?"

"A humanoid like Tezabouh would never have allowed his plan to die with him. Somehow, I think he knew that Verubeal would send someone to help find Nickada and present her plea for help. She told me so. I was too preoccupied to understand it at the time." I ask Ted, "When was the last time you spoke with Tezabouh?"

"The previous second light."

"That's the equivalent of one and a half cycles," Cuz explains.

"Ted, what were Tezabouh's exact instructions to you?"

"There will be visitors on the mountain. Bring them to me."

CHAPTER 43

While Cuz and I continue to probe Ted's memory for clues, we're interrupted by a thunderous concussion that feels and sounds close. A second, stronger one follows, then a third. Large chunks of the ceiling and walls fall around us.

I turn to Ted and say, "Is this place secure?"

"Except for a few low-priority perimeter entrances, all vital areas are secure."

Cuz says, "We need to leave here at once."

I ask Ted, "What's the safest way out?"

"There's a subterranean tunnel system that's not well known. I suggest it will be our safest route." Ted's expression becomes contemplative. "We'll need to go through a secure area, though."

"Is that a problem?" I ask.

"There could be. It's a highly protected area. The auto defense mechanisms may interpret your body signatures as hostile."

"Can't you override or disable it?" Cuz asks.

Ted's showing signs of aberrant behavior. Something is wrong. I think if he's having trouble with the small stuff, how will he react when confronted with a critical problem?

Cuz asks, "Ted, are you concerned that if we disable the security, you'll leave the area unprotected?"

"Precisely."

"Is there a way to enable the system as we leave the area?" Cuz asks.

"No," Ted says, sounding unsure. "It's a fail-safe system. Once the system is disabled, it can't be enabled from the outside."

Cuz seems to consider what Ted said, and asks, "How's the system enabled?"

"Through a multidimensional, holographic, quantum-signature, encryption sequence."

"I see." Cuz appears to understand what Ted's telling him. He explains to me, "It sounds complicated, but it is a simple process. The system has

Ted's body signature stored in its memory. It's designed to recognize a user by their neural energy patterns. It's quite infallible. Everything that exists has a defined energy pattern that makes it unique and therefore uniquely identifiable." Cuz adds, "It's an eloquent system."

"Okay, how'd we get around it?" I ask, anxiously wanting out of there.

"Ted, can you enter us into the system?" Cuz asks.

Ted's eyes look down like a shy child being asked too many difficult questions. "No. Tezabouh is the only one with the authorization."

"Damn," I shout in frustration. "This's getting us nowhere."

Another thunderous concussion knocks us to the ground. The lighting blinks off, and we're engulfed in blackness for a few seconds. The room is illuminated in soft, shadowy lighting. I look around to see if Cuz is all right. He's already standing over me, extending a hand to help me up. We both search for Ted. There is a high pile of heavy-looking material where Ted last stood. We fear the worst has happened. Then Ted's head appears further down the pile.

"Nothing like quick reflexes," he says, brushing debris off his arms and legs.

I ask Ted, "What will the Zenti find in that secure room?"

"It's Tezabouh's laboratory. Over the last hundred and nine cycles, he spent most of his time in there."

Thin shadows became visible outside the great hall.

"We're out of time. We must go," I urge Ted.

"This way." Ted points in the opposite direction from the shadows.

We move as swiftly and silently as possible. All the while, we can hear tools digging and hammering through the rubble a few meters behind us.

Ted leads us through several winding corridors until we approach a dead end. He waves his hand over a small protrusion on the wall to his right. A large metal door appears directly in front of us. Ted stands as a barely visible shower of pale blue light beams seems to penetrate his entire body. The light dissipates, and the door slowly opens.

"Wait here a moment," Ted says as he enters.

A few long moments pass before he reappears and waves us in.

Every square millimeter from floor to ceiling of the room is full of stack upon stack of interlocking cubes. Each cube has a unique color sequence. Inside, the colors appear to be interchanging in random intervals. The interior colors appear to interact with shimmering clouds that pop into existence and then disappear within the cubes. Each cube has a unique cloud pattern that switches with an adjacent one. There is no discernible sequence to the switching, but it seems to be swapping with an adjacent cube first and then randomly to another one.

Cuz is on the other side of the room, slowly progressing down the wall. "This is fascinating," he says.

"What is this?" I whisper.

"It's a quantum memory core," Cuz explains, his eyes fixed on the moving cloud patterns. "Those glowing colored patterns are trillions of particles suspended in a quantum state."

"A quantum state," I half mumble, still gazing at my section of cubes. The shimmering colors are vibrant. "I recall reading an article about quantum computers. Of course, they were more theoretical than actual on Earth when I left. Instead of zeros and ones being used as bits, a quantum computer uses the quantum state of a particle. If my memory serves me, they're called a qubit. So, this is the real thing. How does it work?"

"It's extra-dimensional. Something like your qubit, but it can exist as a quantum-entangled particle, possessing equal superposition in multi-dimensional space. Each particle can contain trillions of bits of data that can be transported or exchanged over long distances, throughout the cosmos, instantaneously," Ted explains with a sense of pride. "It's the culmination of millennia of Tezabouh's research."

"Sounds miraculous. How many particles are in each cube?" I ask, appreciating the genius of the system.

"From what I can ascertain from this small sample," Cuz says, "it's almost infinite. It appears Tezabouh has developed a process of compressing and storing data on a subatomic level in a multidimensional quantum state."

"This is Tezabouh," Ted proclaims, "at least what's left of his conscious energy."

"What do you mean?" I ask, noticing Ted's solemn expression.

"All his thoughts, dreams, and aspirations are contained here, along with the entire collective history of the Venubian system. Additionally, Tezabouh also attempted to gather the entire amassed knowledge of all the intelligent civilizations within the galaxy." Ted's voice trails off, and his expression takes on a look of sincere regret. "He was my brother, my mentor, and he instilled in me more than an automaton's brain. He gave me some of the personality engrams that defined him as a unique being. I'm not Tezabouh, but I have an intimate knowledge of who he was and refuse to allow all that he was to be destroyed or, even worse, taken by the Zenti."

"What do you suggest we do?" I ask.

"We need to preserve his memory," he says emphatically. "But I don't know how we can."

"It's theoretically possible we can upload some essential data streams and archive them into Biomei's memory core," Cuz suggests.

"Does Biomei have a multidimensional, memory-core?" Ted asks.

"Yes. Nickada designed her, and I suspect with Tezabouh's assistance," Cuz says.

"This's all terrific, guys, but do we have the time?" I caution, feeling like the wrench in the works.

"We must make the time," Ted insists.

"I've got an idea," Cuz says, pointing at a console on the other side of the room. "Is that a user interface?" he asks Ted.

"Yes."

"Is it capable of compressing and then converting the quantum-entangled data into holographic, multidimensional data streams without decoherence?"

Ted's expression becomes passive, his eyes widen, and he stares straight ahead as though he's tapping deep into his memory. A few seconds pass before his mouth rolls up into a broad smile as he states, "We can." Ted looks at me as he says, "But we'll have to convert it into quanta or qubits first." "Then it can be formatted for compression and uploaded to Biomei."

"Show me how it works," Cuz says, taking a seat at an interface console.

"I think it would be quicker if I did it," Ted says, moving to Cuz.

I could see an exchange of mistrust between their intense stares.

"Cuz, I agree with Ted. We must begin to trust each other, or we'll accomplish nothing."

Cuz scrutinizes Ted for a beat, then glances at me. I nod for him to let Ted work. He stands away from the console, allowing Ted to take his place.

Ted tells Cuz, "I'll need Biomei's lingual code and quantum signature key."

Cuz stares at me as if hesitant to reveal Biomei's access codes to him. I urge him on with a firm nod.

"To open the security protocol, enter the following sequence: 10 to negative 33 in dimension 7," Cuz says in a quiet, cautious tone. "Once you've established contact with Biomei, I'll transmit the interface authorization." Cuz gives me an uneasy look, then closely monitors Ted's actions.

As Ted opens the transmission portal, we're hit with another hard impact that feels closer and stronger than before. Ted looks up and states the obvious, "They're close." He then returns his attention to the console.

"Can we at least secure the door?" I ask, staring at the open portal.

Ted waves his hand over a small area of the console and then tells us to lie flat on the floor. The entry closes, and a flurry of lasers starts firing from everywhere in the room. After a few seconds, it stops.

"We're now sealed in, but only for a short time," Ted explains, as I watch his fingers moving at a blinding speed over a multi-staged holographic keyboard.

"Can we stand?" I ask, feeling uncomfortable lying face down on the cold floor.

Ted says nothing at first, then he lifts his head and looks over his shoulder at us. "I'm almost through," he says. "I suggest you stay down as a precaution. I've offset the alignment of the lasers as well as the temperature setting. However, they're still enabled and will fire on any movement. The floor is maintaining your core temperature below the laser's pattern recognition threshold."

"Swell," I mumble. "Now, I really feel like a trapped rat." I give Cuz a sideways stare and transmit, *"Have you thought of our next move?"*

"We need to return to Biomei at once," he replies.

"I agree, but how do we accomplish that without giving away her position to the Zenti?"

"Once Ted completes the upload, Biomei will know we're in trouble and will come for us."

A loud hammering sound starts against the door. I strain my neck trying to see Ted from the floor. "How much longer?" I called to him.

"Almost through," he says.

The hammering stops, followed by a hissing sound. Cuz and I both stare at the door, watching its color quickly change. First, it's glowing amber, then turns reddish-brown, and a few beats later, it's a deep ruby-red.

"They're using a high-frequency laser on the door," Cuz exclaims to Ted. "I suggest we get out of here while we can."

"Not yet," Ted insists, sounding most anxious about finishing. "Biomei is about to transmit her confirmation, and then we can blow up this room. Hopefully, with a lot of Zentis in it."

"I hope you thought about an escape route for us," I say.

"Cuz, I need you to crawl over to the linear interface to your right," Ted tells him.

Cuz says, "What about the security?"

"If you crawl with a slow, constant movement, the sensors may not detect you," Ted says, sounding unsure.

Cuz begins his slow crawl. He gets about a meter before he's struck several times by laser fire. After a few more hits, he gets up and walks to the interface, ignoring multiple laser hits from all directions."

"Cuz, are you all right?" I ask in alarm at seeing all the tiny laser holes across his back and down his legs.

"Not to worry. I am unharmed."

"A volley of laser fire started hitting me on the floor. It feels like we upset a beehive. Each laser hit stings but doesn't cause much damage. Then I notice that I have several dozen holes in my arms and hands.

"I impeded the laser's intensity, but they will adjust," Ted explains and then joins Cuz. "We need to create a force field within the room. As soon as we're ready to leave, I'll set the laser to a barrier curtain pattern that will disintegrate anything passing through it. It will only engage if there is no movement within the room."

"I understand," Cuz says and begins to work on the large array of biosensors connected to the interface. The lasers stop firing and are replaced by a wavering electronic hum.

"That should do it," Ted says, taking a final look around the room. He waves his hand over a row of glowing lights. The lighting dims. Ted says, "We need to move quickly." An opening appears behind us—Ted motions for us to go through.

The opening leads directly into a narrow tunnel. The only light is from Tezabouh's laboratory. I look down the tunnel. It's so pitch black I can't see my hand in front of my face. A loud clang like heavy metal falling onto a hard surface echoes through the tunnel.

"They're in the laboratory," Ted whispers.

We listen attentively, waiting for the lasers to do their job. Horrifying screams and the sounds of sizzling flesh follow a warbled buzzing noise. Ted closes his eyes and smiles sardonically as though he's savoring the moment. Cuz and I are surprised at his emotional reaction to something so brutal. At first, I'm taken aback, then I notice Cuz's eyes are closed with his jawline tight. His response seems curious. My emotions seem detached. I can't feel any remorse or regret for our actions. After all, we're killing ruthless monsters. At least that is what I told myself. And yet, seeing Ted's reaction makes me consider whether I should feel something other than numbness.

Unexpected bursts like weapons firing rapidly rang through the tunnel.

"They must be firing at the laser array," Ted explains. "Follow me." The blackness of the tunnel swallows him.

I look at Cuz and say, "I can't see anything. Can you?"

"Concentrate for a moment and allow your photo sensors to adjust," Cuz instructs.

He's right as usual. My eyes adapt, and the blackness resolves into a visible gray. I glance back and can see the dim light leaking from the laboratory. Looking ahead, Cuz and Ted become visible in false colors generated by their heat signatures. The walls and floor of the tunnel are perfectly smooth and present no obstacles. We walk at a rapid pace for a few hundred meters and are startled by an explosion coming from the laboratory. My mouth and nose filled with the bitter tastes and acrid smells of the debris billowing through the tunnel.

I jerk my arm back when an unexpected hand grabs hold of it. It's Ted, smiling from ear to ear.

"I hope we got all of them," he shouts. "Come, the exit is just a few meters ahead."

"He's pretty emotional for an android," I say to Cuz.

"Yes. He's worrisome," Cuz whispers.

"Hurry," Ted calls in a hushed voice.

The wall makes a sharp bend to the left. Once we make our way around the bend, daylight floods in. The light has a relaxing effect on me. The tunnel exits near the edge of a narrow bluff. Looking down, we see Ted already below. He's standing on a small dock, waving urgently at us. There is a large hovercraft tied to the pier. When he sees our acknowledgment, he gets on board and starts the engine. It makes a high-pitched whine as Ted revs it. The craft bobs in the wind-driven ripples of the large lake. Ted pokes his head out under the canopy and points to a trail that leads to the dock.

We find our way down the narrow, winding path and join Ted on the hovercraft. As soon as I untie the lines, Ted throttles up the engines, and we dart across the crystal-clear, blue waters of the lake.

A shattering blast of light strikes the rocks right above our heads. Several more blasts follow. One glance off the bow of the craft, leaving a large, blackened hole. Another splintered the edge of the dock.

The water becomes peppered with near misses. I look back to see what was firing at us. We're already a reasonable distance from the dock. I can only see what appears to be about a dozen small humanoids running down the path, firing odd-looking weapons at us.

"Are they Zenti?" I ask Cuz, feeling an adrenaline rush.

"Yes," he says, frowning, "and now they know who we are."

CHAPTER 44

The only sounds are the hum of the engine and the rustling water. I keep looking back at the shrinking shoreline, wondering about the creatures that have pursued us. In all the distractions and emotional reactions, I never looked my enemy in the face. The one I killed on Delius-5 didn't seem real. It's a hazy memory of a featureless creature. I close my eyes, trying to visualize it. All I can recall is I killed a living creature out of fear and never looked to see what it was.

"You look preoccupied, Phillip," Cuz says, placing his hand on my shoulder. "Do you want to talk about it?"

It's the beginning of the first light. The red giant's dull orange glows in the clear, cool sky as it hovers on the horizon. The new day's bright white crescent radiance shines behind the muscular mountains lining the valley as I study the orange orb's diminishing form, melancholy wells in me. What could've been saved if not for all the violence, hatred, and ignorance? A sigh slips out. Now I see Venubia as a shattered utopia unraveling like a tenuous tapestry woven from a single thread. I wonder if all life is doomed to struggle. Is there no freedom from ignorance or evil?

I gaze at Cuz and, in a low voice, say, "I think I'm feeling a little too sensitive and naïve. Who is the enemy?"

"We all are. There's no right or wrong in war. There's only the destruction of truth and harmony between forces fighting to dominate each other."

"Do all androids believe like you?"

"Need I remind you, I'm not an android," he corrects with a faint smile. "In answer to your question, yes, enhanced-humanoids share a common respect for all life. I can't speak for Tezabouh's androids, though. They seem to have a different perspective on life in general and the Zenti in particular."

"Look," Ted points upward.

Like a shining friend in the darkening sky, Biomei hovers in the distance.

"Our shuttle is over the north wall," Cuz says to Ted.

As we approach the north shore, there's a brilliant flash of light rising behind a low peak. It appears like localized lightning glowing in the area.

"What's that?" I nudge Cuz with my elbow.

"I'm not sure."

"It's laser fire," Ted says, steering away from the shore. "It appears Xandroff is engaging the Zenti."

"I assume that wasn't part of the plan," I say, showing my irritation.

"I tried to warn them the Zenti are not to be trusted," Ted glances over his shoulder as the bright flashes get bigger and more frequent. "They're fully engaged now. We'll have to wait it out."

"I'm not sure that's a good idea," Cuz says. "We need to get to our ship."

"How do you propose we accomplish that without getting in the middle of the fight?" Ted pulls back on the throttle, bringing the hovercraft to a stop.

Cuz gives me a pleading look. He transmits, *"Can you contact Biomei? I don't want Ted to know about my telepathic ability."*

I close my eyes and concentrate on connecting with Biomei. I can't connect with her. While many things could have prevented the link, the fact that I can't at this critical moment is unsettling.

"Can't make a connection," I transmit to Cuz.

Cuz asks Ted, "Do you have a communicator onboard?"

Ted pushes a button on the tiny panel beside the steering wheel. The panel face lifts, revealing a holographic cube. Cuz moves the cube in short clockwise and counter-clockwise movements with his hand. We look up and see Biomei coming toward us. The great ship darkens the reddish-gray sky as she glides over our boat. An aft-hatch opens, and we're bathed in a shower of bright light.

The hovercraft begins to slowly lift upward. Remarkably, we remain balanced as we ascend into Biomei's belly.

"Was that a tractor beam?" I ask, walking off the hovercraft and into the docking bay.

Cuz gives me a puzzled look. "What's a tractor beam?"

"Um, never mind," I say.

"Welcome aboard, gentleman," Biomei greets us. "I'm sorry I couldn't communicate with you earlier. I was in stealth mode until picking up your signal, Cuz.

"That was prudent of you, Biomei," Cuz says.

"We need to go to Tangziah at once," Ted says.

"What's there?" I ask.

"It is the Zenti staging area," Ted says, looking preoccupied in thought.

"Okay?" I prompt Ted to continue.

"Tangziah is on the other edge of Kamertatok," Cuz explains. "A remote and sparsely populated area. A good choice," he adds.

"Precisely." Ted says to Cuz, "They're waiting for Tezabouh's instructions on the counterattack. The plan was to stage an assault on the Zenti forces at Tangziah to draw in all the Venubian joint forces. He wants to align all the major factions in one place and then…" Ted's expression turns pensive, looking lost in thought.

"Yes? And then what?" I nudge him again.

"Ted, is that all the information you have?" Cuz asks.

"Tezabouh was about to download the entire plan into me when he felt your presence approaching. He sent me to you and instructed me to impersonate him. When we returned, Tezabouh was gone. He left me a voice memo instructing me to continue in his place regardless of what happens." Ted's eyes became vacant with an impassive face as if he were awaiting instructions.

"If that's the case, then we don't know if Tezabouh's dead," I speculate aloud. He may be hiding and waiting for us to execute his plan."

Cuz looks closely at Ted and says, "He appears to be in a receiving mode."

"He's not moving or even blinking," I observe. "Could it be Tezabouh is communicating with him?"

Cuz arches a thin eyebrow while staring at Ted. "I'm not sure. It can easily be the Zenti or Tezabouh."

"Why'd you think that?"

"Under the present circumstances, we must consider all possibilities. Biomei," Cuz calls. "Conduct a spectral imaging analysis for data exchange on Ted."

There is a brief pause, then Biomei asserts, "There is evidence of a communications exchange, but the format is unknown to me. I'm now detecting high-frequency quantum particles surrounding him."

"What's the origin of the particles?" Cuz asks.

"Origin is unknown."

"Hypothesize from where such a quantum phenomenon could arise," I suggest.

"Most likely from a subspace disruption," Biomei says, and adds. "I detect a shift in the particle pattern. There's a 99 percent certainty it's a deliberate quantum shift and fits a subspace communication's profile."

"Subspace disruption," Cuz repeats, looking thoughtful. "That's identical to Tezabouh's quantum computer method," Cuz observes Ted for a moment. "It's evident the exchange is intended only for Ted."

"I suggest we wait and see what happens," I say, walking closer to Ted. His eyes appeared vacant, staring straight ahead. "He appears inactive. He's in standby mode. Cuz I think our priority should be in devising a plan to rescue Nicki. Based on the little information Ted has provided, she must be the key to Tezabouh's plan. And that's why he's not here to execute it. He must be in search of her."

Cuz levels his eyes at me and says, in a cautious tone, "Going to Celebus may be exactly what the Zenti want. For all we know, this could be a well-calculated Zenti trap."

"Do you have a better suggestion?"

Cuz stares at me with a placid expression, then cocks an eyebrow and shrugs. "Biomei, set a course to Celebus." He says to me, "I recommend you get some rest. You'll need to be as fresh as possible when we arrive. I'll stay here and observe Ted. I promise to alert you to any significant change."

I nod, feeling both emotionally and physically drained.

"Get me as soon as we arrive," I say to Cuz.

I find my way to the closest quarters. Oddly, it turns out to be my own. The door opens, and the familiar room feels empty without Nicki. I flop on the plush bed and stare up at the ceiling, trying to make sense of what has happened. My eyes grow heavy as I think of Nicki. Her image becomes fixed in my mind as I drift off to sleep.

CHAPTER 45

I'm jolted awake by a sudden shuddering that almost knocks me off the bed. I try to get to my feet but am thrown back when Biomei rolls to starboard—the screen powers on in wide-field view. A swarm of small ships is firing at us in groups of threes. Biomei is weaving her way through the swarm. All at once, there's a bright flash, and the stars blur. My body feels heavy for a second, thinking Biomei must've jumped her engines to escape.

Our situation has me questioning the wisdom of not having any defensive weapons. I take a deep breath. Nicki's voice echoes in my head, reminding me we're a ship of exploration and not war. Besides, Biomei's a pacifist and will object to any weaponry, even though we are on a perilous mission.

Another strong jolt forces me to one knee.

"What I wouldn't give for just one good defensive weapon," I mumble to myself.

The door opens. Cuz looks at me, his brow furrowed in tight lines.

"The Zenti are everywhere," he says.

"Yes, I can see that. Why does it seem they're always one step ahead of us?"

"It appears they have more information than we anticipated."

"Is that your way of saying we've been betrayed?"

Cuz squints and says, "Possibly, but I have no idea who the betrayer could be."

"I've got a theory," I say with a sudden hostility toward Ted.

"Please elaborate."

"Ted must be a conduit to the Zenti. That's the only logical conclusion. His actions have been inconsistent, and we've no evidence to substantiate anything he has told us."

"I'm having trouble believing an android of Ted's development could be manipulated so easily."

"Think about it, Cuz. He's been inexorably present since we arrived on Zenneah. All we know about him is what he has told us. And it doesn't all make sense. Now he's communicating with... who knows? And we're waiting on him like sitting ducks."

Cuz curls his lower lip, then paces the room. I recognize that expression and his pacing. He's emulating me when confronted with conflicting information. It would've been funny if the situation weren't so serious.

"Phillip, we have a dilemma."

"Yes, we do."

"What you're suggesting is that our plan is known to the Zenti and we're executing it. However, knowing this and it being so obvious gives this knowledge a perception of contrivance."

"If that's your way of saying we have been set up, you're correct."

Cuz's posture stiffens, and his expression turns impassive. At first, I didn't know what to make of his abrupt change.

"Cuz," I tap his shoulder. He doesn't react. "Come on, Cuz, don't freeze up on me now." I wave my hands in front of his face. He remains statuesque just like he did in Zenneah. My heart rate climbs a little. "Come on now, Cuz... I need you, damn it."

I studied him for a while, hoping he'd recover. His facial expression is frozen with his mouth open as if in mid-utterance. His eyes are fixed in an unblinking stare. As I examine him closer, he looks much like Ted does. The thought makes me a little numb.

"Biomei, scan Cuz for any anomalous readings, both internal and external."

"He appears to be in a similar mode to Tezabouh's," Biomei says. "I'm getting no responses from any of his internal systems. Stand by, I want to do a more comprehensive diagnostic."

There is a long silence that worries me. Biomei would never have taken so long to do a diagnostic.

"Biomei, are you still there?"

"Phillip, I understand your concern, but I've no idea what's happening."

"What the hell does that mean?"

I glance out the viewscreen. The Zenti ships are gone.

"It means someone, or something, is communicating with him using unfamiliar technology. He appears to be in no danger. All we can do is the same we're doing for Tezabouh, wait and see what happens."

"I can't believe this is happening," I grumble while pacing the room. "Biomei, what's wrong?" She doesn't respond. "Biomei?" My heart is racing as I look at Cuz's frozen form and shout, "Where's all my goddam, enhanced intelligence when I need it?"

"It's within you," a hardy voice says.

I turn to Cuz and am struck by how different he looks. His placid features are now lively, and his eyes glow. As I look closer, his features continue to change. Within a few seconds, he resembles Ted as he appeared before the android army: square chin, prominent jaw, ageless face, and a thick lock of white hair flowing down to his shoulders.

"I am Tezabouh," he announces in a firm voice.

His sudden transformation stuns me. I conscientiously close my open mouth and scratch the back of my head, trying to put things together.

It takes me a minute to regain my composure enough to speak. "Let me see if I understand what's happening," I begin, staring intently at Tezabouh's emulation. "When Ted uploaded, let's say... your consciousness into Biomei, you somehow took control of her, and now Cuz. How am I doing so far?"

"Most astute," he says, looking pleased.

I walk up close and scrutinize this Tezabouh emulation with as much emotional restraint as possible. Our eyes meet for a tense moment, then I pull away and walk around what was, a few moments ago, my best friend. Everything in me seems jumbled into a massive, conflicted lump that settles in my stomach in the form of an intense ache.

I attempt to engage Tezabouh first, with my empathetic senses. Nothing. Then try my telepathic resources, and still learn nothing. It feels as if I'm reading a two-dimensional object. I conclude it must be a hologram. After a second's thought, I dismiss that idea as impractical.

Facing the emulation, I lean in close and ask, "What are you?"

"I'm a program being executed through Cuz."

"Whose program?"

"Mine, of course."

"What's the purpose of the program?"

"To provide the details of a plan to defeat the Zenti, recover Nickada and Verubeal, and save 2.76 billion Venubians, Kaydens, and Klaxons."

"All of that from one program?"

"Yes. If executed precisely."

"Well, then, please, tell me the plan."

"The Zenti believe they have eliminated all the key leaders within the Venubian power base. They have never forgotten, nor have they forgiven me for my betrayal of them in the first Venubian-Zenti war. I'm sure Verubeal has shared the pertinent details of that unfortunate conflict."

I nod for him to continue.

Tezabouh's image turns and faces the viewscreen. "There's so much we could have learned from each other," he laments. He faces me with an intense gaze and continues, "Until now, the Zenti were believed to be a fractured group of desperate scavengers plundering their neighboring systems for whatever they could steal to survive. The Venubians and Kaydens thought their numbers were too small to make up a serious threat. They were wrong. After the last battle, the Zenti scattered throughout the neighboring systems. Although dispersed and disorganized, they were prolific in rebuilding their race, using newfound genetic engineering and cloning techniques."

"Wow," I say, rubbing my forehead. "Are you telling me no one knew about this?"

He nods ruefully. "Recently, they have become united under the leadership of one Zenti, who recognized they were stronger as a well-organized army than a disorganized group, as you so colorfully referred to as pirates."

"They have a leader? So, who is he?"

"Unfortunately, his identity is unknown. I was about to learn it when you arrived. The Zenti perceived your arrival as a betrayal of our agreement and attacked my compound."

"Do you believe that's why they attacked?"

"Yes," he says. "It would seem they were looking for an excuse to get their vengeance."

"How convenient we made it for them." I look Tezabouh in the eyes and say, "It seems the Zenti trust no one and hate with great passion. And I can see why. You have given me no reason to trust you." I jab a finger at him for emphasis.

Tezabouh's image becomes stiff, and he regards me with a brooding expression as though my remark hit a nerve. His features relax, and he says, sounding almost apologetic, "Under the circumstances, trust is tenuous. What proof would you require of me to bridge the mistrust between us?"

"How would you have me answer such a well-crafted question?"

"How elegantly logical of you," the image smiles. His dark, intense eyes soften with a deep sigh. "Isn't the route of all diplomacy compromise? We need to find a common element of agreement."

Interesting, he's chosen a point of simplicity. Compromise indeed. What would be an appropriate compromise? After a bit of reflection, it occurs to me why not ask him what I've neglected from the beginning?

"Release Cuz and reanimate yourself in Biomei's holographic projection area."

"That is agreeable," he says, looking pleased with my answer. "Biomei must transfer my consciousness back into my surrogate."

"Ted?"

"Yes and no. Ted is, well.... It's complicated."

"Yeah. Everything seems to be complicated these days." I let out a heavy sigh. "Very well. I'm sure Biomei will oblige you. Additionally, I want a private interview with Cuz and Biomei to ensure their integrity."

"I must caution there's not a lot of time for a protracted interview, but if this will help achieve our objective, I've no objection."

"Okay, release them."

Cuz blinks his eyes. "I know how this will sound, Phil, but we can trust Tezabouh's emulation."

"Cuz?"

"Yes."

"Are you, yourself again?"

Cuz gives me a careful look and says, "If I understand your query, yes. I'm in complete control of all my faculties."

I walk closer to him and study his face, then do a gentle mind probe, and I let out my breath, sensing the aura of his presence glowing back at me. I pat his shoulder and call to Biomei. "Biomei, did you hear the conversation?"

"Yes, Phillip." Her voice is reassuring.

"What's your opinion of him?" I ask her.

"I've been analyzing Ted's data streams since they've been uploaded into my archives. There appears to be conflicting data as to his actual identity. Although much of the string sequences match Tezabouh's genetic code, there's another distinct sequence I can't access. Phillip, I suggest you be cautious as you proceed with this replication. I'm uncertain with whom you're dealing."

"Interesting. I believe it's Ted you pick up on."

"No. It's someone or something else."

"Come, Cuz. Let's find out what this is all about."

We go to the holography bay, which is in the next corridor.

"Biomei, please open the holography bay-1 and begin the program." The doors open and we're greeted by a different stranger who's laying out a detailed, three-dimensional, topographical map. "Who the hell are you?"

"Allow me to introduce myself. My name is Tezabar, and I'm your strategic guide." He makes a slight bow from the hips.

"The projection looking at me differs from Tezabouh. He appears to be about the same height and build. His facial features have that mature, ageless appearance. His eyes are like two shiny marbles. Unlike Tezabouh's white shocks, Tezabar has black, slicked-back hair. What is most pronounced about this new replication is his disarming persona. And yet, I instinctively distrust him and wonder why.

"Tezabar, where's Tezabouh?" Then I think about Ted. Who the hell is Ted? "Come to think of it, where is he?"

"Tezabouh is missing and believed to be dead. He went in pursuit of Nickada and Minister Uzzendi, and we have lost contact with him for some time," Tezabar explains. "As for Ted, I'm using him as a corporeal surrogate for my consciousness. The consciousness you uploaded into Biomei was primarily Tezabouh's, along with my own. I'm Tezabouh's twin. And how all of this is possible, my new friend is a long story I'll gladly tell you another time."

"There seems to be an abundance of long stories to come," I quip. "Providing we all survive to tell them."

"Point well-taken," Tezabar says. "You have endured through so many contradictions and so little time to put all this disjointed mess together. Now, nothing makes sense anymore." He looks at me with his dark eyes and states in a solemn tone, "You have yet another issue to deal with; one of trust. If what I'm about to say helps at all, I must preface it with a sincere compliment. You have handled yourself honorably. I'm unfamiliar with your species, but I must admit you're among the most resilient I have ever encountered." His eyes glistened at me as he gave me a traditional Venubian nod of respect—fist across the heart and a low bow from the hips.

I return the gesture as expected and say, "Thank you for the compliment, and yes, nothing has made sense other than we're caught up in a well-planned Zenti takeover. Speaking of which, where did all those Zenti ships go? Outside of these obvious facts, I don't have a clue who you are and why you're here."

"The Zenti are still out there. Biomei outran them into this sector. As for Tezabouh, I dismissed his emulation because you didn't trust him, and we don't have the luxury of time to build trust. I have gained an appreciation of how trust is an emotional response for your species. It would have become necessary to reveal Tezabouh's probable demise at some point. I believed that to gain your cooperation, this was the most appropriate time to reveal myself."

"Okay. Tezabouh's dead," I say. "He had a plan, and it's supposed to be the answer to all our problems. I have to tell you that my patience has grown thin, and the last thing I want to hear is more bullshit from a new source." Tezabar's eyes dull a little with an uncertain look. I glare at him and ask, "Do you have Tezabouh's plan?"

"Yes."

"Great. Can you divulge it?"

"Of course."

"Good. Divulge. Enlighten me." I bark, "Give me a grain of hope that we can overcome this… invasion of Venubia."

Tezabar seems unfazed by my sudden outburst and declares, "The plan is flawed." He blinks, then flashes a confident look with his intense eyes fixed on me. "I have a better plan, though."

My mind is rumbling with confusion, and all I hear is *'flawed'.* I get closer to Tezabar, narrow my eyes, and repeat, "The plan is flawed?"

"Yes," he says.

I clench my jaw and get even closer to Tezabar, and in a loud voice proclaim, "If this mammoth ship had one, fucking, useful weapon, I'd attack the Zenti and annihilate them or die trying! Is your plan better than mine?"

"Probably," Tezabar says, flatly. "But first, allow me to help you with this." He reaches his hand out and touches my forehead. "You appear in need of a little energy stimulant. When was the last time you slept?"

"A short time ago, but I didn't sleep well," I mumble, showing my irritation. Instantly, my jumbled nerves and growing impatience, along with the heaviness in my chest, all seemed to have smoothed out. Whatever he did, it relaxed me into a calmer and more focused state. "Thank you," I begrudgingly say. "Whatever you did—I feel much better."

"You're welcome."

"Now to the plan."

CHAPTER 46

Tezabar walks me to his three-dimensional map and describes the placement of the Zenti forces and the captured Venubians. "What you're viewing is the Isle of Tangziah. The Zenti prefer this location because of its remoteness.

"The Zenti are simplistic in their methods but effective. They approached Tezabouh some forty cycles ago with a plan to free him from his exile if he would help them get autonomy and self-rule on Venubia."

"I'm familiar with Tezabouh's deception. The Zenti wanted to conquer Venubia for no other reason than revenge," I interject.

"That has been part of their motivation," Cuz explains, as he joins us, "but only in the sense that the Zenti could establish social order. Anarchy is pandemonium regardless of venue, and the Zenti is next of kin to chaos."

"So, you're saying the Zenti didn't want Venubia for their homeworld?" I speculate aloud.

"Their only interest is Venubia's vast resources," Tezabar explains. "They want to make the Venubians as miserable and homeless as they are."

"I understand. Misery loves company," I add, looking at Cuz. "It's clear the Zenti blame the Venubians for everything."

"Yes," Tezabar says and returns my attention to the map. "We've probed while orbiting this area for the past several ship hours. The imaging you're viewing is the latest reconnaissance mapping."

"A lot is going on," I observe. "Looks like large troop movements. Are those transports as well?"

"Yes, a hundred thousand Zenti troops are readying themselves for battle. Now look over here." He points to the south. "This is what's left of the Venubian forces. A mere ten thousand troops armed with short-range pulse rifles and a few tanks. They're fodder being readied for the slaughter."

"That's ridiculous," I shout in shock. "That's the best the Venubians can muster? They'll offer little to no resistance against such a force. How could the Venubians allow themselves to be such sacrificial lambs? It makes no sense."

"Venubians are pacifists at heart. This meager army is all that remains," Tezabar says.

"What about the Kayden and the Klaxon forces?"

Tezabar frowns. "What remains of the small Kayden forces and their air command are waiting on us to signal them. The Klaxon is a religious pacifist and will not fight under any circumstances."

"Will your grand scheme save those poor fools from annihilation and defeat those bastards?"

"The Zenti have been single-minded in their approach and up to this point haven't thought too far ahead. What I've surmised about their plan is they want to gather all the prominent and most valued Venubians in one place and kill them."

"Just as Tezabouh did to them," I say, eyeing the holograph with contempt.

"You and Biomei are the last two on their list," Tezabar states, ignoring my anger. "They already have all the Venubian and Kayden officials. Last intelligence report still has Nickada prisoner on Celebus and Tezabouh presumed dead."

"I can understand their wanting Biomei, but why me?"

"You're a special case. They perceive you as a possible savior for Venubians. The alien who was prophesied to become the patriarch of the new Venubia."

"Are you saying I'm like a messiah to these people?" That sounded absurd. I narrow my eyes at him. "You're serious about that?"

"Indeed. They want you more than anything. Nothing would better serve their interests than having you publicly executed."

"But I'm none of those things. I'm just an ordinary man who, by a course of strange circumstances, fell in love with Nickada. Why would they perceive me to be more than that?"

"Nickada," he answers.

"Nickada? What does she have to—" Then it occurs to me. "Of course, to give the Zenti a more important purpose than invading and destroying, she allowed them to believe I was the ultimate prize." I shake my head, realizing how foolish this sounds. "Sorry, Tezabar, but this is a little hard for me to accept."

"I understand. As I explained, the Zenti perceives you as the ultimate prize. They've been careful to stay close but refrained from harming you. That's uncharacteristic of the Zenti. They're both curious and cautious about how they should approach you. It seems your encounter with their droid revealed something they've never seen before."

"And what would that be?"

"Human tenacity," he states with an ironic smile. "You never stopped engaging their droid even though you were over-matched by its strength. Frankly, I believe you intrigued them. Most of their prey capitulate rather than fight to the death. Your resilience and unrelenting stubbornness also worry them. They see you as a serious threat. Something they have never encountered or understood."

"Do you think Nickada may have exaggerated my abilities to them?"

"Most assuredly. She gave them exactly what they needed to know to make them fear you. Therefore, you can appreciate how you're at an advantage by being an unknown factor within the equation. Shall we get on with the plan?" Tezabar suggests, pointing at the three-dimensional layout.

I nod absently, preoccupied with Nicki.

Tezabar zooms out of the east end of the Isle. A high cliff surrounds a small lagoon. The wall of the cliff is almost vertical, with only a few trees jutting out of its face. He points to a small hollow below the ledge of the cliff wall.

"There's a multidimensional transponder embedded in this hollow. It's updating Biomei on all their troop movements as we speak. Through the probes, she has telemetry on every organism present." His expression turns solemn. "Nickada was supposed to be transported to this site. Last update, she wasn't there. This suggests the Zenti know of Tezabouh's original plan, and that's why we believe she's still on Celebus."

"How's that possible?"

"The Zenti must have extracted the information from Minister Uzzendi. He and Chancellor Verubeal were the only ones Tezabouh had shared his plan with. Their methods are brutally effective. No one could hold out long under a Zenti mind-probe."

"I'm confused about something," I say. "Why did Verubeal send us to seek Tezabouh's help?"

"She asked you because Tezabouh rejected Verubeal's initial plea. He did exile himself on Zenneah. As I've already explained, he wants to prevent another bloody confrontation. Once he realized the Zenti are intransigent in their vengeance, he decided on a different course of action. He still hoped he could minimize the losses on both sides." He grimaces. "That plan has failed."

"The Zenti seemed to anticipate our every move, and I've no reason to believe they're that intuitive. One thing is bothering me, though," I say, mindful of something Biomei confided in me. "How did the Zenti get hold of the minister's itinerary? I was led to believe it was well-protected because of the minister's great importance."

"With regret, I do," Tezabar says, looking grim.

"So, who's the mole?"

"Tezabouh."

"Why would Tezabouh betray Venubia?"

"He was hoping to reconcile his original betrayal of the Zenti. As I mentioned, he thought he could arrange for the Zenti to win a bloodless coup over Venubia. He knew the minister would break. There would be no alternative but to find a peaceful solution to all the hostilities and reunite the abandoned orphans with their parents. It was a flawed vision from the start. Uzzendi's wife and children weren't supposed to be with him. Tezabouh never considered what the Zenti would do to Uzzendi's wife..." Tezabar closes his eyes for a moment. "When the news reached Tezabouh, he became enraged. That's when he left. The last intelligence report has him surrendering to the Zenti. And we haven't heard from him since."

"You appear emotional about this. It's surprising to see androids with such strong personalities."

"Tezabouh was not a Venubian android. He was a product of careful genetic development."

"Even more developed than Cuz?"

"Cuz is a culmination of many engineering advancements. He's considered a humanoid by Venubian standards. However, he lacks many of the oddities that make humanoids what they are, emotional and logical paradoxes in conflicted states of energy. Tezabouh and I are products of similar biogenetic makeups. Nickada employed the same techniques in your... shall we say, alterations."

"What do you mean?"

"You're an enhanced humanoid, yes? Although you're struggling with your paradoxes, your higher intellect will manifest itself in your personality, and you'll be in total control of your often-conflicted emotional states. This unique quality is beyond the capabilities of Venubian automatons because their innate programming ideology limits them. Mainly, do no harm."

"You speak of Tezabouh in great fondness, and you seem to feel his loss."

"He was my brother, and I'll miss him greatly."

"Your brother?"

"We were engineered and brought to life by the same creator. Although we weren't biologically conceived, we grew up and were schooled together. Over millennia, we explored many worlds, made some new friends, and made a few enemies along the way. Most profoundly, we were the last survivors of an extinct world. Now, I'm the only one of my ancient kind. I am the last Ezdenian."

I look into Tezabar's dark eyes and say, "I appreciate your loss. That's even more reason why we must succeed. We'll lose much more than a world this time."

Tezabar smiles at me, then glances at Cuz. "Let's discuss our mutual problem of trust. It seems to have become a precious commodity of late. The Zenti's mistrust is not without cause. Not that I'm defending their heinous acts or even suggesting they should be given any compensation. They are a plague on our system and need to be eradicated. I'm only illuminating the fact we have made many mistakes in handling the Zenti. I hope in our common cause we can find, if not trust, then cooperation."

Cuz and I glance at each other as if to say, Let's go with him. "Okay. You have our full cooperation. What do you need from us?"

Tezabar eyes us for a second, looking pleased as if he bridged one problem. "Now, I'll try to explain Tezabouh's plan. His original concept was based on a peace initiative with the Zenti. The terms were straightforward. He was to bring Biomei to the Zenti at Tangziah in exchange for Nickada and Verubeal. He expected the Zenti to insist on doing a complete inspection of Biomei before the exchange. They also insisted on all of us remaining on board during the inspection. They want to keep us close as insurance against another deception by Tezabouh. The Zenti are transparent to him, though. He knows once the inspection is completed, they'll kill all of us along with the hostages."

"What about Biomei?"

He casts his gaze down and, in a low voice, says, "They want her for her technologies, which they'll no doubt use to make more battleships. Imagine what a destructive force she can be corrupted into. And Verubeal and Nickada will be—"

"I get it. No need to continue," I cut him off, not wanting to hear any speculation on Nicki's fate.

Tezabar looks up with glowing eyes and says, "We'll force the Zenti into bringing Nickada back so Verubeal, and she will be aboard Biomei. They will find that convenient, and that is when we'll spring our little surprise on them."

"What surprise?" I ask.

"We discovered the Zenti can't tolerate ultraviolet light combined with high-frequency soundwaves. A sustained, simultaneous burst of the right frequencies of light and sound will incapacitate them. It's harmless to

Biomei and us. My brother discovered it in his research on Zenti physiology. It seems like a safe plan. Don't you agree?"

"It sounds lovely," I say. "It's unfortunate the Zenti already know about it."

"Yes, they do, and that's why we'll do it anyway," Tezabar says dryly.

"Why do I feel you have something in mind for me? You're going to ask me to do something dangerous. Aren't you?"

Tezabar's eyes widen. "Yes, I am. But not alone. We'll rescue Nickada and the minister, then tell the Zenti we have recaptured all of you. They will be apprehensive, but the prize is too big for them to ignore. It will seem as if we're honoring the original exchange, throwing you in to seal the agreement. After all, you are a high-value asset to the Zenti. It's, as you would put it, a deal too good to refuse."

"Or be true," I murmur, narrowing my eyes at Tezabar. "I hope I can trust you."

CHAPTER 47

I'm busy packing for our mission in my quarters when the automated voice announces, "Cuz is at your door, sir." He walks in and approaches me with his head bowed slightly, looking deep in thought.

"What's bothering you?" I ask.

"Tezabar's plan."

"I have my concerns... but still, it appears to be our best option. If it will bring this horrible mess to a quick end, I'm all for it."

"It's a risky endeavor," Cuz says, gazing at me with a long face.

"Cuz, you look worried. It's as though you're not emulating but displaying real emotions, and you're using contractions again."

He gives me a curious look, then arches a thin eyebrow. "I'm...." His eyes squint a little, "I'm feeling... concern for your welfare, Phillip."

His whole personality seems to have suddenly evolved. He has become more humanoid in his mannerisms. "Do you realize how remarkable that is?" I smile at the revelation. "This's quite a breakthrough, Cuz." I give him a proud pat on his shoulder.

Cuz regards me with a perplexed look and says, "I don't understand. What's so remarkable about having concern for your welfare?"

"It's because it's a sign of your emotional growth. You're displaying some genuine emotions. Self-awareness is an initial step to becoming human—or I should say humanoid. Emotions define you as an individual. Do you understand?"

Cuz gives me a thoughtful stare, then says with a slight upturn of his mouth, "Yes. I do."

"Cuz, as for the mission, sometimes we have to take risks to achieve our goals."

Cuz nodded. "Tezabar has arranged transportation. He's waiting for us in Shuttle Bay-2."

"We're not going in one of our shuttles?"

"No. He told me he'll explain everything once we're on our way. He wants you to come right now."

"I'm almost packed. Go ahead. I'll meet you in the shuttle bay. There's something I want to ask Biomei."

"I'll tell Tezabar you're on your way."

As I walk to the turbo lift, I transmit to Biomei, *"What do you make of Tezabar?"*

"He's sincere in wanting to help us. But I sense there are underlying reasons for his actions. He's holding something back, I can't read."

"Can we trust him?"

"Yes. But be cautious about how much trust you give him. Be safe, Phillip, and bring back our girl."

I lift my face and give Biomei a confident smile. *"Don't worry. I'll bring her back or die trying."*

What a mess, I thought. We're placing the future of an entire system in the hands of a strange and less-than-trustworthy humanoid.

As I enter the bay, Cuz is powering up the shuttle. Tezabar is waiting in front of the short gangway, looking at me with a crooked grin. When I approach, he gestures with his arm for me to get aboard.

Tezabar takes the copilot seat and tells Cuz to disembark from the bay as he inputs our destination's coordinates into the navigation computer. I take the seat behind Cuz and look over his shoulder to see what is going on.

"These coordinates will take us into the Klaxon system," Cuz observes.

"That's correct," Tezabar says. "We're going to L'hu, which is a moon in the Klaxon system."

"And we're going there because?" I ask.

Tezabar turns in his seat to face me. He arches a bushy white eyebrow and says, "That's where our transportation is. I've arranged with the Klaxon Ambassador to provide us with one of their diplomatic cruisers. Thought we'll travel incognito in style," he smiles. "I'm hoping the Zenti will suspect a Klaxon official is coming to negotiate for Uzzendi and his daughter's release. This will, with any luck, get us to Celebus without having to engage any Zenti defenses, which are formidable."

"What if the Zenti don't wish to negotiate?" I ponder aloud.

"They will. I'm sure of it."

"How can you be so sure?"

Tezabar doesn't answer. Instead, he looks as though he's considering his words.

"Phillip asked a valid question," Cuz interjects. "I'm also curious why you're so confident the Zenti will negotiate. So far, they have honored none of their agreements."

Tezabar considers us with a sly grin and says, "Because I plan to give both of you up for the minister and his family."

"You'll exchange us there?" I say, not surprised. "It never occurred to you to discuss this with us?"

"I thought I already did. So, I'm telling you now. I could have waited until we were on Celebus."

Cuz and I both look at each other for a moment.

"I know what you're thinking," Tezabar says, glancing over his shoulder at me. I can see it on your face, Phillip. You want to know how we'll get all of you off Celebus?"

"That thought did occur to me," I say, sarcastically.

"One of two things will happen. The Zenti will take the trade, then interrogate you to see what information they can extract. Or they'll kill us all."

"Tezabar, neither of those alternatives sounds reassuring." I stare at the back of his large head. "How about telling us how you plan to get us out of the Zenti's control in one piece and with our minds undamaged? From the little I've gathered, the Zenti don't care about how much harm they inflict if it gets them what they want. That frankly scares the shit out of me."

"Me too," Cuz adds with a grim expression.

Tezabar gives Cuz a mystified look with a long, dramatic sigh. "Ye who have little faith, abandon hope in the face of adversity. Or something like that." He shrugs. "I think it's an Earth proverb."

"And what's that supposed to mean?" I snap, growing more irritated with Tezabar.

"It means I've got all of that covered, but prefer not to divulge any details as a fail-safe in the event the Zenti get to you before we can execute the exchange. I will tell you this. You'll have help on the inside." He flashes his crooked smile. "You only have to trust me a little while longer."

"It appears we have little choice." I sigh in resignation.

"I agree with Phillip," Cuz adds, narrowing his eyes. "We are placing our lives in your hands. However, I must express I've reservations about how you will achieve getting us out of a well-fortified detention center."

"I hope you're not full of shit," I throw in, giving Cuz a worried frown.

Cuz says to me, "The trip to L'hu will only take a little over a cycle. You should try to rest while you can."

Cuz's right. I lean back in my seat and try to clear my mind of all the conflicting emotions. I begin Nicki's breathing technique, hoping it will clear my mind. After a few minutes of deep breathing, I relax enough to fall asleep.

***

My eyes jerk open from a disturbing dream about Nicki, but it dissipates from memory as soon as I wake.

"Where are we?" I ask Cuz.

"We're orbiting L'hu waiting on landing instructions," he informs, then gives me a close look and asks, "Bad dream?"

I massage the sides of my head with my fingers, nodding. Then a thought comes to mind. "Cuz, how far is Celebus from L'hu?"

"251.54 million kilometers," he says.

"How are we going to traverse such a distance in a reasonable amount of time?"

Tezabar turns to me with a surprised look. "I thought you already made the trip from Delius-5 to Venubia. It's only a little further."

"I was in hibernation right after we left the Delius system."

"Ah, I understand," Tezabar says. He glances at Cuz and asks, "Do you want to tell him, or should I?"

"I'll explain it," Cuz says. "Phillip, Nickada must have told you about how we use a special gravitational phenomenon to cross vast distances of spacetime almost instantaneously."

"You're referring to the corridors? That must be why the Zenti chose the Delius system. Because of its proximity to a corridor," I surmise, then see Cuz's sudden, uneasy expression.

"I think he's catching on," Tezabar says.

Cuz gives Tezabar a pensive look, then transmits, "*I think I know what Tezabar has in mind. If I'm correct, we must prevent what he intends.*" Cuz turns his attention back to piloting the shuttle.

"We're on final approach," Tezabar tells us.

I lean back in my seat, mulling over what Cuz had transmitted. I could feel his apprehension, which got me rethinking Tezabar's plan. "I'm curious. How are you going to approach the Zenti once we contact them?"

"The Klaxons had sent a message to the Zenti leadership, who are still unknown to us. The Klaxon received a response stating they're willing to negotiate, but it must be in a safe and secure location. The Zenti chose Celebus. They can dictate whatever they want. We have no political leverage over them. However, they're intrigued by our preliminary proposal and have agreed to cease hostilities. At least, for the time being."

"I see. You give us to the Zenti in exchange for Uzzendi and his family. Then what happens to us?"

"I understand your concern, but as I've already explained, the details of the plan need to remain secure while the Zenti detain you. They'll most likely place you in detention and do a preliminary interrogation to determine...." His face screws up as if considering the right words.

"I believe the term you're searching for is pain threshold."

"I was going to say, how much you know." He leans close to me. "I assure you, you'll be rescued in time. Giving any additional details is unwise. We need to protect both the mission and your lives."

Cuz transmits, "*Drop your line of questioning and follow along with the plan.*"

I heed his request, but my insides are turning with an unsettling feeling that there's a good chance, at some point, we'll be double-crossed. Cuz's expression turns passive as though he had placed himself into his security protocol. He must have deduced something and appears to be contemplating our situation. Having seen him in this mode before, I decide not to disturb him.

After a few orbits of L'hu, we do a close flyover of the landing area as a precaution. When we make our final approach, we are directed to dock at a large, domed structure. Once docked, we go to the closest turbo-lift.

"We won't need environmental suits here. The dome is pressurized with a standard atmosphere," Tezabar tells us. Then he looks at me and asks, "Your physiology has been adapted for planetary variances?"

"Yes. And for deep space travel."

He gestures for us to follow him into the lift.

Getting out of the lift, a small group of six Klaxons greets us. Three of them are covered in long, hooded, dark gray cloaks. The other Klaxons are garbed in official-looking uniforms.

I'm intrigued by how different they appear. Their curious bird-like features are fascinating. They are all tall, over two meters, with narrow bodies and long arms, giving them a wiry appearance. They're scrutinizing us with close-set, hawkish eyes set back under a bony brow ridge. Their heads are covered in multi-colored feathers. A thin, curved nose separates their intense eyes rising over a lipless, triangular-shaped mouth set above a pointed chin.

One of the Klaxons removes his hood, revealing a line of bright, blue feathers running through the crown of his large head. Then I notice a flock of large birds flying close to the top of the dome.

"They're a different species," the Klaxon with his hood down explains. "I am Head Minister Erhuardi," he cordially introduces himself. Then he addresses me with his glowing, pale green eyes. "You are the human, Phillip Mann."

"I am," I say. "You know about me?"

"We have heard much of you. You are not what we expected, but we are pleased to meet you." His voice has a soft, melodic tone over my universal translator.

I hold out my hand to him. He stares at it.

"It's a custom among my people to grasp hands together as a gesture of friendship."

He reluctantly offers his hand from under his cloak, and I understand his confusion. His hand has three long, bony fingers with sharp-looking talons.

I pull my hand away and say, "Forgive me. That was presumptuous of me, being ignorant of your customs. What is a proper Klaxon greeting of friendship?"

Erhuardi gives me a pensive gaze, then curls his thin mouth upward into a line that resembles a smile.

"We greet with a sound, which would be hard for you to reproduce. Let's settle on the Venubian sign of respect." He places his left arm across his chest and bows.

We all repeat the gesture.

"Your transportation is at your disposal," Erhuardi says. "All arrangements have been made. I must express anxiety about the success of your task. Also, I have reservations as to the status of Minister Uzzendi and his daughters." He closes his eyes for a moment. "We also want to express our deepest thanks. We wish you success and a safe journey."

He instructs two of the uniformed Klaxons to escort us to the transport. They give the minister a slight bow—one turns and gestures for us to follow.

They lead us to a smaller domed building where we board what Cuz describes as an excursion shuttle. A Klaxon pilot is already aboard. He nods politely as we seat ourselves. The narrow interior only accommodates two rows of seats, which gives it a cramped appearance, but the seats are comfortable.

Once we're all seated, the pilot powers up the shuttle and gets it airborne. As we ascend, I can see through the cockpit canopy an upper section of the dome opening. Then, all at once, we're in the velvet expanse of space again.

I see a sleek-looking silver ship. Its hull arches from amidships to its bow. Two stubby, setback wings tilted downward, reminiscent of a shark's ventral fins. Each wingtip has a large, cylinder-shaped object attached to it.

"What's on the wingtips?" I ask the pilot.

"They are small booster engines."

The aft section terminates in two large, funnel-shaped engine exhaust manifolds. They look like Biomei's fusion-drive engines.

We dock amidships. The pilot wishes us a good journey. I say to him, "Please, send my compliments to the Klaxon Ministry for providing us with such a fine ship."

He closes his eyes and nods, acknowledging my request.

Cuz described the Klaxons as pacifists by nature who have remained neutral regarding the Zenti. After what they'd experienced of the Zenti's brutal treachery, I'd hope they'll reconsider their neutral attitude.

As we enter the spacious interior of the diplomatic cruiser, I say to Cuz, "Is it me, or does this ship's design remind you a little of Biomei?"

"The Klaxons copied this design from Nickada's original plans. It was given to them as part of a reciprocal exchange of technologies."

"It seems as though Nicki's influence is all over the place."

Cuz smiles. "She has affected many."

Tezabar is already busy inputting data from the command pilot's chair.

"Cuz, take navigation and input Corridor 13's coordinates," Ted orders.

Cuz gives me a cautious look. He takes the second chair and inputs the coordinates into the navcom.

I sit in one of the comfortable passenger seats behind Tezabar. Oh, Nicki, I miss you so, I think with a heavy sigh. The well-padded chair is intuitive and conforms to my body, then reclines into a comfortable position.

"Let's go," I say, yawning. Tezabar nods, then powers up the magnificent craft.

CHAPTER 48

Cuz brings me out of deep sleep. "I'm sorry to disturb your rest. We're close to Celebus and thought you might want to eat something before we landed. It may be a while before your next meal."

"Where's the food station?" I ask.

He points aft. "It's behind the second passenger compartment. Klaxons are herbivores, so I created a salad you might enjoy."

"That was thoughtful. Thanks."

I make my way to the food station. An interesting-looking salad is inside the dispenser. I unwrapped it and am surprised it had no aroma. It also had little taste. But that doesn't stop me from eating it.

"So, that's Klaxon cuisine?" I say to Cuz. "It lacks flavor."

Cuz raises an eyebrow and says, "It has a rich flavor. Regrettably, you lack the taste buds to appreciate it. Would you care for some water?"

"Yeah, thanks."

Cuz goes back to the food station and brings each of us a metal container of water. I look at Cuz, perplexed, holding out the container to him.

"Sure, this's water? It feels a little heavy."

"That's because the container has a built-in micro fuel cell used to either heat or chill the water. There's a temperature dial built into the cap. Left for chilled and right for heated."

"What if I want it at room temperature?"

"In that case, push down on the cap, and it will open."

I scrutinize the clever device, then apply a little pressure on the top of the cap, and it pops open. I take a long swallow. It's as refreshing as the water on Biomei. I decide to stand between Tezabar and Cuz and gaze out into space.

"How far are we from the corridor?" I ask.

"Sorry, old man, but we've already crossed it," Tezabar says.

"You needed the rest," Cuz interjects, noticing my disappointment.

"How close are we to Celebus?"

"About 500K out," Tezabar says. "Should be there in under a macron." He stares at me with cold eyes and adds, "You should prepare yourself. This will be an intense experience."

Tezabar angers me with his sharp remark. It sounds more like sarcasm than concern. Cuz squeezes my arm, noticing my evident anger.

"He's only testing your resolve," Cuz transmits.

"I understand, but he also needs to respect me," I answer sharply. I move in closer to Tezabar and narrow my eyes at him. "Let's get something understood between us. Once this mission is over, we'll talk. Until that time, this is my mission, and you'll show me respect, or we'll have that talk now."

Tezabar looks surprised. "No disrespect intended," he says, sounding defensive. "I thought all Earthmen needed to engage in some form of religious ceremony before facing such a perilous situation."

"Really?" I say. "Well, you're wrong. Just do your job, Ted. And don't worry about me."

His bushy eyebrows knit in confusion."

I give him a scornful glance, then say to Cuz, "He's your problem. If he does anything suspicious, shoot him."

Cuz tilts his head with a dubious smirk as if to say, 'You're not serious."

"Humans, they're so emotional," Tezabar complains, letting out a long breath. He turns to Cuz and asks, "Is he always so emotional?"

"Only around people, he distrusts," Cuz explains flatly.

"Do we have any weapons?" I ask Cuz.

"Knowing Klaxon pacifism, I doubt they've supplied us with any."

"Great," I say. "Guess we'll be at the Zenti's mercy."

"Not necessarily," Tezabar says.

"You have something to share with us, Ted?" I say.

"As I intimated before, we have agents both on Celebus and inside the detention center. Please, be patient a little longer."

"I guess I've little choice," I say.

I gaze at the marvelous panorama of the Delius system. At our present distance, I could see Delius-4 and two of its five moons. It looks like a frozen, desolate world.

As we swing around Delius-4's system, Delius-5, with its bright moons shining like colored jewels, comes into view with Thaz-7 looming in the distance. Seeing it from this approach is a different experience. Its vibrant bands of colors are much clearer and brighter than what I saw from Delius-5's surface. It's mesmerizing seeing it in its full enormity.

As we make a close pass of Thaz-7, Celebus comes into view. It's a large moon with a slow rotation and elongated orbit, giving it an intemperate climate.

"We're on final approach," Tezabar informs us. "You should sit, Phillip. I'm taking us in at a steep approach angle to avoid any ground-based detection systems. Celebus has a thick and turbulent atmosphere. Also, there's a large weather system approaching our landing site. Prepare yourselves, things are about to get rough."

Cuz transmits, "*It's a sound strategy.*"

I can't help giving Tezabar a cold stare, then transmit to Cuz, "*That's if we survive the landing.*"

"Prepare, we're entering the atmosphere," Tezabar says.

He didn't exaggerate. The ship shudders and vibrates so violently that it makes me feel as if I have fallen into a giant blender. If it weren't for its strong hull and powerful engines, I don't think we could have stayed in one piece. As we continue our descent, the ship bucks, rocks, and bounces from the powerful turbulence. I think I hear a groaning sound as we increase speed, causing me to second-guess if we'll survive this crazy approach. Tezabar hits the braking thrusters to slow us down. The vibration rises to where it sounds like the ship is about to shatter from the stress. Everything becomes quiet as the ship straightens and glides to a smooth landing.

"We've landed?" I ask, letting out a held breath.

Tezabar also lets out a long breath and says, "Yes. I hope we're still in one piece. I promised the Klaxons I'd return their ship undamaged."

"The ship is the least of our concerns," Cuz says.

Tezabar turns and smiles at me. "I guess he hasn't learned ironic humor."

Cuz looks at Tezabar, confused.

"Cuz, sometimes you're priceless," I laugh, which only seems to add to his confusion.

***

Tezabar leads us into an aft compartment where we find a variety of environmental suits along with food supplies, communication devices, and portable quantum analyzers. Tezabar hands me a suit like the ones on Biomei. It's a bit large, but comfortable.

Tezabar opens a port-side hatch, and a gangway lowers. A howling, icy gale assaults us. My helmet's display shows the winds are gusting up to 60 knots. Dense snow is blowing into our faceplates, limiting our visibility. We have to use our built-in navigational guidance systems to find our way toward the Zenti detention center.

"We need to get into the caves 20 eloms to the east," Tezabar says. "Once we're inside, we'll be updated on the plan."

Cuz and I both nod in acknowledgment and follow close behind Tezabar. It's slow going against the strong winds. Even with my helmet's enhanced optical sensors, I can barely see the low-lying mountains.

"What's an elom?" I ask Cuz over my suit's intercom.

"It's a long kilometer," he answers. "Tezabar is mixing his terms. An elom is a Spacer term that isn't included in your translator's lexicon."

"Spacer terms? Are they something I should become familiar with?"

"It's something you should get familiar with soon, but I wouldn't be concerned about it now."

"Was that your way of telling me I should learn it if I live?" I say sarcastically.

"The storm winds are fiercer. Are you having difficulty keeping up?" Cuz asks, ignoring my comment.

"No. So far, it's only slowing me down a bit." I recall what Tezabar said and ask, "Do you have any idea what he meant by 'we'll be updated? He made it sound as if somebody else would tell us."

"I'm unsure what he meant, but I suggest we let it go for now."

"I hope we're not walking straight into a Zenti trap," I say, thinking out loud.

"I don't believe Tezabar would've gone through such an elaborate scheme to trap us," Cuz reassures me.

"Do you trust him?"

"Up to a point."

"Is there something you want to ask me, Cuz?"

"Do you believe Nicki is still here?"

"I've been trying to reach out to her, but have received nothing to indicate she's anywhere nearby."

"There can be many reasons for that, Phil. They know of her telepathic ability and must have her well insulated."

"I've considered that and many other things. I need to believe she's alive, Cuz."

"We're almost there," Tezabar informs us.

A small topographical map appears in the corner of my heads-up display. It's showing a narrow opening between two jagged-looking outcroppings in the face of the mountain right above the foothills. As we approach the path, the wind shifts behind us. They feel less intense as we get closer to the mountain approach. As we climb, the mountain shields us from the storm. The rocks are icy, making for tricky footing at first, but my intuitive boots produced traction spikes, which ease the climb.

I can see the narrow opening a few meters above us. Tezabar is leading the way, with Cuz right behind me. Tezabar pulls himself up into the opening, then turns and offers me a hand. I grab it, and he pulls me through the opening. I nod in gratitude for the help. Cuz makes his way in. Tezabar gestures for us to follow him deeper into the opening.

"Don't turn on any external lighting," he cautions. "Wait for your autonomic optics to engage and stay close."

We walk in a single file for a while in the dark and empty gray. The path gradually takes a downward slope. The ambient data readings show the temperature is a brisk 14 °C with 24% humidity. As we progress downward, the narrow path opens into a vast cavern. The temperature drops a few degrees, and the humidity rises.

"How come the humidity has gone up? I would've expected a cavern as dry-looking as this would be arid," I said to Cuz over the intercom.

"We're only a few hundred meters above a vast ocean that makes up most of Celebus's interior," he explains. "The waters are heated by a lava core a few hundred kilometers below."

Tezabar turns on his external lights, and Cuz and I put ours on. What we can see of the cavern's interior is magnificent. Everywhere I look, there are vivid, glistening minerals and rocks of all shapes and colors. We appear to be on a large shelf of a cavern wall. I spy narrow pathways leading in all directions into tunnels. The paths disappear within the blackened depths of the tunnel openings.

"Which way?" I ask Tezabar.

He seems to be studying the interior, looking for something specific. After a few long moments of searching, he points his light to another opening on the far side of a wide crevasse in the cavern's floor.

"We must go around. The fissure is too wide for us to jump across," Tezabouh says.

"Which way?" I repeat.

Tezabar points behind us and says, "It's shorter this way." He takes a few steps and stops.

"What's wrong?" Cuz asks.

"This doesn't look right." Tezabar's forehead forms deep lines.

"Tezabar, what's the problem?" I say.

"The strong magnetic resonance of the storm may have thrown me off a few degrees. I think we came through the wrong opening. This doesn't match the map given to me by my contact. That opening is the one shown on my map, but this area looks different. The entrance should be on the opposite wall."

"Okay, let's go," I suggest, feeling uneasy.

Tezabar walks around the narrow lip of the cavern wall.

"Be careful going around this ledge. The rocks are smooth and slippery. It's a long way down from here."

I walk at a deliberate pace, trying to keep my eyes from wandering from the path. It's tempting to take in the grandeur of the interior. I have to catch myself from looking off the path a few times. One time, Cuz catches and steadies me as I step down on a rock, losing my balance. It feels like hours instead of a few long minutes while making our way around the vast abyss of the fissure.

Tezabar stops and turns to us when we reach the opening. "This should lead us to an access point that will place us near the rear perimeter of the detention center," he explains. "Our intelligence has indicated the Zenti do not know of this backdoor into their perimeter." He pauses for a moment and adds, "I've signaled our contact. He told me to meet him at our pre-designated location."

"I guess this was the right path after all," I observe.

"It shouldn't be much further to our meeting location," Tezabar says, eyeing me.

"How'd you signal him?" I ask, wondering what he used and how secure it was.

"You're not the only ones with telepathic communication ability," he declares smugly.

I almost say something harsh, but Cuz stops me with a cautionary glance.

The trail meanders for several kilometers until thin lines of light can be seen, glowing beyond a curve in the path. As we come around the curve, we're suddenly bathed in silver light. I can't see the source of it, but it illuminates the opening. We enter what looks like an abandoned storage area carved out of the bedrock. Beyond the room, I can see a portal to another open, well-lit area.

A silhouette of a humanoid figure is standing near the inner part of the portal entrance. As we approach, the figure strolls toward us. He's dressed in a standard Venubian security officer's navy blue and white jumpsuit. He has a utility belt around his waist. I also notice a holstered sidearm strapped to his leg. When his appearance becomes clear, I can see he resembles a Venubian but has some distinct features that suggest the possibility of a different species. He's taller than the average Venubian and has a head full of curly, blond hair. His oval-shaped head, large, hazel eyes, and prominent frontal lobes are all familiar, but his musculature appears more developed than the average Venubian I'd seen.

"The atmosphere and pressure are standard," Tezabar informs us. "If you wish, you can remove your headgear."

The Venubian gives us a friendly smile and surprisingly holds his hand out to me. I take it, and he gives me a firm handshake.

"I've been waiting to do that for some time. Finally, we meet," he says, still holding me in a firm grip. "I am Karoft," he introduces himself. "First Venubian Security Director and sometimes administer."

"Phillip Mann," I return his greeting. "You seem to know me."

"Chancellor Verubeal has told me much about you. You're now well-known throughout the system."

"I am?" I respond, uncertain how to feel about my sudden fame. "I hope I don't have to beg forgiveness for some of what you've heard," I say with a broad smile.

My statement appears to catch Karoft off guard. "Why not? You're the ambassador from Earth. We're honored by your presence." He places his arm across his chest and nods, giving me a now-familiar Venubian greeting. "The honor is to serve," he proclaims, with a distinct air of pride.

"Please, while I appreciate it, I'm not sure I deserve such high praise."

"From what I've been told, you are worthy. And having our great appreciation for your unselfish service during our great hour of need."

"Speaking of need," Tezabar interjects. "Do you have our weapons?"

"Yes," Karoft says. "And more. We have additional help."

"Really? Who?" Tezabar asks, looking surprised.

"May I present Khezicar of Bylanthia and Sir Bartrk Larzz of Bulvaria?"

The Bylar's fabulous presence enters and is accompanied by a large and powerful-looking humanoid with a bright reddish-orange mane of hair flowing from his head onto his broad shoulders, all the way down his back. Sir Larzz examines me with fierce, red eyes while the Bylar gives me a slight nod of his giant head. They make for an imposing pair of different species. Neither of them looks interested in Cuz or Tezabar. Instead, they intently stare at me.

"Welcome to the fight," I say, at a loss for words.

Neither one says anything. They remain dispassionately scrutinizing me.

"So, this is the Earthman," the Bulvarian said with a resounding roar of a voice. "He looks almost as scrawny as you, Karoft." He lets out a hearty laugh. "Call me Larzz. I hate my formal name." He approaches me and swings his muscular arm out. I stare for a moment, confused by his gesture.

"He's offering you an arm in friendship," Cuz explains.

We grasp each other's forearms. He gives me a powerful squeeze, which I return in kind.

"Oh, you're not as weak as you look," he says.

His fierce eyes soften into a more genial gaze that puts me at ease.

"It's my pleasure to have you on our side," I say with a renewed sense of hope. "I'm thinking we can pull this rescue off." I say to Tezabar, "Okay, what's the plan?"

"Karoft, I believe this is your department," Tezabar defers.

Before he can begin, I blurt, "Is Nicki here?"

Karoft lets out a heavy breath and says, "We're uncertain. We've lost contact with our inside informant a few cycles ago."

"Then there's a good chance the Zenti have discovered him along with our plan," Tezabar says.

"That may be true. Still, we've no reason to believe he isn't keeping a low profile until we contact him," Karoft says. "If the Zenti knew our plan, I doubt we would still be here. In either case, we must proceed with our original strategy. Our latest intelligence has uncovered a Zenti plan to launch a new offensive maneuver against the other planets in our system. There's reliable evidence they've developed a new weapon which can take out an entire planetary defense network in one precise blow."

"I've got an idea what that weapon may be," I say, remembering the strange magnetic phenomenon on Delius-5. "I believe it's a wide-field electromagnetic pulse. Nicki and I noticed a strange magnetic resonance phenomenon when we visited Delius-5."

My stomach aches at the thought of Nicki. I clench my jaw, suppressing a sudden rise in emotions. I don't want to appear emotionally weak to them.

"That seems to confirm what we already received from our intelligence reports," Karoft says. "We're certain the weapon is operational. We also have reason to believe the Kayden system is their next target."

"What about the Klaxons?" Cuz asks. "They have a stake in all of this."

"The Klaxon has not said if they will join our cause," Karoft says. "They're total pacifists. It's not within their nature to take up arms against any enemy, but they have been helpful in other areas. They've provided us with critical intelligence within the sector and have pledged their support, short of providing troops and weapons. I don't believe they'll allow the Zenti to take over their system without resistance. I'm hoping, as are they, we'll end the conflict before that becomes a reality."

I ask, "So, what's our next move?"

"We've discovered a weakness within the Zenti's proximity system. They're using the interior of this moon as their primary base of operations. It provides the perfect environment for weapons testing and development. However, the Zenti didn't take the moon's fluctuating magnetic fields into account. That's why we're 120 kilometers below the surface. They believe the subterranean ocean can absorb most of the planet's magnetic fluctuations. They discovered they were wrong.

"There's a cycle to the core's magnetic fields. It fluctuates from strong to weak. When the field is at its strongest, it creates false alarms within its perimeter protection. It also interferes with standard quantum communications. They've tried to compensate by reinforcing their perimeter with a sophisticated network of optical scanners and infrared video detection.

"We're in a low-energy period of the cycle. We've also discovered the infrared system cannot detect a body whose core temperature is lower than four degrees Celsius. The mean temperature of the interior is 14 UD. Our environmental suits, with some modifications, can lower our temperature to 12.9 UD. It's a narrow margin, but low enough to remain blind to their detection system."

"That takes care of the infrared, but what about the video detection?" I ask.

"It's tied into the infrared system. Their system is based on heat signatures and pattern recognition," Karoft explains. "If we stay below the heat threshold and go slow along the ground, we should remain undetected."

"Won't we be warmer than the ground temperature?" Cuz observes.

"We should be close to the ambient temperature. Maybe just a fraction above the ground, but well below the detection temperature," Karoft reassures.

"What are you thinking, Cuz?" I ask.

"I'm familiar with Zenti detection systems. They're well-versed in countermeasures to their security. I'm concerned that even the slightest differential in temperatures will create an alarm condition. The Zenti are paranoid and always incorporate several layers of countermeasures in all their designs."

Karoft says, "Your point is well taken, and you may be right." He gives Cuz a closer look. "Your genus is unfamiliar. What series are you?"

I was surprised by Karoft's question.

Cuz glances at me as if he's reluctant to answer.

"It's all right, Cuz," I say. "You can tell him. We have no secrets. Especially now."

"I'm a new series of an engineered life-form. I was designed for one individual, Phillip Mann. There are no others in my genus."

"I can attest to Cuz's loyalty and his indispensable knowledge," I add. "He's not only my closest confidant but also my friend."

"Remarkable," Karoft asserts and asks, "Do you have a better alternative?"

"I believe I do," Cuz says, giving me a cautionary glance. "I can alter my body's biological signature to emulate the environment. Also, my biosignature is unknown to the Zenti, and if detected, most likely, will be viewed as an anomaly. This will allow me to circumvent the perimeter security. Once I'm inside the compound, I will locate the nearest network transmitter and disable it; that will permit all of you to enter undetected. The Zenti will believe the transmitter malfunctioned and will send someone to replace it. That will only give us a small window of opportunity."

"How much time?" Tezabar asks.

"A few microns at most."

"That's not enough time to get all of us in," Larzz states.

"That's why I will hamper the Zenti's efforts in repairing the system," Cuz explains.

"And how are you going to achieve that without being detected?" I ask, seeing the risk Cuz was undertaking.

"Accidents happen," Cuz proclaims dryly.

"Any other objections?" Tezabar asks. We all look at each other in silence. "Very well. It appears we have a viable plan. We're out of time, gentleman. If anyone has any concerns or objections, now is the time to speak."

I survey the group and see faces with determined expressions. Never in my wildest fantasies could I have imagined being in such a high-risk and desperate situation. Everything about it feels surreal.

"Failure is not an option," I whisper to Cuz.

CHAPTER 49

Cuz approaches the perimeter from the cover of some large boulders of bedrock that look like leftovers from the center's construction. The rocks are scattered over a large area around the portal and outward toward the fence. It makes for the perfect cover for us to get within a few hundred meters of the perimeter barrier. We spread ourselves out behind the rocks and watch as Cuz crawls to a section of the fence under a sentry tower.

"Keep your heads down," Cuz calls over my suit's intercom. "I can see the tops of your heads. Khezicar needs a better cover."

Tezabar and I are the only ones wearing environmental suits. Cuz suggested we use them for communications, but also, it keeps me warm and dry in the moon's damp and chilly interior. I gesture with my hand for everybody to lower their heads. Karoft understands my gesture, but Larzz and Khezicar look puzzled. Tezabar taps Larzz's shoulder and points to a larger boulder a few meters behind them. Larzz and Khezicar stay close to the ground, making their way behind it.

Seeing Khezicar's head feathers sticking up behind the rock, I signal to him to go further down into a darker area where he can stand. Larzz appears to understand what I'm trying to convey and explains it to him.

I raise my head enough to get a peek at Cuz's progress. He's already inside the perimeter and climbing up the sentry tower.

"It appears as though Cuz got through the perimeter," I tell Tezabar over the intercom. "So far, so good. No alarms."

"It doesn't mean they haven't detected him," Tezabar says. "The Zenti are clever and don't always react as expected."

"You're such a pessimist, Tezabar. Show a little faith."

"Can't help it. It's part of my genetically enhanced DNA."

"There's no sentry posted," Cuz reports. "It appears as though the central courtyard is empty of both equipment and Zentis. This is most irregular."

"Cuz, are there any communications at the sentry station?" I transmit.

There is a brief pause before Cuz responds, *"There's a communicator, but no active communications. I fear the Zenti have already left."*

"The Zenti left?" I relay Cuz's report back to Tezabar.

"That's not possible," Tezabar says. "We would've known if they left. No, this must be a new tactic. They must've known we were coming. We need to find a place to regroup inside the detention compound."

"Cuz just informed me he has turned off the detection system. We can go in now." I stand and study the area around the perimeter. A small domed building a few meters inside the perimeter catches my attention. I point at it and ask, "Tezabar, what's that structure a few clicks inside the perimeter?"

"It's listed as a tactical storage area."

Karoft walks up and gestures for me to remove my headgear. I feel the cold, damp air wash over my face. It has a reviving effect, but I don't want to stay in this climate for too long.

"We need to get moving," Karoft urges. "If this is a trap, we're too exposed here. I suggest we find a place to gather so we can devise an alternative strategy."

"I agree. What do you know about that building over there?" I point at it.

Karoft narrows his eyes a bit and says, "Oh, yes. I've already inspected it. It's a perfect place for us to gather. The Zenti used it as a tactical storage facility, but it has been unoccupied for some time."

I put my headgear back on and told Tezabar, "Have everybody meet in that tactical dome."

"Where're you going?" Karoft asks.

"I want to see what Cuz has discovered. We'll meet you there."

"Don't linger too long. There still may be Zenti troops roaming the compound. Hate to see you guys get into trouble."

"Thanks for the warning. We'll try to be careful."

***

I find Cuz working on a terminal at the sentry station. Looking over his shoulder, I see he's busy on the Zenti network.

"What are you doing?"

"Searching for any pertinent information," he answers, not looking up. "The Zenti have attempted to erase all the files, but must have been in a hurry. They left retrievable data fragments. I'm scanning them and extrapolating the data."

"How long will this take?"

"Not long. Ah, I believe I discovered something of interest," he says, looking pleased.

"Okay. Do you want to let me in on it?"

"Cuz furrows his forehead and says, "Why wouldn't I want to share it?"

"Cuz, it's an expression to get you to tell me what you've discovered."

"I see. It appears from what I could gather, the Zenti have gone. I've also uncovered recent orders in anticipation of our infiltration. There's a small contingent of troops still here, and they're preparing to engage us."

"Does it disclose how many?"

"I couldn't extrapolate that information. There's something else." His expression turns solemn.

"Well?"

"I pieced together directives regarding prisoners."

"Anything about Nicki?"

"They took Minister Uzzendi and his daughters, along with some low-ranking Venubian Officials, back to Venubia. While there's no mention of Nickada, she likely was one of them." Cuz must have sensed my growing agitation and added, "Under these circumstances, there's no reason to believe she's dead. She's too valuable to them and must be alive."

I nod in agreement, then let out a long breath to calm my edginess. I tell myself, stay focused. Keep your mind clear and your emotions suppressed.

"We should join the others," Cuz says. "Based on this information, a Zenti patrol will be searching for us."

"Everyone's in the tactical dome."

From the vantage point of the tower, we survey the encampment grounds for any Zenti troops. There is no sign of activity, which makes me even more uneasy. I want to meet my enemy head-on rather than being surprised by them.

***

We made our way to the domed building without incident. I notice all the buildings are illuminated with a light green glow.

I say to Cuz, "What's powering all those buildings?

"The Zenti incorporates bioluminescent materials in all of its structures. It's energy-efficient and provides excellent lighting."

As we enter the domed building, Khezicar grabs me and raises a razor-sharp talon to my neck. He drops his arm on recognizing me.

I transmit to him through my universal translator, "*I sure hope I never have to fight one of you. You would be a formidable opponent.*"

Khezicar closes his large, gray-green eyes and grunts. "*You are a complicated species, Earthman,*" he transmits in a soft voice. "*I sense many fine qualities about you. It's an honor to fight by your side in our mutual struggle.*" He fans his colorful, feathery crown a few times, then blinks his eyes.

"*That's high regard, coming from a Bylar,*" Cuz transmits. "*They're not free with their compliments. Looks like you made a new friend.*"

"*Interesting,*" I reply while staring at my new, massive friend. Something occurs to me. "*Are you monitoring my telepathy?*" I'm more curious than upset.

"*Always,*" he smiles.

I open my mouth to object, but realize he's only acting in my best interest and drop the matter. I turn my attention to the group of aliens with their eyes fixed on me. Everyone is sitting on discarded storage containers. They are talking in hushed tones full of tension that builds with waiting.

"Cuz has gathered vital information from the Zentis," I announce. They all stop talking and look at me. "From what he has gathered, it looks like the Zentis have left. They may have taken all the hostages with them. Under the circumstances, I suggest we make it back to our transports and head for Venubia. Karoft, can you contact your people and get an update on the situation? Also, a safe place to land near the Capitol?"

"Yes. But suggest there be no communications until we're well on our way," Cuz cautions. "It's likely the Zenti is monitoring all communications in the area."

"Agreed."

"If I may make one small point?" Tezabar says.

"Yes?" I say.

"There's a group of Zenti troops who are waiting for us somewhere in this compound. Most likely right outside this building," he says, in a dry tone. He says to Karoft, "It would be helpful to have the weapons you promised?"

Karoft stands and opens the container he's sitting on. "I was saving these for the right moment," he says, pulling out a large weapon.

"A sonic-blaster," Larzz exclaims, looking at the weapon wide-eyed. "Very nice." He grabs it from Karoft and admires the firearm.

"You have more? I presume," Tezabar says, walking closer to Karoft.

Karoft nods vigorously while opening two more containers. "There are a few plasma cannons and several hand-held pulse-phasers in these containers. I've been collecting them from all over the compound and storing them here over the past few cycles." He gestures for us to take our weapon of choice. As the others are busy choosing their arms, Karoft turns to me and, in a low voice, says, "My inside contact may still be in the main detention center. His intelligence reports have been invaluable to us. I fear the Zenti have captured him and will try to extract information. He knows much." Karoft grimaces. "I'll spare you the details, but their methods are harsh and most brutal with spies. We need to rescue him."

"I'm aware of the Zenti's methods," I say. "But what makes you believe he's still alive?"

"He's a unique individual and..." he pauses as if gathering his thoughts, "let's say he has a high tolerance for all forms of duress. And he's hard to kill. He risked his life to help us. In all good conscience, I can't leave him. There also may be others in there." He lets out a heavy sigh, and his large eyes take on a pleading look.

"What are you asking?"

"I've no right to jeopardize any of you, but I'm not returning without him."

"You're too important to the mission. I can't leave you behind." My innards ache with what I'm about to say. "He's that important to you?"

Karoft nods. "He's that important to Venubia."

I capitulate with a sigh. "How much time will it take to find him?"

"Providing I can avoid any of the remaining Zenti, about a half macron."

Rubbing my chin while gazing at Karoft, thinking his growing angst is transparent. I look at Cuz and shrug. He comes to us brandishing a pulse-phaser.

"Something new has come up?" he says, studying our somber expressions.

"Karoft needs to go after his inside contact," I inform him. "He also believes there may be other prisoners still inside. What do you think we should do?"

Cuz regards us with a contemplative gaze and then says, "If there's a chance others are being held captive, it's our duty to rescue them."

"I knew I could count on you," I grin, patting Cuz's shoulder.

"However, I don't believe Tezabar will share our commitment," he says, noticing Tezabar's brooding stare as he approaches us.

He walks to us, looking at Cuz and Karoft with his cold eyes and frowning. "What are you up to now?"

"There are prisoners still inside the detention center," I volunteer. "One of them is Karoft's informant. We need to get them out."

"Oh?" he says, his bushy eyebrows raised, and with a sneer, goes to a container. He pulls out a pulse-phaser and places it inside his utility belt. Then he looks inside the container next to Karoft and takes out a compact plasma cannon. "I'll see if the path is clear," he tells us, arming his cannon. "I've a strong suspicion the Zenti is waiting for us. Standby for my signal. If you hear weapons fire, come out shooting."

"What about the prisoners?" I ask.

"Once we've established the path is clear, then we'll go after them. If that's all right with you, Prince Phillip of Earth."

"Sounds like a plan." I grin, ignoring his sarcasm, then look at the small, well-armed group and say, "How about the rest of you? Are you for freeing any prisoners?" They all nod, holding up their weapons.

"Gee, I didn't know your royalty," Larzz quips with a hearty laugh. "How do we address you. Your royal highness or sire?"

"Try Phil," I say with a tight smile.

"We'll await your signal," I say to Tezabar.

Tezabar picks up his helmet from a container and puts it on. He glances back at me, pointing at the weapon by my foot, prompting me to pick it up. I toss Cuz his pulse rifle, and we put our headgear back on.

"Ready when you are," I tell Tezabar over the helmet intercom.

Tezabar gives us a quick look over before going out of the building. His body signature appears in the lower corner of my heads-up display.

"The area looks clear of Zenti," Tezabar says. "I'll proceed to the next dome. Standby until I give you an *all-clear* signal. Come out one at a time and head for the next structure. I'll provide cover until you all get to my location."

"Understood and standing by," I reply, then tell Cuz, "I'll go next. Have Karoft and the others follow me, one at a time, with a three-count delay between them. Be sharp. I have a feeling the Zenti are waiting to see our approach before engaging us."

Cuz gently clutches my arm, looking at me with his cold, security protocol eyes, he states, "I think it would be best if I go next, Phillip. I can move faster than any of you and will position myself behind the rocks a little further down from Tezabar's position. It will be a better vantage point for me to observe any activity from the towers and give us two points of cover-fire if needed."

"Be careful," I say, then stand close to the dome's door.

"Are you all right?" Cuz asks. "I'm sensing high levels of stress coming from you."

"It's nervous energy, Cuz. Nothing to worry about."

Tezabar swiftly moves to the next dome without incident. Cuz follows a few seconds behind him.

"All clear," Tezabar calls over the suit's intercom.

I peer out of the dome and can't see any movement. Khezicar lumbers up next to me, closes his large eyes, and nods. I smile back at him, then gesture for him to go to Tezabar's location. He moves with a surprisingly smooth and swift gait.

Larzz comes up and knocks me on the helmet a few times. "For good fortune," he explains, then dashes out the door. Watching, Larzz in amazement as he rumbles like a lion on all fours to Tezabar's position.

Karoft comes up and gives me a warm smile. "I find it remarkable that in the short time I've been observing you, I already see everything in you that Verubeal has described. Universe willing, I look forward to getting to know you much better, my new friend." He pats my shoulder, then runs, staying low to the ground.

With one foot out the door, my body seems to fill with energy. I'm running fast without effort or even breathing hard. Everyone looks surprised when I cross the compound in a few seconds, ducking behind Tezabar.

"Impressive," Tezabar says without sarcasm. "You're full of surprises, Mr. Earthman."

I position myself to Karoft's left and ask, "Where's the entrance to the detention center?"

"It's two levels down. There's a lift inside the main building, which is the large dome straight ahead. It has a separate perimeter detection system that may be problematic. It's the same design as the perimeter system. There's also a tunnel used for heavy equipment transport. The entrance is on the other side of the perimeter and is protected only by troops. That's our best option." Tezabar stands, holding up a hand-held quantum analyzer. He surveys the area with a few quick sensor sweeps. He ducks down and whispers, "Seven Zenti troops are guarding the tunnel entrance and only have one sentry in the west tower."

"I'll take care of the tower sentry," Cuz volunteers.

Tezabar says, "Let's split up into two groups. Larzz and I will go around to the south side. You three go to the north. Cuz, let us know when you've taken care of the sentry. I don't have to remind you, it would be best to take them by surprise and do it quietly."

"You ready?" I ask Cuz.

He gives me a steely-eyed nod.

"You do realize it will be my ass if anything happens to you?"

Cuz smiles, then turns and stealthily gets into position for the sentry tower.

"Are we clear on what we're doing?" Tezabar asks. He studies us for a moment, then stands and rechecks the area with his hi-res binoculars. Tezabar points two fingers at the sentry tower, signaling Cuz to go.

We all stand, waiting for Tezabar's signal. I watch Cuz run, keeping a low profile across the open area. Once he reaches the fence below the sentry station, he pulls out a small reflecting mirror and signals us to go. Tezabar looks at my group next. I led us at a quick pace, but slow enough for Khezicar to keep up. When Khezicar goes by, I quicken my pace.

Karoft passes me, then looks back and gestures to where we should go. I wave him on and stop to see if Cuz has made it to the sentry station. I can't see him, then I see Karoft is already at the side of the detention dome, waving for me to come.

"What were you thinking?" Karoft says irritably. "You could've been seen."

"Sorry. I was trying to see if Cuz—"

"You worry about yourself. Cuz can execute his assignment."

I swallow, realizing the seriousness of my actions. "Sorry. Won't happen again."

Khezicar comes from the other side of the dome and transmits, "*No Zenti. Does not feel right. Believe we are walking into a trap.*"

"He's probably right," Karoft agrees. "Have you heard from Cuz?"

"Not yet, but I think we should stay put until I hear from him or Tezabar."

Karoft tells us to stay put, then ambles around the dome. Khezicar starts to follow, but Karoft stops and throws his hand up for him to stay with me.

I rest my back against the dome's smooth wall, trying to calm my pounding heart. Waiting is torturous. Not knowing what is happening pushes my nerves to the edge. "I wish something would happen already," I mumble.

Khezicar turns and lowers his amber eyes at me and transmits, *"You will not have to wait much longer."*

His comment is surprising, and he's looking at me as if he knows something is up. A second later, the dome rumbles with a stunning explosion—plumes of thick, dark smoke billow from the detention center's entrance.

"Go," Tezabar commands over my intercom.

I hear weapons firing in the background as I jump to my feet. Khezicar is already ahead of me. When I get around to the front, six Zenti troops are firing at us. They're dressed in black body armor, their heads covered by helmets with dark face shields. Khezicar is hit twice but keeps charging toward a Zenti. Khezicar crushes him with a massive blow to the head—a Zenti fires at me. I hit the ground and fire back at him. The pulse laser is more powerful than I imagined. Dark green-blue blood spews from a gaping wound that slices through the Zenti's midsection. I cut it in half, with its upper torso falling to the ground, leaving its lower half still standing. The horrid sight has me grimacing with a sudden wave of nausea. I close my eyes and vomit bitter bile into my mouth.

When I open my eyes, I see Khezicar blow up three Zenti with his pulse cannon. An odd puffing sound comes from behind the few remaining Zenti troops. They turn to the sound. As soon as they get themselves in position, their bodies burst apart with a resounding and powerful thud. Larzz appears through the thinning smoke, pumping his weapon up high in celebration, walking to us. Tezabar stops and stands over the fallen Zenti. He removes his helmet, prodding them with his boot tip as if ensuring they are dead.

When I remove my helmet, I spit out the bitter bile, grab my canteen, and swish out my mouth. Khezicar glances at me as if to make sure I'm all right. I notice blood oozing from a large, blackened hole in the upper part of his torso.

"*You're bleeding,*" I transmit. "*You need medical attention.*"

He shakes his large head and closes his eyes. His body vibrates a little as if he's laughing. "*Not to worry, it is not serious. Bleeding will stop on its own,*" he replies in a calm voice.

Tezabar and Larzz come to us. "Where are Karoft and Cuz?" I ask, feeling nervous about their absence.

"Who do you think blew up the entrance?" Tezabar says, "They'll be along in a moment. Cuz has retrieved more data."

"Somehow that doesn't surprise me," I say. "Are there more Zenti inside?"

"Not anymore. Those appear to be the last of them." Tezabar points to the Zenti I killed and asks, "Your first?"

I glare at his smug smile, looking down at the dismembered Zenti. I'm tempted to kneel and remove his helmet to get a look at its face. My stomach sickens again thinking of the kill. Like on Delius-5, I didn't want the first Zenti I saw to be one I had killed.

"It appears our little plan worked," Tezabar gloats, twisting his mouth into a jeering smirk.

"Right," I answer. "Let's see if any of the prisoners are still alive."

"Karoft and Cuz are already busy doing that."

"Don't you think we should help them?" I eye Tezabar, showing my displeasure. "Never mind, I'll go. But I suggest you guys make sure there are no more Zenti."

Tezabar turns to Larzz, who seems confused by our exchange of words. "Humans, they're so emotional," Tezabar says with his crooked smile.

Larzz shrugs, leveling his fierce eyes at Tezabar and states, in his thick brogue, "I don' think ee likes you."

CHAPTER 50

I walk with care down the ramp into the detention center. The ground is slick with blood, scattered debris, and the stench of dismembered bodies. Entering the center, my senses are accosted by acrid, putrid-smelling air along with creaking and cracking sounds. There is no lighting. I put my helmet back on. Its external lights automatically engage, giving me enough illumination to find my way.

A few meters further in, my foot hits something solid. I look down and see several dead Zenti. The one my foot found had its head and one of its arms blown off. The rest all look mangled and dismembered beyond recognition. All I can see are bits and pieces of the grotesque little aliens. They look more animal than humanoid, which heightens their demonic characterization. Whatever Karoft used to blow open the doors must have been most powerful to cause this much damage.

"Cuz, can you hear me?" I call over the intercom. No answer. Becoming concerned, I reach out telepathically. He responds, putting me at ease. "*Where are you?*" I transmit.

"*Lower detention cell block. Look for a ramp close to the wall past the guardhouse.*"

"*Are there any survivors?*"

"*Yes, there are many, and most need medical attention,*" he transmits with great urgency.

"*I'll be right there.*"

After walking only a few more meters, I hear weapons firing in the distance. It's coming from both behind and ahead of me. I rush toward Cuz's location. The ramp leads to a loading dock. To the right of the pier is another short ramp that leads to a corridor. The corridor brings me to the guard station. The weapon's firing stops. Four dead Zenti are lying on the floor outside the guard station. I hear movement within the shadows of the dark area. I point my weapon toward the footsteps and call, "Who's there?" No answer, at first, then I see Karoft walking into the light of my helmet.

"Hold your fire!" he shouts.

I remove my helmet, and Karoft greets me with a solemn expression. "What's this all about?" I ask, looking down at the dead Zenti.

Like all the others I've seen, they're covered in armored vests and helmets. I have no desire to inspect the enemy. The mangled bodies I had seen on the upper level satisfied my curiosity. I figure it won't be too long before I see a living one up close.

"Cuz sent me to investigate movement," Karoft explains, through heavy breathing. "As I got up to this level, I saw Zenti working inside the guard station. I assumed they were attempting to get their communicator working. They didn't hear me until I kicked something on the ground, which got them firing. I ducked down for cover. When they came out of the station, I killed them with my pulse-phaser."

"Are you okay?" I ask, noticing how red his face looks.

He nods, pushing back a thick lock of blonde hair from his face. "They weren't standard military and lousy shots. Mostly they were only techs," he says, gazing down at his kills. He closes his large eyes and, with a solemn expression, whispers something in Venubian.

"Was that a prayer?" I ask, trying to understand his conflicted mood.

"Of sorts," he answers, looking weary.

"Think these are the last of them?"

"Doubtful. They seem to be scattered all over the complex. Cuz believes some may have gone into the tunnels and are waiting for us to approach."

"What about the prisoners? Can we move them?"

Karoft lets out another heavy sigh. "Best you see for yourself." He gestures for me to follow him. The path is lit with dull, shadowy lighting leaking from the lower level.

As we descend the ramp, the lighting becomes brighter in the lower detention block.

"You got the power back on?" I say.

"This section has an independent power supply. It ensures the cells remain secure during a power outage."

When we reach the detection block, there are scores of prisoners attending to their cellmates. They all look frail, with sunken faces and pale complexions. Their eyes reflect a weariness that gives them the appearance of souls on the fringe of life. Their plight pierces deep in me. I feel their despair and bewilderment.

I ask Karoft, "How did you get the cells unlocked?"

"There's a central controller inside the guardhouse. The Zenti used a simple algorithm that Cuz deciphered," Karoft explains.

"He never ceases to surprise me with his talents."

"In the short time I've spent with him, he has proven to be a trustworthy and valuable partner. You're most fortunate to have him as your aide."

"Aide? Cuz is much more than that. He's become my most valued friend and ally. I trust him with my life."

Karoft doesn't look surprised by my comment. Instead, he smiles approvingly, adding, "It appears Cuz is also fortunate to have such a loyal friend. Even if he's an alien."

Speaking of whom. Where the hell is he?"

"In search of medical supplies. He discovered there's a small medical clinic next to this building. He asked me to have you get the ambulatory prisoners out of here. Also, it would be helpful if Tezabar brought everyone down. We'll need them to assist in getting the sick and injured out. I'm uneasy with our exposure here."

I try contacting Tezabar telepathically. Unlike Cuz, his responses are always dispassionate and blunt, which only reinforces my distrust of him.

As Karoft and I make our way deeper into the cell block, a sudden stench overwhelms us. I cover my mouth and nose with my hand, trying not to gag. Then my jaw drops at seeing great heaps of decomposing bodies in two large cells.

The bodies are laid across the cell floors and piled high. Karoft takes his scanner from his utility belt to determine how long they'd been dead.

"Most have died within the past two cycles. Some longer," he says. His face tightens, then grimaces in disgust at the horrific sight. "This is more confirmation of the Zenti's haste. We must have come ahead of schedule." Karoft stares at the dead masses, in a mournful tone, adds, "They deserve better than to be left to rot. We need to bury them with dignity. Even if it's a mass grave." He turns and, in an emotionally strained voice, says, "Please have Cuz perform a DNA scan for identification purposes. They shouldn't die anonymously. Their families need to know."

"You're right," I say. "Our obligation to recognize their service and to let their families know they didn't die in vain transcends anything else we do here. I'll make sure we find the tools to bury them with dignity."

We return to the upper detention level and are surprised by Tezabar and Larzz, loading a group of ambulatory survivors into three compact transports.

"That was resourceful," I say.

Tezabar grins. "The Bylar is on his way with a heavy tractor with a large bed."

He joins Larzz in helping some weak survivors into the transport.

Surveying the sickly group, I estimate there are over a hundred of them in various degrees of health. The ones who were busy attending to the sick and injured appear barely able to stand.

"So many," I whisper and go back to Karoft. "How do you suppose we can get them off this moon? Our ship can't accommodate such numbers."

Despair rises with a heaviness in my chest, studying the mass of helpless aliens. They're mostly Venubians with a few Kaydens and Klaxons mixed in.

"Is this all of them?" I ask.

"There's a security block the Zenti used for high-profile prisoners. Uzzendi and his family, along with some Venubian council members—" Karoft stops. He must have noticed my jaw tighten and my demeanor stiffen. "Phillip, as far as we know, Nickada and Verubeal were taken separately before the Zenti evacuated this facility. These survivors were used as forced labor. A few may have been low-level diplomats and military leaders who were only useful for whatever intelligence the Zenti could extract."

"Have you attempted to enter the high-security block?" I ask, not wanting to dwell on Nicki and Verubeal.

"Not yet. I was about to ask if you would come with me to see if my contact is there. And any other survivors."

"Where is it?"

"Three levels down. We'll go check it out as soon as Cuz returns with the supplies. In the meantime, why don't you see if you can offer any comfort to some of them?" He turns back to the open cells.

As I help a struggling Venubian, I see Cuz enter, carrying two large rectangular boxes mounted on his shoulders and two full-looking equipment containers dangling on straps from his hands. It appears to be a ponderous load.

"Sometimes I forget how strong you are," I say, holding my arm out to lighten his load.

"Thank you, but I can handle this. Three more containers need to be brought down."

"How did you get all of this here?"

"I located a maintenance dome next to the clinic. There are many heavy and light conveyances stored there. Also, a good number of troop transports and a few hovercraft. Some of them need repair, but many appear operational. Once we attend to the survivors, I suggest we go there and get transportation for all of us."

"Excellent. I'll notify Tezabar and get him to bring the transportation." Finally, we get a break, I think, making my way to the main floor.

Coming out of the dome, I see something like a flatbed transport loaded with supplies. The three containers Cuz needs are lying in front of it. I unhook my helmet from my utility belt and put it on to contact Tezabar.

"Tezabar, what's your location?" He doesn't answer. "Tezabar, this is Phillip. Do you read me?" Either there's radio interference, or he's ignoring me. *"Cuz, I attempted to reach Tezabar. He's not answering,"* I transmit.

"He's not down here," Cuz replies.

His absence makes me uneasy. I survey the immediate area, but Tezabar's nowhere in sight. I try contacting him again, but still get nothing but static. Knowing how essential the medical supplies are, I take the containers down to Cuz and decide to reach Tezabar later.

Karoft greets me as I get to the lower level. "Larzz and Khezicar are working with Cuz on the sick and injured," he informs, and reaches for a container.

"Thanks, but I can handle this. Do you know where Tezabar is?"

Karoft gives me a bewildered look and says, "He's supposed to be helping you."

"He's nowhere in sight. I tried contacting him with no reply." Something occurs to me. "Do you think he's down in the high-security area?"

"Why would he be there?" his expression fills with alarm. "We'd better get down there and see."

"I agree. Give me a micron. Cuz is waiting for these."

"Better see if Larzz or Khezicar can join us. I think we'll need backup," he says.

I find Cuz in a cell, attending to a sick survivor. "Cuz," I call to him from outside the cell.

He turns and sees the supplies. "Just leave them there," he says, returning his attention to the wretched-looking Venubian. Cuz is holding the Venubian's head up and bandaging a long, blackened wound across his forehead. The ghastly, thin patient is lying on a slender, grimy-looking mattress, covering a metal-framed cot. He's groaning in pain, and his breathing sounds ragged and labored.

"Sorry to disturb you from your work, but I need a word with you."

Cuz kneels on one knee next to the cot and administers a hypo-spray, then gently lays the Venubian's head down on a thin pillow. The patient lets out a long, gasping sigh. Cuz runs his scanner over him. He stands, placing the scanner back into its pouch on his utility belt.

"He doesn't look too good," I say, in a low voice. "Is he going to make it?"

"Doubtful," Cuz replies, with an android's detachment. "What's the matter?" he asks, sensing my unsettled feelings.

Karoft and I are going down to the high-security block. We suspect Tezabar is already there, and we're uncertain of his motives."

"I understand, but I can't go with you now."

"That's not what I'm after. I need either Larzz or Khezicar for backup."

"You're worried that Tezabar is doing something counter to our objectives?"

"That's the problem. We don't know. I've tried contacting him, but he's not responding. He doesn't appear to be outside or on any of the other levels."

Cuz arches an eyebrow. "I understand your reason for concern." Cuz looks in Khezicar's direction. "Khezicar would be better suited for what you're seeking. Larzz is busy attending to the survivors on the lower level. He has some medical knowledge. At least that's what he claims. After observing him, he seems competent enough."

"Will update you as soon as I've something to report," I tell Cuz. He motions to Khezicar in the next cell for him to join me. The Bylar lumbers over to us. He regards me with his intense, gray-green eyes.

"I need your help with a problem," I transmit. He lowers his great head closer, looking as though he's waiting for instructions. *Karoft and I are going down to the high-security block to investigate if there are any survivors. Need you to come with us for backup."*

Khezicar blinks his eyes. He walks back to the cell where he was working and gets his weapon, which is leaning against a wall. He gestures with his head for me to lead the way.

Karoft joins me and glances at Khezicar. He gives the Bylar a nod.

"Let's go," I say.

"We need to use the lift on the first level," Karoft explains. "It's the only way to the area."

"That will leave us exposed to any Zenti still down there."

Karoft glances up at Khezicar. "Our big friend said, I don't believe we've any other option other than being ready to react to whatever confronts us."

"It's your party. So, lead on," I urge. *"You understand the risk of what we're doing?"* I transmit to him.

He closes his eyes.

"I'll take that as a yes," I mumble.

We walk around the large domed structure until we come to a recessed set of doors. There is a security panel next to them. Karoft studies it for a moment, then says something to the panel. A holographic cube appears suspended in midair.

"Hope they haven't changed the code sequence," he says, as he waves his hand across the holographic image, causing the cube to spin as he utters a series of clicks and whistles. The cube reverses its spin and disappears.

The doors open. Karoft's knitted eyebrows relax as he lets out a breath in relief.

"After you," he gestures for Khezicar and me to go into the spacious lift. "Better move into the corners," he instructs, tapping another code sequence into a standard keypad inside the lift. The doors close. The lift makes a slight hissing bounce before descending.

We descended quicker than expected, and before we could prepare ourselves, the doors opened. We let out a collective sigh at not being confronted by Zenti troops. The lift opens into a long, dimly lit corridor. Karoft holds his hand up for us to wait until he walks a few meters into the corridor. He takes a few more steps forward, looks to his right, then to the left. He turns back and motions for us to follow him.

We proceed in silence down the corridor until we come to a guard station. The corridor splits into two directions. Seeing no guards, Karoft signals for us to stay as he inspects the area.

"There's no sign of any Zenti troops," he says.

"What's wrong?"

"This doesn't feel right," Karoft says. "The Zenti could have had us at a great disadvantage down here. They must've known we would come down eventually, looking for survivors." He rubs his chin.

"I've got a suggestion," I volunteer. "Let's leave Khezicar here to keep watch while we proceed to the security block."

"Well, that's the problem. This is the block. As you can see, it goes in both directions."

"Okay," I say. "You'll go in that direction," I point behind Karoft, "and I'll go in the other. We'll communicate telepathically, updating each other as we proceed."

Karoft nods. He transmits our decision to Khezicar. Khezicar closes his eyes in acknowledgment and walks to the guard station. He stands with his massive head raised high and his weapon in a ready position.

"Wait, a micron," Karoft snaps as he goes into the guard station.

"Thought of something?" I ask, coming close behind him.

"This is a high-security detention area. There must be plenty of surveillance." Karoft waves his hand over a small display panel full of tiny, colored crystals. With each consecutive wave of his hand, banks of holographic displays power up, building a detailed picture of the entire security wing. First, the corridors came up, followed by the individual cells. The corridors and cells are empty. Then I notice one wing has two body signatures in one cell. The next three only have one signature. All the others are empty.

"Why can't we see their bodies?" I ask.

"It's not a video display system. It's narrow spectral imaging," he explains. "Zenti sees better in infrared. Based on these signatures, the cell with two bodies is Tezabar, and if I'm correct, he's speaking to my inside contact."

"How can you tell it's Tezabar?"

"Notice the blue halo effect surrounding both bodies," Karoft points out.

"Yeah. One seems darker than the other," I say.

Karoft zooms in on the two bodies, "The lighter one is Tezabar. I recognize his biogenic signature."

"The other one's similar," I observe, "but not the same...."

Karoft smiles, "So what does that tell you?"

"They're different series androids?"

"Enhanced humanoid would be more precise. Let's find out what they're talking about."

As I start to go, Karoft holds his arm out for me to stay, noticing something in the next cell. "Just a micron," he says, zooming in on the image. "That's a Vultaran signature," he muses with surprise, then gives me a baffled look. "That's odd," he whispers.

"Sounds like we've more than one puzzle to unravel," I suggest, studying Karoft's baffled expression. "Who should we visit first?"

"Tezabar, he's our most immediate problem. The Vultaran is not going anywhere."

Karoft leads the way down the long corridor. I glance behind me a few times with a creepy feeling that something is watching us. After the third look, I dismiss the feeling like my nerves are playing with me and keep my focus on confronting Tezabar and his mystery friend.

"Going to introduce us to your friend," I say to Tezabar as we enter the cell.

He's not surprised by our sudden appearance. He turns and gives us his crooked grin and says, "Phillip Mann, meet Tezabouh of Ezden." he introduces me to someone who could have been Tezabar's twin.

Tezabouh takes a step closer. "Phillip Mann," he says, in a rich baritone, smiling broadly. "It's an honor to meet you," he states, sounding sincere and holding his hand out. I glance at it for a second, then take it and give him a firm handshake. "You're exactly how I imagined you'd be."

Tezabouh's comment takes me by surprise. I almost ask him what he meant, but catching Tezabar's disgruntled stare, I instead ask, "Is there anything we need to know?"

Tezabar furrows his high forehead into an unsettled expression. His reaction tells me there is a lot we haven't been told.

"I sense a mistrust in you, Phillip," Tezabouh says.

I consider him for a moment, then gaze at Tezabar and say, "Under the circumstances, trust has become a fragile quality. Many of Tezabar's actions have frayed what little trust we had between us."

Tezabar frowns, doing a poor imitation of looking offended.

Tezabouh glances at him, then narrows his gaze at me. His locks of thick, white hair seem thicker and above a thinner brow ridge than Tezabar's, but with the same penetrating cobalt-blue eyes. Although his stare has the same intensity as Tezabar's, I pick up a more sensitive nature about him. His peering eyes seemed to be sizing me up in a single glance.

The longer we gaze at each other, the more I realize some subtle and interesting differences between the two humanoids. Most immediate is that Tezabouh has a tangible quality about him I can't describe. He feels more genuine to the senses. After a few seconds of studying Tezabouh, it became apparent. Tezabar is his clone. I had forgotten that salient fact. Now, being in the presence of the original gives me hope he'd be more trustworthy than his imperfect copy.

"What happened?" Karoft asks Tezabouh.

Tezabouh's wide mouth tightens, giving him an unsettled look. "I underestimated the Zenti's new and cunning leader. I believed I still had their trust. After hearing they had completed the final testing of their new weapon, I checked it out for myself. I should have suspected something was amiss when I saw no guards around the general compound or in the tactical center. I planned to install a small incendiary device into the weapon's processor, hoping it would destroy it and take a few Zenti too. What I didn't realize is they had already shipped the weapon to Delius-5." He lowers his gaze and sighs. "They set me up. The weapon I would have sabotaged was a decoy. And so here I am," he frowns, dejectedly.

"I warned you the Zenti suspected you," Karoft tells him, pointing to the next cell. "Who's the Vultaran?"

"The weapon's designer," he answers.

"How's he still alive?" I say, noticing the Vultarian hasn't moved or spoken.

"Good question, Phillip. Let's ask him," Tezabouh says.

I'm not sure if he was being facetious or sincere, but I ask Karoft, "Let's get him out of there. His knowledge could prove invaluable to us."

"While you're at it. I think it would be a good idea to also let the two Klaxon officials out," Tezabouh says. "They're Uzzendi's associates and responsible for keeping him and his daughters alive."

Karoft goes to the Vultaran's cell door. "This is Karoft, First Venubian Security Director. I'm here to release you," he says, then runs back to the guardhouse. I hear a short buzzing sound. *"Did it release?"* Karoft transmits to me.

To my dismay, the cell door doesn't open.

Karoft steps into the corridor and calls to Tezabar, who's standing, looking on impassively. "Well, do you know the release code?" he asks through clenched teeth.

"If you will step aside," Tezabar moves Karoft to the side. He takes out a device from his utility belt and places it over the door's seal. We hear clicking. The lock rotates, and the door becomes ajar. "It's a simple, but useful device," Tezabar says, holding it out to Karoft as he runs up to us.

I can see the Vultaran huddled in a corner of the cell with his knees curled under his folded arms, his face nestled in them. He doesn't move until Karoft approaches. His head lifts with a startled jerk.

The Vultaran stands, revealing its long, rail-thin frame. Its ebony-colored face is oblong, with a broad forehead and narrow, bony jaw that squares at the chin under prominent cheekbones. His ears are high on his head and pointed. It glares at us with its dark, probing eyes. After a few seconds, he appears less apprehensive, and his eyes take on a soft glow against his dark features. I find the Vultaran to be a strange, almost sinister-looking humanoid. Looking closer, one can see it's frightened and in bad health. Its eyes open wider, revealing their cloudy yellow color, as Karoft holds his hand out to it. It regards Karoft with a sullen expression. Its thin, cracked lips part as if to speak, but instead, it warily studies Karoft. The Vultaran's body trembles, causing Karoft to reach out and bring it closer to him. Karoft speaks in a strange, harsh-sounding tongue that the alien appears to understand.

"He needs water and food," Karoft says to me.

Karoft wraps his arm around him, supporting his wobbly legs. The Vultaran could hardly stand and moved at a slow, painful pace. He gives me a long, sorrowful look as he passes me.

"Release the others," I order Tezabar. He eyes me as he walks over to the other cells and opens them. The two Klaxons come out of their cells on their own. They appear to be in better shape than the Vultaran. They look at me with impassive expressions from under their hooded heads. After staring for a moment, they give me a polite nod as though realizing who I am.

Karoft motions to one of them and somehow communicates with him. The Klaxon takes the Vultaran from Karoft and starts back to the guard station. The other turns for a moment and gives me a close look with his beady, hawkish eyes before following behind his fellow Klaxon.

"What's their story?" I ask Tezabouh, who watches the Klaxons for a moment, then narrows his cold, blue eyes at me. "It's a rather long one. Let's say their pacifism saved them. At least for now."

I return his stare with a contemptuous look, then get closer to his face and say, "That sounds like a typical android answer—conveniently evasive and telling me nothing. Something I expect from Tezabar, but was hoping for something better from you."

Tezabouh arches a bushy, white eyebrow and smiles. "You are emotional. You must learn to rein in your passions, Phillip. They don't serve you well."

He's right. I let out a long breath to release my tension and concentrated on reigning in my emotions. I need to get off this hellhole of a rock. Turning from Tezabouh, I hear Nicki urging me to stay in control of my feelings.

CHAPTER 51

We make our way back to the guard station. Khezicar carries the sick Vultaran cradled in his arms. He informs Karoft that he sent the two Klaxons to the upper level to get medical attention. Karoft instructs Khezicar to take the Vultaran to Cuz. He nods his great head and goes to the lift.

That same weird feeling of something lurking out of sight is hanging around me. I unhook my helmet from my utility belt and put it on. Using the helmet's wide spectrum optics, I walk back into the corridor and scan in both directions. Nothing comes up on any bandwidth. Tezabouh approaches me as I remove my helmet.

"You sense it also," he says, as though he knew what I was feeling. "It's much like an undefinable ethereal presence…" His voice trails off as if he were listening to something.

"Yes. I've been sensing something like that, too… How'd you know?"

"It seems we share a certain," he pauses, "for lack of a better term, intuition about our surroundings."

"Until now, I thought my nerves were playing tricks on me."

"But your instincts have you investigating it, anyway." His eyes soften, and in a low voice, he says, "I sense some of Nickada's training in you."

His observation startles me, "Tell me how you know that?" I snap.

"Let's say her methods are well known to me." His vague answer is disturbing, but he interrupts my attempt to respond by placing his hand over my mouth.

"Not here," he whispers. "Too many wanting ears. I promise we'll have that discussion at a better venue." He gives me a warm smile and pats my shoulder. "I'm seeing why Verubeal sent you. You have a strong spirit and good instincts, but you must promise me to guard your words and be vigilant in whom you place your trust. These are dangerous times that often bring the worst out of even the best of souls."

"Oh, I understand. Speaking of trust. Is Tezabar your clone? And if he is, why did you make him such a disagreeable and untrustworthy surrogate?"

"He's a work in progress," he sighs. "He's based on an experimental design. The Zenti were closing in on our position right as I was completing his programming and was forced to rush his personality matrix. Some regrettable anomalies arose because of this. He was only supposed to buy me time and help you if he could. The other androids saw right through my error and ignored him. That's when you and Cuz came along. I already offered my services to the Zenti under the guise of negotiating a better deal for peace. But once I got an understanding of their plans, I knew there could be no peace. Under the circumstances, I tried another tactic, which, as you now realize, has also backfired." He lets out a sorrowful moan. "It seems my long absence from humanoids has caused me to make some poor choices."

I narrow my eyes. "The Zenti now have a powerful weapon, and we have no viable defense against it. They'll annihilate the entire quadrant if we don't come up with something."

"Well, we're not dead yet," he states flatly. "We still have a formidable army of androids and a handful of resilient, well-trained Venubian-led forces waiting for our signal to begin a counterattack. One more thing, Phillip." He moves me a little further from the group. "Are you telepathic?"

"What do you need to tell me?" I transmit.

"The Zenti leader is different in his approach."

"What do you mean?"

"It's difficult to convey, but he's methodical and focused. It's as if a great mind or minds are guiding him."

Tezabouh's flow of empathy surprises me. His emotions feel real, and he transmits them freely.

"Up to this point," he continues, *"all the Zenti encounters have been random and unstructured, which made them much easier to control. They've constantly attacked with reckless abandon, sacrificing large numbers of troops, then retreating. Their last attack on Venubia was well-organized, methodical, and deliberate in its execution. First, they crippled our infrastructure, then disabled our defenses, and abducted all the*

primary leadership along with the best scientific and technical minds within the system.

"If it weren't for their ruthlessness, I could admire the brilliance of their tactics. If we don't get their leader and whoever else is directing their efforts, our situation will become untenable, and we'll be at their mercy. I don't have to go into detail about what that would mean."

"Yes, I understand," I respond, reflecting on Nicki and all the devastation I'd witnessed during the Zenti's attack on Venubia. Then my thoughts drift to Cuz and those poor, wretched survivors. *"First, we've got to get off this rock. You may not be aware, but we've got many survivors up top who will die if we don't get them out of here."*

"No, I didn't know there were any survivors," he blurts. His long face lines with worry as he speaks. "That's uncharacteristic of the Zenti. They kill everything...." His eyes close for a beat, and his jaw tightens. "Those insidious vermin," he curses. "They left survivors to slow us down. That diabolical bastard! Brilliant, brilliant strategy." He smiles ironically while rubbing his deeply furrowed brow.

"Why do you say that?" I ask, confused by Tezabouh's reaction.

"He's outmaneuvered us at every step. First, he lets me infiltrate his ranks. Then takes me in and fills me with disinformation he knows I'll pass along. Sets me up, then gets me out of the way. Brilliant. Damn him," he grunts through a clenched mouth, then turns and marches off to Karoft. "I know what they'll do," he says.

My eyes widen with a sudden, scary thought. "They're going to Klaxonia and destroy their infrastructure as they did to Venubia's and capture all of their technology, then move on to the Kaydens and Vultarans and do the same to them."

"No. They need no more technology. They're after the corridors." He turns to me and says, "They'll want to go to Earth next. Your planet is perfect for them. Remote and full of natural resources."

What he says makes perfect sense, and it scares the crap out of me.

"You seem sure of that," I stammer, hoping he was only hypothesizing.

"It's the most logical next move. I'm also sure we can stop them, but we must move with all haste." He gives Karoft an anguished look. "I'm sorry, my friend," he says in a low and remorseful tone, "the survivors who are well enough we can take with us, but the others…"

He didn't have to finish. Karoft understands, and his expression becomes grim as he nods.

"No," I shout. "We can't leave them to die." A knot forms in my stomach, realizing what they're saying. I get up into Karoft's face and shout, "They're your people! How can you leave them?"

Karoft's complexion turns gray, and his eyes fill with tears. "You think I don't know that? We have no choice. Ask any one of them, and they'll tell you the same."

Tezabouh turns me by the shoulders to face him. His cobalt-blue eyes study me while keeping his voice low, "War makes us do many unpleasant things, my friend. It forces us to make harsh decisions that affect many souls. You're facing one of many hard choices for the survival of the greater good. You have a saying in your literature, I will now paraphrase: The needs of the many are greater than the needs of the few or the one. It's a truism at times such as these."

"There's another saying that also applies: The strong have a responsibility to protect the weak and the infirm."

My heart aches, and my head feels heavy with all the misery and death surrounding me. *Is there no end to all this horror?* Karoft gives me a tearful, disheartened look. I glare at Tezabouh, then go to the lift.

***

Cuz greets me as I enter the upper level of the detection block. The area is busy with the few healthy-enough survivors attending to the sick and injured. There are many covered bodies. Cuz glances up from his patient, looking eager to talk. He motions for us to walk outside.

"What's wrong?" I ask.

"Do you know who that Vultaran is?"

I shrug, preoccupied with the fate of the survivors.

Cuz pronounces the Vultaran's name with a fluidity of clicks and nasal tones. It's a tongue-twister of a name I wouldn't even attempt to say aloud.

"He's considered one of the foremost authorities on quantum engineering," Cuz explains. He must have noticed my bemused expression, and adds, "If I read your body language correctly, you appear to be preoccupied with something unpleasant. Would you care to share what's weighing so heavily on you?"

"Tezabouh just told me we must leave all those poor, miserable souls behind," I spat out with my heart aching, surveying the dull eyes of the sick and dying. "We need to leave them so that we can catch up with the Zenti. Tezabouh believes the Zenti leader has maneuvered us here as a delaying tactic before their next attack. I agree that we must disable their new weapon before it's deployed. He believes they'll use it to do something in the corridors." My forehead lines as I look at Cuz in confusion. "What I don't understand is why they would need a weapon for the corridors? Do they intend to destroy them? That seems counterproductive for the Zenti."

Cuz doesn't react, at first. His expression seems to glow with an odd excitement. "It's not a weapon," he states, looking intently at me. Then his eyes dim, and his face tightens.

"Cuz, what are you talking about? What's not a weapon?"

He ignores my questions and goes back to the detention block. When I catch up with Cuz, he says, "Hurry, we need to debrief the Vultaran. We'd better get Tezabouh and Karoft. They need to hear him as well."

Following close behind Cuz as we enter the main detention center, I see Khezicar tending to the Vultaran. Cuz has already found Karoft and appears busy talking with him. Searching around the facility for Tezabouh, I see the two Klaxons sitting a few cells down from the Vultaran. Larzz is providing them with food and water.

Tezabouh and his twin are nowhere in sight. That makes me nervous, but my most immediate concern is to find out why Cuz is so intent on speaking with the Vultaran. Hoping Tezabouh will find us, I go back to the cell. As I join Cuz, he's talking to the Vultaran. Karoft enters and nods. He stands next to me and listens to Cuz, who's now speaking to the Vultaran in a strange-sounding language. It sounds both melodic and challenging to follow because my universal translator isn't working. It simply states, "Language is not in the database. There is no linguistic equivalent." What they're saying is more like a code than words. Each of them communicates in flowing clicks, whistles, and nasal tones. It sounds neither linguistic nor musical, but something between the two.

I ask Karoft, "What language is that? It's so strange my universal translator can't even decipher it."

Karoft smiles. "It's an esoteric engineering dialectic. Only a handful of the scientific community still uses it."

"I can appreciate that. It sounds complicated. Do you understand any of it?"

"Only bits and pieces of what they're discussing. From the little I could gather, Cuz is asking him about the device's design and how it can be disabled," Karoft explains, sounding a little unsure of the details. "The Vultaran's explanation is almost beyond my comprehension. While Cuz is using a more current and basic engineering dialect, the Vultaran is responding in a specific vernacular unfamiliar and difficult for me to follow."

"From my end, it sounds more like a noisy stream of random sounds."

"You're correct, in a way. It's a mathematical lexicon expressed in specific utterances. When spoken in a precise order, it can describe a device's design and applications in exquisite detail."

"Wow, that's incredible," I say, scratching my stubble while contemplating the complexity of what Karoft described.

I wait for a break in their conversation, so I can catch up on what has been discussed. Cuz turns his bright eyes in my direction. "I couldn't find Tezabouh or his clone," I tell him. "That's a strange language you guys were speaking."

"It's an older dialect he prefers to use as a security measure," Cuz explains.

"That's why my translator was silent. What have you learned?"

"Aneyhus, that's his informal name, is explaining that the device he designed for the Zenti is not a weapon. However, it's still a dangerous device."

"Okay. What is it?"

"It's a quantum generator. It produces antigravitons, a form of negative energy used to stabilize warped space. The device was developed to stabilize the corridors. It maintains the corridor's structural integrity, preventing collapse when normal matter passes through. Until now, we had no way to control the corridor's functions. We only knew how to locate them and, to a lesser degree, open them. We haven't learned how to control them."

"I don't understand. I thought you guys created the corridors."

"No, they are believed to have been created by a now-extinct civilization many millennia ago. The Klaxon was the first to rediscover them and shared their knowledge with us as part of a mutual exchange of technologies. No one knows their actual origins or how they were created. We have, in the past hundred cycles, mapped out some of their locations. Part of Nickada's primary mission was to locate as many corridors as she could and map them as she explored the outer quadrants of our galaxy."

"I see. So, if I understand what he's implying, the Zenti can now control the corridors with his device? And with Nickada's map, you can also locate them."

"Precisely."

"Why would he give them such power?"

"Not willingly, I assure you. Like Minister Uzzendi, he endured prolonged mental and physical torture until he submitted to their will. The Zenti have perfected methods of extracting information that are beyond cruel but effective. They can now strip information directly from the mind. Needless to say, what it does to the victim."

"That is really shitty. They can keep us from ever getting beyond our system." The revelation struck me hard. Cuz's stiff demeanor is adding to that bad vibe bouncing around in me. *There's more to this, isn't there?"* I transmit, unable to get my words out.

"Yes, but I'd prefer to tell you in private." Cuz's expression remains dispassionate.

"You mentioned when you and Nickada were on Delius-5, there were signs of the Zenti testing an electromagnetic device?" Karoft inquires, sounding like a security officer.

"Yes," I answer. "When we first arrived, there was a strong electromagnetic resonance, which at first, we thought was from a storm, but on closer analysis, the atmosphere and some ground readings all showed it wasn't from any natural phenomenon. Later that day, we believe a squad of Zenti attempted to infiltrate our camp, but we fought them off. The details are all in Nicki's logs. Nicki and I, at the time, thought it might have been a weapons test."

Karoft gives me a calculating look. He then turns his large, gray eyes on Cuz and asks, "What do you think the Zenti have in mind?"

Cuz purses his lips, looking thoughtful before answering, "It would be difficult to speculate on their next move, given how uncharacteristic their actions have been of late. One thing is certain. We need to get out of here and communicate with Verubeal as soon as possible. We also must arrange a pickup point for Biomei."

"Yes," Karoft pulls on his small chin, "You're right. It's all so confounding," he grunts.

"Any idea where Tezabouh is?"

"He mentioned something about scanning the tunnels for explosives. He believes the Zenti wanted to collapse the tunnels as soon as we got far enough inside. It would be a logical ploy for them."

Looking back at all the poor souls inside the detention center gives me a thought. "Are there enough supplies for all of them to survive long enough for us to get back to L'hu and have them picked up later?"

Karoft gives me a contemplative stare before frowning. "Our priority should be to get us off this moon." He lets out a heavy sigh. "Of course, we'll do everything possible to get them back." He pauses a beat, then adds, "I'll get Larzz to help me gather as many supplies and equipment as we can carry. Cuz, I'll need you to get the Vultaran ready for travel. And you," he points a finger at me, "You need to tell Tezabouh we're preparing to leave."

I wait for Karoft to leave, then say to Cuz, "We're alone. Tell me the rest of what you've learned."

"Aneyhus explained he limited the power signature of the device so it would only work for a short time. He convinced the Zenti that the device should not be tested unless near a strong gravitational field, or it will implode. Realizing the Zenti had no one with his knowledge of the device, they had no choice but to believe him." Cuz frowns. "He's dying and is too weak to make the trip. Aneyhus asked me to let his family know he didn't betray them or the Vultaran community. It's apparent he had no choice but to do what the Zenti demanded, or they would have killed everybody. It was a desperate act to buy time for all the survivors."

"Do you believe him?" I ask.

"As we communicated, Aneyhus' intentions became transparent. His biorhythms were normal throughout our conversation. If he were being deceitful or withholding any information, I would've detected it. Vultarans have a reputation for both ruthlessness and deceit in negotiations. But they have always been honorable in keeping their word. Aneyhus hasn't given me any reason to doubt the veracity of what he shared."

"That's good enough for me. I'll find Tezabouh and Tezabar. Something about them being together makes me nervous."

Cuz gives me a cautionary look and says, "If your instincts are telling you to be careful. I suggest you heed them."

"Right," I agree, grabbing Cuz's pulse laser from his belt. "Can't be too prepared," I say, checking his weapon's charge before placing it into my utility belt.

Cuz smiles and transmits, *"Stay connected with me."*

"Yes, mother." An eeriness seems to emanate from the dark depths of that tunnel. As I approach, I find myself pulling Cuz's pulse laser from my belt and squeezing it tightly.

***

When I get within a few meters of the entrance, I see Tezabouh coming out.

"I was coming for you," I tell him. "We're getting ready to leave."

"Very well. Tezabar is completing a sensor sweep of the interior. So far, nothing has come up, which is worrisome."

"How so?"

"The Zenti wouldn't have left without leaving traps for us."

"Could it be they didn't have time?"

"Anything's possible." He looks back at the tunnel. "I've instructed Tezabar to stay behind and keep watch for any Zenti troops."

"You believe they're still in there?"

"I'm sure of it," he says.

"Karoft is waiting for us."

"Was the Vultaran useful?"

"I think it would be best if Cuz briefs you on that. He has a better understanding of what they discussed."

Tezabouh searches my face with his cold eyes. "Why do I sense a disingenuous ignorance coming from you?"

"Trust me, Cuz has a much better grasp of what the Vultaran divulged."

He tilts his head with a faint smile. "If you insist."

We walk in silence the rest of the way.

Cuz greets us with a long, solemn expression.

"What's wrong?" I ask.

"Aneyhus succumbed to his injuries and died right after you left."

"I'm sorry. You seemed to have made a connection with him. It's sad, but it seems like death is winning so far."

"Yes, that's most unfortunate," Tezabouh adds, eyeing Cuz.

"There's something you wish to ask me?" Cuz asks Tezabouh.

"Not now, but we have a lot to discuss," he replies, relaxing his gaze. "Let's get everyone moving. Time is our worst enemy."

Cuz gives me a quizzical glance as though he's expecting me to say something. I tilt my head to the side for him to go back into the detention center. Tezabouh is going to the tactical dome. I watch him for a few moments, wondering if I should join him, but Larzz interrupts the thought when he calls to me.

***

"Phillip, need to show you something," Larzz says, with a growing smile across his massive face.

I follow him around the detention center's central dome to a narrow path. Before proceeding down, Larzz stops and looks back at me.

"Are you expecting somebody?" I ask, turning to take a glimpse behind.

"No. Being a little cautious," he speaks in a hushed voice.

"And why is that?"

"You'll understand when I show you. Come. Stay close."

We follow a narrow path down the side of a tall knoll of solid rock. When we reach the bottom of the path, Larzz stops and turns, holding a pulse laser up. He continues to look back up the path. I watch, unsure what to do, as he appears to be intently listening.

"You hear something?" I ask, scrutinizing his sweaty brow with an uneasy feeling.

He relaxes with a cautious look. "I've been a little... how you say?" he pauses a beat and blurts, "Jumpy. Come, it's only a few meters ahead."

The air becomes warmer and more humid as we come to a big opening in the side of a tall wall of rock. Larzz gestures for me to go in. I hesitate a moment at seeing the interior of the opening is glowing.

"Oh, never mind," he fusses, pushes me aside, and goes in.

Feeling self-conscious, I follow. Once inside, I realize we are in another section of the cavern. A warm column of air blows up from small vents in the hard, stone floor. The yellowish lighting flickers like a candle.

"It's hot in here," I complain, feeling beads of perspiration forming on my forehead. My biosuit quickly cools me down.

"We're over a lava pool bubbling up from the moon's hot core," Larzz explains. "This way." He gestures with his hand.

I follow him as he walks further into the cavern's interior. The walls glisten with light reflecting off multicolored quartz and other minerals. A few more meters in, we come to a large portal.

"I gather we've arrived at what you wanted me to see," I say.

Larzz stares at me with a faint smile, then swings open the portal's heavy door.

Peering inside, I see a vast storage area filled with stacks of devices. Streams of thin wires sticking out. Also, a variety of instruments. Some I recognize as general soil and atmospheric testing equipment, with other stuff scattered throughout its deep interior. Most of it is covered in tarps. Then my eyes lock on a hexagonal-shaped device, sitting on top of a metal table.

"What's that?" I say, going in for a closer look.

"That, my friend, is a quantum communicator," Larzz explains, looking at the device wide-eyed.

"It looks almost like a metal soccer ball. What's it used for?"

"It warps space, creating tiny wormholes that enable instantaneous communication over great distances. It can also be adapted to detect any energy signature."

"Wow, you've made a good find." Studying the shiny piece of technology, I realize how significant this find is. "Larzz, this is quite a strategic device. Why all the secrecy over its discovery? And for that matter, how did you uncover it?"

Larzz pulls on his earlobe, looking as though he's considering his answer.

"I chose well in confiding in you," he smiles, moving closer. He studies me with his intense, red eyes, glowing. "I've been watching you closely, Earthman. You're a complicated species. Also, sometimes too emotional, but I've grown to like and trust you. I understand your misgivings over my actions." He sighs heavily, taking the device from me and squeezing it between his beefy hands. "This device may save many lives. It will give us an advantage over the Zenti, but only if they don't know we have it.

"You've asked how I found it. I didn't. One of the Klaxons I was nursing told me about the device and where to find it. They helped Minister Uzzendi with its development. Uzzendi was incensed about the Zenti after they tortured his wife to death and threatened his children. He had his technicians build in a design flaw that causes the communicator to burn out its power supply after a few microns of operation. The Zenti ran out of time and never resolved the problem. Believing the device was worthless, they left it." He frowns and, in a harsh voice, states, "They still have Uzzendi and his daughters. They will force him to build them another better-performing communicator. So, our advantage has a time limit."

"You're right. They'll develop another device, but why couldn't you trust the rest of us with this information? Especially Cuz and Tezabouh? They have the technical knowledge and can improve the device's design."

Larzz shakes his head, causing his bright mane and thick locks of red hair to flare. "Cuz I can trust, because of his relationship with you, but not that cold, calculating android, Tezabouh. I don't trust him for a micron, or his sneaky clone. They've been playing with both sides for their own reasons. Karoft was the first one I told. I'm telling you this because if anything happens to Karoft or me, I want you to make sure the Venubians get it."

What he says made sense. I understand his distrust of Tezabouh and am not about to defend him to Larzz. My trust in him is tenuous and built on a mutual need to get Nicki back safely.

"Very well. You can count on me, but I need to make Cuz aware of the communicator. I can vouch for his loyalty."

"As you wish." Larzz lifts his great head of thick hair, then pulls a tarp off a desk and drapes it over the device, placing it under his large, muscular arm.

"Let's get out of here," he says, rushing through the portal.

CHAPTER 52

When we rejoin the group, Tezabouh has already gathered the ablest of the survivors. They are preparing everyone to leave. Tezabouh glances at me, then sees Larzz with the device cradled under his arm.

"I see you found something. Anything of interest?" Tezabouh says to me while eyeing Larzz.

Larzz grins and says, "It's a device the Zenti discarded. It may be useful for its parts."

Tezabouh gives us a dubious smile, then turns back to organizing the survivors. "You two had better hurry and get your gear together. We're ready to leave."

"Right," I say, and amble to the detention center.

Larzz comes up to my side and whispers, "Do you think he believed me?"

"Doubtful," I say. "Tezabouh can read right through any deception. It's as though he has a built-in bullshit meter."

Larzz wrinkles his large face. "Bullshit? What is bullshit?"

I laugh, realizing his confusion. "It's an Earth idiom for a lie," I explain.

"Oh," he says, still sounding confused. "Does Earth have many of those idioms?"

"Yes. In many languages, dialects, and mannerisms."

"Mannerisms?"

"Facial expressions and body language." I attempt to give him a better understanding of the complexities of our languages, but noticing his increasing confusion, I decide to drop it.

"And I thought my language was bewildering." He lets out a belly laugh.

"You'd better find a container for that thing and keep it out of sight," I suggest before going in search of Cuz.

One of the Klaxons greets me as I enter the detention block. He's uncloaked, revealing his tight crown of shiny black and red feathers. He engages me with probing eyes. With his head uncovered, he appears different from the other Klaxons. His head and face are covered in small, shiny feathers, and he has a narrow, beak-like nose over a small mouth. I notice two tiny openings on either side of his head instead of pointed ears.

"Do my features interest you?" His voice sounds garbled.

"Sorry. Didn't mean to stare, but you appear different from the other Klaxons I've met."

"My mother is Klaxon, but my father was part Vultaran."

"I thought I noticed some similarities with both species, but didn't make the connection."

"Have you secured the device?" he asks.

"Yes," I answer, surprised. "Are you telepathic?"

"No." He hesitates as if unsure of what to say, then adds, "We're empathic. Larzz was the one I told about the device..." He looked closely at me for a beat, then asked, "How do you know my language?"

"I've a universal translator that converts all forms of language," I transmit.

His stern gaze softens. *"It works well,"* he compliments.

"Larzz has the device and is taking charge of its safety."

"Good."

"How's your associate?"

He blinks his dark eyes, and his expression becomes somber. *"He's not doing well. Has an infection that will require specific antibiotics, which are not available. I fear he will not make it through the next cycle."*

"I'm so sorry to hear that. Don't give up hope. We may find something that may be of benefit." I force a smile of encouragement.

"You are a hopeless optimist." A corner of his small mouth turns upward. *"Nevertheless, I appreciate your words."* He closes his eyes for a second, then returns to attending to his ailing friend.

I search throughout the upper level and can't find Cuz or Karoft. When I start for the lower level, I feel a tap on my shoulder. I turn to find Tezabar staring with his annoying crooked grin.

"What do you need?" I ask irritably.

"Tezabouh wants to see you."

"I'll be with him in a micron. I'm looking for Cuz. By any chance, do you know where he is?"

"Yes."

"Why do I have to pry everything out of you?"

"I don't understand your meaning."

"Tell me where the hell he is!"

Tezabar's bushy eyebrows rise high on his brow. "Are we feeling a little cranky?" he says, mockingly.

I pull my pulse laser out and point it at his head. Tezabar takes a step back, holding up his long hand, smirking. "He's in the main compound area, burying the dead."

"Thank you," I say, placing the weapon back into my belt.

"I was only jesting," he calls to my back.

As I walk to the main compound area, a pungent, smoky smell permeates the air. As I got closer, the air became thicker with smoke. I hear the crackling whoosh of a raging fire. At the burial site, I see Cuz tending to a high pyre of burning bodies. Karoft is operating one of the Zenti construction tractors. He's dumping a huge load of crushed rocks and black lava soil from the massive scoop, topping off a grave next to the burning pyre.

"That should do it," Karoft calls from the cab, looking over the sizable mound of rocks and dirt.

Cuz stares at the smoldering fire next to the mass burial site for a moment before stepping away.

Karoft drives the tractor away and parks it in front of one of the maintenance sheds. He walks up to a small gathering, standing between the large mound and the smoldering fire, with their heads bowed. Realizing what they were doing, I joined them.

"Why the fire and the mass grave?" I ask Karoft.

"The pyre is for the infectious ones, and the mass grave is for the others."

"Is it your custom to say a few words over the dead?" I whisper to him.

Karoft looks up and says, "That's a beautiful gesture, Phillip. Please say an Earth prayer."

My mouth becomes dry, and I feel my face burn, thinking, Why did I open my big mouth? No prayer comes to mind. I find myself at a loss for words.

Cuz must've picked up on my dilemma and transmits, "*I recall reading in your religious literature that Western Judeo-Christian cultures often recite Psalm 23 of David.*"

"*Oh, yes. Of course.*" I let out a quiet sigh of relief. "*Bless you, Cuz, you saved my ass.*"

Cuz squints at me.

I bow my head and begin the psalm, The LORD is my shepherd; I shall not want. He maketh me to lie down in green pastures: he leadeth me beside the still waters. He restoreth my soul: he leadeth me in the paths of righteousness for his name's sake. Yea, though I walk through the valley of the shadow of death, I will fear no evil: for thou art with me; thy rod and thy staff they comfort me. Thou preparest a table before me in the presence of mine enemies: thou anointest my head with oil; my cup runneth over. Surely goodness and mercy shall follow me all the days of my life: and I will dwell in the house of the LORD forever.

"Nicely done, Phillip," Karoft compliments, patting my back. "It's an interesting prayer. We must discuss it when we have the time. It's both poetic and enlightening; a fine example of Earth culture."

"Curious," Cuz says, looking confused. "I read a slightly different version of that psalm. It wasn't as poetic as the one you recited. Is it not confusing to have different versions of your religious texts?"

"Yes. Religion is not only often confusing, but it's also very contradictory in its dogma. Each religious sect has its interpretation of both the words and the meaning of the Old Testament, which is where the psalm comes from. There's also a New Testament that causes problems for many parts of the world. Religion has lost most of its significance for me. I find it too full of stupid superstitions and silly rituals."

"Are you saying you've lost your faith?" Cuz says, sounding surprised.

"No, Cuz, I still have faith. Just not a religiously based one. After all the experiences I've had since meeting Nicki, it's hard to believe in an all-powerful, all-knowing entity. She has changed me in more than physiological and neurological terms. She's changed my whole way of looking at the universe. Of late, I've no idea who I am. However, I'm glad I have you as my trusted guide."

Cuz's forehead stays lined with his eyes narrowing. "Based on what you've expressed, you sound conflicted." He frowns. "But I've come to understand it's a usual emotional state for you."

I laugh at Cuz's honest observation. His expression becomes even more confounded. Placing my arm around his broad shoulders, I say, "Don't try to understand me. It's a waste of your great intellect. Better focus on keeping me from doing something stupid. Make that a priority directive."

"That already is a prime directive," Cuz states.

"Really? And who gave you that *directive*?"

"You did. When we first met."

I consider his answer for a second. "Yep, that sounds like me. Well, keep up the good work."

***

Tezabouh meets us outside the detention center. "I gather you've completed the burial rituals?" he says in a respectful tone. Karoft nods. "We've gathered all the able survivors and have loaded a few small hovercraft with supplies and weapons."

"How do you intend to get the hovercraft through the cavern's narrows?" I ask. "We barely made it through on foot."

"Yes. That's true, but the Klaxon knows of a large accessway to the surface. It's what the Zenti used to get out of here. Like many other things, they've kept it as a guarded secret."

"Give us a little time to gather our stuff," I say, gesturing for Cuz to follow me.

"When we get back inside the detention center," I say to Cuz, "Am I being paranoid, or does Tezabouh's sudden discovery of a better exit path sound a little convenient?"

"It makes me wonder with all his inside intelligence, why he wasn't aware of this other route," Cuz says.

"Those two enhanced humanoids are hard to trust," I say.

"Now, we've no reason to believe they had prior knowledge of its existence. The Klaxon was in a separate cell. Regardless, let's be thankful we have a better exit path."

"I suppose you're right. Let's gather supplies, extra weapons, and get the hell out of here."

Cuz and I gather our backpacks and stuff them with as many small arms as we can find. Cuz also stocks up on food rations and extra water in case of an emergency. Once we have our backpacks to their fullest, we head back to the main compound. When we arrive, Tezabar is already leading a small group of ambulatory survivors toward the cavern's entrance.

"Is that all of them?" I ask Tezabouh.

"Yes," he answers. "A few survivors volunteered to stay behind to tend to the sick and injured. The ones going with us are all skilled technicians and scientists, along with a few who are eager to join the fight."

"Where are Karoft and the other two?"

Karoft and Larzz went ahead to make sure the path was clear. Khezicar and Tezabar were standing guard further up the path.

"Sounds as though everyone is where they're supposed to be." I glance at Cuz and ask, "You ready to get the hell off this rock?"

Cuz nods. As we walk, he looks behind as if taking a last look at the group. I can feel a sense of regret emanating from him.

"I feel you, Cuz. You're gaining some strong emotions, my friend."

He nods somberly. "War has that effect on humanoids."

CHAPTER 53

We go to the far end of the compound, then follow the perimeter fence until we come to a portal built into the side of a high bluff. Tezabar and Khezicar greet us in front of the open portal. Tezabar is wearing his environmental suit.

"I've sent the group ahead and am staying in contact with Karoft," Tezabar says. "Now that you're here, you need to put your helmet on, so you can communicate from the rear. I'll catch up with the group."

"Sounds like a plan," I say, putting on my helmet. "Karoft, this is Phillip," I call over the intercom. "Wanted to let you know I'm bringing up the rear. Tezabar is coming to take the point for the group."

"Good," Karoft answers. "So far, we haven't confronted any Zenti or seen a possible threat. The hovercraft has already passed, and my proximity sensor shows nothing within a hundred meters of the mouth of the cavern. I've sent Larzz ahead, and I'll keep watch until I see the group."

"Be careful. I've got a gut feeling there are still Zenti lurking about."

"Stay sharp. Karoft out."

As we proceeded through the cavern, I got that same odd feeling of a strange presence hovering over me. It isn't a tangible presence, more like a premonition of ethereal energy. What's remarkable is that it seems to get stronger as we go further into the belly of the cavern.

"Do you sense anything odd?" I transmit to Cuz, looking behind me.

"I'm not sure what you mean by odd."

"It's hard to define. It may only be my nerves playing tricks on my mind. Forget about it."

We're making good progress until we feel a strong vibration run across the cavern floor. I turn to Tezabouh and transmit, *"What was that?"*

"There's a vast ocean 2.35 hundred kilometers below. The ocean's depths are close to the moon's hot central core. An ancient lava lake formed this cavern. If you look above and below, you'll see many lava tubes. The tremor was a natural phenomenon caused by the core's superheating of the ocean. During my captivity, I've endured some intense

tremors. This moon is a remarkable world and worthy of study. If I survive this horrible conflict, I hope I'll have an opportunity to return and study this world."

"*I would've thought this would be the last place you'd want to return,*" I transmit with surprise. "You're almost as complicated and conflicted as me," I say aloud, then immediately regret saying it.

A tremor runs under our feet. This one is much stronger. It knocks a few of the survivors to the ground. It buckles my legs, causing Cuz to grab my arm to steady me as soon as we regain our balance and right the fallen, another powerful tremor hits. Almost everyone in the group is affected. Large chunks of rock fall from the ceiling and shatter close to us.

"*We need to pick up the pace,*" I transmit to Tezabouh. "*These tremors are increasing in frequency and intensity.*"

"*I concur. You and Cuz come up to me. I need help with the fallen survivors. A few of them have sustained injuries. One appears to have broken his leg, and another has a badly sprained ankle.*"

"*Cuz, do you have a med-kit on you?*" I ask.

Cuz goes to an injured survivor, kneels next to the Venubian female, and examines her leg. After evaluating the injury, he pulls out a small medical scanner from his utility belt. He scans the agonized Venubian's leg, then pulls out a small med-kit from his belt and opens it. He also pulls out a familiar-looking cube and attaches it to the side of his patient's temple. He looks my way and transmits, "It's a clean, hairline fracture. I've administered an analgesic to relieve her pain and biological nanites to guard against infection and knit the fracture."

"*Can she be moved?*"

"*She will require assistance, but she can be moved in a few microns.*"

"*What about the other one?*"

Cuz walks to the other injured survivor, who's a Kayden. He scans his ankle and performs a similar procedure on it. "Are you feeling better?" Cuz asks him.

Kayden lets out a breath. "Better. Thank you," he says, trying to smile in appreciation. "Let me see if I can bear weight on my ankle."

Tezabouh, while directing the rest of the survivors onto the correct path, turns and calls to me, "I'll help him. I need you two to stand by for the moment. I've sent for Khezicar to help us with the injured."

Tezabouh lifts the Kayden as though he were a sack of feathers and places him on his feet. He cries out in pain as soon as he puts weight on his ankle. Tezabouh cradles the small Kayden like a toddler in one arm while directing the long line of survivors with the other.

A few minutes pass before Khezicar comes lumbering around a large stalagmite. Leaning his long neck forward to avoid contact with the cavern's ragged ceiling, full of pointy stalactites, he walks to Tezabouh and blinks his large eyes. They look as if they were conversing. After a brief conversation, Khezicar flashes his multicolored neck feathers.

He glances my way and waves his head feathers like a friendly wave while blinking his eyes. *"Tezabouh told me of the injured. They need help in moving,"* he relays in a soft voice. *"I require your help."*

"Sure. What do you need?"

He lumbers to the Venubian and leans over him. *"Can you lift him onto my back?"* Khezicar transmits to me.

I pick up the Venubian and place him on Khezicar's upper back just below his shoulders.

"Are you all right?" I ask the female Venubian, who looks as though she's still in pain.

"I'm fine," she answers in a raspy voice. Her complexion appears clammy and ghostly white.

"Hold on tight. Khezicar can hardly feel your weight, so you're no burden for him."

The Venubian gives me a gritty smile.

"Is she securely on my back?" Khezicar transmits.

"She's in a lot of pain." He checks to make sure she's secure. *"She's good to go."*

"I'll have Cuz give him painkillers. Khezicar transmits and goes to Tezabouh, who transfers the Kayden to Khezicar, who cradles him in his

arms. "Go carefully, my friend," Tezabouh says. He says to Cuz and me, "You must go as fast as you can and get out of this cavern."

"What are you going to do?" I ask, sensing something is weighing on him.

Another tremor. This one is stronger and causes a few large stalactites to crash down to the cavern's floor with an explosive force. Another powerful tremor felt like it came from deep within the cavern, causing the floor to swell and crack open into a large fissure close to us.

"You must hurry. Go!" Tezabouh implores us.

"You know what's happening. Don't you?" I say.

"Yes, and there's no time to save the others. I'm begging you to leave. You're both too important to be killed in this hellhole."

"Phillip, he's right, we must hurry," Cuz urges.

"I'll go, but first, tell me what you're holding back."

"There's no time for this," Tezabouh hisses.

"Damn your fucking enhanced humanoid guts! Tell me!" I sharply probe into Tezabouh's mind. I see him wince in surprise at the intensity of my anger.

"Phillip, please let it go," Cuz's plea sounds full of apprehension. *"Don't squander our chance of surviving these tectonic events. They're getting stronger with each wave. We've been living precariously through everything. I'm begging you."*

"No. Not until this bastard tells us what's happening!"

I flash an angry eye at Cuz and can see he's struggling to understand my intransigence.

"The tremors aren't a natural phenomenon," he blurts, letting out a disgusted sigh. "Those bastards perverted the Vultaran's device into a weapon. You must believe me. I had no idea they had activated the prototype. I'm going back to see if I can disable it before it destroys the caverns."

"Let's go," I say, understanding the magnitude of what Tezabouh has said.

"Phillip. You and Cuz must go. It's senseless for you to stay."

"No, it's not," I insist. "Three can cover more ground than one. The longer we stay here arguing, the worse it will be for all those survivors. It's not only the caverns that will be destroyed. The Zenti don't do halfway measures with destruction. They intend to lay this entire moon to waste. And they're probably watching us right now."

"Why do you say that?" Tezabouh asks, giving me an attentive look.

"The tremors began as soon as we entered the cavern," I explained. I ask Cuz, "What are the time intervals between the tremors?"

Cuz's expression becomes contemplative for a moment. "10-mics," he answers.

Tezabouh has a worried look. "We've less than 5 microns before the next event. The device must be on the ground and within 150 meters of the caverns. There are three likely locations within those parameters."

"How certain are you about there being only one prototype?" I asked, coming closer to Tezabouh's side as we ran back to the detention center.

"I'm positive. Only two prototypes were developed. A small, limited-field generator and a wide-field generator. I thought they took both. It seems they only took the wide-field generator. Nevertheless, the small field can devastate this moon within 15 to 20 macrons. It sends out pulses of strong electromagnetic waves that penetrate the moon's interior with V-particles, which are a form of dark energy. The pulses grow more intense with each generated iteration. The waves will grow stronger and penetrate deeper into the moon. Once they reach the moon's core, it will implode, tearing it apart."

A strong vibration ripples under our feet. "Is that another pulse starting?" I ask, rolling my shaking hands into fists, feeling adrenaline rushing through.

"Yes. It's building a new wave," Tezabouh explains calmly. "Phillip, go over to the tactical dome. Cuz, go to the construction warehouse. Use your quantum analyzers and set them to scan for V-particles. I'm going to the high-security detention block. It's the most strategic location for the device."

We all split up in search of the destruction machine.

As I run to the tactical dome, something occurs to me. Why didn't Tezabouh tell us about the quantum generator? He had to have known the Zenti would test it. It also explains why they left so abruptly. They wanted to trap us inside the cavern. The moon's destruction, or at least the caverns, would have guaranteed our elimination. So, why didn't Tezabouh tell us sooner?

I enter the tactical dome and pull out my quantum analyzer, and scan the interior. At first pass, nothing comes up. I increase the scanner's sensitivity range and get a wide range of particles, but no Vs. As I'm about to give up, I pass a small container, and my scanner shows a low saturation of V-particles. I open it and, to my disappointment, find it empty. Frustrated, I throw the damn container across the room.

Just as I start to leave, the hard rock surface vibrates under me. Thin stress lines appear everywhere. I walk with an unsteady gait, still feeling the residual effects of the shock wave. Looking at the interior's surface, I can see lines of splintered rock throughout the compound.

"What the hell was that?"

Cuz is running to me, holding something that looks like a small, rectangular-shaped object in his hand. The object's sides are glowing with a pattern of slow-blinking colored lights.

"What do you have there?" I say over my helmet intercom as he holds out the blinking object.

"It's a temporal synchronization analyzer," he explains. Noticing my absent gaze, he adds, "It's a device that keeps the quantum device within a narrow time interval and frequency to prevent the stream from deteriorating over a set period. This is the device that maintains the intervals between tremors."

"Okay. I understand, but what was that last event?"

Cuz's expression turns a little sheepish, and he says, "I believe it was an inadvertent side-effect from my disconnecting the device during an active event."

"Now the quantum generator is no longer synchronized. What effect will that have on the next event?"

"Unknown. But it may delay it by throwing the time interval out of sync."

"Let's find Tezabouh. I hope you didn't speed things up instead."

"Nothing has happened so far," Cuz says, trying to sound optimistic.

I transmit to Tezabouh, *"Cuz believes he's found the generator's synchronization analyzer and has disconnected it. Where are you?"*

"I'm in the lower security block and have found the device," he transmits. *"You need to get that timer to me right away. Without synchronization, the intervals will become random and more intense."*

"Understood." I give Cuz a worried look and say, "I hope you did the right thing. Let's go. He's in the lower security block."

As Cuz and I run around to the detention center's dome, I'm compelled to peer inside the upper level. A few of the survivors turn from their patients and look at me, confused. I see the entire interior is covered in crisscross patterns of splintered rock. Their sick and injured expressions all reflect a solemn awareness that their lives are in imminent danger and they could do nothing to avert it.

"I think we've discovered the reason for the shock waves. Don't worry; we'll fix it," I shout to them, hoping it'll placate their fears.

When we reach the portal to the security center, it's open, revealing a pitch-black interior. My helmet lights turn on, illuminating the interior of the cavern for only a few meters ahead. Large chunks of rock and materials from the cells were strewn all over the corridor, creating more obstacles to getting to Tezabouh.

"Tezabouh, there's a lot of debris in our way. Can you come out into the corridor so that we can find you?" I transmit to him.

"I'm right here," he transmits, flashing a hand-held light in our direction.

He steps back into the cell where he's working as we get to him. He's kneeling and working on a compact, box-shaped device with a clear dome on top. A small, dish-like antenna is attached to one end.

Cuz and I both shine our suit lights on the generator to give Tezabouh more light to work in. What he's doing looks intricate. He opens one side of the device, revealing an interior full of flat, crystalline cards and familiar-looking small bladders filled with an amber liquid. After inspecting the cards, I discovered they're like the ones we found inside the Zenti droid.

"So, that's the little fucker that's been causing all the headaches," I mumble, watching Tezabouh work.

"If I may be of assistance," Cuz interjects. "I have experience with Zenti technology."

Tezabouh looks up from his work and smiles. "Thank you, but I believe I've altered the device's frequency and output intensity," he explains as he seals the generator and stands, holding it against his side.

"Are you confident you disabled it?" I ask, trying not to show my nervousness.

"Disabled is not the term I'd use. Reducing its intensity and delaying its output would be more accurate. But it's still a destructive weapon. We must go without delay."

Slowed by the debris, Tezabouh turns, holding the generator out to me, and says, "Hold this."

I take the compact destruction machine. Tezabouh picks up the larger rocks and chunks of debris and tosses them into the open cells along the pathway. He clears a ragged path to the corridor. He gestures for us to come. We run to him.

Glancing at Tezabouh through my helmet's transparent faceplate, he seems preoccupied in thought.

"*Is everything all right?*" I transmit to him, removing my helmet and clipping it back to my belt.

"I'm having difficulty contacting Tezabar."

I think for a moment, then tried to contact Karoft. He isn't answering either.

"There might be residual electromagnetic interference," I suggest. By his bemused stare, I realize what a lame remark that was, recalling EMI can't block telepathic communications. "Sorry," I add, embarrassed. "I'm grasping at straws."

"No, there's some merit in what you said. Not in interfering with communications, but rather causing considerable damage to the cavern. Get your gear together and meet me at the opening."

I nod and tell Cuz what we discussed. His face fills with concern.

We gather our gear and supplies and return to the cavern's entrance. There's a great urgency as we proceed into the interior. As we hasten deeper in, we notice large fissures and shattered rock formations on all sides of the pathway. The further we travel, the more ominous the interior looks.

At one point, we're halted by a wide crevasse. We search for a way around it. Seeing that all viable paths are blocked, we unload our backpacks. Tezabouh estimates it's over 12 meters across. An impossible leap for any humanoid, but he bounds over the long traverse with ease. "Throw your packs to me," he calls. Cuz tosses them to him. Once our packs are across, Tezabouh reaches his hand out and, with a faint grin, says, "Now, let's see how enhanced a humanoid you are."

He challenged me, damn it. Not daring to look down into that great abyss, I take a few long strides backward. I close my eyes while letting out a few long breaths to clear my head. Without thinking, I run as fast as I can and leap. I feel myself soar high and outward, almost banging my head on the cavern's roof. I land nearly a full meter past Tezabouh, who's eyeing me, looking impressed.

Then Cuz jumps without hesitation and lands beside me. "Let's go," he urges us.

The massive fracturing of both the ceiling and the floor's rock formations has all but blocked the path. When we make it around the final bend, our worst fears confront us. The roof of the cavern has collapsed, blocking all but a small opening of the exit. The rock is so densely packed that we estimate it would take a full half-cycle to clear an opening big enough for us to pass through. Turning back isn't an option, and once more, we drop our packs and begin lugging and tossing rocks.

We spread ourselves along the great pile of rock and debris with Tezabouh at the top, me in the middle, and Cuz behind me. We maintain a quick pace in our labors, and luckily, none of the loose rocks falls back on us. The opening we create becomes large enough in less than a macron. I can feel the frigid air gushing against my face as we remove the last few rocks.

The moon's intemperate climate makes Cuz, and I put our helmets back on. Crawling through the opening, we're back on the moon's glaring, icy surface. It feels good to be under a sky and sun once more. The sky is crystal-clear, and my heads-up display indicates a stiff wind blowing in from the southwest. The ambient temperature is a balmy -4 degrees C. My relief at being out of that dismal hole is cut short, seeing Karoft lying face down unconscious, and Larzz lying on his back also unconscious, a few meters from the cavern's opening.

Cuz and Tezabouh both rush to them. Cuz attends to Karoft and Tezabouh on Larzz. Karoft is fortunate to be in his environmental suit, but Larzz is exposed to the harsh elements.

I ask Cuz, "How is he?"

"He's alive but has sustained injuries throughout his body. We need to turn him onto his back." Cuz has me kneeling to one side of Karoft while Cuz is on the other side. "I'm going to slowly turn him toward you. Please support his head with one hand while laying him on his back. Ready?"

I nod, placing my hand under Karoft's helmet. His faceplate is shattered, and I can see long lacerations on his face and forehead. The freezing air must've acted as a natural coagulant because the blood is hard-crusted, with no noticeable seepage. Cuz rotates Karoft by his shoulder while supporting his back with his hand. When he gets Karoft on his side, I support and help ease him onto his back. He doesn't stir as we maneuver him.

"I hope he isn't already in shock or even worse, comatose," I speculate aloud. "Do you think he'll make it?"

Cuz runs his med-scanner over Karoft's body. He looks up with a grim expression. "As you feared, he's in shock, but his vital signs are steady. His most serious injuries are to his lower back and ribs. He also sustained micro-fractures to both his lower legs and left arm. It appears from his injuries that he got caught by the collapse of the cavern's roof and must have been halfway out when it fell. Larzz must have pulled him the rest of the way out." Cuz gets out one of his magic cubes from his belt and places it on the left side of Karoft's head. "This will mitigate the pain and temporarily knit the fractures, but he'll need corrective surgery for his back."

We go to Tezabouh and are relieved to see him talking with Larzz. Larzz forces a cheery smile, but his eyes betray his sorrow.

"I guess Karoft owes you gratitude," I say to him.

"No," he responds, shaking his large head full of red hair, "it's I who owes my life to him. If it weren't for his quick action, I would've been buried under that great mass of stone along with the others."

"You mean there are no other survivors?" I ask, feeling my heart sink with the revelation.

Larzz's expression turns dark and solemn. "It happened so fast," he explains, his voice cracking. He lowers his head as if in shame.

I try to console him by saying, "It's okay, Larzz. It wasn't your fault. What happened?"

"One of the Venubians fell, and Khezicar had me carry the two injured survivors. I placed them against the cavern wall by the opening. There hadn't been another shock wave in a few microns. We thought you must have disarmed that horrible device. Khezicar went back to get the fallen Venubian when a tremendous shock wave rumbled through. Khezicar was having trouble maintaining his balance on the trembling floor. He almost made it back. I reached out for the poor wretched soul when... he... he was so close—" his voice trembles, then breaks into a gushing sob.

My heart aches, watching that massive humanoid shaking with tears. I sit next to him on the frigid ground. A thin cover of dust and snow dulls his bright mane. I touch his cold arm and notice a severe head wound. His already flat nose is bent, looking broken. I could see dried blood in and around one nostril and above his mouth. His face has lacerations, and his left eye is black and swollen shut, while his right eye is puffy and dark purple.

"Larzz, you don't have to relive it now. I think we understand. First, we need to get to our shuttle and get back to Venubia."

He tries to smile but can only frown. His eyes narrowed, grimacing in pain. I can sense the deep sorrow he's feeling. Our eyes meet, and Larzz breaks out in uncontrollable tears.

I wonder. How does one comfort a giant?

Cuz comes and transmits, *"We must get them out of this harsh environment. See if you can get him on his feet and walking on his own. Tezabouh will carry Karoft and, if we need to, we'll help Larzz back to the shuttle."*

"How far is it?" I ask.

"Only 4 kilometers. We're on the other side of the mountains, a little east of where we landed."

"Well, at least something good has come of this other route," I say, feeling weary from the constant heartache and death. I stand over Larzz, holding my hand out to him.

He wipes his face with the back of his bulky arm, then gazes up at me with watery, red eyes and forces a thin smile.

"You have a good soul, Phillip," he says, then adds, "but I don't think you can bear my weight in aiding me to my feet."

"Don't let my size fool you. I'm stronger than I look," I say, with a confident smile.

I reach out and get a firm grasp of his enormous hands and place the tips of his feet under my boots for leverage, and pull him to his feet.

"Impressive for a puny Earthman," he laughs, then winces in pain.

I smiled back at him, thinking his laugh was a good outward sign.

***

The going is slow with Cuz and me having to help support Larzz, who's struggling to keep upright. Tezabouh is a few meters ahead of us. We hear a buzzing sound. Tezabouh stops and glances down at the generator. He flashes us an alarmed look and says, "Hurry, the weapon has activated itself."

Cuz asks me to support Larzz while he assists Tezabouh.

"Wonderful," I mumble.

"What is wonderful about the possibility of imminent destruction?" Larzz asks with a bewildered look.

"Um...." I shake my head, realizing how strange my idiomatic expressions are for him. "It's sarcasm. It's a—"

"I know," he interrupts. "Another Earth expression."

"Yes. Soon you'll have an Earth expression for any occasion."

Larzz's appearance goes from enlightened to perplexed again.

I ask, "Now, what's wrong?"

"I'm not sure if what you said was a compliment or more sarcasm."

"Ah, I can see your confusion," I say, curling my lower lip in thought, then add, "That was a little of both."

Larzz looks at me thoughtfully before breaking into a hardy laugh. "And I thought Venubian was a difficult language," he says, holding his side, coughing.

"Well," I shout to them, "what do we do?"

He takes the generator from Tezabouh and places it on the hard snow surface, and studies it.

"Can you stand for a few moments while I check with our brain trust on what they're doing?" I tell Larzz.

"I believe I can," he says, through heavy breaths.

"If you feel dizzy or weak, go down on one knee, and I'll come right back."

"Was that sarcasm? When you referred to them as *our brain trust*?" he calls.

I turn and say with a bright smile, "You're catching on, my new friend. I'm going to join Cuz.

"Okay, you two. We have two seriously injured, and one of them is exposed to the environment and struggling. I suggest you make a quick decision, and let's get to the shuttle."

Tezabouh eyes me with a pensive stare, then looks down at the activated device. "He's right," he grunts. "We have to take our chances and try to make it back to the shuttle. With any luck, we can dump it out an airlock as soon as we're outside of the moon's magnetic field."

Cuz picks the generator up. He asks me, "Can you manage Larzz alone so that I can carry the generator?"

"Yeah."

"We're close to the shuttle," Cuz adds. "Based on our present coordinates, it should be on the other side of that rise."

"Let's go," I say, feeling a little excited as I go back to Larzz. I see him kneeling as instructed. He spits out greenish-red colored phlegm that I believe is blood.

"You look terrible," I say as I wrap his long, muscular arm across my back, bracing my shoulder under his, and I leverage him to his feet. He winces and coughs up more blood. "I'm worried you have sustained some internal injuries. Your breathing sounds labored, and you're spitting blood. So, would you like to tell me about it?"

"I have some broken ribs, and they may have punctured one of my lower lungs," he says through wheezing breaths.

"Lower lungs? How many do you have?"

"Four. How many do you have?

"Two. Never mind that now. Don't talk anymore. You need to conserve as much energy as you can. We're less than 2 kilometers from the shuttle," I add, hoping it will encourage him. "We'll go slow and steady. Okay?"

Larzz's eyes are half-closed, and he looks to be fighting to stay conscious.

"Stay focused. You must remain conscious." I gave him a gentle nudge with my shoulder.

"I am so tired," he wheezes.

"You can't give in. Not yet. Once we get aboard the shuttle, we'll fix you up in the ambassador's suite and let you rest. Stay focused. What's the first thing you want when we get to Venubia?"

"Venubia?" he mutters, sounding confused.

"I know what I want," I say, dreamily. "A long, hot shower with my girl. Followed by twelve uninterrupted hours of sleep and wake up to a variable feast of my favorite synthetic foods."

"Sleep, yes, sleep is wonderful," he murmurs.

Dumbass, you had to bring up sleep. I curse myself. "Sorry, never mind about sleep. Keep thinking about how nice it will be when we make it back to — I see, in the distance, a large, mangled mess that was our shuttle. "No," I whisper, feeling stunned at the sight of all our hopes in ruins. "Those stinking bastards," I hiss, wondering what's next.

CHAPTER 54

Cuz rushes up and helps me bring Larzz to a makeshift shelter he constructed from pieces of the shuttle's hull. He gathers volcanic rock into a pile and heats it to an amber glow with his pulse phaser, hoping to provide a little warmth under the falling temperature. I look to the east and see the small white ball hovering close to the horizon. Its feeble warmth did little against the frigid air. At least the winds lessen. As I walk toward the shelter, I see the generator lying on the ground next to it. The generator stopped blinking and looks inert.

I go to Tezabouh. He's kneeling beside Tezabar, who's lying on the frozen ground. Tezabar acknowledges me with his crooked smile. "It appears as though I will not be joining you in your quest," he says in a garbled voice. "Pity." His voice becomes almost incoherent, sounding like a recording being played at a slowed speed. His intense eyes have softened to a dull gray. For the first time, he looks like what he is: an android losing its power and failing.

I ask Tezabouh, "What happened?"

"He got caught by the collapse, then dug his way out of the rubble. He tried to get to Khezicar, who was struggling to get out from under some debris. When he climbed back in, an aftershock caused another section of the roof to collapse, burying Khezicar and crushing Tezabar's torso." Tezabouh gazes down at Tezabar and, in a mournful tone, says, "He's shutting down, and there's nothing I can do to save him."

"Can he be rebuilt?"

Tezabouh shakes his head. "He was only a temporary surrogate, but I've come to appreciate his uniqueness."

He looks up at me with tearful eyes. It surprises me that he's capable of such an emotion.

"I had no idea you felt so strongly about him," I say, feeling regret about my irritation with Tezabar. "He looked much like you, but his personality differed from yours. Did you design him that way?"

"Thank you for your service," he whispers in Venubian, closing Tezabar's vacant eyes. "In answer to your question, his design was based on my twin brother, whom I lost many millennia ago. I gave him a different personality subroutine, though. I wanted him to have a certain uniqueness of character and personality. Also, I instilled self-awareness and free will, hoping he'd develop a well-balanced personality and respect for all life. He didn't live long enough to acquire sufficient experiences to refine those traits."

"I'm sorry for your loss. While I didn't always appreciate him and sometimes was impatient with his, as you put it, uniqueness. That said, he did have some good qualities." I pat Tezabouh's shoulder. "I saw the generator. It looks deactivated."

He stands, rubbing his square chin. "Cuz theorized that if he scrambled the crystals, it should cause it to go into a standby mode. It appears he's correct. He's a most intuitive humanoid and is loyal to you," Tezabouh adds, sounding impressed with Cuz.

"I've come to appreciate his qualities and uniqueness. The Venubians don't consider him an automaton, but rather a sentient being. A biogenetically engineered life-form is their formal definition of him. Not that dissimilar from your origins, I believe."

Tezabouh arches a bushy white eyebrow, looking surprised at my comparison. "Your observations are correct, up to a point. It's true, I was artificially engineered, but different from Cuz. It's something I'll share with you when this ordeal is over."

"Yeah. I've been hearing that a lot. But under the circumstances, that's a little optimistic," I say. "Considering our shuttle is wrecked. How do you propose we'll ever get off this frozen rock?" I stare at the mangled metal scattered in the snow and let out a heavy sigh.

Tezabouh places his long arm around my shoulders and smiles confidently. "Have faith. Help will come."

"Are you placating me, or do you know something?"

Cuz comes over smiling broadly.

"Why are you so happy?" I ask him.

"You didn't receive her message?" he replies, looking puzzled.

"Whose message?"

"Biomei's. She's on her way."

"Oh man, that's awesome," I shout excitedly. "How are our patients doing?"

"With some immediate medical attention, they should fully recover."

"That's great. Do they know?"

"Karoft does. He regained consciousness long enough to be told. I gave him another sedative, and he's resting. Larzz is more of a concern, though. He has internal damage that will require corrective surgery. He's also well-sedated and resting."

Tezabouh comes to us and says, "Never lose faith. Never give up and always trust your friends."

At first, I don't understand his burst of platitudes until I notice the graying sky blacken. I look up and see one of the most beautiful things in the universe, hovering high above us in the crystal-clear skies. "Biomei," I whisper and then cry out, "Biomei!"

***

"Finally, I can speak with you," she transmits with great joy. *"I've been trying to reach both of you for two cycles. Why haven't you responded?"*

Her question is a little disturbing. *"I'm not sure. When did you reach Cuz?"*

"A few mics ago. On my final approach to the moon." She sounds concerned and relieved at the same time.

"It must have had something to do with the moon. Or maybe something to do with the generator. I don't know. Let's not deal with it now. The important thing is you're here, and I may add, in the nick of time. We've two injured patients who need immediate medical attention."

"I'm aware. I'm sending down a shuttle for you now."

Looking up at Biomei, I see her aft bay doors open and watch an automated shuttle circle out, then straighten its flight path toward us. I look at Cuz with a giddy grin as he was readying Larzz and Karoft for transport.

It only takes a few minutes for the shuttle to reach us. It lands alongside the crumbled hull of the Klaxon shuttle. Its aft-loading door lowers as the side passenger door slides open. Cuz goes inside the shuttle through the loading door. A moment later, he comes out, guiding two antigrav medical gurneys in front of him. He lays the gurneys next to the shelter and calls Tezabouh for help.

I watch them as they lay Karoft and then Larzz each onto a gurney. Cuz connects the built-in telemetry monitors to them and guides both gurneys back into the shuttle through the aft doorway. Once they're inside, my mind turns to the survivors we're leaving behind. I gaze back toward the cavern. My heart becomes heavy with guilt.

"How can we leave them?" I shout at Tezabouh, who's watching me from the shuttle.

A strong gust of air causes me to shiver. It wasn't a shiver from the cold; my environmental suit is keeping me warm. It's one filled with regret. A metaphor of my guilt and resentment of what we're about to do.

Tezabouh comes to me. I can feel him staring at my back. In a low voice, he says, "We'll come back for them. They have sufficient medical supplies, weapons, and enough food and water for many cycles. I promise they won't be forgotten or stranded." He turns me by the shoulders to face him. "You must believe me."

I want to believe him, but it still troubles me that we have to be so callous and leave all those poor souls behind. I turn away from Tezabouh and go to the shuttle.

"So much waste," I mumble, half aloud as Tezabouh sits next to me in the front row.

"War is nothing but abject waste. That's the real horror of it," he states, cocking an eyebrow.

I nod in agreement, then close my eyes as Cuz powers up the shuttle's engines, and we're, at last, getting off that frozen, nightmare world.

CHAPTER 55

"Welcome home," Biomei cheerfully greets us.

"It's good to be home," I say, feeling relieved to be with Biomei again.

"Tezabouh, we are honored by your presence and are here to serve at your pleasure."

I glance up with a bewildered expression and transmit, *"What's that all about?"*

"He's an important and well-respected elder of the planet," she explains.

"Really? I thought he was the one responsible for all of our troubles."

"You have a lot to learn about him. He's not responsible for our present situation and maybe the only one who knows how to get us out of this horrible mess."

"If you say so."

The shuttle bay doors hiss open. Shorty comes with his distinctive bounce, his optical sensor blinking as he walks.

"It is so good to see you again, Phillip," he addresses me with emulated joy. "You appear to be in good health."

"Thanks, Shorty. It's good to be back."

"I am pleased to see you again, Cuz," he says, flashing his optical sensor. Shorty turns to Tezabouh. "It is a great honor to meet you, Master Tezabouh," he makes a short bow from his hinged hips.

"Excuse me," I say, covering a yawn with my hand. "I'm exhausted. With your permission, I'm going to my quarters and trying to get a little rest. Shorty will take you to your quarters." I pat Shorty's head and say to him, "Show our guest to his quarters on deck seven."

"As you wish, Phillip," he acknowledges. "Please follow me, sir," he says to Tezabouh.

"We've much work to do, Phillip," Cuz states. "I don't believe Tezabouh requires a rest period. May I suggest we go to the main bridge and strategize viable plans for a counterattack?"

"That's fine with me. I'll join you in a few hours. I'll have Shorty stay to assist you. He's most resourceful."

"Rest well, Phillip," Cuz calls as I leave the shuttle bay.

"Sweet dreams," Tezabouh adds.

Without turning to them, I give them a backward wave. It feels good to be back on Biomei. I always have a sense of comfort and peace every time I return to her. As soon as I enter my quarters, I strip off my clothes and take a long, hot shower. Coming from the bathroom, my stomach growls, but I'm too tired to eat and settle for a protein shake from my dispenser.

The bed is too compelling. I dive into it, trying to push everything out of my whirling mind so that I can sleep. I try to make myself comfortable, but can't stop thinking about all those poor souls we left behind. Every time I close my eyes, the horrific images of death and destruction dance around in my head. Until now, I was too busy trying to survive to give that insidious reality any thought. The depth and magnitude of what the Zentis are doing are beginning to sink into my consciousness, and it terrifies me.

Finding a comfortable spot, I fall into an exhausted, dreamless sleep. I'm not sure how long I slept, but I'm still drowsy when my eyes open. It takes a concerted effort for me to drag my heavy, lethargic body out of bed. I swing my legs to the side and sit upright, massaging the sides of my head with my fingertips.

"Biomei," I call out. "How long was I asleep?"

"12.23 ship-hours."

"Why did you let me sleep so long?"

"Because you needed it."

I go to the short wall next to my closet and request a sink. A small, oval-shaped sink appears. I request cold water, and I wash up. I dare not ask for a mirror, fearing what I'd see in the eyes staring back at me.

Feeling a little more revived, I head to the small galley down the corridor from my quarters. I'm staring at the food replicator, wondering what I should eat. My stomach's growling again, but I don't want to take a lot of time to eat and order my custom breakfast sandwich with a large coffee. The sandwich is finished in a few large bites. I drink the coffee on my way to the main bridge.

Cuz and Tezabouh are busy working on a real-time, holographic map of the Venubian system. The map is highlighted in different colors. Cuz orders an image of Jo'vah, one of the larger Venubian moons, and a sister moon to Jo'ovf as I join them.

"What are you working on?" I ask, leaning over Cuz's shoulder.

"We're considering several options for staging a counterattack," Cuz explains without looking up.

"What are you planning to do on Jo'vah?"

Tezabouh levels his steely, cobalt eyes at me and says, "Did Verubeal ever tell you about the first Venubian-Zenti conflict?"

"She gave me an overview but didn't have time for too much detail."

Tezabouh arches his bushy, white eyebrows and purses his mouth, looking full of thought. "It was a complex period for Venubia and the Androids," he says. "It was also a few hundred cycles before my time. The Venubian-Android conflict is also known as the Technological Singularity.

"I'm aware of this. So, what's your point?"

"Then you know what happened because of this short and devastating war for Venubia's control."

I nod. Closing my eyes with a painful flashback of the virtual experience.

"Jo'vah was the primary industrial complex used by the Androids in their pursuit of creating a biologically suitable mate for the women of Venubia. From what I've gathered from the surviving data and many personal Venubian accounts, the Zenti were mistreated by the Androids, which was one of the prime reasons for their eventual rebellion and the cause of the second conflict." He lets out a heavy sigh. "If only the Androids could have recognized the Zenti as sentient beings that we're entitled to fundamental liberties, those terrible conflicts may never have gotten so out of control, saving Venubia from so much unforgivable death and destruction.

"We learned nothing from that first horrific war. Even though I was familiar with what transpired, I still made many costly mistakes. Countless lives were lost; almost all the Androids were decimated in the second war.

"The most critical error was believing I could interject myself into the conflict and negotiate with the Zenti. In the end, I took a page from the Zenti and resorted to devious treachery to defeat them. It's one of the major reasons they're so determined to destroy all humanoids and androids alike. Once more, history repeats itself with me in the center, feeling almost as helpless as the last time."

"You said, one of the reasons. What are the other reasons they're attacking?"

Tezabouh frowns, "The Zenti are engineered to adapt to any environment, so they could work and live in a diverse range of planetary systems. Their genetic development permitted them to perform a variety of physical labor, and they are intelligent enough to be resourceful."

His expression turns impassive with his eyes staring outward. "They were given all the physical attributes for survival," he continues in a low monotone, "but none of the mental discipline or emotional experiences for compassion and empathy. For all intents and purposes, we created a psychotic species. The androids never considered the consequences of having the Zenti evolve artificially and thus have no capacity to love, care, or trust. We're paying a terrible price for the Androids and Venubia's greatest folly."

"It sounds more as though you created a race of slaves who rebelled," I interject, but regret it. "Forgive," I quickly add. "That was an unwarranted statement. I shouldn't be judgmental of something I don't understand."

Tezabouh eyes me with a weary expression and declares, "No, Phillip, you're correct. That's what we did. Verubeal must have described the difficulties Venubia faced after the great Singularity."

"She tried, but I'm still fuzzy on why the androids created a genetically engineered species, which I understand, that evolved into the Zenti. Then, after seeing the error of their creation, discard them on a remote world? Their actions seem counterintuitive for such highly evolved androids."

Tezabouh rubs his square chin. "Your insights are poignant and touch the core of the Zenti problem," he observes. "The sentient Androids, like the Zenti, had no real-life experiences to give them insight and a clear understanding of the complexities of humanoid emotions. To say they were immature would oversimplify the problem. They were incapable of organic feelings and needed time to hone their emotional developmental skills.

"The Zenti became frustrated with the matriarchal Venubian society that evolved after the terrible war. When the androids realized the Venubian women's discontent with the Zenti, they took a different approach. Their methods and decisions were based on dispassionate, logical reasoning. They viewed the Zenti as a failed experiment and discarded them. In hindsight, it would have been better if they had eradicated them. For their inexplicable reasons, they didn't."

Tezabouh confirmed what Verubeal had already told me. We're dealing with an enemy that can only be stopped by total annihilation. My mind wanders with the realization.

"Phillip," Cuz breaks the sudden trance I'd fallen into. "Are you all right?"

I blink and ask Tezabouh, "What do you have in mind?"

"We believe we can regroup all the androids on Jo'vah. It will provide the needed resources to repair and rearm them. We have learned the Kayden fleet is regrouping near the Bohari asteroid belt. Biomei has been in touch with Venubian intelligence, and they've been keeping her abreast of all the strategic movements within the system. The Klaxons have agreed to provide us with ships and supplies to aid our cause."

"The Klaxon is getting involved?" I ponder, surprised.

"It appears they've had an unprecedented change in attitude and will give us any support we request, short of supplying troops and weapons. They've learned how the Zenti tortured Minister Uzzendi, his wife, and his daughters. It outraged them enough to become involved. On a positive note, you'll appreciate that they will send a rescue mission for the survivors on Celebus. The Kaydens agreed to send a small fighter squadron to escort the medical transport."

"That's wonderful, Cuz. It sounds like things are turning a little in our favor." I say to Tezabouh, "What are you planning for us?"

"I have an important job for you," he says.

"Yes?"

"I need you to convince Biomei to allow us to install offensive weapons. Otherwise, we'll have to seek different transportation to Jo'vah."

"I'm not sure I'm following you," I say, trying to reconcile what adding weapons to Biomei has to do with her taking us to Jo'vah. After a moment's thought, I understood. "The Zenti have taken over the moon."

Tezabouh nods grimly. "The latest intelligence has the Zenti on the twin moons, Jo'vah and Jo'ovf. It revealed a small contingent of Zenti troops on Jo'vah and a scattering of security forces on the other moons. It appears the Zenti leaders have spread their forces too thin. Besides maintaining an occupational force in Venubia, they are organizing invasion forces for the Kayden system, followed by the Klaxon. We must locate where they're keeping the wide-field generator and take back Jo'vah."

"Cuz, you have a good relationship with Biomei. Why don't—" I stop myself, noticing Cuz's eyebrows raise. "Never mind. I'll talk with her. In the meantime, I suggest you have her set a course for Jo'vah. She won't like it, but she'll agree to the weapons. Are you going to use the droids for the installation?"

"Yes, but I'll be supervising them," Cuz explains.

"You're not thinking of going OVA with them?"

"It's the most expedient way. Unless you have a better idea."

"Do it from the bridge."

CHAPTER 56

Surprisingly, Biomei doesn't argue about the weapons. I only have to assure her they'll be removed after we defeat the Zenti.

"We'll make the Zenti aware of our overwhelming forces and our determination to annihilate them if they don't capitulate," I say, trying to sound confident. "I hope that if we destroy their fleet and scatter their ground troops, they'll be more inclined to agree to a cease-fire."

"You're not as sure as you sound," she says, seeing right through me.

"It may be a bit of a conceit, but I feel our chances are getting stronger by the minute."

"Oh, my dear, Phillip, you're such an optimist," she laughs softly. "That's one of the many things I admire about you. Never change, my dear."

"I love you, too." I grin at a monitor. "I need to get back to work. Oh, one more thing. Cuz is going out with the droids to supervise your weapons retrofit. Please keep a close eye on him. We can't afford to lose him or the droids."

"I keep a close eye on all of you. Don't worry. Cuz is capable and always uses good judgment."

"Yeah, I guess so. Thanks, Biomei."

I amble back to the main bridge full of thoughts, mainly of Nicki. I try not to think of her. Her absence is like a void that can be filled. Each day without her is like cancer eating away at my soul.

"I'm receiving a request to open a communication channel from Zenti command," Tezabouh informs me as I enter the bridge.

"Who's it from?" I ask.

"Alv'Fuerr-Sehm, Leader of the People," Tezabouh translates with a bemused expression. "That's a curious Venubian name for a Zenti."

"Are we finally going to meet this enigmatic leader? Or do you think he's another diversion?" My questions make Tezabouh rub his chin.

"Good question," he says, looking intently at the forward viewscreen, "let's find out. Biomei, open a channel."

"This is Alv'Fuerr-Sehm. I wish to address the Earthman." His voice wheezes with heavy breaths between each word as though he's laboring to speak.

"Do they all sound like that?" I whisper to Tezabouh.

"Yes, they have difficulty with verbalization. Their physiology is more adapted to body language. Until recently, their lexicon was limited to grunts and clicks. However, some of them speak more clearly. Alv'Fuerr-Sehm isn't as advanced in his speech as others."

"I see. It makes me wonder what they must look like. All I've seen of them were mangled messes. Why can't we get a visual?"

"Let's go with audio for the time being. You'll have your visual soon enough." Tezabouh holds his hand up, stopping me from speaking. "Phillip Mann is unavailable," he states, projecting in his rich baritone voice. "You will bring Nickada and Verubeal along with yourself to discuss terms. No others. Is that understood?"

"That is not acceptable!" The Zenti's voice hisses. "You are in no position to demand any terms. You will surrender the ship."

"If Nickada and Verubeal are not brought aboard, we're prepared to destroy this ship along with most of your fleet."

There's a long silence. "We will only talk with the Earthman." The voice stresses '*Earthman*' as though it signifies something of great value.

Tezabouh looks at me and smiles. "Seems like they only want to negotiate with you. Hold on a moment. Let's make them wait before responding."

I'm grateful for the extra time. I need a few minutes to gather myself before dealing with the Zenti.

"Keep one thing in mind. They're more afraid of you than you are of them.

That surprises me.

Tezabouh must have seen my surprise because he adds in a low voice, "Maintain an even, dispassionate tenor to your voice. Reveal no emotion regardless of what they say. Give them nothing they can use against us." He nods for me to speak.

I straighten my posture while taking a few deep breaths to calm my rising nerves. "I am Phillip Mann of Earth," I say slowly, enunciating each word.

There's another long pause, then a raspy voice snaps, "I am Alv'Fuerr-Sehm, the leader of the Zenti, and we demand your unconditional surrender."

"Unconditional surrender is out of the question," I retort forcibly, trying hard to keep my voice even. "Leader of the Zenti. I find that a curious oddity. You're an oxymoron. Anarchy has no leadership." Tezabouh puts his hand up for me to stop.

"We have Venubia's leaders and your Nickada. They will die if you do not comply," the Zenti's voice wavers as he speaks.

"We have no control over their lives, but killing them will accomplish nothing," I state with as much detachment as I can portray, my stomach knotting.

"You will sacrifice your precious loved ones to protect your ship?" The Zenti's voice becomes even more slurred.

"Biomei, mute the channel," I say, feeling a little braver. I say to Tezabouh, "We have them confused by our bluff. Obviously, they've never been confronted with the absurdity of a bluff." Tezabouh and I look at each other in surprise. "I'd love to play poker with these guys. For villainous scum, they seem naïve or ignorant. You know, Tezabouh, I think we got them a little less assured of their position."

"Well done, Phillip," Tezabouh compliments. "While they seem confused, I wouldn't underestimate them. They're adaptive and learn quickly."

"Biomei reopens the channel," I say with confidence. "Alv'Fuerr-Sehm, I have a counterproposal."

"A counterproposal?" he repeats, sounding unsure.

"We wish to create a peaceful coexistence for Venubians and Zentis. You deliver Councilor Verubeal and Nickada to us. In exchange, we'll surrender Biomei, but you must withdraw all your troops back to neutral ground while we negotiate a sensible resolution to the hostilities."

"Negotiations are irrelevant," his voice becomes harsher. "There can be no peace. We already control Venubia. You offer us nothing."

"Then you offer us no other choice. We'll give you..." I transmit to Cuz, *"How's the retrofit coming?"*

"The first stage is complete. Need another forty microns to finish."

"Do it in 30," I demand, then continue my negotiations with Alv'fuerr-Sehm. "40 clicks to reconsider before we unleash Biomei's wrath upon you. Everything will be destroyed, and nothing will be gained. This is my only offer. Agree to our terms or perish!" My mouth becomes dry as I break out in a cold, nervous sweat.

Tezabouh frowns, looking disappointed by the Zenti's sudden change in tactics. "I think they threw back our ruse, my friend. Now we must wait it out and see if they're willing to risk all or back off."

"You're right about their adaptability. In poker, this is known as calling a bluff. I only hope they perceive Biomei as the better hand."

"Poker?" Tezabouh closes his eyes for a beat and then says, "Fascinating." He smiles. "A game of chance played with picturesque cards that require a combination of strategic skills and fortune, played by a group of opponents to win a monetary sum referred to as a pot. I'd enjoy participating in this Earth game with you."

"I'd enjoy that if I could find a way of inhibiting your photographic memory."

"Why would that be a problem?"

"Not now, Tezabouh, it would take too long to explain."

"Phillip Mann of Earth," a new Zenti voice wheezes over the com. "I am Vuansia, chief negotiator for the new Zenti Republic. To facilitate your surrender, our leader has asked me to continue on his behalf."

I look at Tezabouh in confusion. "New Zenti Republic? What the hell does that mean?"

"I guess somewhere in all the turmoil, they formulated a government?" Tezabouh returns my puzzled expression.

"We can't recognize them as a legitimate government. It would give them too much power."

"I think they're trying to legitimize themselves in your eyes to gain respect. Don't give it to them," Tezabouh says emphatically.

"The thought of dealing with a true government is a dual-edged sword. In one sense, a legitimate government would require an organized body of rules or even a constitution. On the other hand, they could use my understanding of government as a ploy to distract me. If they'd organized as a true republic, they would have an elected leader. If that's the case, then Alv'Fuerr-Sehm would be their leader. Our best tactic can be to insist on negotiating only with him. He seems uncomfortable, maybe even a little nervous."

"Yes, you may be correct. Let's insist on it. Also, insist on seeing if Verubeal and Nickada are on their ship and unharmed. We need proof of life."

"Biomei, increase the volume by twenty percent," I say.

"As you wish, Phillip."

"Why do you want the volume increased?" Tezabouh asks.

"It helps to emphasize the point." Tezabouh nods and gestures for me to continue. "Are you telling me Alv'Fuerr-Sehm is the elected leader of your newly established republic?"

"That is correct," the raspy voice says.

"The Zenti have found a common voice to speak for the United Republic of Anarchists? I find that fascinating."

"We have learned to be united in our common cause to regain what is rightfully ours." The voice is stronger and clearer. Different from the strained sounds we heard from the Zenti leader.

"I hope you are a voice of reason rather than demands." I glance at Tezabouh with a sudden thought and signal for Biomei to mute our communications. "I don't think this is a Zenti. His voice has become too regular. Something is wrong."

"I suspect they're using a universal translator, which they're adjusting as the Zenti speaks. Question him, Phillip," Tezabouh urges. "Insist on proof of life."

"Who are you?" I ask.

"I am the voice of the Zenti," he restates, sounding unsure.

"You're not Zenti. I'll only negotiate with the leader of the New Zenti Republic."

"You are in no position to demand anything of us, and we are not obligated to grant anything. Now that we understand our respective positions, let us dispense with these tiresome formalities and establish what needs to be done."

"Wow, he sure caught on fast," I grunt, wiping the sweat from my forehead with my sleeve.

As I was about to speak, a new voice came over the com. "This is Kayden Air Command, we are in position over Venubian airspace, please advise!"

Tezabouh gives me a relieved look and responds, "Kayden Air Command. Do a high sweep of the ground forces and report. Do not engage them. Repeat. Do not engage at this time." Looking pleased, he says to me, "Perfect timing. That should get their attention."

We hear the Kayden aircraft over the monitor, buzzing the Zenti forces. As soon as the Kaydens sign off, I bellow to the new speaker, "Do you want a war, or would you prefer to negotiate an equitable settlement? First, I need proof that Verubeal and Nickada of Venubia are alive and on board your ship."

"Have the Kaydens back off first," he says defiantly.

"They're not there, are they?" I knew it. I can't sense Nicki's presence.

"Do you want to gamble with their lives?" The Zenti asks.

"Last time. Show them, or I'll be forced to open fire. Your ground troops are surrounded."

"If you insist," he responds in a calm voice, "war it is."

"Warning," the auto alert system sounds, "missiles detected 1375K off our port bow."

"Biomei, evasive maneuvers," I shout.

Biomei makes an unexpected, sharp ninety-degree bank. Then she flattens out for a sec before pulling her nose up 80 degrees and engaging the jump engines. We are pinned to the deck under the intense G-forces until the inertial dampener kicks in.

Tezabouh offers me a hand and helps me up. Laser and cannon fire come over the com.

"Does this answer your question, Earthman!?" Vuansia's voice cries in a wheezing laugh.

Tezabouh calls to Biomei, "Give us full visual."

The viewscreen lights up in full panorama view, showing the ongoing battle below. The Kayden squadrons are swarming over the Zenti ground troops. Everything appears to be in a chaotic blaze of weapons firing and intense explosions while troops skirmish for position. The Kaydens are inflicting heavy damage on the Zenti forces as the modest Venubian troops are holding the high ground. They're systematically chipping away at the edges of the Zenti infantry while sending small squads forward, trying to position themselves for a flanking maneuver.

Everything is going well until two large Zenti battle cruisers appear. They dispatched their well-armed fighters against Kayden's small Seteh, and the heavens lit up as the two opposing forces engaged each other. Watching in horror as more of the Kayden fighters engage the Zenti air attack, leaving the small Venubian troops without their cover. At first, the Venubians gain position on the Zenti forces, but they're soon overwhelmed, then slaughtered right before our eyes.

"This is Klee of the Zenti Battleship Anool," a harsh, wheezing voice says over the com. "Prepare to be boarded."

"What!" I shout.

Tezabouh rushes over to Biomei's manual interface and inputs a command on a small, holographic keyboard.

"Biomei, engage audiovisual program, Tezabouh-five."

"Tezabouh-five audiovisual is in standby mode," Biomei responds.

I thought of Cuz and transmitted, *"Are you okay?"*

"Fine. Biomei got us inside before she jumped."

I let out a heavy sigh and asked, *"Did you complete the retrofit?"*

"Only the first stage."

"Okay, come to the bridge."

"It's time to play our trump card," Tezabouh says.

"Trump card?" I repeat in surprise.

"Yes. I've been studying your games of chance ever since you mentioned poker."

"Okay?"

"We need to buy a little time. Let's see who boards us. I'll have Biomei create a special knock-out cocktail for the Zenti. Their physiology makes them sensitive to a specific combination of high-frequency sounds and ultraviolet light. A 30-second discharge of the combined frequencies will incapacitate the boarding party. Once they are knocked out, we can disembark and regroup on Venubia at Cheranlu. I'll send a transmission to Xandroff and tell him to gather the remaining androids on Jo'vah as planned."

"What if it doesn't work?" I probe.

"Then I'm afraid we'll be at the Zenti's mercy."

"They're incapable of mercy. They seem to enjoy killing." Then I thought about Nicki. "Do you think they have Nickada and Verubeal?"

"Doubtful," Tezabouh sighs. "If they had, it would've been to their advantage to show them. I believe they were testing our resolve. And yes, they're remorseless in their vengeance. But I believe they still want you alive."

"But if we fail to knock them out, they'll have us and, more importantly, Biomei. We'll have nothing left to negotiate." I think for a second. "How about a Plan-B?"

"A Plan-B?" Tezabouh gives me an attentive look.

"An alternative in case our initial plan fails."

"Yes. I considered that and couldn't come up with anything effective. What do you have in mind?"

As soon as he asks, my mind goes blank. I don't have a clue. Rubbing my chin in desperate contemplation of the horrors of being at the hands of the Zenti, an idea comes to mind, it's so simple, it frightens me. "Let's not be here when they board." I almost laugh at the irony of the suggestion.

Tezabouh raises one of his bushy eyebrows and smiles. "That's brilliant, Phillip. If we're not here and the Zenti are incapacitated, Biomei can retrieve us. If it fails, she can self-destruct, taking as many of them as possible, leaving them with nothing. We'll still have a chance of rescuing Nickada and Verubeal. It increases the odds a little more in our favor."

My excitement is dampened by the reality of sacrificing Biomei as part of the alternative. I didn't consider Biomei in my impromptu plan.

"No," I say emphatically. "That will not do at all." Looking at Tezabouh's perplexed expression, I explain, "We can't sacrifice Biomei as if she's a piece of technology. She's so much more than her technology. She's a sentient entity and my friend. I didn't consider that when I spoke. We need to find another solution." My insides ache at the thought of using her as a sacrificial lamb.

Tezabouh gives me a thoughtful look and says, "So much emotion for a biomechanical mechanism. I don't understand."

His stiff, aloof mannerisms are very much like the detached android personalities I've become familiar with and dislike.

"Biomei is much more than a machine," I object.

"Maybe," he says, coolly. "If you feel so strongly about it, why not ask Biomei how she feels about the alternative?"

Cuz enters the bridge.

Tezabouh is strategically right. But that didn't change how I feel about asking her. I already knew, given the choice, Biomei would sacrifice herself if it would help us save Nicki.

"Biomei," I say.

"Yes, Phillip."

"Have you been monitoring our conversation?"

"Of course."

Cuz looks puzzled as he listens in.

"What do you think?" Becoming more sensitive to Biomei's interpretation of my voice inflections, I soften the question with, "How do you feel about the situation. I mean, are you confident in our plan?"

"My calculations predict a 95.36% probability that the audiovisual burst will be successful. If it's not, I'll jettison an antimatter stream toward the Zenti battleships and ignite it with a negatively charged plasma burst from my forward thrusters, causing a matter-antimatter discharge. It should be sufficient to destroy all the Zenti ships within a quarter sector."

Biomei sounds confident. She's saying all the right things to put me at ease with the plan.

"And you're all right with it?" I say, and before she answers, I add, "Please, Biomei, tell us the truth."

"Phillip, I'm incapable of giving you anything less than the truth. Why do you question my integrity?"

"It's because you'd sacrifice yourself, regardless of the truth. Regardless of the risks, if you knew you could save Nicki or me," I cry in frustration.

Cuz comes closer and places his hand on my shoulder. "Phillip, we are replaceable, therefore expendable. You're placing too much emotion on something that must be viewed as what's necessary to save us from annihilation."

His words aren't reassuring, but he makes a clear point.

Ignoring my emotional outburst, Biomei responds in a calm voice, "My engine thrust should be robust enough for me to instantaneously reach jump speed for 7.65 milliseconds. Sufficient to clear me of the residual radiation." She becomes silent for a moment. "I've just received an intelligence update. Venubian central control believes the Zenti have reestablished their central command at Cheranlu. Also, there's strong evidence they've secured the perimeter around the Elders Administration Center and are using it as a holding facility for highly valued prisoners. There's a high probability that Nickada and Verubeal are among them."

Tezabouh appears impressed. "Biomei, you're a remarkable entity. It's an honor to know you." He turns to me with a confident smile. "Well, there you have it. It seems the Zenti have set the stage for us. Now we have a clear plan. I suggest we execute it."

"Biomei, please be precise. We all need you." I transmit to her.

"Phillip, have you ever known me to be anything other than precise?"

I smile at her central console, then turn to Tezabouh. "We should go in separate shuttles. Cuz and I will go to the Elder's center and look for Nickada and the Venubian leaders. You need to go to Jo'vah and regroup what's left of the androids and organize a counteroffensive at Cheranlu."

"Something just occurred to me," Tezabouh says, rubbing his chin. "The Zenti are waiting for our next move. They'll pursue you wherever you go. You're their focus. They're determined to capture you for their own reasons. Cuz is irrelevant to them." No offense, he pats Cuz's shoulder.

"I understand and will go alone." I tell Cuz, gazing intently at him, "Try to gather as many troops as possible on Cheranlu. And make sure nothing happens to you. Despite what Tezabouh says, you're indispensable to me, my friend."

"Phillip, Venubia needs you as well. I'll escort you until we've cleared the Zenti fleet."

Tezabouh extends his large hand. "I believe it is your custom to shake one's hand as a gesture of good wishes and respect."

Looking at Tezabouh's cobalt eyes, I firmly grip his hand, and we shake, staring into each other's eyes. His grip is powerful. I also sense something other than bone beneath his warm flesh. Tezabouh gives me a friendly smile and releases his grip. He takes a step back and performs the formal Venubian gesture of respect to us.

We return the gesture, then I call out, "Biomei, prepare auxiliary shuttles for departure."

We head to the aft auxiliary shuttle bay. Biomei positioned it so it's out of the Zenti's view.

Tezabouh looks back at us as we enter our respective shuttles and says, "I believe it is also appropriate to wish one good fortune."

"I believe the term you are looking for is ' good luck,'" Cuz interjects.

"Yes. Good luck, Phillip, and to you, Cuz. I know we'll meet again."

PART V

Zohleemay

CHAPTER 57

The auxiliary shuttle differs from our standard ones in that it's flown manually, and like all Venubian shuttles, it has no weapons. Cuz adapted a sophisticated AI interface into my headgear. The interface allows me to fly like a skilled fighter pilot.

I follow Cuz's shuttle out of the bay. Cuz's voice clicks over my headset and tells me, "We'll only have a few seconds before the Zenti sends a swarm after us."

"They'll go for our engines first," I say. "From what I've observed, they like to disable, then capture like predators after their prey. Do you think we can outrun them?"

"No, but we've better maneuverability. I suggest we go right for their command ship when they dispatch their swarm. It may take them by surprise and disrupt their attack pattern, giving us a small window of escape. The Zenti hasn't displayed a willingness to engage in single combat. I believe you refer to it as a dogfight, which is a curious term for aerial combat."

"There's the Anool, their flagship," I say, seeing Cuz fly parallel to me. He motions for me to get closer.

"Fly tight on me until we're within two hundred meters," he says over the com. "We'll dive under her, then split up. Use your emergency thrusters, along with your primaries. You'll need as much speed as you can get. These shuttles are Kayden design, and can only outrun a Zenti swarm-fighter over a short distance."

"Remind me to thank the Kaydens." I give Cuz the thumbs-up sign.

He looks at me through his clear canopy with a confused expression.

"Thumbs-up is an affirmative acknowledgment," I transmit, then add, *"Let's go get those rotten bastards!"* Then, I frown, remembering we had no weapons.

Cuz gives me an uncertain look and flips up his thumb. "We're being engaged," Cuz warns, pointing upward.

There are at least two squads of Zenti swarms coming toward us. Each squad has four fighters.

"They're sending eight fighters for two defenseless shuttles. Should we feel important?" I transmit to Cuz.

"The Zenti is not taking any chances on you eluding them."

"Well, let's see if we can't at least make it difficult for those bastards," I growl.

"Three hundred fifty meters," Cuz calls out, as the Anool's massive hull becomes ever closer. "Two hundred fifty meters."

The Zenti swarm of six fighters breaks into two equal squadrons. They're closing in on us.

"Cuz, I think we need to increase speed now."

"Hold on a few more seconds," Cuz insists.

The two squadrons make a maneuver and join the other one. They appear to be trying to surround and then separate us. As soon as they break formation, Cuz calls out, "Two hundred meters. Phillip hit the engines."

The interface responds and engages all the engines as I pull back on the throttle. The shuttle makes a slight jerk, and intense G-forces push against me. I see the Zenti break off their maneuver, and then both squadrons go after me. Having a complete operations routine downloaded into my internal compiler gives me a good understanding of the shuttle's capabilities.

"Looks like they want me more than you," I say to Cuz. "At least one of us has a chance now."

"Don't despair. Help is on the way." Cuz points up.

Before I can respond, a squadron of Kayden Seteh fighters flies into view above me. Three Zenti ships go after them, firing all their weapons. My shuttle vibrates under extreme velocity. It only takes a few seconds before the ensuing air battle is out of view.

"Cuz, what's going on? How did they know our plan?"

"I'm a little busy now." The sounds of blasters and pulse cannons are heard in the background. "I'll get back to you. Continue with the plan...." His voice drops out.

I listen to open-channel static for a few seconds, then make a wide bank toward the Elders Administration Center, which is outside of Venubia City. The Center is the seat of Venubia's government. Built on a high plateau, overlooking the rugged Cheranlu mountains to the west, and with a clear view of the surrounding park and woods. It's well-positioned, making it easy to defend. Because of its strategic location, it's the most logical place for the Zenti to hold all the ranking Venubian officials.

My thoughts turn to Nicki. I close my eyes and concentrate on her for a fleeting moment, desperate to make contact. It was a futile attempt, hoping she and Verubeal were among the captives.

The auxiliary thrusters quit on me sooner than expected. The shuttle's still maintaining a good velocity until a hard jolt hits my rear. I command the rearview screen on and see two Zenti swarms closing in on me with their pulse cannons firing.

"Shit," I bark. "Where in the hell did they come from?"

It takes a second to gather my wits. I order the shuttle to flip belly up and make a high-arching dive into the city below. Buildings appear like flashpoints to be avoided. The shuttle responds well under the extreme banks and turns I'm negotiating. Once I get low enough and flying straight, I see the Zenti chasing from behind. That suggests either their ships or their skills are lacking.

I smile, yelling into my headset, "You rotten scumbags are mine!"

The shuttle is making a high-pitched, rumbling sound. What could that be? I wonder, then glance over the instruments. Everything appears normal.

The two Zenti swarm-fighters fly along both sides of me. Their domes aren't transparent, so I can't see what they look like. They're trying to force me to yield to them. I give them a middle-finger salute, then fly straight up and make a steep bank around a high building tower and dive straight down. I watch the Zenti over my viewscreen, split with each making a wide turn. They get behind me in a single file as I try to elude them by flying through several blocks of narrow streets.

My shuttle continues to make that rumbling sound. I turn on the outside cameras and do a quick survey of the shuttle's exterior. I discovered the source of the rumbling in the rear underbelly. The jolt I felt was a hit on the neutrino-array struts. It appears to be still attached, but loose enough to cause it to be bumping against the aft hull section. It also looks unstable and can tear away at any moment.

Another hit. Looking through the viewscreen, I spy one of the Zenti swarms firing at the loosened array from below. I dove, then hit the brakes. The shuttle almost slows to a stop in front of one of the Zenti. I can hear the scream of its engines as the swarm darts upward, trying to avoid the collision.

The second Zenti swarm is diving down right as the other is climbing. I didn't see the actual collision, but I heard a thunderous explosion, followed by a thick smoke trail visible in the distance. Sometimes you get lucky, and sometimes you outsmart your opponent. This time, I think it's a little of both.

CHAPTER 58

The bumping sound gives way to intense vibrations, followed by a shudder as the neutrino array tears away. A cacophony of lights and sounds erupts in the small cockpit. The shuttle becomes unstable. I'm flying less than fifty meters above the ground while trying to calculate how long my shuttle will last. As soon as my mind focuses on the problem, an urgent need to slow down flashes through my mind. A virtual steering controller appears when my interface becomes disabled. I'm surprised by how real the small controller feels. I pull back hard on the stiff rudder control to level out—the shuttle bucks and shakes, feeling as if it's about to rip itself apart.

Checking the area, I see no immediate clearings to make a safe landing. Now, flying a few meters above the streets, I see no signs of life in the area. The buildings are still smoldering from the initial Zenti attack—a disheartening scene, seeing the city in such a state of devastation.

The shuttle gives the last heave and falls hard on a narrow, empty street like a dead animal. The damaged hull slides for almost two hundred meters before skidding off an embankment. Now, I'm airborne again, but only for another ten meters. This remarkable machine ended magnificently by smashing into the only remaining wall of the burnt-out Strategic Planning Office.

What seems remarkable about the whole ordeal is how well the little ship holds together. A foam-like substance cushioned the crash so well that, beyond the experience of the hard impact, I'm uninjured.

The shuttle's dome release is jammed, forcing me to arch my back and push up hard on it. After a concerted effort and some inspired cursing, the dome pops open, slamming on the crumbled hull.

The air's thick with the rancid smells of smoke and decaying dead. The Zenti was thorough. Everywhere I look, I see the devastation. The conflicting emotions of anger and hope rise in me as I walk towards the center of the city. I searched for any landmark that could guide me back to the administration center.

As I wander through the streets in search of the main thoroughfare, I sense a close presence. I stop and look around. There isn't anyone there, and yet I can feel a distinct presence like an aura lurking out of sight.

"Mr. Mann," a wheezing voice calls from behind.

I turn to engage the voice. I pause in wonderment at seeing an awful-looking creature with large, bulbous eyes glaring at me.

"Who are you?" I ask.

"I am Zohleemay, your adversary," he hisses through his wide mouth.

Nothing could've prepared me for my first face-to-face encounter with a Zenti. Describing him as humanoid would redefine the word. He's symmetrical, bipedal, with two arms, and stands about one and a half meters high. Beyond these humanoid distinctions, I find nothing familiar about him.

The Bylars are intriguing, but they have a sense of elegance and grace. What's standing before me looks like a science project gone wrong. Zohleemay is gawking at me with his large, set-back eyes bulging under prominent brow ridges. His oval-shaped head is accentuated by pointed ears positioned high on the sides of his head. Its complexion is pale green, and despite his odd mix of reptilian and insect features, he has smooth flesh, rather than the expected scales or hair. At least, the visible parts. The Zenti has a broad, well-defined thorax, along with torso bulges and underbody armor, giving them a masculine appearance. But their arms and legs are spindly within the form-fitted jumpsuit under the Zenti's body armor. The jumpsuit looks Venubian in design.

They remind me of something I would enjoy squishing under the heel of my boot. Then I realize I'm allowing my human prejudice to overtake my common sense.

"So, Zohleemay, we meet at last." I force a smile while reminding myself that, despite his appearance, I'm talking with an evolved and intelligent being.

"You will come with me," he wheezes.

"Oh? Why's that?"

He slithers his narrow tongue at me. Leaning closer, eyeing me intently, he says, "If you want to live. You will come with me."

"If I refuse?"

Zohleemay snarls his thin lips. "You will be taken by force, or if you insist, killed."

"Given those limited options, I guess I'll follow you."

He twists his mouth into a grotesque smile and gestures with a tilt of his head for me to walk. Then he lifts his thin arm and waves a long, three-fingered hand. Several Zenti holding pulse rifles appear from the rubble, surrounding me.

Looking them over, I start to appreciate how resilient they look. I give Zohleemay a sardonic smile and capitulate to his men.

"I'm yours. For the time being, anyway," I say to Zohleemay.

He nods toward his troops and grunts something. They form around me with two in the front and three behind. We walk for some time before reaching a familiar sight. It takes a moment for me to recognize we're at the Venubian capital. The surrounding grounds are so scarred that their former beauty is barely recognizable. I'm pleased to see the Elder's Center standing almost intact, representing a small sense of hope for Venubia.

"Zohleemay," I call out, as two of his soldiers take a firm grip of my arms. "Why did you spare the capital?"

Zohleemay turns its thin mouth up and says, "Because I want to save the best for last."

I know exactly what that means. And now I also know a little about his plan.

"Poetic justice, eh?"

"What is poetic justice?" he says with a gravelly hiss.

"Never mind; it would be too hard to explain."

The Zenti guards relax their grips, allowing me to walk a little faster to catch up with him.

"We ought to take this opportunity to get to know one another a little better. Don't you agree?"

Zohleemay responds with his bulbous eyes narrowing, looking agitated. He turns to his guards and angrily grunts something. They rush to my sides and grab my arms, slowing my pace. Zohleemay glances back and makes another angry-sounding utterance before walking ahead of us.

Studying him from the rear, I realize how Venubian he looks. Setting aside his pointed ears, the back of his head and torso are Venubian in form. His head is smooth and oval-shaped like any Venubian's, but the rest of him is just plain weird.

As we walk, I study my two companions. The Zenti on my right is taller than the one on my left. There is a noticeable difference in their abdomens. My right-side companion is less fit-looking. He has a bulge about his midsection that resembles the Zenti equivalent of a slight beer belly.

Who do I hit first? I ponder. The one on the right, or the left? I peer back at the three Zenti behind me. They stare straight ahead, avoiding eye contact.

As we approach the Administration building's steps, I make my decision. I twist out of my two companions' grasps, then punch the left one right between his large eyes with the back of my fist while simultaneously kicking the other in his bulging midsection. Both hit the ground hard. The other three guards lunge at me. I duck under the lead one and flip him on his back. Then, I spin with my leg out, kicking the closest one in the chest while chopping the other in the throat with the side of my hand.

The Zenti I flipped struggles to his feet. I turn and kick him under his reptilian mouth, knocking him backward. A fine spray of blue blood comes out of his mouth as he falls to the ground. Zohleemay turns with a pulse laser in hand. His face distorts into a fierce sneer. Before he could make another move, I whirled a hundred eighty degrees, kicking the weapon out of his hand. Then I dive on him, knocking him down. We struggle for a moment. But I outmaneuver him, getting on top, I give him a smashing elbow to his face. A dark blue stream of blood runs from the side of his mouth and small nostrils. The Zenti guards remain immobile as I pick up one of their pulse rifles and nudge Zohleemay with my foot.

He rises, wiping blood from his mouth with the back of his long hand.

"What do you hope to accomplish by this foolish act?" he stammers through heavy wheezes and hisses. His bulging eyes look at me with a cold, calculating gaze. "If you wish to see your precious Nickada and her mother alive, I suggest you give up your desperate act and surrender... quietly."

"What do I have to lose by killing you right now? How do I know they're even alive?"

"They are in there." He points a crooked finger at the center. "All you have to do is follow me."

"Lead on, Zohleemay, and remember I have your weapon pointed at your head."

"You are a challenge, Phillip Mann. You are complicated, but in time, I will learn you as I have learned the Venubians." With a cynical smile, he adds, "You all will come to serve our needs."

"I've heard that line before, and it was as false then as it is now," I say, looking into Zohleemay's distorted face.

Zohleemay takes a step back and scoffs. He straightens his body armor and continues up the Administration building's steps.

The once bright, grand hall is gray and empty. Zohleemay's guards hurry in behind us. I turn, pointing the weapon at them, and say in a firm voice, "I'll shoot him first if you make another move."

They stop and look at Zohleemay as if for instructions. He hisses out a bunch of clicks and whistles at them. They post themselves by the entry.

"They will not follow," Zohleemay says. "What you seek is in the main council chamber."

"Lead on," I say, gesturing with my weapon for him to move.

We walk through a long corridor in silence until we come to the council chamber doors.

"How many men do you have in there?" I ask.

"Enough," he says.

"Okay, this is how we'll do this. You'll walk beside me as though you're leading me in. I'll have your weapon poking your side as a reminder. If they make one move toward me or any of the hostages, I'll kill you."

He gives me an odd look and opens the chamber doors. Nothing could've prepared me for the overwhelming mental shock of seeing hundreds of Venubians squeezed together on the chamber podium and lower floor. The Zenti have them so tightly packed that they can neither sit nor move. Looking at their pale faces, I see a frightened mass of captured souls, waiting for their imminent execution.

I glance up at the upper-chamber level. Twenty armed Zenti troops are looking down on their prisoners with wide, glaring eyes. One could sense they would relish firing on them.

My innards swell in pain at the sight of those Venubians waiting in terror. At first, they don't even notice me, then one frail-looking Venubian woman turns a weary gaze and begins to smile, pointing at me.

"Look," she says in a dry voice. "The Earthman, Phillip. Look. As Verubeal said, he has come to save us." Her voice becomes a little stronger as she continues staring at me with lines of tears rolling down her cheeks.

I don't have time to consider what she meant because all eyes become fixed on me, Venubian and Zenti alike.

Pressing the weapon against Zohleemay's head, I yell, "He'll be the first to die here!"

The Zenti guards point their weapons at the stirring Venubians. I pull Zohleemay back closer, so I can lock the doors. Then my eyes scan the room in search of Nicki and Verubeal. My heart races with the hope of seeing them within the masses. They aren't there. The sickening taste of utter disappointment, hurt, and anger me.

"Where are they?" I say, wrapping my arm around Zohleemay's neck in a tight chokehold.

I wanted to kill him at that moment, but suck down the urge, realizing how stupid that is, noticing half of Zohleemay's troops are pointing their weapons at me and the rest at the hostages.

"Did you expect to find them among the general populace?" He chokes and coughs as I loosen my grip. "You are in no position to bargain. Your best chance is to negotiate with me. If you kill me, my men will kill you, then all of them. Is that what you want?"

"Negotiate? What is there to negotiate?"

"You still control Biomei?"

"No one controls Biomei." Then something occurs to me. "Why do you want her?"

Zohleemay gives me a close look as if he's considering me before answering.

"Biomei is more than a ship. She is a new life-form. She can change everything," he declares, almost sounding like a plea.

"She can change everything, how?"

"There is no time. You must bring her to us."

"And why should I do that?"

"In exchange, you will save Nickada, Verubeal, and the rest of the Venubians." He almost sounds sincere. "You have no other choice. Call her to us."

"Does she know how important she is to you?"

"Why would she?"

"You had her long enough. Did you learn nothing during your capture of us?"

"Once the droid was destroyed, we were cut off from Biomei. What are you saying?"

"You took Nickada, then left Biomei and me. You could've taken us as well?"

"Nickada is Biomei's creator. We believe you both are inconsequential."

"I see. Then Nickada told you nothing."

"She believes we only want revenge when the truth is, we only want our freedom."

"Freedom? You've been free to steal, plunder, and kill everything you've encountered. What more do you want?"

"We want to be free to procreate. To perpetuate our species." He waves an angry hand toward the huddled masses. "But they deny us and condemn us to extinction."

"I don't understand."

"I have nothing more to say. Kill me or accept my terms."

I press the weapon even harder against his head and say, "What can Biomei do for you? Tell me." I can feel a surge of hate well up. Stay cool, I tell myself. *He wants you emotional. Don't let him get to you.* "Let's say, for the moment, I can give you Biomei. Then what will you do?"

Zohleemay remains silent for what seems like a long time. Finally, he says, "I will have Nickada and Verubeal brought to you."

"I've got a better proposal. Why not take me to them?"

Zohleemay looks up at his troops on the upper balcony and grunts something. One of them makes a short bow and leaves.

"Who's that?" I ask. "What did you tell him?"

"The commander of the guard and he will join us here."

"Join us? Why?"

"To kill you and set me free."

"Do you believe your trooper can break open the door and shoot me before I can blow your head off?"

"The commander does not need to break open the door. He has an access key."

"Oh. I guess that simplifies things. One question, though."

"Yes?"

"Why did you tell me this?"

"Because it will give you a few beats to agree to my terms before he opens the door and kills you."

The clacking of the Zenti's boots approaching in the hall worries me. He's moving at a rapid pace. His footsteps grow heavier as he gets closer to the chamber doors. The lock on the door clicks. I hand the weapon to Zohleemay as the wide-shouldered commander pushes the doors open. He enters, pointing his weapon at me.

"Thank you, Commander," Zohleemay says. "I can take it from here." He pushes me out the chamber doors. The Zenti commander snarls, eyeing me. He almost looks disappointed.

"You made a wise choice," Zohleemay says, holstering my weapon. "What you seek is this way." He points up the corridor.

"After you," I say.

"You first," Zohleemay insists, then makes a throaty hiss at the commander, who shoves me forward.

"Okay. You don't have to be so rough." Zohleemay grunts again to the commander, who shoves his weapon into my ribs. "Take it easy, I'm going."

The commander snarls again and shoves me harder. I walk along the dimly lit corridor, thinking of what to do next. I knew Zohleemay won't kill me because he still needs me. For what? I haven't a clue. After walking a little further, I started to wonder what his plan was. The only logical answer is to use me to get to Biomei. So, where the hell is she?

CHAPTER 59

We walk halfway up the corridor when Zohleemay grimaces, placing his hands over his ears, and falls to his knees. Other guards in the hallway also fall, holding their hands over their ears.

"No," Zohleemay screams, his face contorted in pain. He looks up at me with his bulbous eyes wide, then slumps unconscious to the floor.

Kneeling beside him, I feel his neck for a pulse. *Too bad. He's alive.* Seizing the opportunity, I rush up the corridor until I reach another set of double doors. I push on them. They're locked. I bang hard on them, shouting in Venubian, "Is anyone in there?"

Searching up and down the corridors, I see nothing that looks like a holding place for Nicki and Verubeal. I feel sick with despair and frustration until I spot a small staircase at the end of a short hall. *Of course, everything is always stored in the basement.*

A new sense of hope wells in me as I run down the narrow stairway, only to find an exit door. It's also locked. After a few feeble attempts at forcing the door open, I ran back up the stairs and grabbed Zohleemay's weapon. One shot blew the metal door open. I found myself in a small courtyard between the Elder's Center and the government building. Using all my training, discipline, and inner will, I cry out with my mind for anyone to answer. There is none, only an eerie silence that comes after such far-reaching devastation. *They must be close. Why can't I contact them?*

They must be using a cloaking field. Zohleemay knew of my abilities. He must have taken precautions against mental communications. Now, where would he set up a cloaking field?

The courtyard I walk into is small, surrounded by the towering walls of both buildings. *Where can they be? Was Zohleemay taking me to them? Or was he? I wonder, did I blow my chance of saving them?*

Sensing something close stops my second-guessing. Looking up, I see one of the most beautiful images in the universe. Biomei is hovering far above me. The pale light of her anti-gravity beam envelopes me. What a remarkable feeling to become weightless, floating up into the air. In a few seconds, I'm standing in the Main Engineering bay.

"Thank the Universe. You're alive," Biomei's warm voice greets me.

"Biomei, where have you been?"

"Looking for you."

"We were worried," Tezabouh said as he joined me in engineering. "Cuz and I traced your engine signature to the crash site. We became concerned when we lost your transponder signal."

"Transponder? What transponder?" I ask, narrowing my eyes.

"The one I installed into your forearm," Tezabouh says.

"My arm?" I study them for any puncture marks.

"You're left," he says, pointing at my forearm.

I scrutinize it and see nothing. "Where?"

"I injected it subcutaneously while you were sleeping. It leaves no mark on the skin."

"You could have asked first."

"Biomei insisted on not waking you."

"It's undetectable by usual scans. We thought either the Zenti found and disabled it, or there was a strong dampening field surrounding you. In either case, we knew we needed to find you quickly."

"Thanks." I let out a heavy sigh as my heart beat hard in my chest. "The high-frequency burst worked. How long do we have?"

"Less than two macrons," Biomei says.

"It must be a cloaking field they're using," I suggest, thinking aloud. "They never examined me or even had time to do so. There was no way I could communicate with Nicki, and she's down there. I know it." I look around and ask, "Where's Cuz?"

"He's monitoring the Zenti's communication channels," Biomei says.

"Cloaking field?" Tezabouh rubs his square chin. "It must be the quantum generator." He arches his bushy eyebrows and says, "It can disrupt the quantum signature of almost anything by creating a deflecting field around whatever is inside its perimeter. That's the most logical place they're hiding her and the weapon."

"Tezabouh, don't all dampening and cloaking fields have to have a distinct electromagnetic signature?"

"They do. But the quantum generator they're using has some unique properties and deflects anything hitting its fields..." He rubs his chin again, "However, it's being used as a morphing field, and we can detect that."

"Morphing field? Is it like Nickada's morphing ability?"

"A general morphing field is nothing more than a rearrangement of atoms into a specific structure. Simply, it's an elaborate disguise. Nickada uses a more complex biological morphing matrix. It requires a remarkable amount of concentration and physical energy. But morphing physical space and inorganic matter only requires a specific energy stream to maintain a projected field... Interesting." He smiles, looking as though he had a sudden revelation.

"What's interesting?" I ask.

"The Zenti must have acquired the expertise to use the quantum generator as a quantum projector. It's not a morphing field we should search for. We need to look for a fluctuating quantum signature."

"Where could they get that information?" I ask, then after a second's thought, cry, "Those fucking, bastards! They must have forced everything they could out of her. She's the only one who knows how to convert the generator." My heart aches, realizing what terrors Nicki must have endured." I say to Biomei, "And now they want you."

"I'm aware of Zohleemay's maniacal quest to possess me. And Phillip, something you should know. Zohleemay is male, and they aren't genderless as I first believed."

"I don't understand."

"All Zenti are male in gender, but also are sterile," Tezabouh explains. "For their reasons, the androids made them that way."

"You realize that's the underpinning reason for their rage."

"Yes. You are right in that regard," Tezabouh admits.

I tell Biomei, "Zohleemay mentioned you're the key to their freedom. He believes you're a new species of life that can solve all of their problems."

"The Zenti only want to extract my biogenic matrix and pervert it into a new prototype," Biomei snaps. "A ship like a super-entity, which is both immortal and invincible, making it a living weapon of mass destruction. They're vile, untrustworthy predators, incapable of living in peace. We must stop them."

"Biomei, you surprise me," I say. "I never would have believed you capable of such deep prejudice against any species."

"Sorry, Phillip. My emotions run awry concerning the Zenti. They've always been a plague against peaceful coexistence. You know their history now. They infect like a virulent plague and kill everything in their vicious wake. As much as the thought disturbs me, there is no other solution than their total eradication."

Tezabouh comes close to me and speaks in a soft voice, "You've only been exposed to the Zenti for a short time. Biomei has dealt with them for many planetary cycles. During that time, they have been destroying and pillaging every species they have encountered.

"It's been said that the final solution of failed politics is war, and total war means total death and destruction. In a real sense, the Venubians are facing their Armageddon if we are unsuccessful. Our failure will mean there's no future for Venubia and all the civilized worlds within the quadrant." He levels his cold eyes at me and, in a solemn tone, says, "If they learn how to control the corridors, that will also make Earth vulnerable, my friend."

"I understand the situation, Tezabouh. We will not fail," I say with great conviction. "Biomei, we must find Nicki now. Once Zohleemay regains consciousness, he'll kill her and all the captives."

"Biomei, bring up the west side of the Capitol building," I ask. After studying the holographic map for a moment, I point to the west wall. "Tezabouh, look. If the capital building was destroyed, why does this section appear intact?"

"Yes. That must be it. Biomei, magnify sectors 214 by 618 by 44," Tezabouh requests.

The picture enlarges, revealing a pixelated image.

"A solid structure shouldn't do that," I say. "Biomei, go to infrared imaging from the opposite angle."

The image shifts, revealing a false-colored image of a cylinder-shaped device lying against the west wall of the building.

I tell her, "Enhance and pan the area, please."

The image pans and then zooms in on two Zenti guards lying on the ground to the right of the cylinder.

"That looks like a good candidate for our generator," Tezabouh says. "Biomei, prepare a shuttle." He says to me, "Shall we take a closer look, Phillip?"

***

We land close to the Capitol building. Tezabouh hands me an odd-looking weapon.

"What is this?" I ask, studying its simple design. "It looks like a tube with a sight mounted on it."

"It's an antique of sorts, but effective," Tezabouh explains. "Please note there's a safety device on one side, and behind it, there's a selector switch. To disengage the safety, press the center of the selector switch. Slide the switch forward, and it's at full strength, backward stun. I suggest you keep it set at full strength. Now, look through the sight."

Everything appears to be right in front of me. The lens adjusts to my eyesight. As I move the weapon about, there's almost no lag in visual perception. I could shoot the eye out of a Zenti from a hundred meters.

Tezabouh continues with his instruction, "It's equipped with infrared and daylight photo optics with auto-range detection and is accurate up to 200 meters. It's capable of firing at a hundred twenty bursts per second with a recharge rate of fifty nanoseconds."

"Fifty nanoseconds, that's almost instantaneous," I say, surprised. "This's a nifty weapon. Why isn't it still in use?"

"Its dependence on direct sunlight made it a liability. Over time, a more versatile photon design replaced it. The improved version uses a biometric interface that requires a little time to adapt to its user. So, this version is more immediate."

"I see. Is there anything else I should know?"

"Be sure to make your shots count," he cautions.

We go to the east side of the Capitol building, where a group of Zenti troops greets us. Tezabouh and I fire at them. Our weapons make an odd puffing sound, like compressed air being released in small, rapid bursts. It fires with no recoil, and it's accurate. We mow the Zenti down before they can get a shot off. The burst makes a clean, lethal penetration right through the Zentis' armor and flesh like a laser through thin metal.

We scan the area for more troops. "It looks like we took them by surprise," I say, feeling a surge of energy running through me.

Tezabouh takes another close look around.

"They must have been a returning reconnaissance detail," he surmises. "We should go before they're missed."

As we approach the east gate, we hear voices and a mechanical whining. Looking around, I spy a group of Venubians walking towards us. They look dazed and walk with an unsteady gait. I start for them, but Tezabouh holds me back.

"Wait," he says, eyeing the weary group. "This doesn't look right."

"They need our help," I object, not understanding Tezabouh's sudden reluctance.

We hear weapons firing—the helpless Venubians scatter. Powerful blasts shred their bodies. Seeing them slaughtered like that enrages me. I break Tezabouh's grip and run towards them, screaming, "You, dirty, rotten scum."

Tezabouh calls for me to wait, but I'm too incensed and run with my weapon ready to shoot at the first Zenti I see. To my surprise, it's Zohleemay.

He makes a sinister curl of his mouth and, in a raspy hiss, says, "They are but the first. Do you need to see more?" His voice pierces through me like a dagger in the heart.

"Zohleemay, you coward—you, villainous bastard!" I scream at him. "How could these defenseless souls cause you any harm? You're insane with hate." I fire at him, but my blind passion leaves me short of the mark, allowing him to dive out of the way and escape.

"This's not the way," Tezabouh says, placing his hand on my shoulder, squeezing it hard to get my attention.

I knock his arm away, glaring. "We need to kill him. We must go after him now," I shout.

Tezabouh pulls me close and, with his mighty arm, holds me tight against his chest like a father restraining an irate child. In a calm voice, he says, "I know how you feel, but vengeance is not what's needed. Clear resolve and smart thinking are essential now. No matter how much your emotions tear at you, you must contain yourself. Remember Nickada's training. Rein in your emotions, or I will render you unconscious." His grip tightens across my chest to the point where I can hardly breathe. "Do you understand?" He squeezes tighter. My head starts to feel light.

I nod, with a pleading look for him to let go.

He releases his crushing grip. I take a few deep breaths, trying to clear my tight chest and quell my raging passions.

"You're right," I admit, through heavy breaths. "But they were helpless, and he killed them without hesitation. His belligerence is beyond reason."

Tezabouh narrows his gaze at me and says, "We must fight him on our terms, not his. We've got a more pressing issue."

"Yes?"

"Why is he conscious?"

"Did we miscalculate?"

"No. However, there could be another explanation."

"What's that?"

"Zohleemay may be the only conscious Zenti. Suggesting he may have enhancements of his own."

"Great. Just what we need, an enhanced and crazy Zenti."

"Let's determine if there are any others who are conscious before going after Zohleemay."

I glance at the dead bodies. They're all reduced to bloody, dismembered parts spewed across the scarred ground. The scene is a gruesome reminder of how expendable life becomes in war. It's called collateral damage. What a euphemistic term for carnage and waste of the innocent. Knowing there's nothing I could've done to save them isn't comforting. I now know revenge is an empty pursuit. But saving Venubia would at least give meaning to their death. There isn't much solace in that thought either.

A deep, mournful sigh is all I can muster. I tell Tezabouh, "Lead on."

He pauses to look at the dead on our way to the small courtyard. He looks back at me and says, "This is a perfect place for an ambush. Knowingly walking into an ambush has two predictable outcomes. The bushwhackers get you, or you get them."

"Bushwhackers? Now, that's a term I haven't heard in some time. Did you get hold of some Earth-style westerns?"

"Biomei's library is full of that genre. She has become partial to them," Tezabouh says, pulling on his earlobe.

"Interesting choice on her part," I add.

"Interesting, in what way?"

"They deal with some common human themes, good versus evil, and all the romantic heroism of the struggle. In a real sense, they're almost like morality plays. But that's a discussion for another time. Do you think it may be a good idea if we split up and take different approaches?"

"No. Zohleemay is alone."

"You sound sure. Why?"

"He would have delegated killing the prisoners if he had any troops available. No. I'm sure he's baiting us. I believe that's the appropriate term for this situation."

"I agree. So, why are we playing into his trap?"

"By playing along, he must reveal something of his plan. That'll give us options to act on."

"That's true, providing we don't get killed in the process."

"Death is irrelevant," he says flatly.

"Well, that's reassuring, "I say, eyeing Tezabouh with a sarcastic smile.

Tezabouh motions for me to move behind him as he maneuvers along the east wall that leads to the back of the courtyard. When he reaches the end of the wall, he peers around the side to see if Zohleemay's there.

He tells me, "Go to the opposite side, I'll cover you."

I nod and run with my weapon pointing toward the courtyard. It appears empty. I see Tezabouh move into the center. He makes a 360-degree sweep, taking in everything he can. He relaxes and says, "He's not here. Let's go inside."

We meander through the corridors of the administration center. Every few hundred meters, we come across unconscious Zenti troops. Tezabouh and I pick up their weapons and dispose of them in disposal units along the way. We know we're only making a modest dent in the Zenti's arms, but we hope it will buy us a little time. And time has become a precious commodity.

"Tezabouh," I say, "by my calculations, we've less than twenty microns, and we only covered a few floors."

"What do you suggest?"

"We need to split up. I don't believe Zohleemay is here, but there are more Venubian hostages. Zohleemay must have separated Nickada and Verubeal from the main group. You look for the prisoners here."

"And you?"

"I'm going to the Capitol building. The generated field was used as a decoy. He was counting on us discovering it. He used it to lure us here. Now that he has killed the first group of hostages, he wants us to find the second. My instincts are telling me Nickada and Verubeal are not in that group. We only delayed his plans with the audiovisual burst. We didn't foil them."

Tezabouh seems to ponder my plan for a moment. "I agree in principle, but believe we still should stay together. Nickada and Verubeal are our primary aim. Whatever is in here will keep."

We rush to the capital through some interconnecting subterranean tunnels that Tezabouh knows about. They lead us to a sublevel beneath the main foyer. We take a narrow staircase that leads to the back of the grand foyer. There are about a dozen unconscious Zenti troops scattered throughout the room, and more on the steps of the large horseshoe-shaped stairway.

"Twelve minutes," I whisper to Tezabouh.

Tezabouh gestures with his hand for me to take the right side of the stairs while he takes the left. We climb in haste. When we reach the top, Nicki's presence overwhelms me. It rushes through me like a powerful narcotic. I'm high on Nicki's energy.

Tezabouh notices my sudden grin and calls, "What is it?"

"Nicki... she's close, but I'm not getting any thought transmissions. She's either unconscious or unable to communicate."

"Try to focus on her," he suggests. "Conscious or not, she's still generating biorhythms."

I close my eyes and concentrate. I can sense her presence, but her mind and body feel somehow separated. The idea of her mind and body being apart frightens me at first. Then I remember something that Nicki once told me. She could shut down her streaming consciousness. It's a type of transcendental meditation used to relieve stress. I remember how hard she tried to get me to do it, but I can never shut down my mind as she does. An intense wave washes over me.

"It's her," I exclaim. "Nicki, she's three levels up." I become giddy with her discovery.

"Caution, my friend. Let's not go with emotion," Tezabouh says, stepping in front of me to look up the staircase.

"Why can't I communicate with her? Tezabouh, I fear there may be something wrong."

"What do you fear, Phillip?"

"The Zenti don't have telepathic abilities. So, she wouldn't be concerned with them intercepting our transmissions. The only other explanation is she can't communicate, and that's serious. I fear the Zenti did something to her."

Tezabouh frowns. "We must proceed carefully, or we may endanger her further."

"Let's go."

We climb the stairs, expecting Zohleemay's sudden appearance. The upper levels are veiled in gray, shadowy light. We can only see a few meters ahead. As we reach each landing, a tenseness has my heart beating faster and harder. Tezabouh and I peer down the corridors of each landing. We search within the shadows, only finding gray and empty hallways. When we approach the fourth floor, Nicki's presence becomes even stronger. I sense she's under duress. I transmitted to her that we were on our way. She doesn't reply. Is she being protective? I think, protective of what, though? Herself or us?

"Which way, Phillip?" Tezabouh asks.

I don't have a clue. Closing my eyes, I concentrate on Nicki, taking in the faint sensory output of her erratic biometric waves. All of a sudden, her body's production becomes so strong that I can almost breathe her in. I realize all I need to do is let my subconscious lead me to her. If I clear my mind, I can let her body signature guide me. Taking a deep breath, I let go of all my conscious energy and allow my subconscious mind to wander.

I only go a short distance before something miraculous happens. Nicki's delightful pheromones fill my olfactory senses. Like a dutiful hound dog, I follow my master's scent.

"This way," I say, tapping Tezabouh on the shoulder while sniffing.

Tezabouh looks at me curiously and asks, "Are you all right?"

"Yes, but don't ask. I'll explain later." I sniff deeply, and Nicki's scent becomes stronger, along with sensing her biorhythms. "Hurry," I call to him.

As we go cautiously down the shadowy corridor, a thin line of light glows on the floor. We walk toward it, and Zohleemay bursts into the corridor, holding a pulse-phaser to Verubeal's head. The light from inside the room glows like a spotlight on Zohleemay's contemptuous sneer and Verubeal's pale face.

"Come, join us," he wheezes, his bulging eyes leering at me.

Tezabouh and I walk up to him. I survey the room. A hibernation chamber from the ship is in a corner. I start toward it, but Zohleemay pushes Verubeal in front of me with his weapon still pointing at her.

"No, Phillip Mann from Earth. We haven't finished our negotiations."

Looking at Verubeal, I sense she is undaunted by her capture. Her majestic spirit is most evident in her eyes. She smiles warmly at me, showing no fear. Her bravery strengthens my resolve in not giving in to Zohleemay.

"What are we negotiating?" I ask, staring intently into his face, trying to read his distorted features. He shows me little beyond his contempt for us.

"Biomei, for her and Nickada," he hisses.

"Let Verubeal go, and let me see Nickada, then we can talk.

"You'll see her soon enough. The question is whether she will be dead or alive."

I make a move toward the hibernation chamber, but Zohleemay thrusts his weapon out, making me back up.

"Let Verubeal go. Consider it a goodwill gesture."

Verubeal lets out a little gasp as Zohleemay wraps his arm around her delicate neck, tightening it. His eyes dart between Tezabouh and me, looking uncertain. He blinks and then, as if he reconsidered his actions, he slowly relaxes his hold on her. "Here's your goodwill gesture," he says, shoving Verubeal to me. I pull her close, and we hug. Tezabouh takes her to the side.

What at first I perceived as anger became more apparent as frustration in Zohleemay. He also appears frightened and irritated. Of what, I'm uncertain.

Tezabouh takes Verubeal down the corridor. Zohleemay stands with his weapon in hand, his eyes narrowing into a penetrating stare. His body slumps as he stares at me with a weary, almost despondent gaze.

I study him for a moment, thinking of what to say. "You look tired and defeated, Zohleemay." I try a little armchair diplomacy. "Why not surrender and disarm your troops, and we'll work together in finding an equitable solution to our differences?"

He rolls a side of his reptilian mouth up into an ugly sneer. "I would rather die than submit to a Venubian sense of justice. They want to rid themselves of their mistake. The last thing they want is our survival. Venubians are not the magnanimous, enlightened race they pretend to be. They are cold, calculating, and selfish people who want a slave race to attend to their needs. They're cowards and lust for power, but don't have what it takes to do it themselves, so they created us to fight their wars to maintain their leisurely lives. Art, science, culture. Those are their professed mantras. Enslavement, cruelty, and guilt are their reality! They don't deserve to live!"

"You're a liar," Verubeal shouts, bustling back into the room. "We gave you a chance for life and purpose, freedom to do as you will, and you returned all we've done with resentment and ruthlessness."

"You gave us nothing but servitude!" Zohleemay hisses, shaking his weapon at Verubeal.

I move between them, holding my hand up to Zohleemay.

"We need to calm down and work with our intellects rather than our emotions," I say, feeling a little hypocritical, then turn to Verubeal, giving her a stern look.

"Why do you perceive yourselves as slaves?" Verubeal asks after regaining her composure.

Zohleemay glares at her. He takes in a deep breath and exhales in a disdainful growl, "You dare to ask such a question?"

"We did everything we could after the first war to make it possible for you to live free in your world," Verubeal states, in a calm but firm manner. "You chose not to accept it. You've rejected all our efforts to help you create a livable coexistence."

"Yes," he grunts, with a cruel smile. "You gave us a world to tame. And only gave us enough supplies to survive for a while. But the one thing you never gave us was a chance to perpetuate ourselves. You knew we only had a few generations before we would die off." His bulbous eyes narrow into a glaring stare at me, and he says, "They did nothing to help us!"

"Die-off?" Verubeal's mouth opens, and her face blanches, looking shocked and confused. "Die-off, how?" she repeats.

"Do not play ignorant with me," he croaks, spraying spittle from his mouth. "Are you denying any knowledge that we are without viable reproduction?" He walks up close to Verubeal and squints. "The androids created a single-gender, sterile race. We had no means to procreate. Our cloning has gone beyond the limits of viable cellular replication." He turns his angry eyes toward me. He points at Verubeal while shouting at me, "They knew we would die out. Without genetic diversification, there are no mutations, and eventually, our mitochondria would break down, making our cells inert. We were designed to die!" Then, in a low and mournful tone, he says, "We were just an experiment for their curiosity."

"I didn't know. I didn't know," Verubeal cries. "We would've never done such a thing." She lets out a heavy sigh. She bows her head in thought and speaks in a reflective voice, "But the Androids were capable of such a dispassionate act. They decided your fate based on their own rules of logic." Verubeal's eyes welled with the revelation. "They worked in their secretive ways without regard to our needs or desires." She looks at Tezabouh. "For all their advanced wisdom and regard for life, they are still machines, incapable of understanding our need for self-determination."

Zohleemay appears unmoved. "They were monsters of your creation, and you must pay the price for their treachery."

"They weren't monsters," Tezabouh defends. "But, yes, they didn't understand the consequences of their actions until it was too late." He turns a wide-eyed gaze at Zohleemay and smiles ruefully. "You were made as best they knew how. Look how long you've survived. We now have the technology to fix our mistakes. Give us a chance to correct a terrible mistake. We can give you what you want."

Zohleemay sneers. "Do you take me for a fool?" his voice vibrates and whistles. "You betrayed us the last time. I won't be maneuvered into another one of your clever Android traps."

"So be it. Die," Tezabouh says flatly.

I listen to them in despair. They're all victims of the Androids. Xandroff's androids said, 'War was not an option to Tezabar and allowed the Zenti to slaughter them. I wondered if they did it out of a sense of guilt? But that would be illogical. So, what did they mean?

CHAPTER 60

A thunderous explosion sends a shock wave, knocking us hard to the floor. I'm the first one up. Zohleemay struggles to regain himself. I pick up his weapon, place my foot on his back, and tell him to stay put. He appears in no condition to object. He lets out a quiet moan as I lift my foot off his back.

Tezabouh attends to Verubeal. I rush to the hibernation chamber. My heart races, seeing Nicki's lovely face in repose under the transparent dome. I study her for a moment, trying to revive her with my mind, but she lies in a deep sleep, unaware of my wanting presence. With an anxious finger, I touch the dome's release button. It opens too slowly in my eagerness to hold her.

I gaze at her still form, longing to feel her in my arms. She appears thin and frail. Her chest moves up and down as she struggles to take her first breaths of the ambient air. Her large eyes roll under her closed lids, showing she is coming back from her deep sleep. My mind whirls with nagging *what-ifs*. What if her memory is damaged, and she doesn't remember me? What if she's not my Nicki, but something the Zenti created to kill me? What if I'm becoming ridiculously paranoid?

I lean in and kiss her. She opens her eyes with a gasp.

"Nicki, you're back." She gives me an absent stare. She looks at me as if she doesn't know who I am. My heart sinks. "Nicki, it's Phillip."

She mouths my name, showing no sign of recognition, then tries to sit up. I help her. She starts to shiver. After a few minutes, her symptoms became familiar. Pale, clammy skin with chills and disorientation. All the familiar signs of hibernation shock.

"Tezabouh, I need a blanket or jacket." He hands me a Zenti trooper's jacket. The irony not being lost on me, I drape it over her trembling body. Her skin is the color of chalk, and her dull eyes are staring unblinkingly as if she isn't aware of her surroundings.

Knowing what she's going through makes the matter worse because I feel so helpless. All I can do is keep her warm and calm until her body recovers.

Tezabouh and Verubeal join me. Verubeal says, "She needs electrolytes and complex proteins, or she'll go into systemic shock."

"What caused that explosion? It felt stronger than the others," I ask Tezabouh.

"Neither the Zenti nor the Kaydens possess such a powerful weapon," Verubeal interjects.

"What are you suggesting?"

Tezabouh gives us a thoughtful look and says, "There's only one logical suspect."

"Who?" Verubeal and I say together.

"The androids. They're the only ones who have that technology. The discharge pattern is consistent with a quantum grenade. Albeit a small one."

Verubeal's eyes widen in surprise. "I thought you said Xandroff refused to fight?"

"His exact words were, 'War is not an option. We inferred it meant nonaggression. Xandroff was being literal in his intent. He's executing my original plan against my wishes. He decided to stop the war before it could escalate further by eliminating the Zenti."

"We must go as soon as possible," Verubeal says.

Looking at Nicki's condition, I say, "She needs time to recover. Moving her could be detrimental."

"Not if we can get basic nutrients in her," Verubeal explains. "Her metabolism is resilient." She smiles at her daughter and runs her hand down her cheek. "She'll recover soon enough."

"I'll be right back," Tezabouh says.

"Remove the attachments, Phillip, and get her out of that chamber," Verubeal says.

I do it and cradle Nicki in my arms. She clutches her arms around my neck like a frightened child clinging to a parent. I hold her cold, quivering body close, both to give her the benefit of my body's warmth and satisfy my longing to embrace her. As I lie her on the bench, she looks up and smiles, running her hand down my cheek. I kiss her forehead.

Verubeal stands next to me and grasps my hand. "She knows you're here," she tells me.

"Thank you. I feel so helpless not knowing what I can do for her."

"The Zenti must've kept her in a hibernated state to hide her from us. They're paranoid by nature and see everything as a conspiracy against them."

"Why is Biomei so important to them? Zohleemay said she's the key to their survival."

"I'm uncertain, but I know Nickada used some biogenetic engineering techniques the Androids created for the Zenti. Beyond that, I don't know why she's important. I believe it may be more complicated than her technology, though."

"Biomei is still a ship to them?"

"They know Biomei is much more. She's a true sentient life-form."

Verubeal's use of the word sentient strikes a chord in me. "So, what you're saying is Biomei is another type of life, like Tezabouh and the Zenti?"

"She's an independent, living entity, but different from Tezabouh and much different from the Zenti, and us."

"No. No. Please help me. Help me," Nicki screams, her body convulsing.

I gather her into my arms and hug her tightly. "It's over, Nicki. You're safe now. You're with Verubeal and me. Everything is all right."

She mumbles incoherently. Then her eyes rolled back into her head and shut. She becomes still. A surge of panic runs through me.

I look at Verubeal in alarm and say, "She's not breathing, and her body has gone limp."

Verubeal forces one of her eyelids open and calmly says, "She's going into shock, where's Tezabouh? We're running out of time."

"Here, attend to her. I'll see what's holding him up."

As I turn toward the door, I notice Zohleemay's gone. I wonder if he is occupying Tezabouh.

Another tremendous jolt strikes the administration building. This time, the walls crumble around me. I glance into the room where Nicki is. It appears intact. Verubeal nods at me, indicating they are all right.

After the dust and debris had cleared, I could see a thin stream of light giving the corridor enough illumination to find my way. The ceiling and stairwells remain intact, but everything surrounding them seems to be in pieces.

When I reach the staircase, I hear footsteps above. It sounds like only one person. Not knowing who it is, I proceed with my weapon ready. On the next level, I take in my surroundings. No one is there. Tezabouh greets me as I come down from the level above. He's holding bottled water and packages of standard field rations.

He tosses one of the packages to me. "Zohleemay is loose," he warns.

"Yes. I know." I toss the package back, letting out a heavy sigh. "Nicki is in shock, and I forgot about him. He's my problem now. You need to get to Nicki and Verubeal. Please take good care of them."

"No need to worry," he says. "Get Zohleemay." He grabs my arm and adds, "Don't hesitate. If you get the shot, kill him." He quickly descends the stairs.

I call down to Tezabouh, "Where did you see him?"

"He's heading south."

I go to the nearest stairwell and rush down. After climbing over and around collapsed walls and ceilings, I make my way outside the capital building. I walk close to the side of the building. The air is heavy with acrid smoke and fine debris, causing my nose and throat to burn. The burning stops almost as quickly as it starts. I follow along an old stone path that leads me to the other side of the Administration Center.

The sky's a glowing red with the coming of the second dawn. It feels like being inside a schizophrenic dreamscapes—vivid colors dancing in a desolate landscape of mangled corpses and demolished buildings. The price of war is everywhere and profoundly influencing me. Bleakness seems to be the only real thing I see, like a living nightmare imprinting its images on my psyche. I have to give myself a moment to refocus and rid my mind of the disturbing reality.

Coming from the north, I hear heavy equipment moving along with the rhythm of marching footsteps—all the distinct sounds of the advancing android warriors. Not sure if I'd be perceived as friend or foe, I avoid them.

I ponder where Zohleemay would go. Not wanting him to find me, I attempt to open myself to something Nicki had tried to teach me with little success. She wanted to have me connect with the universe's conscious energy. It requires something I haven't learned yet: the ability to focus. The process is called hazsolm or *quiet mind*. An ancient form of Venubian mysticism I never took seriously. I close my eyes and concentrate on Zohleemay. Nicki's voice is telling me I must allow my spiritual energy to reach out and find Zohleemay. I wonder if it could draw him to me. I hear Nicki's voice again. She's telling me to trust my instincts. Loving her as much as I do, I trust her spiritual belief more than anything else at this moment.

She is alive in my head. Her thought transmissions are rambling at me.

"Phillip, Zohleemay is close to you. Stay where you are. He's looking for you!"

"Nicki, I'm so glad you're back! How do you know he's close?"

"Zohleemay forced me to mind-merge with him, and I know his mental signature. He'll not stop until he gets what he wants. He wants you as a hostage. Allow him to take you. It's the only way we can defeat him and his followers."

"Where is he?"

"He's a few hundred meters north of your position."

"And how do you know that so precisely?"

"His signature is strong."

"I see. I'll do as you suggest, but I think it's best we cease further communications."

"Do you think that's wise?"

"Trust me."

"As you wish."

That wasn't Nicki, but Zohleemay. Zenti isn't supposed to have telepathic abilities, but Zohleemay has demonstrated he has a working knowledge and is using it well. He didn't know Venubians transmit their emotions within their transmissions. A telepathic kiss is as real as a lip-to-lip one and more sensual because it comes from a different energy source.

His transmission feels cold and devoid of emotion. Zohleemay somehow extracted some of Nicki's energy patterns and is trying to use them against me. Maybe I should have played along. It may have been the quickest way to find him. The risk is the same regardless of who saw whom first. We are destined to conflict at some point, and the sooner it happens, the better.

CHAPTER 61

As soon as I walk into a small courtyard where the gazebo is, I see Zohleemay. He turns and looks at me with eyes expressing all his hate, disillusionment, and desperation. Blood runs down one side of his distorted face and out of his nose. He glares at my weapon, poised by my side, waiting for my move. He's like a wounded animal ready to attack, but too weak to put up a winnable fight.

Pointing a crooked finger at me, he wheezes something in Zenti too incoherent for my internal translator, but angry enough in tone to understand.

"Look at you," I shout with deliberate smugness. "What have you gained for your people? You're defeated and still unwilling to concede. You can have peace and freedom if you only work with the people you want to destroy."

"Is that what you believe?" he spits out.

"I see no other logical explanation."

"You arrogant Earthman. You dare judge us when your world is in a state of turmoil."

"Yes, I can judge as a citizen of a corrupt world and know that absolute power corrupts absolutely. That's a universal truism. No one power or belief may dictate what is true and what is just. The majority must always consider the minority as an equal voice of reason. Every living being has the right to live the way it wants if it doesn't interfere with the rights of others. That's the only true universal law."

"You are as naïve and ignorant as the Venubians you defend. The androids reign and have absolute power over everything. They are the ones responsible for all the death and destruction. Your precious Venubians created them and protected them over the past two millennia. Now they want to use them to erase the source of their greatest mistake. A convenient war, wouldn't you agree?"

I shake my head at his belligerence and say, "Convenient for whom? Certainly, not the Venubians and all the other worlds you've slaughtered. I've no reason to believe you. You've demonstrated a willingness to plunder and destroy anything of value for your purpose. I've seen no remorse or mercy for the unfortunate souls you encounter. How can I believe you to be victims of anything other than your psychotic reality?"

Zohleemay narrows his cold eyes. Studying him, I wonder if he's contemplating his next words or move? I can kill him where he stands, but instead decide to be proactive and reach my hand out to him, gripping my weapon with the other.

He considers my hand with an eyeful glance, then asks, "What do you want?"

"I can put an end to the hostilities with a single shot to your head." That gets his full attention. "But more than anything, I want peace for both the Venubians and the Zenti. The only logical end to the course we're on is death and destruction for everyone. War's only purpose is war itself." I relax my grip on my weapon, hoping to show my sincerity. "It represents the ultimate failure of communications and an inability to resolve differences between ideologies. I offer my hand as the first gesture of peace. Let us end the hostility now. I beg you. End it now."

Zohleemay appears more confused than moved by my plea. He almost looks disappointed by my sudden pacifism.

"There can be no peace. Peace is defeat and servitude for the Zenti."

He lunges for my weapon. I step aside, and he falls to the ground. Before I can draw my pulse laser, he springs to his feet, then throws himself at me. Like a tight bundle of fused hostility, we fall hard to the ground. His bony hands are desperately grasping for my weapon as we struggle, rolling on the cold, damp ground. He wheezes his rank breath in my face. Snarls and hisses like a wounded animal fighting for its life. I wrench his hands off me and pin him tightly to the ground. He's no match for my size and strength. I grasp his thin neck and squeeze until I notice his greenish skin brighten and his breath becomes labored. Part of me wants to end him, but I still hold a glimmer of hope for a peaceful resolution.

"Will you yield?" I shout into his distorted face. He blinks his eyes in capitulation. I relax my grip, pressing my laser against the side of his head, and tell him, "Get up."

He flounders on the ground as I stand over him. I hold my hand out to help him. Zohleemay grabs my arm and jerks me forward, giving my midsection a jarring blow with his foot. I lose my balance for only an instant, but it's enough for him to get away.

"Fuck!" I shout in frustration at my naivety, then chase after him.

I see him go into the south side of the admin building. I follow him through a dark corridor that takes me to the other side of the building. I see the north stairwell exit door closing. A misdirection, I think.

The soft, evening air greets me as I rush out the door. A sweet scent drifts in on a light breeze and is quickly overwhelmed by the putrid stench of decay. A thunderous shockwave from above gets me looking eastward. The dim sky fills with flashes from the distant bursts of lasers and plasma cannons firing. The aircraft is out of sight, but it sounds like Zenti and Kayden fighters are fully engaged in battle.

I search for Zohleemay, but he's nowhere in sight. He couldn't have gone far. A wall of bright, white lights approaches from the west. The familiar hollow footsteps of marching androids accompanied the lights. The lights and sounds intensify at an alarming pace.

Hissing and groaning noises mingle with the heavy footsteps. At first, I can only make out what appears to be a large, shadowy mass approaching in opposition to the barely visible androids. It looks like a great, murky, moving monster forming within the blackness of the night.

A sudden laser blast illuminates the area, revealing a great gathering of charging Zenti troops. The light dissipates, but the multitude of Zentis moving in the dim light is all around me. Zentis' shadowy forms are flanked by their armored vehicles. I can do nothing but watch and listen in bewilderment.

From the corner of my eye, I see Tezabouh approaching. He stands next to me and whispers, "They're executing my plan after all."

"Your plan, what do you mean?"

"I knew the Zenti wouldn't negotiate. Their single-mindedness made them determined to rid themselves of both the Venubians and the androids. We needed a common cause to unite both armies, so they would all be gathered in one place at the same time. What the Zenti didn't foresee is the possibility of additional forces." He grins at me. "And you, my friend."

"I understand how the Kayden could be perceived as a force, but what do I have to do with any of this?"

"Your love of Nickada and her deep devotion to you made this possible. Determined love and devotion are formidable forces and beyond the Zenti's comprehension."

"So, I was the perfect bait for the trap," I say and grimace, feeling used by everyone.

Tezabouh arches an eyebrow and says, "In a manner of speaking, that's accurate."

"We must get Nickada and Verubeal out of here. Can Nickada travel?"

"It'll be best to stay put for now. If all goes as planned, this will be over soon."

We stand like anxious bystanders, observing the escalation of opposing forces. We're surrounded by Zenti, androids, and their machines, now immersed in the fury of battle. The sky becomes a raging inferno as Zenti ships burst into flames and crash in the near distance. As Tezabouh predicted, the battle doesn't last long. Within minutes, there's an eerie silence that falls upon us like a death shroud.

The second light rises in the north. A bright blue sky becomes clear in the early morning light. It also lights up the desolation of the recent battle. Not a single living Zenti could be seen among the rubble and masses of mangled bodies. Androids are lying among the fallen—hundreds of them, with their shiny, clad bodies broken open by sonic cannons.

As the sun rises, piles of dismembered limbs glisten under the bright sunlight. Body parts from both humanoids and machines are scattered in little mounds, looking like pieces of a perfect tapestry of war.

"So, this was your plan?" I say, recoiling at the devastation. "Leave no Zenti alive?"

I feel like a hypocrite because just a short while ago, I wanted them all dead. Reality has a way of quickly adjusting one's perspective.

"Not quite, Phillip. The plan was to destroy their ability to wage war. As we speak, the Kayden are bombing their homeworld and all their colonies. I knew once the Zenti had believed they could occupy Venubia, their forces would be thinned out on all their other occupied worlds. It was an all-or-nothing calculation, and you made it possible."

"Me? How?"

"Biomei downloaded a well-constructed plan for the Zenti to find within your implanted compiler. Nicki did not know of this. The memory loss you experienced after the Zenti encounter was deliberate. I arranged for the Zenti to find Biomei and take Nickada. This made it possible for you to go to Venubia and execute the implanted plan. The nanovirus was an unfortunate delay. As was Uzzendi's abduction."

"Are you telling me everything I've done was by prior design?"

"Well, not quite. There is no way of predicting how unpredictable you are. After all, I did not know about human behavior. I was relying on Nickada's empathic transmissions as guidance. Nickada was also unaware of my plan."

"So, how were you able to be so in tune with Nickada without her knowledge?"

"I know everything about her."

"How's that possible?"

"Because as I told you before, she's my daughter."

"That's not possible," I mumble, dumbfounded. "You're an android."

He lets out a heavy sigh. "I have tried to tell you. I'm not an android. I'm a biologically engineered life-form."

"She has none of your features—or personality." It's inconceivable that he could be her father. I stare heavily at Tezabouh and ask, "Does she know?"

He lowers his gaze. "No. And she's never to know. I share this with you because you need to understand how unique she is. You must promise you'll never speak of this with her."

"Don't you think she deserves to know the truth?"

"I created Verubeal to be my wife, and Nickada was conceived through natural biological means. It was an unprecedented event. But what is truly remarkable is that two biogenetically engineered life-forms could conceive a baby through natural intercourse. Nickada is the only one of her kind. Because of the growing social tensions that developed between the self-aware Androids and the populace, Verubeal and I protected Nickada from the truth. We implanted false memory streams in her. She believes her father was a diplomat who was killed during a peace negotiation with the Zenti during the first conflict. She was young at the time and only had limited contact with me."

"So, what happens now?" I ask with my eyes still fixed on him.

"We pick up the pieces and begin anew."

How can I go on with Nicki, knowing such a secret? Looking at all the devastation around me, I mumble, "Oh, brave new world that hath such crazy humanoids in it."

"What was that?" Tezabouh says.

"Nothing. Just me thinking aloud."

As Tezabouh and I survey the surrounding ruins, a group of Venubians staggers out from the Elder's Administration Center. At first, they seem dazed and disoriented. Once they see the multitude of fallen bodies all around, one by one, they go among the bloodied masses in search of survivors. A disjointed effort to give what little aid they can provide. It's a scene of humanoids at their humblest. Victims in search of other victims to render assistance, regardless of species. It reflects what I've come to believe made Venubians so special: their compassion toward all life.

Tezabouh looks on, trying to remain dispassionate. Still, his eyes betray a sense of pride as he watches the Venubians discovering with excited joy a few living souls to render some meager assistance.

The sky fills with many ships, both protective and paramedic. A scene full of carnage changes to a venue of desperate salvage, like a cleansing wave of healing upon a war-torn land of animosity.

"So much hate and waste," I say to Tezabouh. "Now I hope the Venubians can finally forge a lasting peace and rebuild a true Utopia."

Tezabouh nods in agreement. He turns around with his weapon poised, then relaxes seeing Nickada's glowing face. My heart races, seeing her up on her feet, looking at me with a radiant smile. We embrace tightly as if trying to absorb each other's essence. Feeling her presence energizes me. The smell of her hair lifts the heavy despair I'd been feeling and fills my heart with joy.

She wraps her arms around my neck and pulls me in close for a passionate kiss. Everything that has happened, all the waste and pain, dissolves into a distant memory. I can't imagine my life without her.

While gazing into her eyes, I glimpse a figure running towards us. The glare of the sun hides its identity. Distracted by holding Nicki for the first time after such a long and stressful ordeal, I pay no attention to it. We continue to kiss and embrace with intense passion. At that moment, nothing could break the spell we were under.

As I open my eyes to take another look at Nicki's beautiful face, he's upon us. Zohleemay stands a few meters from us, leering with a grotesque sneer. He holds out a percussion grenade in his clenched fist. His eyes are full of burning hate. Zohleemay released the detonator pin from the grenade and let it fall to his side. There's no time to react. Tezabouh sees it, but Nicki pushes him aside.

"No!" I scream my heart out as the grenade explodes. It's force tears into me with a moment of searing pain, then unconsciousness.

CHAPTER 62

I wake with a deep sense of remorse and loss from a dark, dreamless void. I sit up on the edge of a large, round bed, trying to gather my thoughts. My body has a familiar feel. It's the same as the first time I regained consciousness on Biomei. The revelation strikes a chord within my numb senses. *They rebuilt me again. Once again, I'm a reborn, enhanced humanoid...*

I'm unable to summon an emotional response. It seems my emotions are as numb as my senses, leaving me with nothing but questions and emptiness.

The room's familiar, but it isn't my own. I walk around. My arms and legs feel heavy, and my movements seem perfunctory. Staring into a full-length dressing mirror across the room, I take inventory of myself. Everything appears to be the same. However, I sense a strange difference.

I walked closer to the mirror and stared into my reflection. Studying my impassive face, I notice something familiar in my eyes. They remind me of Cuz's when he first gazed at me. They are as absent from feeling and expression as he was. *Where are my emotions? Where am I? What has happened?*

Then a sudden and most profound thought shocks me. Who am I? I knew some things about myself, but a lot is missing. Not like amnesia; more like selective memory loss. The harder I try to recall any memories, the more frustrated I become. After pondering my condition, it's obvious. The techs performed a deliberate memory block, and it was done by a skillful hand.

A steady, warm breeze is blowing in from the open doors leading out to a terrace. My attention is drawn to a lovely Venubian female who comes in from the terrace. She's dressed in a light, flowing gown that clings to her long, graceful body. Her face looks familiar.

She smiles and says, "Good, you're awake."

She seems to know me and is glad to see me, but her long face betrays her smile, telling me something is wrong.

"How long?" I ask as if she knows what I'm asking.

"Two cycles," she says, then noticing my confused look, adds, "Three earth days."

"That seems like a long time to be asleep."

She nods, letting out a long, sorrowful sigh.

"Come over here and sit down." She pats the bed. "There's much I must tell you." She looks away as if to avoid my eyes.

I sit next to her and turn her face to me. A line of tears runs down her cheeks.

"What is it?" I say. This woman knows me, so why don't I know her? Looking closer at her soft features and large, engaging eyes, I ask, "Please, I want to help you, but you must first tell me who I am and what's happened?"

She hands me a familiar-looking cube and states, barely above a whisper, "Everything you need to know is in here. Lie down and close your eyes. Once this device is activated, all your missing memories will be downloaded. Phillip, my heart aches for you. I want you to know I'll always be here for you. Try to understand, desperate times often require great sacrifices."

I have no idea what she's talking about. We stare at each other for an awkward moment. Her large, gray eyes are rimmed in red and full of woe.

I recline on the bed. She affixes the cube to my left temple.

"Call me when you finish." She kisses my cheek before leaving.

***

It felt like being descended into hell. The killing, the destruction, all the waste, and all for what? Nothing was won, and so much was lost. I relive the entire horror with dispassionate objectivity until it's over.

I sit up on the edge of the bed and wait for Verubeal to enter the room. *"Now that my memories are restored, I can redirect myself."* I transmit. *"My mission is clear. Zohleemay must be found."*

"Is that all you can think of?" Verubeal frowns. "Revenge is a hollow pursuit. It resolves nothing and leaves the vindicated emptier than fulfilled."

"You misjudge me. It's not revenge I seek, but justice. Zohleemay must be brought to justice. How else can Venubia ever find peace? If he is free, there can be no real peace. You of all people should appreciate that."

"All I know is the war with the Zenti has taken everything I ever loved and held dear. You are all I have now. I don't want to lose you on an empty quest for justice."

"You have already lost Phillip Mann. He no longer exists. Everything he was is gone. What you see before you is a mechanically engineered replica of Phillip with his soul ripped out."

"Phillip Mann is still who you are. All his memories, feelings, and qualities I admire are inside you. It defines who you are. You may not feel it now, but in time, your true nature will surface."

"Until that time, I'll require a new identity."

She places her hand on my shoulder and, in a warm voice, says, "Venubia needs heroes now." She takes my hand and leads me to the terrace. I hesitate at hearing the murmur of a large gathering. When I step out onto the terrace, the scene below is eerily familiar, but I can't remember why. As far as the eye could see, a great multitude of Venubians, Kaydens, and Androids are looking up at me. They start chanting, "Uzil, Uzil, Uzil."

Their voices sing out like a reverent hymn that echoes into the far distance. They continue to call out that word over and over as I stand numb, ignorant of its meaning.

"What are they saying?" I shout to Verubeal.

"Uzil, it's an ancient term that means hero or deliverer."

"No. I'm no hero and not a messiah," I shout at Verubeal, then turn, shouting to the crowd, "I've done nothing to deserve this. I'm not your hero or deliverer. I'm an ordinary Earthman."

The crowd cheers and hoots louder, drowning me out. I can't think of anything meaningful to say over the raucous gathering. I stand frozen in bewilderment, forcing a confident smile while waving in acknowledgment. After a few minutes of trying to look humble, I go back into the room.

Verubeal narrows her large eyes into a puzzled look. "I don't understand why you refuse to accept your great accomplishment," she chides. "You're the deliverer of Tezabouh's Plan." She elevated Tezabouh's Plan as if it were something sacred. "You made our victory possible. Why can't you accept what you have done?"

"Because Tezabouh used me and installed his plan without my knowledge. I did nothing other than look for Nickada. There is no bravery or selflessness in anything I've done. My love of Nickada and nothing else is what drove me." *Every time I say her name, my heart aches.*

Verubeal gives me a proud smile with tears in her eyes. "See, that's Phillip talking now. You're so modest and good. I thank the universal forces that caused Nickada to bring you to our world. Even though you refuse to acknowledge your wondrous powers, I will always see you as the hero of the final Zenti conflict. Whether you like it or not, your story is now part of the Venubian collective memory. You'd better get used to being a hero."

"I never want to get used to it, and the conflict is not over until Zohleemay is found."

As I speak, I keep expecting Nicki to run into the room and ease my pain. I also know I have to let her and Phillip Mann go. Neither is part of me anymore.

"If you no longer want to be Phillip Mann, what name shall we bestow upon you?" Verubeal squints her eyes as if sizing me up. After a long, unwavering gaze, her eyes widened as if she had decided something. "Territaff," she states with a sense of pride.

"Territaff," I repeat. "It has a nice ring to it. What does it mean?"

"The literal translation is the body of the planet, but it also can mean Earthman."

I smile at the underlying irony of the name and like it.

"Territaff it shall be."

I nod at my reflection in the mirror.

Verubeal walks up behind me and runs her hand through my thick, black hair, and frowns.

"What's wrong?"

"Your hair is a mess. Sit down, you need a haircut."
"You cut hair?"
"Who do you think taught Nickada?"

THE END

The saga continues with book 3, Mr. Territaff: The Vultaran Dilemma, coming early 2027.